O9-ABE-095

*A Haven on
Orchard Lane*

Books by Lawana Blackwell
───────────────────────

A Haven on Orchard Lane
A Table by the Window

THE GRESHAM CHRONICLES

The Widow of Larkspur Inn
The Courtship of the Vicar's Daughter
The Dowry of Miss Lydia Clark
The Jewel of Gresham Green

TALES OF LONDON

The Maiden of Mayfair
Catherine's Heart
Leading Lady

www.lawanablackwell.com

A Haven on Orchard Lane

LAWANA BLACKWELL

BETHANYHOUSE

a division of Baker Publishing Group
Minneapolis, Minnesota

© 2016 by Lawana Blackwell

Published by Bethany House Publishers
11400 Hampshire Avenue South
Bloomington, Minnesota 55438
www.bethanyhouse.com

Bethany House Publishers is a division of
Baker Publishing Group, Grand Rapids, Michigan

Printed in the United States of America

All rights reserved. No part of this publication may be reproduced, stored in a retrieval
system, or transmitted in any form or by any means—for example, electronic, pho-
tocopy, recording—without the prior written permission of the publisher. The only
exception is brief quotations in printed reviews.

Library of Congress Control Number: 2016930583

ISBN 978-0-7642-1793-7

Scripture quotations are from the King James Version of the Bible.

This is a work of fiction. Names, characters, incidents, and dialogues are the product
of the author's imagination and are not to be construed as real. Any resemblance to
actual events or persons, living or dead, is entirely coincidental.

Cover design by Jennifer Parker

16 17 18 19 20 21 22   7 6 5 4 3 2 1

For Buddy,
my sweetheart and best friend.

1

If one would drown one's sorrows with music, the music must be loud.

On the seventeenth of February, 1880, if Charlotte's fingers had not pounded out Haydn's Andante with Variations in F Minor so forcefully, the score would not have slipped from its stand. She would not have heard hoofbeats.

They halted in the snow-frosted carriage drive instead of carrying on to the stables. Visitors were rare, thus curiosity led her from grand piano to window. She pushed aside a curtain and watched a coach sway to a stop behind a pair of horses. The driver hopped down from the seat and opened the door. His passenger stepped to the ground, looked up at the house.

She could almost read his expression. Her first sight of sixteenth-century Fosberry Hall had taken her breath away, with its four storeys of honeyed limestone, gables and projecting windows, and verandah with wide steps.

Charlotte crossed the Belgian carpet and eased open the parlor door.

Alerted by a bell in the kitchen, Mrs. Trinder moved soundlessly up the hall.

"Good morning." The man's voice resonated from the porch. "My name is Milton Perry, calling for Lady Fosberry. Here is my card."

"I'm afraid Lord Fosberry is away."

This was news to Charlotte, but Roger was not one to inform her of his comings and goings. Nor was she one to ask.

"That's quite all right. As I said, my business is with *Lady* Fosberry."

"Lady Fosberry is not available," Mrs. Trinder said and began closing the door.

The male voice quickened from *andante* to *allegro*. "I have an urgent message, if you would but—"

"Here I am, Mrs. Trinder," Charlotte sang, stepping into the hall.

Mrs. Trinder turned, cheeks as ashen as her hair, veined hand still grasping the knob. "Lord Fosberry insists upon receiving guests in person, Your Ladyship."

"The gentleman appears to be *my* guest."

"But—"

Charlotte stepped closer, touched her shoulder. "I'm still the lady of the house. Now, if you please?"

The housekeeper stared at her for a moment before moving aside.

The visitor at the threshold was well dressed in a black Chesterfield coat. From a high forehead flowed oiled salt-and-pepper hair, dented from the crown hat tucked inside his arm. Above a trim beard, his cheeks were ruddy from the cold. One gloved hand held a narrow leather satchel.

"What an honor, Lady Fosberry," he said with a little bow.

"Thank you." She took the proffered card from his gloved hand. *Milton Perry*, it stated. The urgency in his hazel eyes intrigued her, and after all, she had not had a caller in two or three years. "Come in, Mr. Perry."

"Thank you."

She stood to the side. "Will your driver care to wait in the kitchen?"

Stepping into the hall, he replied, "You're very kind, but I shan't be long, and he has rugs."

Mrs. Trinder watched with an aggrieved expression, not offering to take his hat and coat. Charlotte did not have the heart to force the issue.

"Wait and remove your coat in the parlor, where it's warmer." She led him down the hall and opened the door.

Mrs. Trinder, lagging behind, cleared her throat and said when Charlotte turned, "His lordship will be displeased."

"I'll explain to him that I insisted . . . that I *bullied* you, Mrs. Trinder. Will that suffice? Now please, return to your duties."

In the parlor, Mr. Perry stood before the fire in pinstripe suit, his coat, hat, and gloves draped across a sofa arm.

"I had forgotten how cold the north can get."

She seated herself in one of the plush green Venetian chairs.

Mr. Perry came over to fold his limbs into the adjacent chair, resting his satchel upon his knees. "You managed that situation well, if I may say."

Tempting, it was, to explain, *"Mrs. Trinder is pleasant on the whole, but as she has been in my husband's employ for thirty years, she naturally defers to him."* But this visitor was a stranger. Enough of Charlotte's private life had been bandied about over the years.

"What brings you here, Mr. Perry?"

He nodded. "Mrs. Perry and I had the pleasure of seeing you in several productions. You had such presence onstage."

That raised in her no small suspicion. Was he a reporter? If so, she would show him the door, then apologize to Mrs. Trinder. "You're very kind. And once again, may I ask the purpose of your visit?"

"But of course." He took an envelope from the satchel and left his chair to hand it over. "I own a courier service in London."

Charlotte's breath caught at the sight of the return address. "The Lyceum."

"Mr. Irving sent two telegrams himself before contacting me," Mr. Perry said, seated again. "I dispatched a messenger here on Tuesday, but he was turned away."

Henry Irving took over management of the Lyceum two years ago, according to *The Times*. She had shared the stage with him on several occasions, most recently eight years ago as his mother, Gertrude, in *Hamlet*.

Charlotte worried the edge of the envelope with her thumb. Her hopes had been dashed so many times. Stalling, she said, "I received neither telegram nor message."

"So he assumed." Mr. Perry hesitated. "Is it possible your husband . . . ?"

She felt a sick chill. "It is not only possible but probable."

"I'm sorry to hear it. In any event, I'm not as easily intimidated as my staff, and as dependability accounts for the success of my business, I caught the very next train to Lincolnshire."

"Impressive. But what if my husband had been here?"

Mr. Perry smiled. "Over an hour ago, I hired a local courier to deliver a message from one Maxwell Simpson, Esquire, requesting an audience with Lord Fosberry over a matter of supreme importance at Three Horseshoes in Halton Holegate."

"I was playing the piano and did not hear. But pray, who is Maxwell Simpson?"

"My sister's husband in Yorkshire. I daresay he'll miss the meeting."

Charlotte smiled. How good it felt to do so!

Mr. Perry's brows drew together. "Which leads me to ask if our high jinks will cause you any harm. Is Lord Fosberry a violent man?"

"He is not." Roger's wit was his weapon of choice.

She gave that a second thought. Roger would connect Mr. Perry with the fool's errand. He owned guns for hunting. Surely he would not use them against a person, but then, his behavior had surprised her before.

"Still," she went on, "you mustn't tarry. I'll read this after . . ."

"Will you read it now? Mr. Irving awaits your reply."

Pulling in a deep breath, she opened the envelope.

Dear Charlotte,

I pray this finds you in excellent health. And I dare to hope . . . would you care to take a break from country life to play Gertrude again? An unfortunate attack of palsy has forced Mrs. Rathbone to quit midstream, and while Mrs. Overton is a competent understudy, she has not the audience loyalty you commanded. A prompt and favorable reply would put me forever in your debt and bring joy again to London audiences!

Her nausea gave way to light-headedness. She had read in *The Times* weeks ago of the revival of *Hamlet* at the Lyceum, never daring even to dream she would be associated with it. "He offers me a part."

Mr. Perry smiled and withdrew more papers from the leather case. "He sends the script so that you may refresh your memory."

She took it from him and pressed it between her hands. She could almost smell the gaslights.

"I'm authorized to purchase a railway ticket and would consider it a privilege to escort you to London."

London!

How wonderful would it be, Charlotte thought, to have a reason to wake in the morning! To go through the day free of self-recrimination for having blundered yet again into the biggest of mistakes!

To be with people!

And yes, to see *Charlotte Ward* upon the marquee!

The dream faded like stage fog. While her face was free of

11

wrinkles but for the corners of her eyes, and her ash-brown hair only enhanced by the few strands of gray, there was another issue. She pressed her elbows into her sides and felt the flesh yield. "I've gained two stone, at least. They're unaware."

"You're still beautiful, Lady Fosberry."

"Not enough." Audiences would not fault her for her fifty years. *Fifty-one in August!* After all, the part was for a grown man's mother. Yet they would expect someone attractive and regal.

Mr. Perry was a stranger. But there was no one else in whom to confide her angst. "I've let myself go. Terribly. I'm . . . fat."

"I must disagree."

"Yes, you *must*," she said with frown. "Because a gentleman is constrained to say otherwise."

"On the contrary, I'm unfailingly honest." He winced. "My brother-in-law's fictitious message notwithstanding. If I may be so bold, you're, well, Rubenesque."

"Rubenesque." What every woman wanted to hear. With knees creaking, she heaved her Rubenesque body to its feet. "Please convey my deepest regrets to Mr. Irving. If you will see yourself out . . ."

She, who could produce copious onstage tears, wanted no witness to those now prickling the backs of her eyes.

He rose slowly. "Should you not *speak* with him, at least?"

Attempting to say a word would unleash the flood. She pressed her lips and nodded toward the door.

"I'm sorry to have distressed you." Mr. Perry collected coat, gloves, and hat, and backed across the room. Just before the doorway, he paused. "Lady Fosberry, my dear wife is a stout woman. I daresay she weighs much more than do you."

Charlotte could pull in only shallow breaths.

"She purchases certain undergarments at ladies' shops. To make herself appear smaller."

That was the icing on the cake. Of course she knew of corsets, but she had never needed one. A hundred years ago, that life seemed.

Why will you not leave!

Mr. Perry was the epitome of male discomfort: eyes not quite meeting hers, fingers plucking at coat buttons. "Forgive my indelicacy. But it would be a tragedy if you gave up without a try."

The tears eased, though the back of her throat ached.

A fireplace log collapsed with a hiss into the bed of ashes.

"How can it hurt?" he asked.

How could it hurt? In so many ways! She had only to picture Henry Irving rejecting her. The return train ride. Roger's smug look.

"I'm afraid that I'll fail."

He nodded. "I understand. I do. For years, I kept books for Harrods, chained by fear to a job that I despised. One day, I realized it was far better to fail than to spend the rest of my life wondering what would have happened *if*."

If.

She imagined herself in the years ahead, browbeaten into a shadow of the woman she once was, sick with longing for paths she had not chosen.

Drawing in a deep breath, she said, "When does the first train leave tomorrow?"

His brows rose. "Why, at eight. Shall I come for you?"

"I will meet you. My husband will not welcome you back onto his property."

"That's sooner than I could have hoped. Will you not need more time?"

The thought of *more time* was not appealing, considering that it would be spent beneath the cloud of Roger's anger. Besides, more time would give footholds to fresh doubts.

She shook her head.

"Very well, Lady Fosberry. I'm staying at Red Lion Inn, should you need to contact me."

She glanced toward the window. "You must go now."

He thanked her and left.

As hoofbeats sounded again, Charlotte sank to her knees, rested her head against a sofa cushion, and wept. The spiritual numbness that had gripped her for so long loosened its hold. God had not forgotten her after all.

Dearest Father . . .

How good it felt to pray!

She had been a believer since age fourteen. A common assumption was that actors and actresses led immoral lives. Many did, which was the reason her circle of friends in the profession had always been small. But her parents were faithful churchgoers, no matter how late a Saturday show ended, and no matter where the tour had them temporarily planted. Over her mother's constant but pragmatic Anglican objections, her father chose whichever congregation was near enough to the theatre to allow them to be in costume for the Sunday matinee.

Thank you for your kindness, in spite of my wallowing in my own misery. Now please give me the strength to do this.

2

Charlotte spent the remainder of the morning laying out clothes. She could have assigned the task to upstairs maid Alma Willis, but word might have gotten out. She wished to speak with Roger before sending for her trunk.

A rap at the door gave her a start. Alma's voice came through. "Shall I bring up a tray, Your Ladyship?"

"Yes." Charlotte eyed the clothes upon the bed. "On second thought, I'll go myself."

A single impulse propelled her down the stairs, past gilt-framed and somber Fosberrys from generations past. *Food.* Tight nerves made her ravenous.

Savory aromas greeted her in the paneled dining room. The table stretched out to accommodate sixteen, but the cloth was laid with one place setting. Footman Jack Boswell hastened in, slump shouldered and seeming older than his thirty-odd years. He had been doing the work of two ever since a financial snag had forced Roger to sack the second footman, along with the butler, under gardener, and two housemaids.

"I beg your pardon, Your Ladyship," he panted. "Lord Fosberry ordered a tray in the library."

"That's quite all right." She slipped into the chair he held out for her. As he moved over to the sideboard, she said, "Has God ever surprised you, Jack?"

"Surprised me?" He lifted the soup tureen and shook his head. "I can't say that He has."

"Well, you're young."

"Begging your pardon again, but I feel anything *but* young."

Charlotte clucked her tongue sympathetically. "Don't give up your faith, Jack. I learned today that we cannot imagine what's around the corner."

"Yes, Your Ladyship," he said with little conviction.

How could she fault his lack of optimism, when Roger insisted upon carrying on as if Fosberry Manor were fully staffed? With just the two of them, they could make life easier for the servants, but her suggestions were brushed aside.

Meals, for example. There was no reason they could not serve themselves from the sideboard for every meal, not just breakfast.

But what a relief, that Roger intended to sulk! Food and terse discussion did not mix well. And she could have seconds without having to endure his comments.

Seconds.

She had not even had soup, and she was anticipating seconds. In spite of a huge breakfast just hours ago. Was food more important than this opportunity handed to her?

But there was not time to shed but two or three pounds, she reminded herself, for she could be onstage within the week.

Better than gaining two or three. There seemed no in-between.

"Jack?"

He paused halfway from the sideboard with a steaming soup dish upon a tray.

"I believe I would care for tea only."

"Tea, Your Ladyship?"

"Yes. Black, and on a tray that I can carry upstairs."

"With a sandwich?" His surprise was almost comical. "Biscuits?"

"No, thank you."

She had to flee these aromas from whichever delights waited under covered platters.

With tray in hands and head held higher, she again passed the stares of Fosberry ancestors. No food had ever tasted sweeter than this victory!

Two hours later, Charlotte found her husband in the conservatory, fussing over his beloved pink, red, and white camellias.

"Roger?"

"I'm occupied," he said.

"Something important requires your attention."

"Are there no hams in the larder that require *your* attention?" He chuckled at his own witticism and waved a hand with a flourish. "No cakes in the breadbox, no tarts in the window?"

He can't hurt you anymore, she said to herself yet felt the sting.

Roger Fosberry, Viscount of Spilsby, was a mildly handsome man for his sixty years, a trim six feet tall, with fading auburn hair as thick as a young man's. He had been widowed two years when Charlotte met him at the wedding of his niece once removed, actress Lillie Langtry.

"You'll adore Uncle Roger," Lillie had enthused those five years ago. *"He was so tender with Aunt Helen when she was struck with a cancer."*

After years of resisting matchmaking attempts from friends, and direct flirtations from men, Charlotte found herself charmed by Roger's devotion to his late wife and his talk of his life on an estate in Lincolnshire.

She could imagine reading in the garden. Picnicking on the riverbank. Gathering berries in the woods. Breakfasting in the conservatory. Strolling through golden fields. Going to village fairs. Wholesome activities she had read of in novels but never had time to pursue.

After decades of pretending, what would it be like to be simply herself? After two marriages to actors whose moods were tied to the volume of the applause they received, how would it be to have a companion with nothing to prove?

The newspapers made much of the wedding, quiet affair though it was. The caption in the *Times* read *Charlotte Ward Becomes Lady Fosberry of Spilsby. Third Time Lucky?* During those first halcyon months, Roger taught her to play chess, to ride, to tell the difference between a larkspur and a delphinium. He brushed her hair evenings and asked to hear her theatre experiences. They shared a hymnal during services at St. James.

He encouraged trust so much that she allowed herself to cry on his shoulder over the losses she had experienced. He knew of loss as well, and the comfort they gave each other strengthened their bond.

She had not minded his disinterest in entertaining. They were lovers cocooned by polished walls and pampered by servants. The times he was away seeing to tenants and farms, she simply read, took walks, played piano.

It was the beginning of their second year, when she was as besotted as a young maiden, that he came to her in tears. "I so wanted to spare you this, Charlotte, but I'm on the verge of bankruptcy. I've become a cliché—land rich, capital poor."

None of his doing, he assured her. The price of wheat had fallen. If he did not lower rents, he would lose farmers to rising factory wages in Norfolk. He could not sell off some of his land because the estate was entailed.

She was glad he had come to her. Having paid her own way most of her life, she was beginning to feel like a kept woman. The estate was her life too.

Ignoring a little warning voice in her head, she cleaned out her account, over six hundred pounds. She commissioned the sale of her London townhome, bringing in another hundred pounds. To do otherwise would have been to admit she had sold her birthright for bad pottage.

Yet again.

Perhaps Roger had not married her for money, she thought, watching him inspect a leaf for who knows what. Perhaps self-loathing lay at the root of his increasing coldness, humiliation for having had to ask for help.

Or it could be that he had grown resentful that she was not Helen, the love of his youth. Whatever his reason, he had chosen not to share it. Silence was cruelest for the monsters it bred.

As intimacy waned, food became more than sustenance; it became her solace. He mocked her lack of restraint and the bloating of her body, complained at having to pay a dressmaker to alter gowns and, eventually, sew new ones. He undermined her confidence piecemeal, so by the time she realized she would never see her money again, she could not think of returning to London.

Until today.

"I've been offered a part in *Hamlet*," she said. As if he had not read the telegrams.

He straightened, and his brown eyes mocked her. "As what, dearest? The castle?"

"You will not take this away, Roger," she said over the bile in her throat.

He plucked a white camellia, twirling it in his fingers. "Out of the question, Charlotte. I'll not have my family name subjected to ridicule."

"I would use *Ward*, as I have from the beginning. *My* family name."

"Everyone knows I'm your husband. You'll not make a fool of me."

She swallowed and forced breath into her lungs. "That would be the utmost irony, wouldn't it?"

Snorting a bitter laugh, he dropped the bloom to his feet. "It was *The Era* that made fools of the both of us."

"The theatre paper?" She blinked. "What does—"

"I never read such rubbish, but Helen subscribed to follow Lillie's career. She read an article to me about how the Shah of Persia was so moved by a performance that he gifted you a ruby . . ."

"A ruby . . ."

". . . stored in a vault in the Bank of London and insured by Lloyd's of London for fifteen thousand pounds."

A sharp laugh left Charlotte's throat. "You believed this?"

He shrugged. "I never read where you denied it."

"I would have had no time for my career if I had tracked down and denied every falsehood. It would have been futile in any case. Most people want to believe the sensational. Why did you not ask about it before we married?"

His silence spoke volumes. Any questions about her finances would have aroused suspicions. She had prided herself on her ability to spot fortune hunters.

Pride truly did go before a fall, as Scripture warned.

"Were no wealthy widows pursuing you?" Charlotte asked. "You're a handsome man but for the coldness in your eyes when your true nature reveals itself."

"There were some." He shrugged. "Lady Blake."

"Lady Blake? Who wore a different stuffed bird on her hat every Sunday?"

He had the grace to look embarrassed. "So she's fond of birds."

"I expect the birds would dispute that." Charlotte sighed. "Then why me?"

Another silence, but the fictitious ruby had taken on a life of its own and stood between them.

"I'm grateful your little gift helped me keep the estate, mind you," Roger said at length. "I have but to wait out the price of wheat, and this place will be restored to its former glory."

She felt no remnant of love, but that he could be so blasé

about taking her savings stung more than any insult he had ever thrown her way.

"What I cannot understand," he went on, head leaned thoughtfully, "is why you had so little, in light of your successful career. The ruby notwithstanding."

"I *have* a successful career," she corrected. "I'm going to London."

"You neither drink nor gamble," he went on, "and your house was modest, all things considered. You own few baubles . . ."

What had she done with the bulk of her money? Had he but asked, she would have explained. If he had really *known* her, he would have figured it out long ago. For such a self-congratulatory man, he could be quite obtuse.

"I'm going to London, Roger," Charlotte repeated. "In the morning."

"Hmm . . . well, there's the rub. How will you get to the station?"

"The landau, of course."

He shook his head. "Allow me to disabuse you of that notion."

"What do you mean?"

"*My* landau. My driver. My horses."

"You're not serious."

"Utterly serious. You're free to walk. Twelve miles would do you some good."

"You can't keep me prisoner, Roger."

His brown eyes narrowed. "By the by, I sent my own message to your prankster, Mr. Perry, that you've changed your mind . . ."

Charlotte felt as if the breath had been knocked out of her. Mrs. Trinder must have listened at the door.

". . . *and* that I shall have him arrested if he trespasses again. Chief Constable Bickerton and I were boyhood schoolmates. Have I never mentioned that?"

I will not allow him to see me cry, she thought even as tears stung her eyes, blurring his face.

"Why?" she said thickly. "You don't even *like* me."

"Nonsense. You're my wife." He could have commented on the weather for all the affection in his tone. "But in due time, if you choose to leave, I'll not prevent it."

Due time . . . meaning when *Hamlet's* run was over.

He nodded as if reading her mind. "I forbid you to make a laughingstock of me. London papers are sold in Lincolnshire too, as you're well aware."

"Roger . . ." She swallowed past the lump in her throat. "I'm begging you."

"Enough, Charlotte." He returned to inspecting his camellias. "You'll thank me one day when you've returned to your senses."

◇◇◇◇

The sound of soft rapping penetrated Charlotte's mind. She opened her eyes; they burned as if rubbed with sand. It was incredible that she had managed to fall asleep across the cluttered bed.

"Your Ladyship?" came from the door.

Charlotte lifted her head. Her neck ached from using her arm for a pillow. Beyond the open curtains, the frigid winter had sunk into early dusk. "Go away please, Alma."

Yet the knob turned, and the door eased open. Alma entered, carrying tray and candle. Closing the door with her foot, she said, "I brought supper."

"I'm not hungry," Charlotte said, raising herself to sit.

"Yes, Your Ladyship."

Alma set the tray upon the dressing table bench, lit the bedside table lamp, turned, and smiled. She was twenty-six, tall and thin, with a light brown topknot and unfailingly equable disposition.

"Alma, I have no appetite." Charlotte's throat, however, was parched. "Just some water."

The maid filled a beaker from the carafe. As Charlotte drank, Alma said, louder than necessary, "Now then, see what lovely trout with Dutch sauce Mrs. Fenn made? And some nice artichokes with poached eggs."

Charlotte saw no such thing, only Alma's face looming close.

"Oswald will take you to the railway station," she whispered. "If you wish to go."

"But how?" Charlotte whispered when she could speak.

"He'll be waiting at the verandah at four in the morning."

"Why would he?"

Stableboy Oswald Green was an affable young man, but her interactions with him were limited, especially since Roger had stopped taking her riding.

"Lord Fosberry sent him to town with a message, and the man he brought it to offered him a job. He's to send a coach. What shall I say to Oswald, yes or no? You can't bring a trunk."

A trunk meant nothing, compared to freedom. But there was another factor to consider. She would be burning bridges. Roger would never allow her to return.

What, then, if Henry Irving deemed her too large? She had but six pounds sterling and some loose coins.

The knot in her stomach grew. As unpleasant as the *now* was, the future's pitfalls were shrouded in fog. *Show me what to do, Father!*

No voice spoke from a burning bush, no heavenly vision appeared, but in her mind's eye, she envisioned herself on her knees in the sitting room that morning, gushing a prayer of thanks. If she believed this opportunity to be a gift from God, she must not balk because it was not wrapped in layers of certainty.

She took Alma's rough hands. "Yes."

Alma smiled. "Shall I help you pack?"

"No. The less time you spend with me, the better. And if this causes you any trouble, write to me in care of the Lyceum Theatre."

23

"I shall be fine." Withdrawing her hands, Alma stood straight again and said in a louder-than-necessary tone, "Will you not eat, Lady Fosberry?"

"I have no appetite." She adored trout, but her insides were so wracked that there could have been an anthill on the dish for all the appetite it induced. Which was fortunate, for the quest to shed some weight was renewed.

Alma took the tray and sent her another smile from the doorway.

Charlotte stared at the closed door and fought temptation to call her back. Fear rattled its bones at her like a gruesome skeleton.

She was limited to what she could carry. She rose, lit another lamp, and opened the door to her wardrobe. Standing upon tiptoe, she latched onto the handle of her French Morocco-leather traveling bag and tugged, catching it in her arms. It would be her only luggage, with space for hair and tooth brushes, underclothing, a nightgown.

But first . . .

Moving over to the belongings spread upon the bed, she opened the lid to a flat rosewood box and moved aside papers stiff with age. The oval frame was tarnished, but she had been warned long ago that to take it apart for polishing would damage the sepia photograph. She held it to her cheek for a moment and then packed it into her bag through a haze of fresh tears.

3

Charlotte did not return to bed, lest she not wake. Her mind was beset with doubts and fears in any case. Bag packed, she sat at her writing table and read the playscript.

The lines came back to her.

Your mercy overwhelms me, Father.

From two until three o'clock, she glanced often at the mantelpiece clock, wishing the hands would hurry. At three, she padded to the bathroom. She cleaned her teeth, bathed with facecloth, and fastened her hair into a fresh chignon.

Back in her bedchamber, she pulled on a sea-green poplin gown that would travel well, a gray wool coat with hood, and calfskin gloves. She wondered, then, which shoes to wear. The clock struck a quarter of four. *You should have thought of this hours ago.*

She would have to move through the house in stocking feet. There would be no time to button her warmest boots on the verandah. She decided upon the worn low-cut balmoral boots with the elastic side gussets. They would fit more easily into the top of her open bag as well.

Taking up holder and candle, she eased open the door, moved the bag through it, stepped out, and closed it just as quietly.

Years of having to be silent offstage paid off, for she knew to place her weight upon the pads of her feet.

Darkness magnified the silence, as well as the thumping of her heart. The hall clock chimed four as she started downstairs. Without a free hand to grasp the banister, she resisted the temptation to hurry. She crept into the silence of the entry hall and opened the door.

Frigid air assaulted her and blew out the candle. Charlotte had no choice but to carry on in the dark, setting bag upon verandah to close the door. The stone below felt like ice through her wool stockings. She knelt to feel for the boots in the top of her bag and pulled them on.

There was no sign of Oswald in the velvety blackness. She could not be more than five minutes late. Had he assumed she had changed her mind?

Or had he changed his? He was surely as anxious as she was.

Please, Father, he has to come, she prayed even as her eyes caught sight of a flickering in the distance, past the row of windows at the east corner of the house. As still as held breath, she watched lamplight sway slightly to and fro. She recognized Oswald's lanky form when he was some forty feet away, though a hat covered his carrot-red hair. She felt her way down the three low steps and met him. With her free hand, she gathered up as much of her coat and gown as she could manage.

He held a bag as well. They slogged though six-inch snow, past the carriage drive into the lane, where bare linden branches loomed. She was full of questions but held her tongue.

At length, he whispered in a cloud of vapor, "I'm sorry I cannot carry your bag, Your Ladyship. Can you walk a mite longer?"

"Yes," she whispered back, though the cold tormented her feet.

They continued on for what seemed an hour, shivering and panting, but what was more than likely ten to fifteen minutes.

She looked over her shoulder. No windows were illuminated in the mass of blackness.

"Not much longer," he whispered. "They cannot come too close to the house."

Finally, they reached Ashby Road. They turned to the west, toward Spilsby, walking in the middle between hedgerows. She saw light ahead, heard the soft whinny of horses. Several paces more, and a coach appeared. A dark form hopped down from the lamplit driver's seat. As a man entered the light from Oswald's lantern, Charlotte recognized him from having delivered Mr. Perry yesterday.

"Lady Fosberry? I'm Guy Heaton."

He helped her into the dark coach. "My apologies, but the road is too unsteady to attach a lamp in here."

True to northern dialect, he pronounced *road* as *ro-ad*.

"But there are rugs to warm yourself," he went on.

"Thank you," Charlotte said, voice shivering.

Inside the coach, she unfolded a wool rug and burrowed herself to the neck. Oswald leaned his head in to set the bags upon the floor. "I'll sit with the driver."

"Must you? I'd rather not be alone."

"Of course, Your Ladyship."

He spoke to Mr. Heaton and then came inside and wrapped himself in a rug. With creaks of wood, the wheels began a slow trundle. About a mile up the road, the team picked up speed to a trot.

"It's too dark to run them," Oswald said. "But we've plenty of time."

"It's a wonder they can see at all," Charlotte said, relieved at not having to whisper yet struck by the strangeness of her voice, as if she had not spoken for days.

"Horses can see better in the dark than people."

Blackness had faded to dark blue when the coach came to a halt. Through the window, Charlotte could vaguely make out the short canopy between the pitched roofs of the modest main station and the stationmaster's house.

A busy day lay ahead. They would take the train from Spilsby to the market town Firsby, then on to Lincoln to meet the London and North Eastern Railway.

Mr. Perry rang less than twenty-four hours ago, she marveled.

Mr. Heaton opened the door, took the bags that Oswald proffered, and set them upon the cobblestones. "Keep the rugs. Mr. Perry bought them for the train. I must go and fetch him now."

"I beg your pardon for the wait," Oswald said as they shared an iron bench beneath the canopy, swaddled in rugs. "The stationmaster should open up in an hour or so. But I could rouse him, say that Lord Fosberry's wife—"

"No!"

He looked embarrassed. She had not intended to spit that out so sharply. Softening her voice, she said, "It's been a long time since I've watched the sun rise. So, Mr. Perry offered you a job."

"He said he could always use good riders."

She hoped Mr. Perry had not made his commitment for her sake.

"It's an answer to prayer," Oswald went on. "Seven years is a long time to clean stables."

Charlotte had to smile. "I should think seven *minutes* would be a long time to clean them."

He smiled back. "I don't mind hard work, but there wasn't much leave for advancement. Mr. Douglas is as healthy as I am, even though he's been stable master since before I was born. Not that I would wish anything upon him."

"You're setting out on an adventure."

"I've put aside wages for years in hope of starting over in London. I can scarcely believe I'll soon be walking the streets of Oliver Twist and David Copperfield."

"You're a reader, then."

"Aye, Your Ladyship." He paused. "You're setting out on an adventure as well. Are you at all afraid?"

Petrified, she thought. But she didn't wish to give vent to her fears, not now, when any moment she could hear hoofbeats.

Oswald gave her a sidelong look. "The lamp belonged to Mr. Heaton. He lent it to me yesterday. Wouldn't want you to think I nicked it from his lordship."

"I would never have assumed so," Charlotte said, meaning it. It was obvious that this young man had character. Not that she had been the best judge over the years, but even an off-key piano could sometimes strike a proper chord.

She lowered her chin to cover a yawn with the rug.

"Rest your eyes, Your Ladyship," Oswald said. "I'll keep watch."

"I'm quite sure I can't." But folding arms and lowering her chin again, she sank into a muddled half slumber.

"Good morning?"

She roused herself and looked up at a thickset man in a coat and bowler hat.

"I'm Mr. Sparks. Would you care to wait inside?"

The town of Spilsby was waking to their backs: sounds of wheels and hooves upon stones; St. James's six bells striking a quarter past seven.

"Thank you, yes." She gave Oswald a gentle elbow and smiled when he snorted awake. Inside the station house, Mr. Sparks offered tea. The familiar warmth of the cup in her hand was reassuring.

Still, her insides flinched every time the door opened.

A handful of passengers assembled upon the benches. Charlotte drew some curious looks, but no one ventured over. She did not think her nerves could stand the strain of polite chatter.

The young man with her studied the door just as intently.

Roger can make a scene, but he cannot force us to return, she had to remind herself.

She felt better at the sight of Mr. Perry approaching. Charlotte held out her hands; he set his grip upon the floor and took them.

"So here you are. Please forgive my not accompanying the coach. I took to heart Lord Fosberry's threat to have me arrested."

"I understand."

Releasing her hands, he took a purse from his waistcoat pocket and turned to Oswald. "Mr. Green, go and purchase three first-class tickets to King's Cross."

Oswald looked at the coins in his hand. "Third is fine for me, sir."

Mr. Perry smiled. "Just don't become accustomed to it, my good man."

"Are you all right, Lady Fosberry?" he said to Charlotte as they shared a bench.

"Quite, thanks to you." She had to address the question in the back of her mind. "Did you hire Oswald for my sake?"

He shook his head. "My couriers ofttimes deliver money and valuables; thus, integrity is vital. I can teach a man to ride but not to be honest. I was having my pipe in the courtyard when he rode up. His horsemanship was obvious."

"But how could you discern his integrity?"

"After I read Lord Fosberry's letter, I offered him five pounds to get word to you that I would take this to the local authorities. He turned down the money and warned that Lord Fosberry and the chief constable sometimes ride together. Whilst I pondered what to do, he came up with the plan. I had given no indication that he would be offered a position."

"God sent you and Oswald," Charlotte said. "You're surely angels."

Mr. Perry chuckled. "Mrs. Perry would beg to differ."

Midday London glistened from morning rains. Two gray horses pulled the coach along Euston Street, among hansoms and drays and costermonger carts and omnibuses. Charlotte alternated between watching familiar landmarks and Oswald's glowing face.

Up the Strand toward Wellington, Charlotte kept her eyes to the window and was rewarded with the sight of the six Ionic limestone columns of the Lyceum's grand portico.

The coach rocked to a gentle stop. The cabby opened the door and offered his hand. She handed him her bag, stepped out onto the pavement, and turned. Both men were half rising as if to accompany her.

"Kind sirs, it is time to return to your lives." She smiled at Oswald. "Your new life."

"Your bag . . ." they said in unison.

"Is not heavy. I shall give your names to the box office, and I do hope you will attend a performance as my guest and stay for refreshments backstage. And Mr. Perry, that includes Mrs. Perry, of course."

"We should be delighted," Mr. Perry said, settling back into his seat.

Oswald nodded. "Godspeed, Lady Fosberry."

"Thank you," she said. "But it's *Ward*, if you please. I left Lady Fosberry back in Lincolnshire."

A sunken-cheeked woman was mopping the lobby's marble floor with wide swabs.

"Waste of effort," she hissed through gaping teeth. "Tonight there'll be two thousand pair of boots mucking it up."

"Good morning?"

The woman turned, hand to throat. "Oootch! You gave us a fright!"

"I beg your pardon."

"Ah, no matter. Box office ain't open for—" She studied Charlotte's face. "Would you be . . . Missus Charlotte Ward?"

"Yes. Here to see Mr. Irving."

The aged eyes traveled the length of her, or rather, the breadth of her.

Charlotte stood straighter. "Will you direct me to his office?"

"I am here, Charlotte."

Henry Irving strode into the lobby from the side door. He was as handsome as ever, even though some gray had cropped up in the hair parted above his long face.

"Good morning, Henry."

He took her proffered hand in both of his. "So, Mr. Perry pulled it off."

"It was quite an enterprise."

"You've put on some weight." He was not one to mince words.

"Too much?" she asked, resisting the urge to fold her arms across her body.

"'Tis the bane of bein' woman, Mr. Irving," the cleaner offered. "My George once could put both hands round my middle."

He gave her a bemused look, and she snorted and returned to mopping.

"I've had nothing but tea since your letter," Charlotte said. "I'm determined to make myself thin again. And I intend to buy a corset."

"No, not necessary," Henry said. "Our dressers will truss you up."

Charlotte's breath caught in her throat. "I may stay, then?"

"But of course. It's an honor to have you. Can you be ready Saturday night?"

Three days away? "I can be ready tonight."

Finally, he smiled. "We must inform the newspapers and squeeze in a rehearsal with the cast. I'll have someone carry you over to the Mona Hotel in Covent Garden. Rehearsal at one o'clock on Friday."

With a wave of his hand, he turned. Charlotte watched his retreating back.

"This is as a dream," she said.

The woman with the mop snorted. "If this be a dream, dearie, give us a good pinch."

4

Backstage at the Lyceum was an anthill of activity one hour before curtain. Actors and musicians, wardrobe and hairdressers, managers and stagehands traveled the labyrinthine passageways and narrow staircases at half trot.

The hairdresser had just left Charlotte's dressing room. A silvery crown perched upon her coiled hair. She closed the door and practiced projecting her voice while using only the upper portion of her body.

> "Doctor Foster
> went to Gloucester
> In a shower of rain.
> He stepped in a puddle
> Right up to his middle
> And never went there again."

A whalebone corset constrained her lower lungs. She had arrived three hours ago in order to have the full attention of the dressers. Tucking and tugging and grunting, they had managed to transform her into Gertrude without having to let out any seams in the loose-flowing blue brocade gown.

Her hands went often to her waist. The firmness was comforting. The hunger pangs had finally eased last night, along with the blinding headache. How good to feel in control! She could do this for as long as it took.

"Come in!" she said when someone rapped at her door. One of the assistants, a wizened, affable fellow named Bayard Rook, entered with a bouquet of roses.

"From His Highness," he announced.

"How lovely."

It seemed unpatriotic to set the vase upon the floor with the half-dozen others, so she pushed aside jars and bottles upon the dressing table.

Welcome back! the card read simply, signed *Edward*.

Edward VII, Prince of Wales, was a great patron of the arts. The flowers meant he and his entourage would be in his usual box 1. She was accustomed to royalty in the audience. This was, after all, London.

She continued breathing techniques.

"Doctor Foster
went to Gloucester . . ."

Half an hour later, Mr. Rook knocked again and stuck his head around the door. "It's time."

Meaning, time to assemble in the greenroom. Her fluttering of nerves mingled with relief that the waiting would soon be over.

"You're stunning, Mrs. Ward," Geoffrey Fisher called from his open door. He would soon be King Claudius to her Queen Gertrude. He sat upon a stool as a woman dresser stitched an apparent rent in the sleeve of his tunic.

"Why, thank you, Mr. Fisher," Charlotte said and floated down the corridor, buoyed by his compliment.

The hum of conversation met her ears. A pair of young

actresses stood at the greenroom door, wearing silks appropriate for Ladies of the Court.

". . . didn't realize it was missing until I looked into the mirror. They were cheap as last week's trout, but the jade matched my eyes."

"Well, mind you keep the other, or the missing one will turn up next day. It always happens that way."

"Mrs. Ward!" exclaimed the one with green eyes. "I didn't have the chance to speak with you yesterday. My aunt took me to see *The Octoroon* when I was but seven. We waited at the stage door, and you were so kind. I kept the program you inscribed for me."

Charlotte smiled. "And now here you are, an actress yourself."

The young woman sighed. "Standing about with no lines."

"Now there. William Shakespeare thought enough of your part to include it, so let's hold our head up high, shall we?"

"Thank you, Mrs. Ward." Smiling, the two stood aside to allow her entrance.

Gentlemen and gravediggers, lords and ladies conversed in worn chairs and sofas before the fireplace, or sipped from beakers of water on the table. There was no need to be silent as yet, for from the theatre came faint sounds of voices and shuffling of feet. Most actors had been in the production since its inception, thus there were few frenzied scans of playscripts.

"Ah, and there you are," called Tom Folks, soon to play Horatio. He crossed the room and handed her an envelope bearing her name.

The sight of the familiar bold script sent a chill through her. "Where did you get this?"

"I was the first one here." He motioned toward the far wall. "It was attached."

Through the costumed bodies, she spotted what appeared to be her trunk. Her constrained lungs labored to pull in breaths. Surely he would not give up so easily and extend an olive branch. Did he intend to shake her nerve?

Brows rose beneath Tom's flatcap. "Mrs. Ward?"

"Just . . . an old acquaintance. If you'll excuse me." Walking over to a relatively quiet corner of the room, she broke the seal and opened the vellum paper. She could not stop herself from reading. If he were out there in the audience, she must know.

My Dearest Charlotte,

You did not think I would miss your opening night, did you?

I understand aging has been difficult, but I believed you above corrupting the virtue of a servant barely out of boyhood. Alas, the proverb rings true: The leopard cannot change its spots.

I am too decent a man to exact revenge, hence your trunk. However, in my grief, I did pour out my heart to a very sympathetic reporter for The Daily Telegraph.

She gasped.

Conversations tapered. Eyes turned toward her.

Mr. Irving entered in flatcap and a shortcoat befitting the prince. He looked about and barked, "And who died, pray?"

"It's nothing," Charlotte said when nods were directed her way. She forced a smile. "A ghost from the past. Prince Hamlet and I have that in common."

That brought on a smattering of laughter. Henry crossed over to her and said, "Your husband?"

She hesitated, nodded.

"Give it to me." He crossed over to the fireplace and threw page and envelope into the flames. Upon his return, he quoted one of his lines. "'The play's the thing.' Yes?"

"Yes. I won't allow him to win."

He nodded. "And so he shan't."

"'The play's the thing,'" Charlotte said under her breath, and then again.

—◇◇◇—

Stagehands sprang into action once the blue velvet curtain ended act 1, scene 1. Thanks to ingenious rolling platforms, the exterior of Denmark's royal castle became the interior room of state in seconds.

"Shall we, my dear?" Geoffrey Fisher asked in the wing.

Charlotte tucked her hand into his arm. They walked onto stage right and over to gilded thrones. Henry Irving stepped to his mark and winked at her.

Her heart welled with gratitude. She would be the best Gertrude ever played. He would not regret believing in her.

The curtain rose.

And then, miracle of miracles, hearty applause! *Not for me*, Charlotte thought, but when Mr. Fisher pressed her hand into his side, she knew that it was. She could feel her face glowing.

What have I ever done to deserve such grace, Father? Her prayer was brief, for the audience was silencing. She took as much breath as the corset allowed and delivered her first line.

"Good Hamlet, cast thy nighted colour off, and let thine eye look like a friend on Denmark!"

The scene went well. She *was* the Queen of Denmark, not Charlotte, aging, unloved, and betrayed. The applause as the curtain lowered was intoxicating! She could have danced for joy!

Do you hear, Roger?

She would not appear again until act 2, scene 2. Which gave her time to picture the aftermath of Roger's deed.

The Daily Telegraph was well circulated. Lies set in newsprint might as well be carved in stone. Other publications would follow suit. Yes, she could fight to clear her name, which would amount to a retraction on some later page, but she would be fighting against the adage of *Where there is smoke, there is fire*. Who had the most credibility? A respected member of the peerage, or a thrice-married actress?

And how long before the gossip reached Cheltenham?

Another chill caught her, though the theatre wings seemed as hot as an oven.

She wouldn't believe it.

But why would she not? They were essentially strangers.

Too soon, the curtain opened again on a castle room of state, where Claudius and Gertrude would ask courtiers Rosencrantz and Guildenstern to seek out the source of Hamlet's distress.

Charlotte's distress was acute. Sweat trickled between her shoulder blades. The gaslights made her nauseous. But she kept her eyes upon Geoffrey Fisher as he began his lines.

"Welcome, dear Rosencrantz and Guildenstern!"

She had performed in far worse condition. Hives, a broken ankle, toothache, even the onset of pneumonia.

Four months of morning sickness. Even so, she could not recall nausea *this* severe, nor such a lump in her chest.

Silence.

She blinked, looked about. Actors waited. Out in the darkened seats, uneasy anticipation was palpable.

"Good gentlemen, he hath much talked of you," she said hastily.

Too hastily.

She could not believe this. Past fame or not, one more mishap and Henry would replace her with Mrs. Overton, who waited somewhere backstage.

Taking a quick breath, she continued. "And sure I am . . ."

What next?

The actor who played Guildenstern held two discreet fingers beneath his chin.

Charlotte was both grateful and resentful. This was a part she could play in her sleep.

". . . *two* men there are not living . . ."

The lump welled from chest to throat. Nausea overwhelmed

39

her. She gulped air, tried to continue. The young actors before her traded worried glances.

She could picture Roger out there, smiling.

". . . two men there are not living . . ." she repeated, digging fingernails into her palms, "to whom he more adheres. It will please you . . ."

The line was supposed to be *if* it will please you. Those things happened. Never to her, but she knew that it was best to carry on.

". . . to expend your time with us a while . . ."

Guildenstern's eyes fairly bulged. She had left out a whole line!

From a seat out in the darkened audience, surely no farther away than the third row, a pair of hands began clapping. That led to murmurs from all over and rustling in seats.

You're a professional, Charlotte reminded herself, blinking tears.

What was the next line?

"Curtain!" came from the wings. Mercifully, pulleys began humming, and the curtain started lowering.

She buried her face in her hands. As curtain met stage, despair seized her with such violence that every nerve in her body felt on fire. Yet her teeth chattered, and she felt pressed upon from all sides, as if under water.

The pair who had dressed her, Mrs. Dowey and Miss Wren, hurried onstage. Mrs. Dowey touched her shoulder. "Come, Mrs. Ward. Let us see after you."

Charlotte gaped at her.

She was led to the wing in a fog. She felt damp cloth against her skin, clothes being loosened, others pulled over her head. Whimpering, she was escorted into a carriage. A ride through gaslit streets. A cot with starched sheets. A spoonful of bitter liquid pushed past her lips. And blessed nothing.

⤖◇⤕

As Charlotte eased into consciousness, dream characters floated about speaking bits and pieces of sentences. She had the vague notion of yet another carriage ride through dark streets. She had no concept of time, save light and shadows. At length, she regained some lucidity, and was informed by a Dr. Jacobs that she was in an isolation room at Royal Free Hospital in Hampstead.

"You've been here two days. You spent three in a ward in St. Thomas' Hospital." His brows joined and sprouted like weeds above narrow eyes, but his voice was soothing. "Reporters became nuisances, so you were brought here in secret under the identity of Mrs. Iris Jones."

"Why can't I remember?" Charlotte asked.

"You were treated with opium for exhaustion and melancholia."

"Opium! I don't want—"

"I discontinued it when you arrived. I wish to see how you respond to bed rest."

That was a relief. She had witnessed the results of opium addiction firsthand. "I have very little money. A brooch and bracelet in my bag, wherever it is . . ."

"There is only a small fee for the use of this room, as technically you're not an isolation patient. Mr. Irving intends to pay it on behalf of the Lyceum and asked that we protect your identity."

"How kind."

"He asked me to assure you that the production went on the night of your unfortunate departure. And that your trunk and belongings from the hotel are being stored at the theatre."

"Henry Irving is a good man." Charlotte sighed. "And I'm a charity case."

Dr. Jacobs wagged a finger at her. "Few of us go through life without needing assistance at some time, Mrs. Ward. My mother was a widowed parlormaid, and her employer kindly paid for my education. No doubt you've helped others as well."

Charlotte thought, shook her head. "I'm afraid not. Oh, little encouragements to fellow actors here and there, but nothing to the degree of your employer."

"We do what we can, Mrs. Ward. And your time on earth is not up."

Being that poverty was all Charlotte could see for her future, it was unlikely she would be able to help anyone. But such thinking exhausted her, and she was grateful when Dr. Jacobs left and she could sink back into sleep.

The following day, or it could have been the same day, for she had lost all sense of time, she tried to figure out what she would do after leaving the hospital. The thought of trying to find another acting job made her physically ill, yet the thought of asking Roger to take her back was far worse, if he would even deign to do so.

No letters arrived.

"Few know you're here," Dr. Jacobs explained when Charlotte asked. "I'm certain they're being held at St. Thomas's. Shall I inquire?"

She was tempted. Perhaps some of her old acquaintances had written? Theatre people were generous, as a rule. She had but to ask, and hospitality would be offered.

But for how long? There was a not-too-fine line between houseguest and burden. Especially when that houseguest was almost penniless.

Self-recrimination filled her prayers.

I never asked you once if Roger was the right man for me. Or if it was your will that I should marry again at all.

Her most frequent prayer was not for herself, however, but that the faculty of Cheltenham Ladies' College, one hundred miles away in Gloucestershire, were too busy educating young minds to read theatre columns from London newspapers.

5

The sun had started glazing the neo-Gothic windows of Cheltenham Ladies' College when Rosalind approached the main entrance on Thursday, the fourth of March.

"Good morning, Miss Kent," said sixth-form prefect Carina Hadley. "Miss Beale asks to see you."

Lectures were to begin in half an hour. Rosalind hastened to the principal's office, pausing in the open doorway. Dorothea Beale removed her reading spectacles and smiled up at her. The calm, almost placid face belied the intensity of her decades-long struggle for women's educational rights.

"Do come in, dear. Did you take your stroll?"

"It was invigorating," Rosalind said. "I spotted a song thrush building a nest."

"It's a wonder you haven't caught your death in those damp fields."

"It energizes me for the day. And where best to speak with God?"

After seven years on staff, minus four months tending her ailing aunt, Rosalind could speak easily with Miss Beale.

"Well, you're the picture of health and serenity. There must be something to it." Her face became serious. "Do sit, dear."

Rosalind slipped into the chair facing the desk. Miss Beale's gray British shorthair cat, Hetty, raised her head long enough for a disinterested look before resuming her lie-in on the windowsill.

"Is something the matter?" Rosalind asked.

Miss Beale passed a newspaper clipping across the desk. "It's from *The Times*."

With a sense of dread, Rosalind scanned past a glowing account of Henry Irving's *Hamlet* and found her mother's name.

> As to Charlotte Ward's portrayal of Gertrude, I can only echo Hamlet's words: "O, woe is me, to have seen what I have seen!" While one cannot logically fault any person for aging, one must wonder when our beloved Lady Charlotte's legendary passion for acting gave way to passion for food. The brain may process only so much information at one time. Could it be that a craving for after-party cake dominated Mrs. Ward's to the detriment of her lines during Saturday's ill-fated performance?
>
> All criticism aside, we are encouraged that Mrs. Ward sought treatment at St. Thomas' Hospital. We hope she will grace the boards again, as she did so eloquently in the past.

"He's encouraged," Rosalind muttered as all serenity from her stroll escaped her. "What a hypocrite."

"It *is* cruel. There are a couple more reviews of the same ilk in other newspapers."

"Why didn't she stay in Lincolnshire? Whatever was she thinking?"

Rosalind had used the surname of her mother's maiden aunt, Vesta Kent, since childhood. Miss Beale was the only person at the college aware of her family connection.

"Your mother and I are the same age," Miss Beale said.

"When you feel past your prime, you wonder how many opportunities you have left."

"One more opportunity to bask in the glow of everyone's admiration."

"That hardly seems the case now, does it? I wonder if she has anyone to offer support."

"She has never lacked for support," Rosalind said, setting the clipping onto the desk. "I'm certain she's home again, being consoled by her husband. He'll buy her a gold bracelet or some such bauble, and she'll recover."

Miss Beale picked up another clipping and passed it to her. "That one is ten days old. Last night, I decided to catch up with news of the world. This one is from *The Daily Telegraph*."

The second clipping contained an etching of her mother and Lord Fosberry from their wedding day. The headline read

LORD FOSBERRY HEARTBROKEN OVER CHARLOTTE WARD'S DESERTION WITH YOUNG SERVANT

Rosalind's face went hot. "How could she!"

"Wait before you pass judgment."

"I'm grateful Aunt Vesta isn't around to witness this. She always said my mother had no morals."

"The same Aunt Vesta who shamed you for going to college?" Miss Beale asked.

Rosalind cast about in vain for a reply. She regretted being so forthcoming during her interview those seven years ago, though that very openness had helped land her the position. When Miss Beale asked, "*How are you different from the thirteen other qualified young women who have applied for this position?*" Rosalind had answered, "*Because I value education so much that I fought for it tooth and nail.*"

Face burning, she attempted to read the article's first sentence.

"Here, I would rather you read this one from six days ago,"

Miss Beale said, holding out a third clipping. "It sheds some light."

This one contained an interview with a Mr. Milton Perry and an Oswald Green, a former servant of Lord Fosberry.

"Lady Fosberry was the soul of goodness, like Lucie Manette in *A Tale of Two Cities*," claims Mr. Green. "That is why we want to set things right. There was never any untoward action on her part to me, nor any of the other menservants."

Mr. Perry, who admittedly had never met Lord Fosberry, detailed his and Mr. Green's parts in assisting Mrs. Ward in her escape through the dark winter's night. It seemed some intrigue from a play.

The article ended with a question: *Where is Charlotte Ward now?*

Rosalind pushed aside another tug of pity. "No doubt one of her theatre friends is hiding her until this blows over."

"Spring lectures conclude Wednesday next," Miss Beale said. "I started out teaching mathematics. It would be gratifying to have a classroom again for a bit. And I haven't forgotten how to give examinations. That would give you five weeks."

"To see after my mother, you mean," Rosalind said. "No, thank you."

"I realize you haven't a close relationship."

"We have no relationship."

She should be grateful that her mother had turned her over to an aunt twenty-six years ago, instead of leaving her on the steps of an orphanage.

"I can hardly fault your bitterness," Miss Beale said.

"I'm not bitter. I simply have no interest."

"Again, I understand. But you are now living the days your mind will revisit during old age. Will you wish you had reached out to her? Regret is a bitter pill."

When has she reached out to me? Rosalind thought. But sitting across from Miss Beale, whom she admired more than any person on earth, she felt vindictive and petty.

"I don't even know where to find her."

"Someone does. You could start with the theatre."

Rosalind sighed. "I'll go."

"That's our girl."

"But what if she doesn't want me?"

Miss Beale was opening her mouth.

Cutting her off, Rosalind said, "It happened before."

"I trust this time will be different. Why don't you pack a few things in a valise? If you see that you need to stay, we'll send your trunk."

"My trunk." Rosalind sighed. Five weeks with a stranger.

"There, there now," Miss Beale said. "If she needs to leave London, I could ask about for a nearby house to let."

"Miss Beale, I cannot have my mother in Cheltenham," Rosalind said. "Lord Fosberry is surely aware of my existence and location. What if he's vindictive enough to inform reporters?"

"Very well." Miss Beale pursed her lips. "You may find helpful an agency that lists lodging opportunities. Just today, I saw an advertisement in *The Times* for one on Charing Cross Road. I shall find it for you."

⸎

The Great Western Railway wound through fog-shrouded farms and hedgerows. *London will be even drearier,* Rosalind thought. All this effort, just to find that her mother had bounced back. She was a tough old bird.

Please let it be so, she prayed.

Did not Scripture say that God would supply the desires of a believer's heart? Rosalind was far from perfect, but she had lived a clean life, had cared for Aunt Vesta during her declining weeks, had passed up an offer of marriage to a man of means, simply because he was unkind to a shop assistant.

Not the only reason, she conceded.

Still, she had asked for very little. Now she was asking to be on the return train tomorrow to resume her unfettered way of life.

6

"Help!"

Charlotte's cry tore from her as a whimper. The passengers carried on boarding as if a scowling man was not forcing a woman across the platform.

"No!" she attempted, frustrated at her frozen throat.

"Get onto the train, Charlotte!" Roger barked.

Charlotte burst into tears. "Oh, please! Help!"

She heard a woman's voice, and her arm felt a nudge.

Roger, the passengers, the train lingered but a sickening moment and faded. Heart pounding, she listened to the quiet and remembered she was in the hospital.

"Mother."

Charlotte opened her eyes and blinked at the young woman looking down at her. "Rosalind?"

"Good morning, Mother." Her daughter's voice held no warmth.

She had changed a little in four years. Gone was the long, severe plait in favor of a cluster of ringlets at the nape of her neck, and fringe above twin slashes of brow. In the morning sunlight from the windows, a hint of red softened her hair's mahogany brown.

"It's really you!" In spite of her hope that news had not reached Rosalind, Charlotte was seized by joy. She sat up, moving her covered legs to the side of the cot.

Her daughter took two steps back.

Charlotte's heart sank, but what could she expect? With a forced smile, she said, "But how did you know where to find me?"

"Mr. Irving, once I convinced him I was your daughter. I've come to ask if you need anything."

Tense silence followed. A telling silence.

Charlotte shook her head. She owed her as much, and more. "No, nothing. Thank you. But it is good of you to ask. Please . . . how are you?"

"Very well." The green eyes made a quick shift toward the door.

"Are you on school break?" Charlotte babbled on, loath for her to leave.

"Not quite yet."

"Then, how did you . . ."

"Miss Beale. The principal. She offered to take my place."

It was this Miss Beale who had prevailed upon her to come to London, Charlotte suspected.

"Your doctor says you cannot stay much longer," Rosalind said. "Where will you go?"

Another tense silence. Where would she go, indeed?

But this was not her daughter's problem. What was Rosalind to do, bring her to school?

"Home," she said brightly.

"To Lincolnshire, you mean." Rosalind sighed. "Mother, Lord Fosberry accuses you of adultery. It's in the newspapers."

Charlotte's stomach tightened as if someone had punched her.

"Were you not aware?"

"No. That is, he threatened, but . . ."

Was this another reason her mail was not forwarded? If she had received any at all.

Her daughter studied her face. "It's not true. Is it?"

"Never!" Charlotte said. "Please believe me. He's being vindictive because I left him."

"Have you somewhere else to go?"

Be brave, for her sake! Charlotte ordered herself. She was an actress, after all. "Oh, I've been at a nice little hotel in Covent Garden. Perhaps they've kept my room for me."

Rosalind's shoulders rose, then fell. "Mother, Dr. Jacobs also said you have no money."

Charlotte opened her mouth to protest, but tears betrayed her. She groped beneath her pillow for a handkerchief, wiped her eyes.

"What happened?"

"Roger . . ." Charlotte croaked. "My acquaintances don't know I'm here. Surely some have written . . . offered . . ."

Her daughter sighed again. "I must make some arrangements and retrieve your things from the theatre. Hopefully I can come for you in a day or two."

"No! I will not be a burden to you!"

"Too late for that," she said in a flat voice. She turned and walked out without a backward look.

Looking back was all Charlotte could do.

The only child of touring actors, she started out in pantomimes at three years old until her first speaking part at age nine: Mamillius in *The Winter's Tale*. At sixteen, she played Juliet to twenty-five-year-old Emory Gilroy's Romeo in Manchester. Youth and the romance played onstage so blurred the lines of reality that she ignored rumors of opium-fueled visits to seedier parts of town. The marriage endured but five months. Years later, she learned he had died of syphilis in a sanatorium.

At nineteen, she landed a minor part in London's Theatre Royal Drury Lane, and a year later, married actor Patrick Dowling. Nine months later, Patrick celebrated the imminent arrival of what he hoped would be a son by stealing a boat with a pair of friends for a drunken midnight lark on the Thames. The only one of the trio who could not swim, he was buried the day his daughter was born.

She was pink and downy, with studious green eyes, a shock of dark hair, and long, elegant fingers. Charlotte named her after Rosalind in *As You Like It*. Newspapers played to the public's appetite for morbid sentiment, running accounts of the brave young widow left to carry on after such tragedy. Theatre Royal offered her a lead part in *The Lady of Lyons*. Seven evening performances and six matinees weekly left little time for mothering. When eight-month-old Rosalind wept for the nursemaid every time Charlotte attempted to hold her, she sent both to live with her late mother's sister in Coventry. She sent letters, gifts, and cheques, and buried her guilt over infrequent visits by throwing herself into her career.

When Rosalind was twenty and had just begun teaching, Charlotte received a heartbreaking letter asking for no further contact. *Now that I am a grown woman and can support myself, we may stop this mother-daughter charade.*

After two letters Charlotte sent to her were returned, unopened, she wrote to her aunt to ask permission to set up a legacy in her name. Aunt Vesta, past seventy, agreed. The two thousand pounds emptied Charlotte's account, but she made good wages and believed there were enough years ahead to save for old age.

At Aunt Vesta's funeral three years later, Rosalind was civil but not warm.

But what could Charlotte have expected?

If I could but live those years over, she thought, tearing up again.

Time was a steep downhill path, and regrets were the stones that cut one's feet near the bottom.

7

Waterloo Bridge Station was thick with humanity: porters wheeling trolleys of luggage; anxious mothers holding the hands of restless children; harassed fathers encumbered with satchels, rugs, and hatboxes; voices shouting farewells and admonitions over the whistle of the London and South Western Railway express locomotive.

After turning her mother's trunk over to a porter, Rosalind hurried to the bench near the refreshment room. Her mother sat staring at her gloved hands, camel coat over the blue poplin gown the hospital had stored, and the narrow-brimmed hat with half veil that Rosalind had purchased.

"It's time to board, Mother," she leaned to say.

Her mother turned her face up to her, eyes hidden by the veil, but tension obvious in her frown and clasped hands. "I cannot do this."

"What do you mean?"

"I'm fatigued. Please take me back to the hospital."

"That's impossible." Rosalind looked over at the waiting train. "Come, Mother. Everything will be fine."

Her mother labored to her feet. Rosalind switched her valise to her left hand so that she could take her arm. They wove their way through the crowd. The front-facing seats of three second-class compartments were filled. In the fourth, a young man and woman and a girl upward of two had claimed, incredibly, the rear-facing seat.

The final boarding whistle shrieked while Rosalind considered seeking another compartment. Small children tended not to travel well, in her experience. But forward-facing seats filled quickly, and she was in no mood to gamble. The child's behavior could go one of two ways, but nausea was a certainty. Chiding herself for not waiting closer to the tracks, she assisted her mother up the step and settled beside her.

The train had no sooner hissed out of the station than the girl began moving from one window to another.

"Look, look, look!"

Rosalind attempted to focus upon the passing cottages of Wimbledon and Surbiton, the fir-tree forests and undulating chalk country, while her boots were stepped upon and her nerves as taut as harp strings. Attempts the mother and father made to restrain the child brought on ear-splitting shrieks. At length, both sank back into their seats with weary eyes and apologetic smiles.

Perhaps I was meant to be a spinster after all, Rosalind thought.

Into an hour, the child's chattering was shrill, her activity frantic. Just as Rosalind was at the end of her tether, the tot climbed into the space between her parents and fell asleep. She slept all the way to Salisbury Station, looking like an angel, no less, lashes resting upon rosy cheeks.

"Are you all right?" she asked her mother on the station's wooden platform as they waited to change trains.

Her mother gave her as much of a blank look as the veil would allow. "Um . . ."

"The wee wild child."

"I'm sorry. I didn't notice."

What were you thinking of? came to Rosalind's mind. But to press would be to imply that she cared. She motioned toward the redbrick station house. "Let's have sandwiches."

One hour later, they shared a carriage to themselves on the train bound for Port Stilwell. Rosalind removed her pattens, propped stocking feet upon the facing seat, and sighed with contentment. Now that she could command a window to herself, she watched the succession of valleys threaded by streams and flanked by wooded hills, hamlets of color-washed cottages, and red plowed fields hemmed in by hedgerows.

"Have you ever been to Port Stilwell?" her mother asked.

"I have not," Rosalind replied.

Silence. Then, "What's it like, I wonder?"

Rosalind gave her an aggrieved look. *Why don't you wait and discover for yourself?*

"I'm sorry," her mother said.

The sadness in her tone pricked Rosalind's conscience in spite of herself. Softening her voice, she said, "It's a fishing town on the Devon coast."

That it was one hundred and thirty miles from Cheltenham was its biggest draw.

"I see."

It seemed the appropriate time to inform her. "I've let the rooms under 'Kent.' You may wish to use that name as well."

"Very well."

Resentment took over again, and she could not resist adding, "After all, what's one more name change?"

Her mother stared at her hands. The dart had found its mark, but the victory felt hollow.

She has no right to make you feel guilty, Rosalind reminded herself.

After a few stilted moments, though, she said with some degree of gentleness, "In other words, they won't know your identity unless you decide to inform them."

"Never," her mother said hoarsely.

They sat in silence until the train crawled into a little wayside station.

"Well, this is it," Rosalind said.

She exited the compartment and looked southward. Port Stilwell lay in a valley, guarded by hills that folded one upon the other and faded into the clouds. Past thatched cob and stone cottages, a shingle beach glistened in the wide gap between silvery gray cliffs, and beyond, blue waters.

She turned to the open compartment. "Mother?"

Her mother stepped onto the platform.

Three fellow passengers traded greetings with a man with grizzled cheeks, bowed with age but apparently hale and strong. He approached Rosalind and her mother, touched the brim of his cloth cap, and said with a slight burr of the tongue, "I'm Septimus White. Mrs. Hooper had me fetch you. I'm married to her cousin."

"Thank you for coming, Mr. White," Rosalind said. "My mother has a trunk."

"Aye. I supposed."

He led them to a wagon hitched to two dray horses. A dark-haired boy of about sixteen gave them a shy smile.

"Mr. Plummer is who carries people from the station, but he's down at the guildhall, working the election," Mr. White said. "My grandson Amos and I have just the fish wagon. 'Tis a mite gamy, but we spread a canvas and put in a bench for ye to sit on."

Amos helped the porter heft up the trunk, set a footstool on the ground, and hopped into the bed to offer Rosalind's mother an arm. With Mr. White's added assistance, she stepped up to the bench and moved to make room for Rosalind.

Herring gulls filled the air with discordant screams, but it was a strangely welcoming sound to Rosalind's ears. As the wagon trundled through the countryside, the coal smoke of the train faded, replaced by the overwhelming odor of fish. The horses picked up their pace. Rosalind gripped the bench to steady herself, and felt a loose bit of something. Fingernail?

She brought it before her eyes, squinted at a scale. Naturally, considering what this wagon delivered. Curiosity made her shift sideways and raise the cloth. Several scales were caught in knife scars in the weathered oak.

In silence, her mother watched, as if too intimidated to ask.

"This is not a bench," Rosalind said. "It's a table for cleaning fish."

Her mother shifted to the other side to look.

"It's at least scrubbed clean," Rosalind went on.

"Give or take some scales," her mother observed, squinting at one clinging to a fingertip.

"I would rather give them, if it's all the same."

Her mother chuckled, and Rosalind could not help but smile.

"Thank you," her mother said, wiping her eyes beneath the veil.

For what? Rosalind thought. The shared humor? Taking her from London?

She sobered. What an unburdening it would be just to forgive. And biblical. But so hard to put into practice when the offending party had yet to confess the wrong. When the offending party seemed *oblivious* to the wrong.

Rosalind turned away to concentrate on their surroundings. They were moving southward, toward the sea, passing thatched cottages with prim little gardens and fishing nets hanging out to dry. Blue jerseys fluttered like flags from wash lines.

Minutes later, the wagon turned left past a pillar-box and started up a gentle hill. Cottages gave way to rows of stunted trees with spindly bare limbs.

"Apples," Mother murmured.

"Is that what they are?"

"The blossoms will smell heavenly, come spring," she said.

Whether to cheer her or herself, Rosalind did not know her well enough to tell.

Just past the orchards, the lane ended at a two-storey, half-timbered cottage of striking yellow cob walls, with a thatched roof and small porch.

A block of cheese wrapped in twine, Rosalind thought.

Red pansies sprouted from window boxes and lined a stone walk to the wicket gate.

"The advertisement said 'tucked-away cottage in seaside Port Stilwell,'" Rosalind muttered. "It quite left out the part that you could quarantine smallpox patients."

"I'm glad for the seclusion," her mother said, pushing her veil back over her hat. "But is it too dear?"

"It's reasonable."

Mr. White tied the reins, and he and his grandson hopped down to help them from the wagon. There was a slight stir from within the cottage; then the door opened and a tall woman stepped across the porch and up the stone path.

"Welcome!" she cried, face wreathed in smiles. "Welcome, Mrs. and Miss Kent! I'm Aurora Hooper. I trust your journey was agreeable?"

Rosalind winced inwardly at Mother's not seeming to notice the proffered hand. She offered her own to Mrs. Hooper. "Quite, thank you."

"Very good!" The woman's soot-colored hair was gathered and ironed into corkscrews above her ears as was stylish twenty years ago. They bounced as she spoke, which was incessantly. Her small eyes, like shiny blue marbles, darted back and forth until they rested upon Mother's face.

"Have we met before, Mrs. Kent?"

Rosalind held her breath.

"I don't believe so," Mother murmured.

Mrs. Hooper angled her head. "Are you quite certain? One of Thomas Cook's exotic tours, perchance?"

"My mother seems to have one of those faces," Rosalind said. "Your cottage is quite colorful."

Mrs. Hooper gave a lusty laugh. "Just wait until you see inside."

Leaving the men to the trunk, she led them across the porch and into a hall with a narrow staircase, coat rack, and carved walnut mirror. A door was set into each side. She opened the one to the right and led them into a parlor redolent of beeswax and old wood.

A Louis XIV sofa in burgundy velvet, a settee in gold brocade, an overstuffed chair in multicolored paisley, two walnut armchairs upholstered in green silk, side tables, and a tea table were arranged around a patterned rug of reds, greens, blues, and browns. A low fire snapped in a stone fireplace to their right. Against one sage green wall sat a pianoforte, near a checkered draughts table and two wooden chairs.

"A pianoforte?" Mother said.

"Do you play?" Rosalind asked before thinking.

Mrs. Hooper continued as if she had not heard. "My husband and I enjoyed collecting things from our travels." Walls were covered with plates and platters: blue delft windmills, green dragons, Asian gardens, Bavarian children, pink landscapes, peacocks, roses, and even one commemorating Queen Victoria's coronation.

Through a wide arched doorway, a dining room was visible with wooden table and chairs, sideboard, and a glass-fronted cabinet filled with china.

"Quite nice," Rosalind said, for the whole effect was cheerful.

"My dear Vincent was keen on colors; the bolder, the better." Mrs. Hooper's mouth was smallish for her round face, but her smile exposed long white teeth. "That's why the drapery shop did—does—so well. He passed on two years ago, God rest his soul."

There was no opportunity for condolences, for she carried

on without seeming to draw breath, "I pray you don't mind solitude."

"I don't mind," Mother said quickly.

Mrs. Hooper smiled at her. "Vincent liked people but desired peace and quiet at the end of the day. I moved above the shop a year ago. Got weary of trudging the mile to and fro, being apart from town life. My grandchildren pop in for sweets, and I take meals at my son's restaurant. But an empty house doesn't age well. I'll need this place when I'm no longer able to keep shop. Mr. and Mrs. Knight were my first and only lodgers. They stayed nine months whilst he designed and built the latest cobble winch."

Cobble winch?

Rosalind had no opportunity to ask, because Mrs. Hooper went on.

"I'm afraid we have no books, but there is a lending library in town." She shrugged. "I donated my Vincent's collection before deciding to take in lodgers. Doesn't it always go that way? You toss something out and then find a need for it! Have you grandchildren, Mrs. Kent?"

"I'm not married," Rosalind said before her mother could reply.

"There's a pity," Mrs. Hooper said, giving her a wink. "But that will change in due course. Once word gets out of a new girl, the locals will swarm like wasps about jam cake. I daresay our fishermen are not as fussy as them gents up in London."

"Mrs. Hooper, I'm not looking for—"

She held up a silencing finger. "Yes, yes, dear. Just bear in mind what I've always said . . . every year past twenty, a girl's chances of finding a husband are halved."

"I'm twenty-seven."

Rosalind may as well have said *"I have the plague"* for the shock in Mrs. Hooper's face.

"Do not give up hope, child! There is still time!"

Not according to your arithmetic, Rosalind thought, restraining a smile.

Her mother's numb expression tightened. Softly, evenly, she said, "My daughter aspires to be more than bait for local fishermen. And any Londoner would be honored to—"

"Mother." Rosalind touched her sleeve, heartened at being defended so.

She abandoned you, she reminded herself.

"But of course," Mrs. Hooper said with hand upon bosom. "Far be it from me to suggest otherwise."

Mr. White leaned his head through the door. "Aurora . . . the trunk?"

"Well, Septimus, bring it!"

We haven't seen the rooms, Rosalind opened her mouth to say, then closed it. Unless they were uninhabitable, which was unlikely, she had no choice. What was she to do? Bring her mother back to school with her?

Besides, in a hurry to get the thing done, she had telegraphed Cheltenham after visiting the agency, asking that her own trunk be delivered.

"I must nip back to the shop," Mrs. Hooper said. "My housekeeper will attend you." She raised her face to trill, *"Mrs. Deamer!"*

Footfalls sounded from the entry hall. "Now, you must say naught of prison or prisoners . . ."

"Why would—" Rosalind attempted.

". . . larceny or stealing. Anything such as that."

"You have a criminal in your employ?"

"Not *Mrs. Deamer.*" Face flush with excitement, Mrs. Hooper hurried on with a softer voice. "But when her husband was Lord Mayor of Plymouth—"

The door opened, and a woman entered wearing a white apron over a dress of fine blue broadcloth with small white flowers.

"Ah, Mrs. Deamer," Mrs. Hooper said with a conspiratorial

glance at Rosalind and her mother. "Please show Mrs. and Miss Kent their rooms. Must fly."

Thus she did, leaving Rosalind with overwhelming relief that this woman did not reside here.

Her mother's expression betrayed the same. Not that she gave a whit, Rosalind reminded herself. And not that she herself expected to spend much time here.

"Welcome to Port Stilwell," Mrs. Deamer said.

She was about forty, with charcoal-colored hair combed from a pronounced widow's peak into a chignon. Thin dark brows and sparse lashes contrasted oddly with eyes the color of weak tea. Her saving grace was flawless skin and a fine nose, though over thin lips. Rosalind, who preached good posture to her students, appreciated that Mrs. Deamer's was especially erect.

They followed her back into the hall and upstairs to a landing with a linen cupboard against a back wall, and two doors on either side. Mrs. Deamer went to the right and opened the door to a decent-sized bedroom, papered in a rosebud pattern and furnished with a bed, chest, wardrobe, washstand, and a long mirror. Open curtains, rug, and counterpane were of the same cheerful colors as the parlor.

Lovely, Rosalind thought.

In the second bedchamber, Mrs. Deamer went over to a window set in the south wall, with a cushioned seat below and a small half-moon table to the side. "The view is better from this room."

Rosalind and her mother joined her. Past treetops and rooftops, in the long gaps between cliffs, the water was dappled with shafts of light and color: blue, green, and even dashes of mauve and brown.

"Lyme Bay," Mrs. Deamer said.

"Beautiful," her mother said with more animation than she had used all day.

The housekeeper leaned over the seat to raise the glass, letting in a great draught of damp, chilly air carrying scents of Scotch firs and the sea.

"This one should be yours," Rosalind said.

"No . . . I'd rather you—"

"You'll spend far more time in this cottage than I will."

Her mother's face crumbled.

Rosalind sighed to herself. What did she assume? That they were to live here, happily ever after?

"Perhaps you would care to rest for a while?" Mrs. Deamer suggested.

"May we leave the window open?" her mother asked.

"It's your room," Rosalind reminded her.

Her mother sat upon the window seat. Rosalind and the housekeeper carried on with the tour. One of two doors across the landing opened to a bathroom with a sink and mirror and claw-foot tub with gleaming copper pipes. The other, to a third bedchamber.

"This is Mrs. Hooper's."

"Does she stay here often?"

"No, never." Mrs. Deamer's expression gave no indication of her feelings. "She hopes to acquire another lodger."

"Oh. I didn't realize." Rosalind tried to imagine another person sharing bathroom, stairs, and parlor. How would her mother cope?

"Miss Kent?"

She sighed. "Please take no offense, Mrs. Deamer, but I made the decision to come here in haste. And I assumed we would be the only lodgers."

"I see." The housekeeper gave her a sympathetic nod. "It may not happen. Port Stilwell isn't as touristy as Dartmouth and Torquay or even Seaton. The beach isn't sandy for bathing. Artists tend to stay at the inn because of the cliffs. Still, there will always be that possibility."

You're doing the best you can for her, she reminded herself. *It's wasteful to pay for an empty room.*

"Would you care to see the kitchen?" Mrs. Deamer asked.

"Mrs. Deamer!" boomed from below.

"I beg your pardon." The housekeeper moved toward the landing. "Mr. White?"

"We canna carry it up," he growled. "Amos will not assist."

"I'll be right there." Mrs. Deamer gave her an apologetic look and then started down the staircase. Rosalind followed.

Septimus White stood scowling across the trunk at the boy holding the other end.

"I gave my word to Grandmother." Amos's face was ruddier than the old man's, his voice trembling but stance firm. "The stairs will do him in. He'll be abed for weeks."

"Very well, Mr. White. Leave it." Mrs. Deamer turned to Rosalind. "I'll unpack and carry up her belongings."

Grunting and heaving, Septimus and Amos lowered the trunk to the floor on the side of the staircase, before a cellar door. They mumbled a unison "good day" and left.

"Shall I show you the kitchen first?" Mrs. Deamer said to Rosalind.

She opened the door opposite the parlor. The room was as cheerful as the rest of the cottage, with flagstone floors, sea blue cupboards, a carved rosewood dresser, oak worktable with chairs, and a huge shiny range. Dried herbs were strung across a window with cheerful yellow print curtains, and copper pots hung from a rack.

"Where do those doors lead?" Rosalind asked.

"The one on the left, to the garden. And the other, to the pantry and larder, and cook's bathroom and bedchamber."

Rosalind became aware of surprisingly few visible items for food preparation even though supper was but two, three hours away. Yet no pot simmered on the stove, no heat radiated from the oven, and no bread rose on the table.

As if reading her mind, Mrs. Deamer said, "Our cook, Coral Shipsey, was visiting her family in Buckfastleigh when your telegram arrived. She's due back late morning. Mrs. Hooper's son is to send supper from his restaurant."

"How thoughtful," Rosalind said on their way back toward the hall.

Mrs. Deamer gave her a droll smile. "But I'm afraid you're at my mercy for breakfast tomorrow. I'll try not to scorch the porridge."

Rosalind decided she liked this woman. She smiled back. "I'm actually of the toast-and-tea persuasion. I'm not certain what Mother takes."

She gave herself a mental kick. How long would it take to remember to guard her tongue! Casting about for a change of subject, she noticed a keyhole in the door. Half joking, she said, "Are we to be locked out between meals?"

That brought another smile from the housekeeper. "According to Coral, Mrs. Lightman, now head cook for the restaurant, did not want the family trooping through when she was working, so she insisted upon the lock. The bathroom was added at her prompting as well. But never fear, Coral is quite happy for guests in the kitchen."

Back in the hall, Mrs. Deamer opened the trunk and took a bag from the very top.

"Here, I'll help," Rosalind said, taking the bag from her. If any memorabilia or playscript turned up, it was likely to be inside. She could take charge of it and deflect any curiosity. "*My mother was an avid theatre-goer,*" she could say in all honesty.

8

Charlotte pulled her wrap tighter. The cool air bathed her face, the sight of distant blue water soothed her eyes, and the gulls were music to her ears. And yet the knot in her chest grew. Tennyson's poignant lines came to her mind.

> *Break, break, break,*
> *At the foot of thy crags, O Sea!*
> *But the tender grace of a day that is dead*
> *Will never come back to me.*

Why had her body not protested against her mind's agenda those many years ago? Arms that had cradled, lips that had brushed against perfect little ears, breasts that had nourished.

"I should throw myself from a cliff," she muttered.

"Surely not, Mrs. Kent."

She turned toward Mrs. Deamer, at the wardrobe shaking wrinkles from Charlotte's mauve silk gown.

"I forgot you were there."

"Quiet as a mouse, and you learn all sorts of things."

Charlotte frowned. "You overheard Mrs. Hooper. What an odious woman."

"I'm grateful that she gave me employment."

The housekeeper hanged the dress upon a hook and took a step closer. "If you'll pardon my saying so, Mrs. Kent, change is frightening. Particularly when it's thrust upon you."

Certain that she referred to her own experience, Charlotte said, "What keeps *you* going?"

"My faith. It truly sustains me."

"You're never bitter?"

"There are times I must remind myself not to be. That it cannot change the past." She shrugged. "Or a person."

"I'm so sorry."

Mrs. Deamer shook her head. "You're very kind, but *you* were the one contemplating suicide."

"I wouldn't actu—"

"Mother?"

Charlotte and Mrs. Deamer turned heads toward Rosalind, carrying the framed photograph from the trunk.

"Me?" Her expression was unreadable. "Why have you kept it?"

Charlotte's mind barely registered movement, the soft closing of the door with Mrs. Deamer's exit.

"To comfort me."

"Comfort *you*," Rosalind said with bitter smile.

"But it has been my torment, daughter."

"Why did you give me up?" she said thickly.

"It tore my heart out." Tears pricked Charlotte's eyes. She pulled the handkerchief from her sleeve and blew her nose.

"Why, then?"

"I had to work. Aunt Vesta offered a safe place for you."

"Why did you stop visiting?"

"I *lived* for those visits. But Aunt Vesta said it would ruin you to have others know of your mother's . . . moral failings. That no decent man would want you when you were old enough to marry." She swallowed, her throat a tight lump. "And you seemed so happy."

"I *was* happy," Rosalind said with a triumphant look. "Aunt Vesta *doted* on me."

Charlotte's fingertips brushed the top of the window seat. Sapped of strength, she longed to sink back into its cushion. In less than a fortnight, she had lost her footing in the world. She had dropped into her daughter's orderly life and was resented for it.

Just take me now, Father, she begged from her heart while her daughter's eyes burned into her. *I have nothing. No one.*

And from her heart, God seemed to say, *A mother puts her child's pain above her own.*

She could barely draw breath. She thought back to her own childhood. Chaotic at times, living from trunks and crowding in with relations the times between roles. She had laid her head upon many a strange pillow, yet always secure in her part in the family.

Not only had Rosalind been denied a mother, but a father. Could an aunt, no matter how loving, fill those voids? Patrick's drowning was not Charlotte's doing, but it should have made her all the more eager to parent her child.

"I have no right to ask forgiveness. But I beg you not to despise me."

Her daughter stared, face unflinching.

"Because you were always in my heart, I convinced myself our bond would transcend the separation. If I could only go back, Rosalind, I would have kept you so close. No matter what it took."

Rosalind seemed to be struggling to contain herself. "Easy to say it now."

"Then why does it hurt so?" Charlotte rasped.

Her daughter's expression softened only briefly. "You're trained to cry on cue, Mother."

"You think I'm acting?" Charlotte gulped in a ragged breath. "I deserve that."

"I don't know what to think." Her daughter moved to the chest of drawers, laid the picture upon the top, and turned for the door. "I'm going for a walk."

"Now?" Charlotte asked through her tears but received no reply.

Tea arrived within seconds, as if Mrs. Deamer had known it would be needed. She placed the tray upon the half-moon table and, pouring tea into a Minton lovebird cup, said, "You'll enjoy the garden when the weather warms."

Charlotte nodded dully.

"The armchairs are perfect for sitting out with a book. Cream and sugar?"

"Yes, please," she murmured. *Why not?*

"And there's a table with chairs on the terrace," Mrs. Deamer added while stirring.

She accepted cup and saucer, and took a sip. "Thank you."

Mrs. Deamer straightened. "You're welcome. I'll bring up more clothing now."

Suddenly reluctant to be alone, Charlotte said, "I loved our garden in Lincolnshire. For a while."

"I had a giant copper beech in Plymouth." Mrs. Deamer gave her a wistful smile. "The shade kept everything else from thriving, but I did so enjoy reading beneath it."

"We appear to have much in common. Have you any children?"

"I was not blessed with children."

"Rosalind is my only child." Charlotte sighed. "We've been estranged for years."

"Indeed? And yet she's here with you."

"Under duress."

"But here all the same," Mrs. Deamer said, glancing at the window. "Do you know how long she intends to be out?"

"I don't." Charlotte's pulse quickened. "Is there danger?"

"Evening temperatures drop swiftly."

"Surely she'll return before sunset."

Mrs. Deamer nodded. "Surely."

9

Rosalind's mind worked best in concert with her feet. They carried her past cottages alongside Fore Street and then quaint shops with bow windows, Saint Michael's with its narrow Saxon stained-glass windows and bell tower, the post office, and the guildhall, where men stood in a queue outside a door beneath Gladstone and Disraeli election banners. Absently, she returned the occasional nod or greeting.

She had relocated Mother with surprising ease. Mrs. Deamer seemed competent to care for her. Why not take the train tomorrow and resume her classes?

Because Miss Beale would be disappointed.

And approval from the only real mother figure Rosalind had ever had was important.

She had lied to her mother from spite. While Aunt Vesta had fed and clothed her, she was a critical soul who so feared her following in her mother's footsteps that she forbade her to play with boys even as a young child. Novels were forbidden, lest they cause aspirations toward the stage. Outdoor play was restricted to the garden for fear she would fall in with a rough crowd.

Embraces were few and far between, limited to times of sickness or injury, such as the time she fell from a tree at age seven. Strokes of her forehead and clucks of sympathy as the doctor set her arm were followed by bed without supper because her ascent up the tree had exposed her knickers to possible passersby.

She could envision her aunt discouraging her mother from visiting. *What would you have done in her place?* she asked herself.

"She could have drawn me aside," she muttered. "Asked if I were hap—"

"Why, Miss Kent!" a voice trilled.

She winced, turned.

Mrs. Hooper stood outside a shop, smiling and waving. "I was draping cloth in the window, and there you were! Having a look about?"

Rosalind stepped back and managed a smile. "It's a charming town. Where is the library you mentioned?"

Mrs. Hooper pointed southward. "Three shops down, over the solicitor's office—Mr. Lockhart is his name. His family owns the orchards before my cottage, though you'll never see him set foot in them."

"And is there a bookshop? I'd like to send a postal card to the head of the school where I'm employed."

It would have to wait until tomorrow, for she had brought no money along, but as long as Mrs. Hooper was so obliging with directions, she may as well ask.

Mrs. Hooper's smile remained but no longer matched the expression in her marble eyes. "There is one, but I'm certain there are no postal cards. Only books, quite expensive, and you seem too sensible a young woman to buy what you can read for free. As for the cards, you can purchase them cheaply at Clark Mercantile."

She's concerned I'll not be able to keep up the rent, Rosalind realized.

"I'm quite frugal," she assured the older woman. No sense

71

mentioning Aunt Vesta's legacy, or it might give her ideas about raising the rent once they were settled.

"But of course you are," Mrs. Hooper said, her face smoothing. "You should go to the beach early one morning and watch the cobles."

"Cobles?"

"Boats. The fishermen bring in their catch from the night before. It's quite a sight, all the hustle and bustle. Mrs. Kent would enjoy it as well." She pursed her lips. "You're from Cheltenham, yet your inquiry was from London. Is that where your mother lived?"

"Only briefly," Rosalind replied with stiff smile. "I'll leave you to your window-dressing. Thank you for the information."

Teeth clenched, she continued down the pavement. That was one woman whose approval she cared for not one whit.

Fore Street ended at Lach Lane, and beyond, a beach was cradled by cliffs on either side, with huge stacks of rock isolated by the waning tide. The air was fresher and cooler past the chimneys. She crossed the lane and sat upon one of four public benches. Salt breezes chilled her cheeks and coaxed all thought of Mrs. Hooper from her mind.

At least forty boats of all colors rested upon the shingles. A few men in blue sailcloth smocks were checking nets and rigging. She imagined the rest were preparing to take their suppers before going out to earn their livings.

Supper, she thought. She rose and continued down Lach Lane, intent upon finding a return street that did not pass Mrs. Hooper's shop. A half-dozen pleasant homes lined the town side before she came to a signpost reading *Kleef Lane.* Before her on the opposite corner sat a large hotel with cob walls and a slate roof, appropriately named Sea Gull Inn. She turned to the right, assuming that Kleef Lane ran parallel to Fore Street.

Fewer shoppers were out, and several windows were dark. She sniffed, and then again. *Why didn't I bring a handkerchief?*

Desperation caused her to swipe at her nose with the side of her hand.

Blood?

Hand cupped beneath nose, she entered the next lit shop beneath a signboard that read *Pearce's Books*. In spite of the nosebleed, she could smell paper and ink, leather and cloth. To her left, a man stood before a counter, cutting twine from a pasteboard box. A medium-sized dog with tan fur lay at his feet.

"If you please?" Rosalind said.

He whipped a handkerchief from his coat pocket. The dog reached her first and raised up upon its hind legs to lick her free hand.

"Down, Jinny," said the man.

And then to Rosalind, as he handed her the handkerchief, "Should you not tip your head?"

Instead, she held the cloth below her nostrils and pinched just above. At length, she felt safe enough to test a clean spot on the white linen. Nothing.

"Leaning back causes it to go down into your throat," she explained. "Thank you for your help. I'm quite humiliated."

"But why?" he asked.

"To have such a defect."

"Everyone has at least one," he said. "I can't whistle."

"I also can't ride backward in a train."

"I suppose that means carousels are out?"

"They are."

He gave a sigh. "Well, you have me there."

That made her smile.

His smile curved toward bespectacled green eyes beneath a shock of hair the color of wheat. The clean-shaven face, with cleft chin and faint laugh lines, seemed tanned by the sun yet was not leathery like a fisherman's. He stood average height for a man, about four inches taller than she.

The dog sat before her and thumped her tail. She had long

pendant ears, black expressive eyes, silky tan fur, and legs that appeared awkwardly long for the rest of her.

"Aw, lovely pup you are." She leaned to pat her head gingerly; she had had very little contact with dogs in her lifetime, Aunt Vesta preferring cats. Many cats. "What breed is she?"

"Some Spaniel, some Labrador retriever . . . with a fair dose of anyone's guess."

Either Jinny did not care for that description, or she had had enough of the head patting. Her paws clicked against the floor on her return to her spot before the counter.

"Are you recovered?" the man asked Rosalind.

"I think. But I can't say the same of your handkerchief. I'll replace it."

"Please don't. I have enough hankies for the whole town's sniffles, as well as the rare nosebleed. My grandmother never took to knitting or to embroidery but needed something to do with her hands in the evenings."

"You're very kind . . . Mr. Pearce?"

"Why, thank you. And yes, I'm Jude Pearce."

"I'm Rosalind Kent."

"Are you visiting Port Stilwell?"

"Just for a bit. I teach in Cheltenham, so I will be there during school terms."

"What subject, might I inquire?"

"Mathematics."

"Very good. Are you staying in the inn?"

"My mother and I have taken rooms at Mrs. Aurora Hooper's cottage. Are you acquainted with her?"

"I am," he said with no change of expression.

A display rack upon the counter caught Rosalind's eye. "Why, you *do* carry postal cards."

"I always have. Along with an assortment of stationery and art supplies. Books alone would not bring quite the profit to keep this place going."

"She must have been misinformed."

"*She?* Meaning Mrs. Hooper?"

"I asked if there was a bookshop that sold them." She kept the rest to herself.

"Interesting." His eyes were smiling now. "Rosalind . . . from *As You Like It?*"

"My mother is fond of Shakespeare."

"As was my grandfather. He read to us evenings. The Bible and Shakespeare."

"While your grandmother hemmed handkerchiefs."

"A woman on a mission."

He had mentioned both grandparents in past tense. She wondered where his parents fit in. "And what did you do?"

"As little as possible, I'm afraid. I was a shamefully lazy boy."

She motioned to the rows of books "You seem to have caught on."

"When it dawned upon me that avoiding work was more tedious than actually working."

She laughed. "I think that epiphany comes to most of us at some time."

"Thankfully so," he said, "as I have this affinity for food and shelter."

Rosalind was enjoying the repartee; however, she was keeping him from closing shop. Besides, it was not proper to be chatting like schoolmates with a man she had just met, albeit a chivalrous one. She could almost see Aunt Vesta's frown.

"Well, good day, Mr. Pearce."

"And to you, Miss Kent." He moved to the door, opened it, and looked out. "It'll be dark very soon. Please allow me to escort you to Mrs. Hooper's cottage."

"Thank you, but I'll make it there. I walk fast."

"But wait," he said and moved over to the counter. He brought back a postal card of the beach and the cliffs beyond. "This is a good one."

"I shall have to buy it another day."

"My *welcome to Port Stilwell* gift. Do go home straightaway. It would be best to go northward to Fowler Lane, then turn eastward and continue on to Fore Street."

"Thank you. I know the way from Fore Street."

"Very good. And I hope you'll stop by again."

As a customer, she thought. She thanked him again and set out.

Past Saint Michael's, where the shops of Fore Street gave way to cottages, she slowed her steps at the sight of two young boys scrubbing a picket fence before a two-storey cottage on her left. She drew her wrap tighter. They should be indoors, not out in the chill dusk sloshing water from a bucket.

She paused and cleared her throat. Both heads whipped around.

"Um, can you give me directions to Orchard Lane?"

"It's but one lane beyond, miss," said the elder, motioning with dripping rag. He seemed but ten, with brown hair and ears that stuck out a bit.

The younger, copper-headed and freckled, nodded. "Are you lost?"

"Not anymore, thanks to your help." Taking advantage of this brief communication, she said, "Shouldn't you be at your supper?"

"I said a naughty word, miss," the youngest said.

"Albert . . ." cautioned his brother.

The younger sniffed, swiped his sleeve under his nose. "Didn't know it was. I heard a fisherman say it when his cart-wheel broke. Mum said if Teresa says it, she'll skin me like a hare."

"That's enough, Albert!" the elder boy hissed. "Please go, miss."

Rosalind continued on, sick at heart. But perhaps it was not as it seemed. Boys were more prone to mischief than girls, or so it appeared from casual observation. And as to the threat, exaggeration often accompanied anger. It was very likely that the boy had been warned not to swear.

A shiver went through her. *His punishment is to catch pneumonia?*

She turned. The two gave her stricken looks as she approached.

"I'm sorry, but your parents surely don't realize your clothes are wet. I can't go to a warm cottage whilst you're out here."

"We've almost finished," the elder pleaded. "Please go."

The cottage door opened. A woman stepped out, haloed by lamplight behind her. "Danny! Albert! What's going on?"

Rosalind swallowed her anger, waved a hand, and chirped, "Hello . . . I was asking directions."

She dared not look at the boys but could feel their relief.

"I shall go now. Good evening!"

As she walked up Orchard Lane, the moon sailed out from behind heavy clouds, making the apple trees ghastly in the silver light, as if prepared to uproot themselves and skulk toward her. Gravel crunched beneath her feet. And then in the distance, a figure moved. Rosalind's breath caught in her throat.

A masculine voice called, "Miss Kent?"

"Yes?" Rosalind called back, weak with relief.

Amos White drew closer.

"I carried supper over. Your mum's frantic over your whereabouts."

Rosalind thanked him and walked faster. Light shone from every window in the yellow cottage. Mother and Mrs. Deamer stood outside the gate in the glow of the lantern Mrs. Deamer held.

"Rosalind!" Mother cried.

Surprised and moved by the distress in her voice, Rosalind found herself saying, "I'm sorry I worried you."

"I wondered if you'd decided to return to school." Her mother sniffed. "But Mrs. Deamer reminded me that you would not have left your bag. Then I thought of the cliffs."

"They can be slippery," said the housekeeper.

"I'm fine." Impulse prompted her to lift her hand, yet Rosalind stopped herself from patting her mother's arm. "Let's go indoors."

In the dining room, she told the women of the nosebleed and then the boys.

"At this hour?" Mother asked.

"Perhaps they were being punished?" Mrs. Deamer suggested. "And the parents did not realize they were soaked?"

"Perhaps," Rosalind conceded. *At least they weren't being beaten. Or worse.*

Mrs. Deamer served from the sideboard a clear gravy soup, beef rib roast, sea kale, and potatoes. She placed a small silver bell near Mother's bread plate. "I shall be in the kitchen. Please ring for dessert."

"Is it on the sideboard?" Mother asked.

"Yes. Mrs. Lightman's excellent rhubarb tart."

"We'll serve our own. Take your supper at your leisure."

"Why, thank you." Mrs. Deamer left the room.

Rosalind could not help but grudgingly admire her mother's kindness, enough to engage her in conversation. She took a spoonful of soup and said, "I passed several men queued to vote."

Her mother gave her a blank look.

"For prime minister."

"Ah." She nodded. "I lost all sense of time in the hospital."

"We'll subscribe to a newspaper or two. You can catch up."

"You mustn't waste any more money on me."

"They aren't expensive."

"Yes. Thank you." Her mother moved her spoon through her soup.

"What is it?" Rosalind asked, once again annoyed at herself for caring.

Looking up again, her mother said, "I don't want to seem ungrateful. Please subscribe for yourself if you wish, but I would rather not read the London news."

"Very well. There may be a local newspaper. But . . ."

She stopped herself from saying, *Surely the critics have moved on.* To her knowledge, Mother did not know of the scathing reviews. While she felt justified in the fiction of Aunt Vesta's doting nature, Rosalind had no wish to inflict more pain. Mother was, after all, a human being.

Another thought came to her. "Should you not be aware if Lord Fosberry makes more accusations?"

"No." Her mother gave a little shudder. "There is nothing I can do if he does. He haunts my dreams. I can't allow him to rob my waking moments."

Rosalind watched the spoon moving, the pain upon her mother's face. She softened her voice. "The soup is good."

Her mother leaned to taste. "Quite good."

They finished their soups. Setting aside her bowl and picking up fork and knife, Rosalind said, "May I ask why you stayed five years? You've divorced before."

After a moment, her mother replied, "Having divorced makes the thought of a second more difficult. You feel a failure once again. In any case, by the time he revealed his true nature, my money and any courage I thought I possessed were gone."

You could have written to me, Rosalind thought. But would she have responded?

Yes. Sent money at the very least.

Or would she have? Perhaps not the Rosalind she was of just days ago, carrying the mental image of a mother who had not lived up to the duties God had assigned to her.

Not everything is black and white, she realized.

"Everything will be all right," she found herself saying.

Her mother's eyes glittered. "Thank you, Rosalind. And for rescuing me."

"You're welcome." But she was not accustomed to so much sentiment. She busied herself by cutting up a potato. "We should finish supper before it grows cold."

10

On Tuesday morning, ten-year-old Danny Fletcher opened his eyes and noticed the tepid sunlight slanting through the curtains. Pulse quickening, he rolled over and shook his brother's shoulder.

"Albert!"

Albert's lashes trembled, but soft snores continued from the mouth bowed against the pillow.

Another shake, and this time Danny's whisper was more urgent. "Wake!"

The six-year-old's blue eyes opened, blinked at him. Filled with tears.

Danny groaned. "No . . ."

Albert's voice was small, thick. "I'm sorry."

Danny released his grip to pat the bony shoulder. "No matter. I should have woken. But hurry!"

Two sets of feet eased to the chill floorboards. Danny tugged off the bedding and went around to his brother's side. With soft grunts, they folded and flipped the thin mattress.

From behind the chest of drawers, he pulled the wadded sheet he had taken from a clothesline weeks ago. He was certain that stealing a sheet was a more serious sin than stealing food. He could only hope Mother would have the chance to explain to God that he had to protect Albert.

They made the bed again. There was no disguising the odor, but the room had smelled this way since Albert was four and their stepmother declared him too old to wear nappies to bed.

Danny shoved the damp sheet behind the chest. He would wait for an opportunity to spread it out in the attic. She never went up there.

He and his brother climbed back into bed. Only the hem of Albert's nightshirt was damp. He knew without being told to lie on that side.

They stared at each other. Danny could hear the faint chatter of Teresa, aged eighteen months. He smiled to himself, picturing her latest achievement, patting the garden door and saying, "We go?"

He could not smile *at* her, not without risking his stepmother accusing him of motives he did not understand.

Albert's eyes filled again. "What if she feels my shirt?"

"She won't."

She was loath to touch them, even while using the stick. She had her ways, however. Almost every corner of the cottage had nicks in the cob walls.

Albert had it the worst. Danny knew in his heart that the bedwetting wasn't the only reason. How many times, back when they used to go to church, had people exclaimed over Albert's freckles and red curls? Over how much he resembled Mother? Stepmother's lips would press together as if she had tasted vinegar.

Why this was so, Danny could not fathom.

Oddity upon oddities, he could recall when his stepmother was kind. That was back when she arrived because Mother's stomach was growing too big and her ankles too puffy for her to keep house.

He kept Mother's image in his mind. Gentle, smiling, embracing. Her face was sober in the photograph he had discovered last year in a snuff tin tucked into the toe of an old skate on a cellar shelf. Though she did not smile, her eyes danced.

Father was the only person who could have hidden the photograph. Danny dared not ask. Not that Father had ever lifted a hand to him. He was a clerk at the bank and naturally soft-spoken. But absent in a way that Danny could not understand.

Did Father blame Albert? After all, by some mystery, his infant brother had appeared the same day Mother died. But surely not, because Father treated both sons with equal indifference.

His shoulders could still feel the touch of his father's soft hands when Albert was still an infant. Miss Sabrina Walsh was to become his mother, he had said. *"We need her and may as well make it proper. Besides, she lost her own mother as a child, so will help you to cope."*

Three sharp raps and his stepmother's voice broke into his reverie. "Wake up!"

Fortunately, she did not open the door.

They dressed quickly. Danny helped Albert bathe with a flannel and cold water from the pitcher, then ran a comb across both their heads.

As happened more and more lately, Father had left when they entered the kitchen. Stepmother was preparing their lunches at the table: shilling-sized spots of jam on slices of bread that she dropped into treacle buckets.

She looked up and said, "Eat your porridge. You'll be late."

They had plenty of time, but she wanted them away. Still, she seemed of a pleasant enough temperament, though that could change in an instant. Danny was careful to ignore little Teresa. Plump, pink-cheeked, and with her mother's blond hair and violet eyes, she played with a stack of wooden blocks, hooting with laughter when they fell. One look from him would bring her toddling over, babbling and hoping to play.

The porridge was cold, and worse, had burnt spots. As

ravenous as he was, it was all he could do to choke it down without allowing it to touch his tongue. His warning look to Albert was not necessary, for his brother spooned in mouthfuls and gulped, eyes tearing.

At least their stepmother was as stingy with the porridge as with the lunches. Danny carried bowls and spoons to the sink, thanked her again, and took up the buckets.

"Thank you, Mother," Albert said as well.

"Does my little mite need a clean nappy?" she cooed to Teresa.

The bells of Saint Michael's were chiming nine o'clock when the boys reached the weathered stone Augusta Silcox School, named after the founder years before they were born. Children were assembling at the steps before the two front doors, the left leading to the two classrooms of the infant school. Danny handed Albert his bucket and admonished him to be good for Mrs. Fairburn. The warning was not necessary, for Albert adored his schoolmistress, even though she was old and had a shrill voice. She was equally kind back when Danny was in her class. He wished he had some way to repay her. If only he had fishing lines! He would catch her the biggest fish in the bay!

He took his time shuffling over to the grammar school door, waiting until most were inside before joining the end of the queue.

Would that he could run off and hide in the cliffs! His classmates gave him wide berth and made up taunts such as "Jugears" and "Louse-head," even though, to his knowledge, he had never had lice.

Worse was "Stinky," for he suspected it was true. Elsewise, why would the schoolmaster always be so cross with him?

"All at attention for 'God Save the Queen'!" Mr. Clark barked from the front. He would not sing until he had absolute silence.

Danny's stomach pinged like a rusty spring. Someone giggled, and Mr. Clark scowled at the entire class.

The sleepiness, the taunts, the slaps, the worries for his brother, and the longings for his mother were more than Danny thought he could bear at times.

The grinding hunger was worse. His stomach growled again. More giggles, and this time Mr. Clark's scowl found its mark.

11

Coral Shipsey arrived at the yellow house at ten past eleven, and mental images of the plump, rosy-cheeked, mature cooks of Charlotte's past evaporated.

Nineteen, she was, with wide hazel eyes and a fair complexion marred only by a faint strawberry mark between her cheek and left ear. She was short, with a shapely figure. Honey-colored curls spilled from a ribbon.

"If you could bear ham sandwiches for lunch, I'll make it up to you at supper with stewed eels and pork cutlets," she said in a girlish voice after Mrs. Deamer made introductions in the parlor.

"But of course." Charlotte smiled. "I wasn't expecting someone so young."

The girl nodded. "I was scullery maid for Mrs. Lightman from age twelve. She liked to teach, and I wanted to learn."

"Good for you," Rosalind said.

She turned out to be a decent cook, especially with pastries. One day, confidence and experience would make her an excellent one, Charlotte thought.

On Saturday morning, five days after arriving in Port Stilwell, Charlotte sat at her writing table and penned a letter.

Dear Mr. Irving,
   May God bless you for not abandoning me in that hour of need. I am quite well, tucked away in Devonshire. I pray that your production is continuing well. I shall always regret failing you, yet such failure brought a silver lining, as my dear Rosalind has come back into my life. I feel most blessed.

She signed her name and folded it into an envelope. Should she include her return address? She decided against it. Why lay that burden on him? And there was always the chance of its being misdirected. He would understand and likely not even notice.

Her thoughts were becoming calmer after but five days of simple routine.

While she enjoyed meals and desserts, she no longer felt the drive to dull her senses with visits to the kitchen betweentimes. She reckoned she would never be thin again but felt the upward spiral was over.

She could appreciate the quiet of Mrs. Hooper's parlor and chats with Mrs. Deamer. Life would be almost perfect, she thought, if Rosalind were not so clearly wishing to return to Cheltenham.

That first supper had turned out to be an anomaly. All conversations since had been polite and cautious. She could sense her daughter was under tremendous pressure, so she did not attempt to force interaction.

She brought the letter downstairs and found Mrs. Deamer holding the front door for Amos White and another young man as they carried through a trunk.

"Hello, Amos," Charlotte said as they lowered it to the hall floor. "How is your grandfather keeping?"

"Very well, Mrs. Kent," he said, straightening. "This is my cousin, Billy."

Billy, short and muscular looking, doffed his cap and nodded.

"We can carry it upstairs this time," Amos went on.

"Is Miss Kent resting, do you think?" Mrs. Deamer asked.

"I'll go and see," Charlotte said.

"Would you rather I did?" But of course Mrs. Deamer sensed Charlotte's reluctance to be a nuisance to Rosalind.

"No, thank you."

Charlotte went upstairs and knocked. Rosalind answered holding a novel and wearing her usual polite, patient, but oh, so opaque expression.

"Your trunk is here."

"It is?" Rosalind looked past her and turned. "I'll just put this away."

Charlotte moved into the room and watched her place the book onto the seat of her chair.

"Amos brought a stronger back along this time. They're able to carry it up."

"What a relief."

When her daughter turned, her face said otherwise. Charlotte had seen that same expression many times in mirrors at Fosberry Hall.

"May we speak first?" Charlotte said.

"Speak?" Rosalind gave a little shrug. "Very well."

Charlotte closed the door, turned. "Have them take it back to the station."

"I beg your pardon?"

"And go with them. Catch the next train to Cheltenham."

Her daughter stared at her.

"You've done enough. It's time to get on with your life."

"But you need me."

"All I need . . ." Charlotte's throat thickened. ". . . is for you to be happy. I shall be fine."

Rosalind looked tempted, then shrugged again. "Spring lectures have concluded."

"I'm sorry. Truly I am." Charlotte reached for the knob.

"Wait."

She turned again, noticed a sheen in her daughter's green eyes.

"You would do that for me?"

"Oh, Rosalind," Charlotte gushed, feeling the sting of tears. "Anything."

Her daughter watched her with a tense expression, as if working up to saying something unpleasant.

Charlotte braced herself.

"I lied to you. Aunt Vesta held her cats in higher esteem than me."

An ache stabbed Charlotte's chest. "I'm so sorry! My poor girl!"

Lips trembling, Rosalind said, "I'm not saying this to hurt you, Mother. I just want you to know that you were missed . . ."

Charlotte put her hand to her mouth and choked back a sob.

". . . and that I'm grateful for this chance to be with you."

Had her ears betrayed her?

Rosalind sniffed and gave her a teary smile. "May we begin again?"

"Yes, please!" Charlotte cried as they went to each other's arms.

She held her daughter for but a moment, relishing the tears this time. A tentative knock sounded. Rosalind stepped away, patted her arm, and opened the door.

"Forgive me for intruding," Mrs. Deamer said, "but the boys must return the wagon soon."

"Of course," Rosalind said, hurrying past her.

Footfalls sounded upon the staircase. Charlotte wiped her eyes and blew her nose under the housekeeper's worried gaze.

"Is everything all right?" Mrs. Deamer asked.

Charlotte smiled. "Yes, quite all right."

Mrs. Deamer returned the smile, clearly happy to hear it, and Charlotte thought, *I pray I can say the same for you one day.*

⟡

Conversation over lunch was considerably lighter. Charlotte prevailed upon Rosalind to tell of her school experiences, even of the former beau who apparently could have been one of Roger's disciples.

Afterward, she sat in Rosalind's chair and watched her unpack the trunk.

"Will you go to church tomorrow?" Charlotte asked.

Placing a folded nightgown in a drawer, Rosalind replied, "Yes. There is a Congregationalist chapel, Saint Paul's."

"But Aunt Vesta was Anglican."

"I became Congregationalist while at college. And you?"

Still so much catching up to do! Charlotte thought. "Anglican. But I visited some Congregationalist churches over my childhood. As long as Christ is preached, I'm fine. And I'd rather be with you . . . if you're agreeable?"

Rosalind smiled. "It would be my pleasure."

An unsettling thought struck Charlotte. "But what if I'm recognized?"

"You could wear your veil."

"Yes. But for how long? Months and months? Torture! And will I attract the attention I wish to escape?"

Rosalind stepped around the bed to lean against the post, and folded her arms. "May I be frank with you, Mother?"

"But of course."

"After an absence of five years, you had the one performance."

"Part of a performance," Charlotte corrected.

"And what are the chances that someone from Port Stilwell was there?"

"Remote, at best."

"Even if so, such a person would have been out in the audience. Not up close. As for anyone recognizing you from newspapers, when were the most recent engravings printed?"

"I suppose that would be my wedding to Roger."

Her daughter mugged a frown. "Blackbeard."

"Quite appropriate. But some may have been printed again whilst I was in the hospital."

"Hmm. Well, in them . . . were you . . ."

Charlotte had to smile at her discomfort. "As thin as a reed. I never thought I would be grateful for the extra weight."

⋅⋅✦⋅⋅

Charlotte asked Mrs. Deamer about the minister the next morning over breakfast. She had fallen into requesting Rosalind's usual toast and tea, and was discovering, oddly enough, that she was not hungry two hours later, as when after a laden platter.

"Mr. Moore is his name, according to Coral. She could show you the way, but she leaves early for choir."

"I've seen it," Rosalind said, wearing a bottle green silk that enhanced her eyes. "North of the shops on Kleef Lane."

Mrs. Deamer nodded. "Tragically, his wife has a cancer and is not expected to live beyond summer."

"How sad," Rosalind said. "Have they any children?"

"I believe he has a married daughter in Cornwall and a son at Oxford."

"Are you Church of England?" Charlotte asked, just as Rosalind had asked her.

Teapot in hand, Mrs. Deamer replied, "All of my life. But I haven't attended here."

"Is it because you don't wish to go alone?" Rosalind asked. "We could walk you there on our way and meet you afterward."

"You're very kind." She hesitated, as if considering whether to share something. "I almost never venture into town. Coral does the shopping."

Gently, Charlotte said, "Is this because of your husband?"

Mrs. Deamer hesitated, then nodded again.

"But surely no one here knows."

"They know."

Rosalind's glance at Charlotte had *Mrs. Hooper* written all over it.

❖

Saint Michael's bells peeled out an Anglican five-note call in the distance. Saint Paul's Congregationalist Chapel was of gray stone, with slanted red-slate roof, long mullioned windows, and a painted coral door beyond an arched porch. Worshipers socialized in the yard in loose knots: families with young children, weathered fishermen in faded suits, their wives in colorful wraps. Charlotte pretended not to notice glances sent their way. She could not afford friendships, people with whom to monitor every word.

"Good morning, Mrs. Kent, Miss Kent!"

They turned to smile at Coral Shipsey. She stood with a man so handsome as to be beautiful. Tall and slender, he had full lips and hooded amber eyes beneath a halo of flaxen curls.

"May I introduce Noble Clark?" Coral said, fairly glowing. "He's schoolmaster at the grammar school. And lead soloist here."

"Singing is my passion," he said.

"I anticipate hearing you, Mr. Clark." Charlotte offered her hand. "My father oft said that hymns are the sermons we remember the longest."

"Well said." He wrapped long, soft fingers around hers. "I shan't disappoint you."

But his eyes were upon Rosalind.

"I noticed you on Monday, Miss Kent, near the seashore. Do you stroll every day?"

"I try, weather allowing," she replied. "But usually mornings."

"There is a lovely path to the west, along the cliffs, that I would be happy to show you on Saturday."

Charlotte could not help but notice Coral's rigid posture.

"That's very kind of you, Mr. Clark," Rosalind said with polite aloofness. "But I find solitary walks to be most advantageous to the mind."

"You'll be late for choir," Coral said, touching his shoulder. She softened her voice. "We mustn't disappoint Mrs. Kent."

"Yes, of course." He raised his chin and turned on his heel without another look at either of them.

"That was disquieting," Charlotte leaned close to say when he was out of earshot.

"What else could I have said?" Rosalind asked.

"You were as kind as possible."

They entered the church. At the end of the fourth row from the back, an older woman smiled at Charlotte.

"You may sit here," she said in a startling Prussian accent, nudging the man with her to slide to the right.

Charlotte smiled and entered the pew with Rosalind following. "Thank you."

In the loft, five women, including Coral, and two men, including Noble Clark, sang "Go Not Far From Me, O My Strength," accompanied on the organ by a young woman. The congregation joined them for "Come Thou Fount of Every Blessing," and then Mr. Clark stepped from loft to podium.

> "Lead, kindly Light, amid the encircling gloom,
> lead Thou me on."

His tenor was clear, sweet, and on key, at least for the majority of the notes.

> "The night is dark, and I am far from home;
> Lead Thou me on!"

An elbow nudged Charlotte. The woman beside her rolled her eyes and whispered, "His uncle is churchwarden."

Charlotte nodded

Aldous Moore was of medium height and stoop shouldered, and while his gait was weary, his voice matched his kind smile. The subject of his sermon, he announced, was the pursuit of holiness, key Scriptures from the Book of Matthew.

"'Blessed are they which do hunger and thirst after righteousness,'" he began, and Charlotte found herself saying a silent prayer for his wife. Cancer was a terrible disease.

After the closing hymn, Charlotte turned to the couple who had surrendered their seats. "Thank you."

The man leaned forward, smiled, and said in an accent like his wife's, "It was our pleasure. Our daughter, Gisela, is the organist."

"She played very well," Charlotte said.

"We have the butcher shop down the street," said the woman. "Grundke's."

Mr. Moore stood outside the door, beneath the arched porch.

"Welcome to Port Stilwell, Mrs. Kent . . . Miss Kent," he said after Rosalind's introduction. "May I call upon you soon?"

Charlotte offered her hand but shook her head. "Thank you, Mr. Moore, but you have enough on your shoulders for the time being."

He gave her a sad smile. "Thank you for understanding."

"That was thoughtful of you," Rosalind said when they were out of earshot. "At least he has children. To comfort him . . . later."

"He will have to comfort them as well," Charlotte said. "It is hard to lose a mother."

"I can hardly remember Grandmother Ward."

"You were but five the last time she accompanied me to Aunt Vesta's. It was shortly afterward that pleurisy took her."

"I'm sorry."

Charlotte's eyes began to smart. "At least mine didn't leave by choice."

"You *had* no choice that you could see."

Overwhelmed by such forgiveness, Charlotte had to dab her eyes with her fingertips.

Rosalind linked an arm through hers. "Mother?"

Charlotte patted her arm. "I'm all right. Thank you."

"Imagine such cheek from Mr. Clark!" she said in an obvious attempt to lighten the mood.

"'A man wrapped up in himself is a very small bundle,'" Charlotte said.

"Shakespeare?"

"An American, actually. Benjamin Franklin."

"Ah . . . the kite and electricity fellow. Should I apologize to Coral?"

"Apologize? You did nothing wrong."

"I wouldn't wish resentment."

"Especially from one who prepares your food," Charlotte quipped before sobering again. "I saw resignation and pain in her eyes, but no resentment toward you. After all, you cut him off quickly."

Arm in arm, they walked in companionable silence a bit longer, and then Rosalind asked, "Do you think of my father?"

"Yes, at times."

"Aunt Vesta said he was drunk when he died."

Charlotte sighed. "She should not have burdened you with that. He was celebrating your imminent birth. As a rule, he drank rarely."

"Tell me more."

She started from the day she met Patrick, during rehearsals for *The Man in the Iron Mask* at the Adelphi. Leaving out a volatile temper and capricious moods linked to performances, she spoke of his always having coppers in his pocket for beggars, his visiting his aged parents every week, his love for a clever riddle.

"He never had the chance to hold me," Rosalind said.

"There's a pity."

"You spoke of his parents . . ."

"Gone. No other family. A sister who perished from whooping cough." She sighed. "I'm afraid I'm all you've got, family-wise."

Rosalind squeezed her arm. "You'll do nicely."

12

That afternoon after Rosalind left for a walk, Charlotte played the pianoforte for a bit and then went up the staircase to the attic. She studied the four closed doors before taking a chance on the first one on her left.

Mrs. Deamer answered with book in hand.

"Oh good. You weren't asleep," Charlotte said.

"I enjoyed your music."

"Thank you. I realize it's your afternoon off, but I came up on the off chance that you'd fancy a game of cribbage. But you're reading."

The housekeeper held up the book. "*The Cossacks,* by Tolstoy. My fourth read through. I kept but a few novels, which I now regret."

"I brought none," Charlotte said.

"Would you care to borrow one of mine?"

"Thank you, that would be lovely."

Mrs. Deamer stepped back. "Do come in."

The room was small, with a ceiling that slanted to a four-foot wall with two dormer windows. A Bohemian-looking woven blanket was spread upon a mattress with an iron bedstead, a comparatively subdued rug of blues and greens and browns upon the floor. Against one wall was a wardrobe and chest of drawers. A chair and washstand were against the other, beside a framed picture of daisies in a vase.

The books stood upon the chest of drawers, propped between two cast-iron bookends in the shape of owls: a Bible in black leather, three novels by Tolstoy, one by Trollope, and another by Wilkie Collins. Charlotte had read all but Trollope's *The Small House at Allington*.

"Thank you," she said, pushing the books together to fill the gap. "I'll leave you to your reading."

She was at the door when Mrs. Deamer said, "My parents would not allow us to play cards on Sunday. It rather stuck with me."

"I see."

"The subject of draughts, however, was never addressed."

Charlotte smiled. "I shouldn't wish to tempt you down the path to perdition."

"I've witnessed others on that path, and it does not appeal to me. I would enjoy a game."

At the draughts table in the parlor, Charlotte took twelve round pieces each from the wooden box, kept the black, and handed the tan across the board. Placing game pieces upon her squares, she said, "Are your parents still living, Mrs. Deamer?"

"They are not. And yours?"

"Gone many years. I had no siblings. Have you?"

"I have a brother, Charles."

"Does he live nearby?"

The draughts pieces clicked upon the table. "He's in Dartmoor prison. He was my husband's secretary and involved in his crimes."

Charlotte put a hand to her bosom. "My dear."

Mrs. Deamer shook her head. "I almost drove myself mad, thinking that if I had not married Lowell, my brother would not have been offered the position."

"But that wasn't your doing."

"It was in that I pledged myself to a man with no more thought than as if I were picking out a bonnet. That he was handsome and charming was enough. Character? I scarcely knew what it was."

"How old were you?" Charlotte asked.

"When I married? Eighteen."

"That says everything. No one should be allowed to marry before the age of thirty."

"Hear, hear."

"Hmm. Considering my last marriage . . . sixty."

Mrs. Deamer grimaced. "I'm sorry."

"I say that in jest. We wouldn't want to wipe out the earth's population in one generation, would we?" Charlotte hesitated. "Regarding your brother . . . whilst your marriage gave him opportunity, it would have meant nothing if the inclination was not there as well."

"Yes, I realize that now," Mrs. Deamer said.

"When will he and your husband be released?"

"My brother, in fourteen years. My husband, twenty-three. They have served but one. Mrs. Hooper has agreed to my visiting both every four months, an absence of three days. I went last just before you arrived, so I will not need to leave again until July. I hope that is agreeable to you."

"But of course," Charlotte said.

They began the game, and Charlotte moved a piece diagonally. "How did you come to be employed here? And you must shush me if my prying goes too far."

Mrs. Deamer made a move at her end. "I came to be in Mrs. Hooper's employ when she sent a letter of sympathy after the sentencing."

"How did she know?"

"It was in newspapers all over Devonshire, probably even as far as London. Or so I'm told. I could not bear to look at them."

"How well I understand," Charlotte said.

"Mrs. Hooper and her sister, a Mrs. Caswell, were on the same tour of Egypt as my husband and me six years ago. There were fifteen of us; naturally we became well acquainted."

"I see." She had also lived well, Charlotte thought. Proof that security in this world was a tenuous thing. But unlike Mrs. Deamer's, her own reduced circumstances had led to something positive.

"In my reply to her letter, I asked if Mr. Hooper could possibly use an assistant, as I'm quite knowledgeable of fabrics. She wrote back that he did not, but then sent another letter saying she was considering opening her home to lodgers."

She slid her draughts piece to a side square. "My pride suffered. But other positions for which I had applied had not replied. I was living with friends who were clearly uncomfortable with the notoriety attached to my husband. In any case, I could not take advantage of their hospitality forever. It has worked out well. My responsibilities are lighter than they would have been had I been in charge of cooking and laundry."

"I'm sorry for all you went through," Charlotte said. "But I am glad to know you. I believe we shall become good friends."

"Why, thank you, Mrs. Kent. That would please me."

"It would please me if you were not so good at this game," Charlotte grumbled lightly, seeing two of her draughts pieces cornered.

Mrs. Deamer laughed, the first Charlotte had heard.

They played on.

Charlotte was pleased, finally, to have a piece crowned on Mrs. Deamer's side of the board. At length, she said, "You've shared your story. It's only fair that I share mine."

It was a relief not to keep it bottled.

"I will never tell a soul," Mrs. Deamer said.

Charlotte smiled at her across the board. "I believe you."

Late the following morning, Mrs. Deamer introduced Charlotte to Amy Hugo, who arrived in a horse-pulled cart with *Clive Hugo Laundry Service, Port Stilwell,* stenciled upon the side. She collected the wash Mondays and delivered on Thursdays.

"I'm pleased to meet you," said Amy, a pretty, dark-haired girl. To Mrs. Deamer, she said, "I'll gather the kitchen linens first."

It was from the kitchen that Charlotte heard voices as she was reading *The Small House at Allington.* Rosalind was upstairs, changing shoes after her walk.

"You want to see the poems he gave to me?" Coral's high voice shouted.

"You wrote 'em yourself!"

"Excuse me," Mrs. Deamer said and hurried from the parlor.

Soon there was silence. In time, Mrs. Deamer returned. "They were fighting over some town swain."

"I thought as much," Charlotte said. "Mr. Clark."

"You've met him?"

"At Saint Paul's. He has an unfortunate passion for singing."

"I heard voices," Rosalind said from the doorway. "What is going on?"

Charlotte sighed. "As we suspected, Mr. Clark may not be so noble."

13

"You stopped in just in time, Dr. Harris," Jude Pearce said on Thursday, the eighteenth of March. "Your book arrived in yesterday's shipment."

From behind the counter, he produced *Studies in the History of the Renaissance* by Walter Horatio Pater.

"Good enough." The doctor, with a wild, graying beard, was one of his best customers. He had no interest in the lending library's "musty old collection of romantic novels," nor in being scolded again by the librarian for leaving snuff stains on pages.

His knees creaked as he knelt to scratch behind Jinny's half-perked, half-flopped mongrel ears. Digging into his coat pocket, he said, "Fancy a chocolate?"

Jinny trembled with happiness, but Jude said, "Sorry, Dr. Harris. It's bad for her stomach."

"Aye, most pleasures are," the man grumbled while getting to his feet. "Sorry, Jinny, I'll bring kippers next time."

"You'll have a friend for life."

Dr. Harris left, and Jude began arranging copies of Disraeli's *Endymion* in the window. He admired the man as a writer but was glad Mr. Gladstone had won the election as prime minister, for he considered Mr. Disraeli's foreign policies ill conceived.

Movement caught the corner of his eye. He looked up and spied Phoebe Drummer leave Owen's Bakery, look over her shoulder, and cross Kleef Lane.

Her face turned toward the window. He stepped backward, said to Jinny, "Is she coming here?"

Jinny raised her head, cocked an ear forward.

Force of old habit prompted Jude to smooth his hair with his hands.

The door opened, and Phoebe stepped inside with a swishing of skirts. "Jude."

"Good morning, Phoebe."

Jinny raised herself and trotted over, tail wagging.

"So, you remember me, do you, girl?" she said, patting behind Jinny's ears.

Phoebe was lovely still, with a dimpled smile and dark blond hair caught up in a jeweled comb. She straightened, closed the door behind her, and glanced about.

"Good! You're alone. But I shan't stay long, or Father will notice."

"Yes?" Jude stood rooted to the spot.

She moved closer. "You look well."

"As do you. I've heard you have a son."

"Edward, after his father. He's nigh four weeks old. Mother's watching him."

"Very good."

She rubbed her sleeved arms. "Dr. Goldsberry said it's too soon to be up and about, but my lying-in was so long that I thought I should go mad. When Mother came to visit, I gave Nanny the day off and talked her into bringing us back with her."

The way her words rushed out was unsettling, as were her frequent glances to the window.

"Phoebe," Jude said gently, "why have you come here?"

Her hazel eyes pooled. "I've thought often of you lately. Of how cruel, how cowardly it was of me not to speak with you in person. Especially as you were mourning your grandfather."

She referred, of course, to the letter slid beneath his door last year, informing him that she had accepted Edward Drummer's proposal of marriage. Edward Drummer! The part owner of the quarry was twice her age, and oddly enough, the same man of whom she oft complained, for his bold stares whenever she served him in her father's bakery.

But Phoebe feared her father's disappointment more than anything and could not stand against his conviction that the races should not mix. It mattered not that Jude was but one-quarter Indian, nor that his half-caste mother had been honorable and loving to her family.

The wedding was grand, he had heard. Now Phoebe and Mr. Drummer and their child lived in a servant-infested house in Seaton, twelve miles to the east.

"You've forgiven me, then?" she was saying.

"But of course."

Her lip trembled. Tears spilled. "I thought my baby would make me happy. He's a sweet little fellow, mind you, but I cry every night. Edward's losing patience with me."

He handed her a handkerchief, experiencing brief *déjà vu*. She blew her nose into it and wadded it with trembling fingers.

"I'm so sorry, Phoebe," he said.

Moving forward, she rested her head upon his shoulder. He allowed it but for a moment, then, with great restraint, held her shoulders so that he could step back from her.

She gulped a breath. "Mother says melancholia happens often to new mothers. That time will heal."

"Your mother is a wise woman." He waited a second. "Does he mistreat you?"

"No." Her voice was a squeak, and she blew her nose again.

"He gives me anything I want. But his breath is vile, and he drones on and on about the goings-on in his beloved quarry. And his hands . . ."

"Phoebe," he said, "your family wants what's best for you. Allow them to help you. Because I can't."

"I know," she rasped and gave a little shudder. "You loved me. And I threw it away like so much rubbish!"

It grieved him to see her this way. But after a year, he dared not peel the scar from his heart and allow those old feelings again. To what end? She was another man's wife.

Softly, he said, "Any moment someone could walk in. If word gets back . . ."

"Yes." She sighed and went to the door. Turning, she gave him a sad smile. "The eyeglasses suit you, Jude."

The timing of her departure was fortuitous, for but two minutes later, Mrs. Fallon from the Sea Gull Inn arrived for the half-dozen books she had ordered for the inn's little library for patrons. Jude closed shop and carried the books back for her, Jinny trotting ahead.

On their return, he left Jinny outside and stopped into Grundke's for a thick slice of ham for his lunch sandwich, and some beef bones for the dog.

"I just took bratwurst from kettle," Mrs. Grundke said.

Jude smiled. "Never mind the ham and bones. I'll have two."

He stepped back onto Kleef Lane carrying the paper-wrapped parcel and noticed a woman staring into the window of his shop.

No!

He thought to duck back into the butcher's, but then Jinny let out a bark and bounded ahead.

Traitor!

Aurora Hooper patted Jinny's head and waved at him.

Can this day get any worse?

"Good day, Mrs. Hooper," he called while struggling to fish his key from his pocket.

She hurried toward him and snatched the parcel. "Allow me."

He unlocked the door and turned to offer a few brief civilities. But she followed him inside.

"Thank you, Mrs. Hooper," he said again, taking back his parcel. "We mean to take our lunch upstairs. But if there is a particular book . . ."

He was going through the motions. Mr. Hooper was the reader of the family. *God rest his soul.*

She waved a dismissive hand. "Mr. Hooper was the reader of the family, God rest his soul. I have something to show to you."

From a blue embroidered reticule, she withdrew a small black pasteboard folder with gold trim. She was holding it out, so he set his purchase upon the counter and took it.

"Your being keen on dogs, I thought you would appreciate this photograph."

Not quite following, he opened the folder to a sepia-toned girl standing beside a potted fern and holding a Yorkshire terrier.

"A handsome dog," he said, thinking of his bratwursts, growing cold. "But one is enough."

She laughed and cuffed his arm. "Such a jokester you are, Mr. Pearce! This is my grandniece, Bernadette Caswell. Daughter of my sister's son in Portishead. She turned eighteen on Sunday past."

"Lovely girl."

"The exact age of our beloved queen when she assumed the throne."

"That is so." He handed the photograph back to her. "Thank you for—"

"*And* . . . she visits next month for Saint George's Day. The picture does not do her justice, Mr. Pearce."

"No doubt," he said, hoping this was not leading where it seemed to be.

"When you see her, just try and stop yourself from falling in love."

Jinny let out a little yip. She was fond of bratwurst too.

Jude sighed. "Mrs. Hoo—"

She wagged a finger at him. "I know what you're thinking. Will lightning strike twice? I assure you, Bernadette's family is quite cosmopolitan. Your drop of Indian blood matters not one whit. Indeed, one would think you were Spanish at first glance."

Jude's jaw ached from clenching it. "I'm one-quarter Indian, Mrs. Hooper, not just a drop. And I'm not ashamed of my heritage."

"Nor should you be," she said quickly, hand to bosom. "I've toured your country, remember, and met the loveliest—"

"England is my country," he cut in.

"But of course." Now it was she who sighed, small blue eyes shining. "I meant no offense, Mr. Pearce. It's just that you're a good man, well respected in Port Stilwell. I should like my niece to have as wonderful a marriage as I had."

His umbrage toward her softened. "No doubt she's a lovely young lady, Mrs. Hooper. But I'm almost twice her age."

"That's no problem. Bernadette is mature for her years."

"Indeed? As am I. Which means I prefer women twice *my* age."

Mrs. Hooper blew out an exasperated breath. "Jesting again, Mr. Pearce! Phoebe Drummer wasn't older than you."

"And that didn't exactly turn out well."

"Because she's a childish twit!"

"That's not fair, Mrs. Hooper."

"Bernadette, on the other hand, was head girl at her school."

He opened the door. "Good day."

"Good day yourself," she said petulantly, then turned to raise brows. "And all the same, we shall see you on Saint George's Day!"

"Not if I see you first," Jude muttered to the closed door.

He turned the *Will Return in Half an Hour* sign at the glass and carried the food up the staircase.

Jinny reached the landing first and turned to thump her tail.

"Yes, yes," Jude said. "I'm miffed at you for giving me away, mind you. I should eat both brats myself."

Idle words. Jinny knew that, for she gave his leg a loving nudge when he reached the top.

14

On the twenty-first of March, Rosalind and her mother started out again for Saint Paul's. This time, Mother seemed more at ease, walking more slowly, even returning greetings sent their way.

"I'm glad you're more comfortable," Rosalind said.

"I believe you're right. The possibility of anyone recognizing me is remote. Of course it helps that you're at my side. Why notice an old face when you can look at a young one?"

Rosalind clucked her tongue. "You're beautiful, Mother."

"And you're kind, daughter."

Noble Clark sang again, almost reaching the high notes of the *Gloria Patri*.

The title of Mr. Moore's sermon was "Consistency in Our Walk," based upon the example of Daniel, and how being faithful in everyday things made his faith strong enough to endure times of great testing.

Noble Clark was no Daniel, Rosalind thought as she happened to glance back on their way homeward and noticed him chatting up a beaming Amy Hugo.

Rosalind had looked back, not to spy, but in hopes of catching sight of Mr. Pearce. She had not seen him last week either, but then, it was difficult to spot faces from behind.

"Is something troubling you?" her mother asked.

"Mr. Clark is with Amy this time" was Rosalind's evasive reply.

"I suppose there'll be another row in the kitchen tomorrow." She was wrong. It took place in the garden.

"So there you are, Jezebel!"

Amy's voice. The endearment floated up to Rosalind, who was brushing her teeth. She spat out tooth powder and went to the window. Carefully, she raised the window glass. There being no theatre in Port Stilwell, one had to take one's entertainments where available.

"He takes pity upon you!" Amy shrieked. "How can you not see it?"

"Pity!" Coral hissed. "How dare you!"

"Everybody knows you were born on the wrong side of the blanket! That's why Mrs. Hooper got you so cheap!"

"I should slap you for that!" Coral said. "At least I don't have to scrub clothes! What will the carbolic soap do to your hands in ten years?"

"Speaking of hands, he held mine whilst walking me home!"

"No doubt you flapped it out there like a flounder till he had no choice!"

"Well, he took lunch with us too!"

Where is Mrs. Deamer? Rosalind thought. As interesting as the drama was, she did not wish to see them resort to blows. Should she call out?

Another voice saved her the trouble.

"Ladies, ladies!"

Her mother stepped into view. The two young women silenced themselves, though even from one storey above, Rosalind could see the tension in their postures.

"I'm sorry, Mrs. Kent," Amy said, lowering her head.

"I'm sorry as well," said Coral. "Will you speak to Mrs. Hooper?"

"Of course not," Mother said. "Although it's a wonder everyone in town did not hear you. This young man . . . has he mentioned marriage?"

"Yes!" both chorused, then gave each other hard stares.

"Indeed? For how long has he held out hope to the both of you?"

"Nigh two years," Amy said after a moment.

"Because she won't leave him be!" Coral said with hands upon hips.

"I didn't force him to stop by Mum's!" Amy shot back. "And he says I'm prettier than you!"

"He said your ears stick out like coach doors!"

"Young ladies!" Rosalind's mother interjected. "I don't wonder he won't make up his mind. He's enjoying the attention you lavish upon him."

Rosalind smiled, chin resting upon the windowsill.

"If he *firmly* commits to one of you," Mother went on, "the other will give up in due time. Where is the thrill in that?"

"Begging your pardon, Mrs. Kent," Amy said at length. "If *she* would just stop badgering him, he *could* make up his mind."

"And if *you*—"

Mother held up a silencing hand. "What if you *both* ceased badgering him?"

They stared at her.

"When he is no longer the fox to your hounds, he will be forced to choose."

"How would we go about that?" Amy asked. "If I don't allow him to walk me home, what's to stop *her*?"

"The same here," Coral said.

"You walk with each other," Mother replied. "It will rattle his world."

"I'd rather keep company with a snake!" Coral exclaimed.

111

"As would I!" said Amy.

"Very well, then go on this way for another two years." Mother took four steps toward the cottage. "You're obviously enjoying this as much as Mr. Clark is."

"Wait, Mrs. Kent . . . please."

Mother turned toward Amy, the speaker.

"It's wretched! I don't sleep nights."

"Wretched," Coral sniffed.

"Well, there you are. You have something in common, besides a fondness for reptiles. I shall be interested in seeing what you do about it."

After a moment of silence, both mumbled in unison, "Yes, Mrs. Kent."

Mother folded her arms. "By the by, Amy . . . I'm not choosing sides, but one cannot choose the circumstances of one's birth. It's not Christian to hold that against a person."

The laundress nodded, head lowered.

But Mother wasn't finished. "And Coral . . . I never look down on anyone for working hard, as Amy does. Better to have rough hands than idle ones."

By the time Rosalind caught her curls up into a comb, slipped on her bronze-and-white-striped silk gown, and hurried downstairs to the parlor, Mother was sitting ensconced on the sofa, reading calmly as if she had been there all morning.

"I saw what happened out there," Rosalind said, slipping beside her.

"Did you?"

"From the window. You gave wise counsel."

Mother lowered her book and smiled. "Thank you. Experience is a good teacher, though the tuition can be painful to pay."

"Where was Mrs. Deamer?"

"Dusting lamps. We were having a chat when we heard the girls. I entreated her to allow me to intervene."

"Will they take your advice?"

"Who can say?" She sighed. "But I will tell you that men such as Mr. Clark are not suited for the long haul. So it may be that the loser is the winner."

⚬⚬⚬

The following three days brought rain showers, impeding Rosalind's walks. She finished *Off on a Comet* from her belongings and *The Moonstone* from Mrs. Deamer's limited collection.

Good Friday was fittingly overcast but without showers. Saturday dawned sunny, as did Easter morn.

There were two surprises in the dining room.

First, the bowl of colored eggs upon the table.

"Lovely," Rosalind said to Mrs. Deamer as she slid into her chair. "Coral must have stayed up for hours."

"I think not," Mother said, taking her own chair. "Show us the evidence, Mrs. Deamer."

The housekeeper wiggled her fingers. The tips were faintly stained, with a brownish mingling of pink, green, and blue.

Rosalind took an egg from the bowl. "Will it not wash off?"

"This was the best I could do," Mrs. Deamer said. "Fortunately, my gloves will conceal them in church."

That was the second surprise.

"You're going?" Mother asked.

Mrs. Deamer gave her a careful smile. "Actually, may I accompany you? I cannot in good conscience miss Easter. But I'll sit by myself."

"You'll not only walk with us but sit with us," Mother said.

"Thank you," Mrs. Deamer said after a moment.

Mother smiled and closed her eyes.

> "Sleep, sleep, old sun, thou canst not have repassed,
> As yet, the wound thou took'st on Friday past,
> Sleep then, and rest; the world may bear thy stay;
> A better sun rose before thee to-day."

113

Mrs. Deamer's eyes shone. "John Donne."

Rosalind looked up at her. Mrs. Deamer had obviously not been born into service.

The three of them set out later. They had to pick their way on new grass bordering the still-drying lane. Townspeople gave each other greetings outside Saint Paul's, and Rosalind's mother responded in kind.

"You're quite chipper this morning," Rosalind said.

"How can anyone be less than optimistic on this day, with its new beginnings?"

Yet not all beginnings were appreciated. Noble Clark stood in his usual post, looking as perplexed as a cat with a wooden mouse.

"Over there," Mrs. Deamer whispered with a nod toward the churchyard.

Coral and Amy stood under the lych-gate, chatting as if best friends.

Perhaps, Rosalind thought later, seated between Mother and Mrs. Deamer, that explained Mr. Clark's failure to attach his voice to many of the notes to "Christ Arose."

"I almost pity him," she whispered to Mother.

Pews were filled with worshipers as Rosalind scanned backs of heads for Mr. Pearce.

Could he be Anglican? Methodist?

She realized with some guilt that Mr. Moore was well into the sermon on gratitude for the cross by the time she gave it her attention.

I do thank you, Father, Rosalind prayed silently. *If you choose never to answer another prayer of mine, your gift of salvation is enough. More than enough.*

She was out in the yard when Mr. Pearce approached.

"Miss Kent," he said. He looked handsome in a black suit and blue-and-gold cravat. Jinny stood close by his side, panting happily. "How good to see you again. I wondered if you had returned to Cheltenham."

"I leave in a fortnight," Rosalind said before introducing him to her companions.

"I'm pleased to make your acquaintance," Mother said, offering her hand.

"And I yours, Mrs. Kent," he replied. Mrs. Deamer did not offer hers, so he gave her a respectful bow of the head.

"And this is Jinny," Rosalind said.

"You're a sweet pup, aren't you?" Mother crooned, leaning to pat her head. Jinny licked her hand.

"Jinny . . ." Mr. Pearce admonished.

"Please don't scold her," Mother said. "I take it as a compliment. 'Nature teaches beasts to know their friends.'"

He laughed. "Shakespeare."

"Mr. Pearce's late grandfather used to read Shakespeare to him," Rosalind said.

"Shakespeare and the Bible," he said.

"That's quite a legacy," Mother said.

"Thank you."

"I did not notice you inside," Rosalind said and then wished she had not.

His bespectacled green eyes met hers. "I saw you. I ofttimes slip in at the last moment. Jinny tends to dawdle on the way."

"Would you care to take lunch with us, Mr. Pearce?" Mother asked.

He gave her a regretful smile. "Thank you, but I've been invited to dine with the family of Mr. Black, the chemist. In fact, I must excuse myself and catch up to them."

"But of course," Mother said.

"I hope I see you again," he said to all but looked directly at Rosalind.

Her heart gave a little flutter. She was surprised that, in her advanced spinsterdom, her heart remembered how to do so.

15

"Did you say there is a lending library here?" Mother asked Rosalind over their usual toast and tea on Tuesday morning.

"On Fore Street, toward the beach," Rosalind replied.

"I finished *The Small House at Allington* last night. I would like to get the final book in the series, if possible. Mrs. Deamer may care to read something new as well."

"Why don't we go after breakfast? Surely we qualify as Port Stilwellians. I have some banking business to tend as well."

"Um . . . I thought you might take care of that for us after your morning walk."

"This would be my morning walk."

"I shouldn't wish to hold you back."

Rosalind sighed. "I leave in less than a fortnight, Mother. You should become familiar with the town. Unless you plan on venturing out only on Sundays."

Her mother nodded. "You're right. It's time to learn my way about."

Half an hour later, they pulled on boots and coats and set out down Orchard Lane, then south onto Fore Street. Smoke rose from cottage chimneys as fires welcomed fishermen trudging home after their night at sea. They touched the brims of their caps as they passed.

Rosalind passed the boys' cottage with her usual pang of sadness. She had not seen them since the evening of the fence washing. The first shops came into view. Beyond, the bay rippled and sparkled like silver in the sun. She stopped before the door to Lloyd's Banking Company, LTD.

"I'll wait," Mother said.

"Actually, I shall need you to come with me. We'll set up an account you can draw upon."

"Thank you, but I shan't need money."

"You can't be certain of that. What if you see something you'd like to buy?"

Her mother looked away. Her shoulders rose, fell. "It grieves me no end that you're forced to support me when it should be the reverse."

"I'm happy to do so," Rosalind said. "What else is money for? To sit in the bank's dusty vaults?"

"You'll need it during your old age. I warn you, it comes sooner than you think."

"As long as I don't lose my senses and buy diamonds, I have enough." She took her mother's arm. "Please?"

Mr. Fletcher resembled more a highway foreman than a bank clerk, with his pockmarked cheeks, thick moustache beneath bulbous nose, and thin brown hair plastered above a wide face. But he was dressed dapperly in a gray suit and had the clean fingernails and manners of a gentleman.

"Welcome to Port Stilwell, Mrs. Kent," he said to Mother with a smile after Rosalind explained her mission. "It will be our pleasure to serve you."

"That wasn't so bad, was it?" Rosalind asked when they were back again on Fore Street.

"Thank you, Rosalind," Mother replied in a subdued tone.

Knowing how difficult this was for her, Rosalind did not press for conversation. They continued on to the corner of Fore Street and Lach Lane, where the Maude Harris Lending Library was situated above the office of John Lockhart, Solicitor.

Mother turned to her. "I gather you've not visited Mr. Pearce's shop again?"

Rosalind shook her head.

"Perhaps you should buy yourself a book."

"I should, to repay his kindness," Rosalind said, her thoughts having taken her there more than once. "But will he think I'm forward?"

"For purchasing a book?"

"It's just that . . ." She took in a deep breath. "Coyness is not a skill I possess."

"Be glad for that," Mother said.

"I so enjoyed conversing with him. I'm sure it was written on my face. What if he assumes I'm . . ."

Mother smiled. "*Badgering* him, as Amy Hugo would say?"

"Precisely."

"If you enjoyed yourself, it means he enjoyed himself as well. A good conversation draws energy from both sides."

Her mother rested a hand against the small of her back. "I'll find my way upstairs. You go and purchase your book. What have you to lose?"

~◁◇▷~

Outside Pearce's, Jinny raised head from paws and got to her feet. Rosalind knelt to pat her head.

"You're a good pup."

The animal wagged her tail.

Inside, Mr. Pearce bade her good morning. He was assisting a well-dressed young couple, so Rosalind looked through the shelves.

"This *Baedeker's Guide to Northern Italy and Corsica* gives you everything you could wish for," he was saying, "Maps and railway timetables, hotels and restaurants, and the operating hours of museums and galleries."

The young man snickered. "I daresay we won't visit museums and galleries on our honeymoon."

The young woman let out a stream of high-pitched giggles. *Father, please strike me mute if I ever twitter like that,* Rosalind prayed under her breath.

"Then, Thomas Cook's guide is more concise," Mr. Pearce went on.

After the couple left with their purchase, he came over to where Rosalind was inspecting a copy of *Roget's Thesaurus.*

"I'm sorry you had to hear that, Miss Kent."

"Thomas Cook does not offend me," Rosalind said, reshelving the book.

He laughed appreciatively. "May I take your coat?"

"No, thank you. I shall need to join my mother soon."

His smile was so warm that Rosalind became a little flustered. *You're twenty-seven years old!* she chided herself.

"I thought to buy a book," she said.

"You've come to the right place."

"I've just recently finished *Off on a Comet.*"

"Ah, Jules Verne."

"A student lent it, and I rather enjoyed the departure from drawing-room intrigues and penniless heiresses. Have you any of his others?"

"I have them all," he said, moving to the second bookshelf. "And I've read them."

"Thus you would recommend . . ."

He took down a cloth-covered blue book. "*Around the World in Eighty Days.* Can you guess why?"

"Because it's also an adventure?"

"There is that." He smiled again. "Because there is a main character who is a woman. Mr. Verne apparently held to women staying home, for the most part."

"I'll forgive him that," Rosalind said, "as long as his stories entertain."

He escorted her to the counter, where she took two shillings from her reticule. He was gathering her eight-penny change from a metal box when Jinny's muffled barks sounded.

"Shall I?" Rosalind asked.

"If you please?"

She moved over to open the door. Jinny trotted inside and showed her gratitude by licking her hand. "How long have you had her?"

Mr. Pearce came around the counter. "The summer before last, I was out for a stroll on the cliffs, and she came out of nowhere and stuck to my side. I did all I could to chase her away, but to no avail. When no one replied to the notice in my window after several weeks, I put it away and decided it was meant to be."

Rosalind's mother opened the door and stepped into the gap. "I asked directions of the librarian. Good morning, Mr. Pearce."

"Good morning, Mrs. Kent," he said. "Won't you come inside?"

"Are you quite sure?" She nodded at the two books tucked into her left arm. "I have just patronized the competition."

"You're always welcome here. I've donated books to the lending library."

"Clearly an exceptional man," Mother said.

"You flatter me, madam," he said with a smile and then glanced at the wall clock. "I wonder . . . would you both consider joining me for lunch? There is a good café, Flores, but four doors up the lane."

"Can you leave the shop untended?" Rosalind asked.

"A fellow must eat."

As tempting as it was, she thought of the meal that Coral would be preparing.

"I'm afraid it's too late to give notice to Miss Shipsey, our cook," Mother said, voicing her thoughts.

"Thursday, then? That would give her time to plan around it."

Mother smiled and gave Rosalind a little nod.

"We would be delighted, Mr. Pearce," Rosalind said.

On their way back to Fore Street, Mother showed her the two books. "*The Last Chronicle of Barset* for myself. And *A Narrative of the Life of Frederick Douglass*, as requested by Mrs. Deamer. Then we can swap. She's been rereading the same books for a year."

"It's sad that she's forced to be such a hermit," Rosalind said.

"She doesn't have a daughter to pry her from her shell." She hooked her arm into Rosalind's. "If you wish, I will find some excuse to stay home on Thursday."

"Please don't. It wouldn't be proper. And he invited *us*."

"Very well. I would certainly like to know more about the man who's set his cap for you."

"He's simply being hospitable. It's good for business."

"And I have a twenty-inch waist," Mother said.

They were two shops down from the bank when Mr. Fletcher stepped out and held the door. An infant carriage appeared, pushed by a scowling woman.

From where did she know her? Rosalind walked every day, weather allowing, and faces were becoming familiar. It was the sour expression that made her difficult to place, for most in Port Stilwell were open and friendly.

". . . and if you won't, I'll go up there this very minute and give him a piece of my mind!"

Rosalind frowned. But of course! That voice!

"You can't be coming here and making another scene, Sabrina," Mr. Fletcher said. "I'll get sacked!"

"Then behave like a man and speak with him!"

"You gave him to understand he's not to call again. What more is there to say?"

"That I don't appreciate no vicar nosing into—"

"Please, people can hear—"

Mr. Fletcher glanced over his shoulder, and Rosalind was too slow in looking away.

"Coward!" the woman called.

He gave Rosalind and her mother an apologetic look before returning to the bank.

Rosalind felt a wave of queasiness.

"That poor Mr. Fletcher," Mother said.

"Those poor boys."

"I beg your pardon?"

"The fence boys. She's their mother. He must be their father."

"Oh dear."

"No wonder they were so fearful, living with such a harpy. Let's walk more slowly. I shouldn't wish to catch up."

"That would be uncomfortable," Mother said.

"I'm not worried about discomfort. I'm worried that I might say something to her that a Christian woman should not say."

16

"How kind you are," Mrs. Deamer said in the parlor when Charlotte handed her the book. "Did Miss Kent find one as well?"

"She purchased one from Mr. Pearce. She and I are to have lunch with him Thursday, by the by."

"I'll inform Coral."

Charlotte looked toward the door and unburdened her mind to her. "Do you know anything of him? He seems a decent man, but I've learned not to judge a book by its cover."

Mrs. Deamer shook her head. "Coral may. Shall I ask her?"

"I'm not sure. What if she puts two and two together?"

"Casually? For my own sake?"

"Well, if you could be discreet."

"I'll be most discreet."

"Thank you," Charlotte said. "I wouldn't want Rosalind to know . . . unless it so happens that he has a shady past. In which case I will do all in my power to discourage her. As I wish someone had when I was young and in love."

"Does she love him?"

"No, of course not. But the best time to help one see clearly is before infatuation has clouded the vision. Don't you think?"

"I wholeheartedly agree," said Mrs. Deamer.

"What are you two plotting?" came from the doorway.

Charlotte smiled at Rosalind. "Ladies don't plot. We conspire."

"Well, lunch is ready, and it smells heavenly."

Coral served a fine meal of stewed mutton kidneys, mashed turnips, carrot pudding, and warm, yeasty bread with butter. Charlotte was relieved that they had not given in to the temptation to accept Mr. Pearce's invitation, and happy to inform Coral that she could have an easy day on Thursday.

That afternoon, after Rosalind had set out to post a letter to Miss Beale, Mrs. Deamer brought Charlotte tea in the parlor. "I've spoken with Coral."

"Do sit down," Charlotte said.

Mrs. Deamer took the paisley chair. "Mr. Pearce was once engaged to a young woman who left him for a wealthy man."

Sad though it was, Charlotte was relieved. Decades in theatre had taught her that not all men preferred women.

Mrs. Deamer hesitated. "There is more."

<hr />

In dressing gown and slippers that evening, Charlotte tapped on the door to her daughter's room.

"Come in."

She entered to find Rosalind seated against her pillows, reading by lamplight.

"I saw the light beneath the door, or I would not have disturbed you."

"You're not disturbing me." Rosalind set aside the book and drew up her knees. "Come, Mother, sit. You can't sleep?"

Charlotte sat and swiveled to face her. "My conscience troubles me."

"Your conscience?" Rosalind smiled. "What dastardly deed have you done?"

She took a deep breath and admitted the mission she had entrusted to Mrs. Deamer.

"She didn't . . ."

"You mustn't fault her," Charlotte hastened to say.

Rosalind sighed and rubbed her forehead. "It's Aunt Vesta yet again. When I was in grammar school, she inquired into the background of my dearest friend and discovered her grandparents had divorced. I wasn't allowed to play with her. She even had the schoolmaster move our desks to opposite sides of the room. Naturally, the other girls took her side, and I had no friends."

"I'm so sorry, Rosalind," Charlotte said. "If I had only known."

"You *would* have known if . . ." Rosalind closed her mouth, shook her head. "No, I won't throw that at you again. But, Mother, how could you do this!"

Charlotte's eyes and nose stung as Rosalind's image blurred before her. "I didn't want you to be hurt."

"I *shall* be hurt if word reaches him that my mother is sizing him up for husband material."

"But that won't happen. Mrs. Deamer made it as if she were asking for her own sake."

"And what reason did she give for asking?"

"None. She simply worked it into our lunch plans. She's bright enough to pull it off."

Rosalind blew out a breath. "I'm fatigued, Mother. Go back to your bed."

"Rosalind, please forgive—"

"Just leave. Please."

Charlotte nodded and returned to her room. She lay in bed and wept into a handkerchief. Her first attempt at actual mothering had failed miserably.

Why must I ruin every blessing you send me? she prayed.

More so, why had she allowed Rosalind to shoulder the burden of her existence? She was a leech, a ball and chain.

She heard her door open and Rosalind's whispered, "Mother? Are you awake?"

"Yes," Charlotte rasped.

She could see her daughter approach in the feeble light from the open windows.

"How do you sleep?" Rosalind said. "It's freezing in here!"

"I have overwhelming episodes of heat at times. As if walking into an oven."

"Seriously? Are you ill?"

"No, not at all. It comes with age for women, I'm afraid." Charlotte moved over and folded back the sheet and quilts. "Here, it's warm."

Rosalind dashed into bed and covered herself to her neck. "I shouldn't have lashed out at you."

"You had every right."

"It's just that I don't want to frighten Mr. Pearce away before I get to know him."

Charlotte waited to collect her thoughts.

"Mother?"

"You do like him?" Charlotte asked.

"Well, yes."

"Because he's pleasant? Skilled at conversation? Good manners?"

"Are those not good reasons?"

"You would have described my three husbands," Charlotte said. "And two were rotten to the core beneath those surface charms."

She heard her daughter's sigh.

"What did Mrs. Deamer learn?" Rosalind asked. "Tell me everything. What has Mr. Pearce done? Left wife and children? Been to prison?"

Charlotte smiled to herself. "His reputation is sterling. He's a decent Christian man who took tender care of his grandparents and practices fair business dealings with everyone in town."

Rosalind let out another breath. "I would have suspected as much."

"He's suffered some sadness too." She told her daughter of the broken courtship . . . and the reason for it.

"Indian? I thought he was simply well sunned."

"Does that matter to you?" Charlotte asked.

"It doesn't," Rosalind said. "He mentioned grandparents but not his parents. . . ."

"His grandfather was a soldier in the East India Company and fell in love with one of his captain's servants. She had no family and was considered an untouchable. When his service was concluded, they married and he brought her here. Their daughter married a missionary, returned to Cawnpore with him, and bore three children."

"Did you just say *Cawnpore?*"

"You know what happened there? You were but four in 1857."

"History class. Everyone knows of the uprising. Men, women, even children were chopped into pieces."

"British soldiers found him in the back of a cupboard, where his mother had hidden him. But his parents were killed, and the older sisters in their hiding places."

"What horror! The poor man."

"It's a terrible thing." They lay in the darkness, the weight of such tragedy heavy in the room. At length, Charlotte said what she felt she must. "Rosalind?"

"Yes, Mother?"

"I don't wish to sound cold. But just as charm and wit and even good reputation should not be the foundation for your affection, neither should pity. Ofttimes women feel a need to rescue and confuse it with love."

Rosalind sighed again. "I don't understand your meaning, Mother. What, then, should be the foundation for affection?"

"For now, *time,*" Charlotte said. "Time for your fine mind to learn more of him, before you involve your heart."

Silence ticked between them.

Charlotte went on. "There would be far less pain in the world if everyone did so."

Her daughter shifted beside her, and Charlotte's own heart felt a pang. She had overstepped herself yet again.

And then Rosalind twined her fingers through hers.

"I promise to try to keep my heart far removed from my brain. At least for the time being. Thank you for the counsel, Mother."

"Thank *you*."

"Why do you thank me?"

Charlotte squeezed her hand. "For allowing me the privilege."

17

"Finished, are you, girl?" Jude said when Jinny trotted from behind the counter, licking her chops.

"I beg your pardon?" His elderly patron sent him a severe look over the book in her hands.

Jude winced. "Forgive me, Mrs. Lassen. I asked Jinny if she finished her lunch."

"Ah . . . good dog!" she said with softened tone. She handed Jude the copy of *The Ingoldsby Legends* and counted out seventeen pennies from her purse.

"Thank you, Mrs. Lassen. I hope you enjoy the book."

She patted his shoulder. "Such a nice young man you are."

When she was on her way, he looked northward and smiled. Mrs. and Miss Kent were but one block away. Miss Kent lifted a hand. She looked fetching in a gray wrap over a mauve gown, a straw bonnet perched upon her head.

He returned the wave and stepped back into the shop.

"Jinny! We have an engagement."

With his hand, he smoothed his hair, wishing he had thought to bring his comb downstairs. "I should buy some oil. I've not courted in so long. How do I look?"

Jinny's yip seemed complimentary.

"But then, you wouldn't insult the hand that feeds," he said, turning his sign. He locked the door, and he and Jinny met the two at the whitewashed cob exterior of Flores.

The women patted and cooed over Jinny. When greetings had run their course, Jinny flopped down beside the door, and they entered.

Port Stilwell boasted three dining establishments. Jude's choices were limited to two. At Hooper's Restaurant, there was the risk of the owner's mother inviting herself to the table and talking a blue streak. Of the remaining two, he had chosen Flores over Sea Gull Inn because the proprietors were longtime friends.

"How lovely," Miss Kent said as they entered. The restaurant's interior was in contrast to its plain exterior. Red cloths covered eight round tables, a fresco of fishermen bringing in their catches covered most of one wall, and tall ferns fanned out from floor vases.

Patrons sent smiles or halloos from three tables. Mr. Lockhart, the solicitor, waved. Savory smells drifted from the kitchen, from where a dark-haired woman in white apron called, "Good day, Jude!"

"And to you, Mrs. Galvez." He pulled chairs from a table near the fresco, one on either side of him.

"Is *Flores* a Spanish name?" Mrs. Kent asked when they were seated.

"It is, indeed," Jude said. "Over two hundred years ago, a Spanish ship wrecked off the coast, and the sailors made it ashore."

"They stayed on?" Miss Kent asked, then shook her head. "Foolish question. There were obviously no ferries."

"Not at all, Miss Kent. I should think the only foolish question is the one we won't ask for fear of seeming foolish."

"Thank you, Mr. Pearce."

He loved how her smile made her bottle-green eyes into half-moons. For a moment, he forgot his subject of conversation. *Don't stare like a schoolboy!*

"A plague had killed over half the men here months earlier," he said when his mind returned to him. "The sailors were welcomed as much-needed laborers. Quite a few here have a Spanish branch in our family trees. My great-grandfather's name was Leiva."

Mrs. Galvez, with many Spanish branches in her tree, brought over a pot of tea and a hand-printed menu.

"So! You have some new friends. It is high time!"

Jude laughed and made introductions.

"Who painted the fresco?" Miss Kent asked.

"My husband, Paul, a genius with paints as well as with pots and pans." She rested a hand upon Jude's shoulder. "Jude's mother—Hansa—was my schoolmate, may God rest her soul."

She crossed herself and walked away, and Mr. Lockhart gave him a grim nod on his way out. Mrs. and Miss Kent exchanged stricken looks.

"I'm so sorry, Mr. Pearce," Mrs. Kent murmured.

"Please, don't be." He picked up the menu. However Continental the interior, the hand-printed card listed typical English fare. He hoped they would not be disappointed.

"The fish was pulled in from the sea this morning."

The women followed his lead and ordered baked turbot and lobster sauce when Mrs. Galvez returned.

"Good choice," she said and walked to the kitchen, still clucking in sympathy.

"She was obviously very close to your mother," Miss Kent said.

"I appreciate the sentiment." Jude leaned to whisper, "You're both so kind. But I really just want to show you a pleasant outing."

131

Both nodded, and after a moment, Miss Kent said a little too brightly, "I've read that fish is good for the intellect. The dining hall at Cheltenham serves trout from the River Chelt at least once weekly."

"Trout," Mrs. Kent said equally brightly. "Did you know that their colors and patterns can change with their environments? They act as camouflage."

"I wasn't aware of this," Jude said.

She smiled at him. "We are not the only creatures who are fearfully and wonderfully made."

Returning her smile, he said, "What led you to choose Port Stilwell?"

"My mother required a more sedate locale," Miss Kent said. "For her health."

"It seems a very nice town," her mother said. "I intend to learn more about it."

"From where did you move?"

"Spilsby. In Lincolnshire."

Her thumbnail made little half-moons in the lemon rind upon her saucer. From her posture, it seemed she held her breath, hoping he would ask no more questions.

Mrs. Galvez brought platters of fish with boiled potatoes, carrots, and dressed cucumber. After her first bite of the turbot, Miss Kent said to her, "Delicious! Please convey our compliments to your husband."

She pushed back a strand of graying dark hair. "I had many suitors in my day. Paul was the only one who could cook. I'd had enough of cooking, helping feed nine brothers and sisters. I made him promise I would never have to light the stove before I would marry him."

"Mr. Galvez is a good man," Jude said and felt her hand upon his shoulder again.

"This man is a good man too," Mrs. Galvez said to the women. "He took care of his grandparents. They cared for him too. I remember as if it were yesterday . . . everyone abuzz over the little boy who was rescued from those terrible goings-on."

She patted his shoulder yet again and left.

Jude stifled a sigh and looked at his companions. "I suppose I should explain."

Yet how to do so, without seeming to ask for pity?

Miss Kent said, "We know, Mr. Pearce."

But of course. How could they not when they rented rooms from Port Stilwell's most notorious gossip?

"Such savagery!" Mrs. Kent said.

He gave her an appreciative smile. "I was consumed with hatred most of my life. Lately I have come to understand the frustrations of those who rebelled. Many of our fellow countrymen glean great riches while impoverishing them; even now, they are treated as inferiors."

"All the same, I doubt I could be as charitable," Miss Kent said.

He nodded. "It took much prayer. The hatred was a ball and chain, and I'm glad to be shed of it."

The two looked at him with such understanding, he found himself going on.

"Yet though the hatred is gone, I confess to difficulty with Christ's commandment to forgive. It was my parents and sisters who lost their lives. Forgive my bluntness, Miss Kent, but if someone strikes *you*, have I the right to forgive him?"

After a space, Mrs. Kent said, "Perhaps your obligation is to forgive the part of the injury that was yours. The loss of your family?"

"And it seems you've done so, by letting go of the hatred," Miss Kent observed.

"Perhaps." Silence followed as Jude cast about in his mind for a lighter subject of conversation. At length, he asked Miss Kent, "What led you to teach mathematics?"

"I've enjoyed numbers since the day I first realized two fingers plus two fingers equals four. Algebraic and geometric equations are marvelous puzzles. It's very satisfying to open other minds to those puzzles."

"I'm impressed."

She eyed him in mock suspicion. "Now you flatter me, Mr. Pearce."

"Not at all. I made fair enough marks in mathematics, but we were never the best of friends."

"What led you to open a bookshop?" Mrs. Kent asked.

"Grandfather encouraged it. I have always enjoyed reading and had no desire to blacksmith, as was his trade. But after university, I lectured on literature at Eton until five years ago, when Grandmother's failing health necessitated my return."

"What a good grandson you were," the older woman said.

"They were all that I had left. Even when I was away, I felt anchored by them. The world is very different without family."

Miss Kent's eyes were glistening, he realized.

He blew out a quick breath. "I'm not usually so morbid. It's just that you're such good listeners."

The women gave him tender smiles, the kind that only women could give.

"You weren't morbid at all," Miss Kent said. "My mother is all I have left. I would be bereft without her."

Now both sets of eyes glistened.

Later, when they stepped out onto the pavement, Miss Kent and her mother offered hands and thanked him again before giving Jinny parting pats.

Unlocking the door to his shop, Jude looked back. The two were walking northward arm in arm, engaged in conversation.

As if sensing being watched, Miss Kent slowed her steps and glanced over her shoulder. Their eyes met. Chagrined at being caught staring, he raised a hand sheepishly.

She smiled back.

He grinned and watched her turn again.

They had exchanged a brief, wordless message, and Jude floated into his shop on an inexplicable and most welcome wave of wonder.

18

From the parlor came six faint chimes of the wall clock. Rosalind burrowed into the covers and tried to capture some more sleep, but her mind would have none of it and carried her again to her chair across from Mr. Pearce in Flores.

She flipped her pillow to the cold side. It did not help. Some ten minutes later, she thought, *May as well walk*. She had never set out this early to watch the cobles come in. Why not now?

Her limbs rebelled against throwing back the blankets, and she shivered all the way to the bathroom. Back in her bedroom, she pulled on stockings and a dress, and tied her hair with a ribbon. No sense in a comb, since dampness would wreak havoc anyway.

Fingerlike branches of apple trees pierced the fog shrouding Orchard Lane. A cloud of wood pigeons rose from her right and flapped away, crooning. Upon reaching Lach Lane, she walked the ridge just above the beach and watched boats being winched from the high water onto the shingles, accompanied by the creaking of chains, shouts of hoarse voices, and the snorts of dray horses hitched to wagons. Fishermen in blue worsted shirts scurried about, scooping fish into barrels.

Beyond the activity, fog blurred the line between sea and sky, and the cliffs dawned a soft azure.

I shall miss this place, Rosalind realized, smiling at the recollection of Miss Beale practically forcing her onto the train four weeks ago. No matter where her path might lead her in years to come, Port Stilwell would forever be connected with making peace with her mother.

And with, incredibly, after all these years surrounded by women and immersed in education, feeling something for a man. A man whom she suspected felt something for her.

Do men have this intuition too? she prayed. *Or did you give it to women as compensation for having to wait for men to take the lead in courtship?*

Or am I being ridiculous? Please don't allow me to be ridiculous!

However much Rosalind liked Mr. Pearce, she avoided Kleef Lane. It was unbecoming to lurk, especially when she had dressed in haste.

But there would be nothing wrong with inviting him to dinner. Surely she and her mother had incurred a social debt with yesterday's lunch?

Some shops had opened on Fore Street, including Mrs. Hooper's. On impulse, she went inside.

"Out and about early, are you, Miss Kent?" Mrs. Hooper said while smoothing a length of brocade that overlapped her cutting table.

"I wanted to see the boats come in before I return to school."

"Oh, to be young again!" Mrs. Hooper chuckled. "Although you're actually a bit long in the tooth, aren't you?"

I will not lose my temper, Rosalind thought.

The older woman's marble eyes scanned her. She clucked disapproval. "All the more reason you should take pains with your hair, if you expect to catch anyone's eye."

"I didn't go out there to—"

"I have a niece in Portishead who won't take one step from the house without every curl in place. I hope no one saw you, dear."

You want her to grant a favor, Rosalind reminded herself with clenched teeth.

"Here, you may as well lend a hand," Mrs. Hooper said.

Rosalind went to the far side of the table, took hold of her corner of the cloth, and helped to overlap it.

"My assistant—Betsy Garner—feels unwell." Mrs. Hooper snorted. "There's the one thing about being young that I *don't* miss! I trust the cottage is satisfactory?"

"Most satisfactory," Rosalind said and then voiced the question that had propelled her inside. "I wonder . . . are we permitted to entertain guests?"

"Entertain? As in charades?" Mrs. Hooper laughed and waved a dismissive hand. "Of course I know what you mean. Just give Mrs. Deamer an extra half crown for the household account for each guest. And of course you must give Coral notice."

"Thank you." Rosalind did not argue that the rent did not decrease when she was away, even though there would be one less for meals. Wages had to be paid whether Coral cooked for one or for ten. "I'll not keep you."

"By the by," Mrs. Hooper went on while stacking the folded cloth upon a shelf, "who are these mystery guests, pray tell?"

Rosalind hesitated. That same intuition she had thanked God for just minutes ago seemed to warn again. With all honesty, she replied, "We haven't invited anyone. For future reference."

"It's good for your mother to have friends when you're away again. I don't wonder she's lonely. Mrs. Deamer is pleasant but speaks hardly a word. Coral Shipsey is dense, as if one's trying to converse with a cabbage."

Maintain a pleasant expression, Rosalind willed herself. "Well, good day."

Her mother was up and dressed, reading on the parlor sofa by the light of the windows as a low fire licked coals in the grate.

"I knocked and peeked in. Assumed you were walking."

"I'm sorry I held up breakfast," Rosalind said, hanging her wrap upon the rack. "Or have you had yours?"

"Coral offered, but I asked her to wait."

A light tapping sounded. Coral, who had obviously kept an eye out for Rosalind, entered carrying a tray with a teapot and cups, toast, and marmalade.

"Did you enjoy your walk, Miss Kent?"

"I did, thank you," Rosalind replied.

Coral set the tray upon the tea table. "When you return from the school, all the flowers will be abloom. Takes your breath away sometimes."

"She's a pleasant girl," Mother said, taking up the teapot when she and Rosalind were alone again.

"Mrs. Hooper said speaking with her is like conversing with a cabbage."

"How cruel!"

Rosalind spread some marmalade on a slice of toast. "I would rather converse with a cabbage than with Mrs. Hooper, the old trout."

They smiled in complete accord, and Mother handed her a filled cup and saucer. "When did she say that?"

"This morning." Rosalind took a deep breath. "I stopped by her shop to ask permission to have a guest. What would you think of our having Mr. Pearce to dinner?"

"Hmm." Her mother stirred her tea. "We lunched with him only yesterday. As the Baird said, 'Wisely and slow. They stumble that run fast.'"

"*Hamlet?*"

"*Romeo and Juliet.*"

Rosalind rolled her eyes. "I suspect Shakespeare had few friends."

Her mother smiled.

"It's just that I leave in ten days."

139

"Wait four or five, then?"

"I suppose you're right. You do like him, don't you? I refer to Mr. Pearce. Not Shakespeare, whom I *know* you adore."

"I like Mr. Pearce very much." Mother sighed. "And please forgive my overbearing ways. You're far wiser than I was."

"I'm not so sure how wise I am at all. So I'll concede your experience."

Perhaps some time for reflection would be best, she thought. After all, Shakespeare knew something of love.

⚬⚬⚬

Rosalind stopped at Mr. Pearce's shop on Tuesday afternoon of the following week.

"How good to see you again!" The hint of relief in his voice was gratifying and made her glad she had waited.

Even Jinny seemed happy to see her, but then she wagged her tail just as enthusiastically for the half-dozen women of various ages who entered before Rosalind could extend the invitation.

Mr. Pearce murmured an apology. She nodded and moved to a far corner, thumbing through a copy of *Insectivorous Plants*.

The women desired to purchase a birthday gift for a fellow member of the Port Stilwell Gardening Club, they informed him. After some discussion and debate, they settled upon *My Garden: Its Plan and Culture* by an Alfred Smee. Mr. Pearce wrapped it in brown paper, determined how much two and seven would be divided by six, took money from each hand, and counted out change for most, blushing charmingly when one older woman patted his cheek and said, "What a pity that you have no wife to help you, Mr. Pearce."

When they were gone, Rosalind hastened to say, in case others were to enter, "Would you care to have dinner with us on Thursday at seven?"

"Why, thank you," he said. "I shall be delighted."

The warmth in his green eyes behind the spectacles weakened

Rosalind's composure, and she blurted the next thought that entered her head.

"We serve ourselves from the sideboard, by the by. It seems silly for Mrs. Deamer to have to wait upon just the two of us."

"Quite reasonable. And I'm used to dishing up my own plate."

"Will you be able to find your way homeward after sunset?"

"I'll carry a lantern."

"And if it happens to rain . . ."

"Umbrella *and* lantern." He folded his arms. "But are you certain you *want* me to be there, Miss Kent? You're not obligated. The luncheon was my pleasure."

"Yes, of course." She gave a sigh. "I've obviously grown rusty at this."

"At inviting a man to dinner?"

"Well, yes."

"And how did that work out before?"

"We're no longer together, so . . ."

"The cad!" he muttered, smiling.

"It was my decision to end it."

"Indeed." Rubbing his chin, he said, "Hmm . . . that puts me under quite some pressure. What mistakes did the other fellow make? Did he chew openmouthed? Drink from his soup bowl? Blow his nose with the tablecloth?"

She had to smile. "His table manners were impeccable."

His feigned disappointment so amused her that she decided to toss him a morsel. "You don't happen to believe that you could run the country better than Parliament, do you?"

"Why, no," he said. "Britain would be in utter shambles with me at the helm."

"Very good," she said. "We shall look forward to seeing you on Thursday."

19

Clouds hovered in a pewter sky on Thursday but held their rain. Rosalind spent the day composing lesson plans for the upcoming term, took her usual walk, played cribbage with her mother, and later, changed into her favorite gown, of brown grosgrain trimmed with blue ribbon. Her mother and Mrs. Deamer both offered to style her hair, but she decided being at ease would be more important than balancing unfamiliar curls and braids. She clasped her hair into its usual comb.

Mr. Pearce knocked promptly at seven, dressed in a black suit with a white waistcoat, starched white shirt, and blue- and yellow-striped cravat.

"Please do come in, both of you," Rosalind said.

"Jinny's fine out here." And indeed, the animal had already settled herself beside the door.

"Coral has saved some tidbits and means to invite her into the kitchen later. Will she follow a stranger?"

"She would follow Guy Fawkes for a treat. Wouldn't you, girl?"

Jinny's tail thumped an affirmative.

In the dining room, the sideboard boasted boiled mackerel

with butter, oxtail soup, potatoes and carrots, and artichokes with white sauce. Her mother stood at the wall, straightening a Wedgwood platter depicting Robin Hood and Maid Marian.

"Mother?"

She turned, moved around the table, and offered her hand, "How very good to see you again, Mr. Pearce."

He returned the greeting and allowed her to lead him over to the sideboard.

At the table, he related more Port Stilwell history, particularly of the quarry, a vast network of tunnels one mile to the west.

"The Romans were the first to appreciate the limestone of this area. It's fine-grained and soft, so it can be sawed with relative ease but hardens when exposed to air. Many of southern England's cathedrals and a number of other grand buildings are constructed of it."

"Are visitors allowed?" Rosalind asked.

"I'm afraid not. It would be interesting." To Mother, he said, "By the by, what will you do while Miss Kent is away?"

"I shall have to keep myself occupied to make time go faster."

"The Saint George's Fair is on the twenty-third. It draws visitors from all over. I keep the shop open for that reason."

"I'm not too keen on crowds, but I may give it a look-over. I do have a project in mind. I'm thinking of asking Mr. Hurst to teach me to garden. He comes Tuesdays."

"Port Stilwell has a gardening club. I should be happy to introduce you to the chairwoman."

"Thank you, but I would prefer not to commit to the social side of it. Just soil my hands a bit. Grow some vegetables in particular."

"I didn't realize you liked the outdoors, Mother," Rosalind said before thinking.

Her mother gave her a knowing smile and said smoothly, "You're never too old to acquire a new interest."

Mr. Pearce nodded. "I fully intend to take up ballet one day."

Rosalind joined her mother's laughter and asked, "Can you stand on your toes?"

"How do you think the books reach the top shelves?"

Smiling, Rosalind went to the sideboard to serve the raspberry jam tartlets with clotted cream and bring the dish of almonds and raisins to the table.

"May I ask you about your family?" Mother said.

"But of course, Mrs. Kent," he replied.

"Were your mother and grandmother treated well here in Port Stilwell?"

"Very well. For my grandmother's part, perhaps because of the novelty of her. She continued to wear the sari until the day she died. Mr. Hooper kindly ordered Indian fabrics for her. My mother chose to dress like her schoolmates. She was beautiful, I've been told by more than a few who remember."

"Where did she meet your father?" Rosalind asked.

"At Stonehenge, actually. They were both on school-day tours and were introduced by a mutual friend. They exchanged letters for two years before my grandparents consented to his visiting her here."

"From where?"

"From Somerset. Bridgwater."

"You said you have no more family. Did your father's parents pass on recently?"

"I'm not certain."

"You're not certain?"

Rosalind groaned inwardly. *Mother . . .*

Mr. Pearce smiled and nodded at his empty dish. "Forgive my lack of etiquette, but the tartlets were delicious. Do you suppose I could have another?"

"Let's all have another," Rosalind said and started to push out her chair. "Coral will be delighted."

"No, allow me," he said, rising.

While he was at the sideboard, Rosalind leaned close to mouth to her mother, *No more questions!*

She gave her an apologetic look and nodded.

Mr. Pearce brought the tartlets and bowl over, dished out one for each, and dolloped clotted cream on top. Three forks cut into three crusts, and they chewed and swallowed as one.

"My father's parents disowned him before I was born, hence my ignorance of how they're faring."

"But why would they do such a thing?" Rosalind asked in spite of herself.

"I suppose because he married a woman of mixed race. Grandfather wrote to my parents when I arrived here but never received a reply."

"You've never heard from any other family members?" Mother asked.

"Father had two younger brothers. Perhaps they feared their father's opinion."

"May I be so bold as to ask why you've never contacted his brothers yourself?"

Mother . . . Rosalind thought again, warning her with her eyes.

"My grandfather made the attempt," he reminded her.

"Years ago," she said. "How many? Twenty?"

"More than that."

"People can change."

"My address has not," he said gently.

"The letter could have been misdirected. Anything could have happened."

"Mother," Rosalind said. "Mr. Pearce is not comfortable with this discussion."

"On the contrary," he said, giving her a reassuring smile. "I appreciate Mrs. Kent's concern."

He turned again to Mother. "If, by some chance, my grandparents have undergone some miraculous change of heart, that doesn't negate the fact that they caused my father much pain. I would feel disloyal for attempting any sort of relationship."

"Your loyalty is to be commended." Her voice softened. "I wonder, what do you suppose your father would say to that?"

He fell silent for a moment. "I've never asked myself that question."

Rosalind pressed her fork into her tartlet for wont of anything else to do. What was she to say? She rather agreed with her mother but felt they had not been acquainted with Mr. Pearce long enough to be inserting themselves into his family dynamics.

Was this what she could expect of herself twenty-three years from now? Did all older women feel obliged to share their opinions with such shattering directness?

To her great relief, her mother said, "Forgive me if I've pushed too hard, Mr. Pearce. It's just that I have only recently learned to believe in miracles, and I would wish one for you. But I shall speak no more of it."

He nodded. "I promise to think on your advice."

"Good enough!" she said and turned to Rosalind. "You're very quiet, dear."

"Am I, now?" Rosalind said with a benign smirk that made her mother and Mr. Pearce laugh.

They chatted on, mostly about favorite books. At length, he pushed back his chair and said with seeming reluctance, "Thank you both for a lovely evening."

Rosalind led him to the kitchen to collect Jinny.

"Miss Shipsey has been giving you treats, has she?" he said.

"Just a few," Coral admitted. "And then a few more."

"Will you need to be carried?" Rosalind asked Jinny, scratching behind the dog's ears.

"Please don't give her ideas," Mr. Pearce said. "I'm certain I'm as full as she is."

Past the porch, the sky was black and starless. She was glad he had brought a lantern. "I apologize for my mother's persistence."

"There is no need to apologize," he said. "Unlike the gentleman you so wisely stopped inviting for dinner, I'm aware of how little I know. I'm grateful for counsel from those with my best interests at heart."

Rosalind smiled and offered her hand. "Good night, Mr. Pearce. I'll see you Sunday."

"Very good." He took her hand in both of his, then hesitated. "If you wonder why I don't ask to sit with you during church . . ."

"No," she cut in, though the question had crossed her mind.

"It's just that gossip is the main entertainment here. It's best, in my mind, to wait a bit. But if I'm wrong . . ."

"You're not," she said, meaning it. They still knew each other so little and did not need the pressure of other people's expectations.

"But may I write to you at Cheltenham?"

"Yes," she said, glad for the darkness, for surely her face glowed.

<hr />

On Sunday, Mr. Pearce arrived just before the opening hymn and slipped into the back pew. Rosalind sent a glance over her shoulder and saw that he was looking at her. He smiled.

Afterward, he waited outdoors, Jinny at his side, to trade greetings with her, Mother, and Mrs. Deamer, and to again wish her a safe journey.

"He's such a nice man," Mrs. Deamer said on their way out of the yard.

"Miss Kent?"

Noble Clark's voice. Rosalind turned, hoping Jude had not heard. But he obviously had and sent her a maddening smile from the near distance.

"Good morning, Miss Kent. Might I have a word with you?"

"Why, certainly, Mr. Clark," she replied, looping her arm through her mother's on one side and Mrs. Deamer's on the other, just in case either had any thought of wandering away. She did not have to glance sideways to see the glint in Mother's eyes. And she knew in her heart that Coral and Amy were watching.

His smile exposed his multitude of teeth. "Will you walk later? I could do with some exercise myself."

"How kind of you," Rosalind said. "But I'm afraid I shall be staying close to home today. I leave for school in the morning, so there is much to do."

The fact was that she had planned to walk and resented being forced to abandon doing so in order to be truthful.

"Leave?" His eyes dulled a little, even though his smile still stretched across his teeth. "Will you return soon?"

"Not until half-term break in late May."

"May I write to you?"

"I do love 'It is Well With My Soul,'" Mother cut in. "I'm glad you chose that hymn."

Mrs. Deamer jumped in as well. "The story behind it is so moving."

"Why, thank you," Mr. Clark said, lowering his lashes. "I give all credit to Christ."

Christ would have sung in tune, Rosalind thought. "If you'll forgive me, Mr. Clark, I must hasten home."

"Um . . . yes," he sputtered but pressed on. "May I write?"

"I'm afraid schoolwork dominates my time," she replied as gently as possible. "Good day to you, Mr. Clark."

Just before turning onto Fore Street, they heard Coral's voice. "Miss Kent?"

Rosalind paused and turned, as did her mother and Mrs. Deamer.

Panting, Coral caught up with them.

"I'm sorry for Noble," she said.

"I'm sorry too," Rosalind said as they fell into step. "I assure you, I've done nothing to encourage him."

"Of course not," Coral said, giving her a sad smile. "And *that's* what encourages him."

Rosalind glanced at her mother, on the far side of Coral and Mrs. Deamer.

You haven't any advice to offer?

Two hours later, over a lunch of pea soup and boiled bacon cheek with sprouts, she realized the reason for her mother's restraint.

"You won't be here this time tomorrow. It's all that's been on my mind this morning. I can scarcely remember poor Mr. Moore's sermon."

"I could look for a place while I'm there and send for you," Rosalind said. "A pleasant cottage that I could visit."

She could see her mother's shudder.

"Or not," Rosalind went on.

"It's just that I feel safe here. As much as I want to see you . . ."

"I understand."

"Selfish, when my moving close would be easier for you."

"Coming here during breaks will be no hardship," Rosalind assured her.

Her mother smiled. "Might a certain man have something to do with that?"

"He may," Rosalind admitted.

"So, Noble Clark is growing on you."

Rosalind laughed. "I shall miss you, Mother."

20

Danny was especially vigilant to watch the amount of water Albert drank upon the evening of April twenty-second, waking him before sunrise to use the chamber pot.

When the sun rose, they made the bed with more than usual care, with Danny smoothing wrinkles and making certain that the quilt hung evenly on both sides.

He washed his face at the washstand, then used the same flannel to wash his brother's.

"Is my hair flat?" he asked Albert after pulling a wet comb through it. Though they had a bowl and a pitcher—which held but two inches of water because of a crack—they had no mirror.

"It's pointing there," Albert said, indicating the crown of his own head. "Will there be pony rides?"

"I've said to you again and again," Danny whispered after a glance at the door, "say nothing. I'll do the asking."

He combed his hair again, patted it to be sure, and then combed Albert's.

"And don't look so eager!" he hissed.

"But I *am*!"

Danny sighed. Albert still did not grasp that their stepmother would take it as a sign that they expected permission to be granted. *Presumptuousness* was a big word for young boys to know, but it was one she used often. They had no right to presume anything.

"Just imagine it's an ordinary day."

But the day did not begin ordinarily. Father sat at the head of the table with tea and a newspaper. Their stepmother held Teresa upon her lap, feeding her coddled eggs. She actually smiled when Teresa chirped, "Dinny! Aber!"

The smile was for Teresa, but at least she did not seem angry with Danny and his brother.

"Good morning, Mother and Father," they said in semi-unison.

"Good morning, boys," Father said.

"It's on the stove," their stepmother said, then turned again to Father, "The pink chair has a loose spring and sinks when you sit. This one in the advertisement is quite elegant and guaranteed for forty years."

Father gave a little nod and took a bite of bacon. Danny went to the stove with his brother trailing. Albert knew not to sit at the table without him. The porridge in the pot would have been a meager serving for one, but Danny spooned it into two bowls. One piece of bread lay beside the burner. He tore it in half.

He carried the dishes to the table while Albert pulled out chairs. Once upon a time, Father complained over the sparseness of their plates. Now he seemed not to notice. It would be no use reminding him of it, Danny thought. He had eyes.

And she would make them pay later, so it was best to say nothing.

Perhaps their stepmother was right and they did not deserve more. Good children were not burdens to their parents.

"They send fabric swatches by post," she was saying. "Green would go well with the rug, I think. Or stripes. I would have to see the swatches."

"Can the pink chair be repaired?" Father asked around a mouthful of bread.

Teresa lunged for the spoon in the saltcellar and happily banged the table.

Danny attempted to grow smaller in his chair.

"Is there to be nothing in this house that's *mine*?" his stepmother asked over dull thumps of pewter against cloth.

"But of course, Sabrina." Redness spread from father's collar. "It's just that we never have callers, so I don't see the need."

"And whose fault is—"

"I'll buy the chair," he cut in tightly.

"Everyone comparing me to your sainted Marjorie!"

"I'll buy the blasted chair!"

Albert shifted in his chair and tapped Danny's arm.

Danny shook his head and spooned some porridge into his mouth.

"May we go to the fair?" Albert asked. "And have a penny for pony rides?"

Their stepmother wheeled to face them and hissed, "Go wherever you wish! As long as it's out of my sight!"

She heaved Teresa to her shoulder, her chair toppling against the flagstones, and fled the kitchen. Elbows upon the table, Father buried his face in his hands.

Albert was opening his mouth again. Danny poked his arm and shook his head.

"But the penny . . ."

"It's as much fun to watch," Danny whispered, knowing it was not true.

In spite of the knot in his stomach, he finished his porridge and took up the bread. He halved it with Alfred on their way out the door. As they reached the gate, Danny could hear panpipes and drums. In spite of himself, he smiled.

"Can you hear that?"

Albert nodded, freckled cheeks bulging.

"Boys!"

They turned to look at their father, standing in the open doorway. His face was crimson, but he looked more resigned than angry. Danny and Albert walked back to him.

"You shouldn't upset your mother that way."

She's not our mother, Danny thought as his lips forced out, "I'm sorry."

Father sighed. "Mind you remember next time."

"May we go now, Father?" Albert asked with a look over his shoulder.

Danny elbowed his side.

"Here," Father said and held out two pennies in his palm.

Danny stared, too stunned to move.

Taking command of the situation, Albert scooped the coins and handed them over to Danny. "Thank you so very much, Father!"

Even for boys with but two pennies between them, Saint George's Fair was a merry outing. Stalls sold shell purses and baskets, china ornaments and paintings, food and sweets. The nine-member Port Stilwell Band played tunes in the gazebo on the green while Morris dancers in costume hopped and wove. The drama of Saint George, patron saint of England, slaying the dragon and saving the king's daughter was especially thrilling. Then there were sack races. Danny was too timid to participate but enjoyed watching people stumble toward the finish line.

And finally, when the queue to ride the ponies had shortened, they spent a halfpenny each on a ride, ten laps around a makeshift arena.

"What will we do now?" Albert asked afterward.

"Are you hungry?" Danny asked as his own stomach growled.

"I am!"

They walked past stalls of fried fish and chips and meat pies, boiled cockles and crabs and shrimps, the aromas overwhelming the salt air.

"Meat pies, meat pies, two for a penny,
Squealing pork and cackling henny!
Buy some now; don't delay.
The finest that you'll find today!"

The song, or at least the voice, sounded familiar.

"Meat pies!" Albert chirped.

Mr. Clark, Danny realized. But although the tune was merry, the face wore the same frown he wore in school. He was leaning against a frame post with arms folded while his father, owner of Clark Mercantile, tended a paraffin stove.

Danny's heartbeat quickened. He took Albert's arm and pulled him to the side.

"Let's get Scotch eggs."

"Aw, but we have eggs all the time."

"But not *cooked.*"

One way to fill their stomachs was to slip into henhouses when owners were indoors. Danny reckoned he had eaten so many that his scalp would go bald one day. Or sprout a stem, for in the fall, unguarded apple trees abounded on Orchard Lane.

From the corner of his eye, Danny watched a man and woman approach the stand. Mr. Clark stopped singing, took their penny as if it were tainted, and wrapped two pies in newspaper. He handed them over without a word.

Mr. Clark's father barked from the stove, "Look lively, you imbecile!"

He shot back, "It's difficult to look lively whilst singing that ridiculous song! I shall hear it in my sleep! Why hasn't Mother come to relieve me?"

How odd, Danny thought, *to hear a grown man behaving so childishly.* His stepmother would have slapped him twice for whining so.

"Your mum's tending shop! She cannot be in two places at

once, can she? And we wouldn't have to do this every year if you didn't dress like a duke!"

"And how am I ever to become famous if my clothes are shabby? You may as well accept that I'm going places, Father!"

"And you may as well accept that we've got competition! So, commence to singing!"

Crimson faced, Mr. Clark turned again to the counter and leaned against his post.

"Meat pies, meat pies, two for a penny,
Squealing pork and cackling henny!"

A man walked over to buy four pies. The schoolmaster served him and boomed an unsmiling "Thank you, Mr. Brown!"

"Aye, that's better," said Mr. Clark's father, taking off his apron. "We've enough cooked for a bit. I'm going to see after yer mum."

He left the stand and passed Danny and Albert with a grim nod.

"Please, Danny?" Albert said.

Danny sighed and fished the coin from his pocket. He held his breath as his brother skipped over to the stand.

"I would like two."

Mr. Clark yawned. "Let's see your penny."

Albert, in the process of raising his hand, flinched.

No . . . no . . . no, Danny thought.

"I've dropped it, Mr. Clark," Albert said. "You seen it roll, didn't you?"

"Run along with you, boy. I'm wise to your trick."

Danny swallowed his fear and rushed over. "I beg your pardon, Mr. Clark, but Albert had a penny. Our father gave it to us."

Mr. Clark sent a sweeping look downward and shrugged.

"You seen it roll!" Albert cried with a burst of tears.

A shadow fell over the counter.

"Why, Mr. Clark."

Danny looked over his shoulder and into the face of a plump woman with kind gray eyes.

Mr. Clark straightened and cleared his throat. "Um . . . good day to you, Mrs. Kent."

"I could not help but overhear. The young man has lost his penny?"

There was no humor in Mr. Clark's nervous chuckle. "There never was a penny. The children of this town are full of tricks. You dare not turn your backs to them."

"But you didn't turn—" Albert said.

"My brother could have dropped it on the way over," Danny said, taking his arm. "He's but six. Thank you, Mr. Clark."

A firm but gentle hand clamped his shoulder.

"How many pies would you care to have?"

"Oh. No, thank you," Danny said.

Wiping his eyes, Albert turned to look up at the woman. "We were to buy two, missus. But four would be better, if you please?"

She chuckled and let go of Danny's shoulder to dip her fingers into a purse. "They'll have eight, Mr. Clark. Here are four pennies."

Mr. Clark shifted and looked down at his feet. He dipped down, held up a penny. "Ah, will you look at that? I must have stepped upon it."

"Imagine that. Here are three, then."

He shifted again. "Two, actually. A discount for your trouble, Mrs. Kent. It's the least I can do."

Mr. Clark wrapped the pies in newspaper and handed them over to Danny. "There you are, lad."

"Thank you and good day, Mr. Clark," the woman said. Her hand clamped upon Danny's shoulder again, tugging gently so that he could do naught but turn with her, Albert following. The warmth and aroma of the bundle were gratifying. They stopped on the far side of a cockles stand, their vision of the pie booth blocked.

"Let's chat for a moment, shall we?" the woman said.

In spite of her kind eyes, her tone was as authoritative as Mr. Clark's. Danny looked up at her with a faint heart, and Albert pressed into his side.

"Thank you, missus," he said, wishing he could recall her name.

"It was my pleasure." She smiled. "I'm just glad I decided to venture out. My name is Mrs. Kent. And you would be . . . ?"

"Danny Fletcher. This is Albert."

"Do you live on Fore Street?"

Danny's heartbeat quickened.

"Well?" she said.

He could feel the heat in his face. As well-meaning as she was, no good could come from her visiting his home.

She nodded understanding. "I'm simply curious. Two helpful lads pointed the way home to my daughter some weeks ago."

How could he repay her kindness with less than the truth? "Um, we do."

"Then you know of the yellow cottage on Orchard Lane, beyond the trees?"

He nodded.

"You must come there if ever I can help you. Now, enjoy your pies."

Enjoy they did, seated upon the crumbling hearth of the Bickle cottage on Mercer Lane, five cottages east from the school. In the unlikely chance that Father and their stepmother had made up and decided to come to the fair, Danny did not wish to explain so much food.

The thatched roof of the cottage had burned away before Danny was born, and according to Father in a rare talkative mood, Mrs. Bickle's son moved her to his farm in Branscombe and never got around to repairs. At times, the cottage was the boys' refuge from their stepmother's fury, when older boys were not lurking about with handmade pipes and Three Castles cigarettes. The plum tree in the jungle of a garden fed their bellies when in season.

"Will we go back now?" Albert asked between licks of his fingers.

"In a bit," Danny said, resting his back against the stones. For the present, he wished nothing more than to savor the fullness of his belly.

"Maybe the lady will give us more pennies. She said we should go to her—"

"No!" Danny said. "She said it only to be kind. You don't trouble people who are kind."

"But why not?"

Danny sighed. "Because they'll grow to resent you."

As had happened with their stepmother. That was just how life was.

21

Patron saint of shopkeepers, Jude thought as the coins accumulated in his money box. The Saint George's Fair drew country folk from miles about, and most considered ambling in stalls and shops part of the day's festivities.

Aromas wafting in through the door enticed, but serving the seven patrons browsing his shelves was more important than dashing out for lunch.

Still, Jude's stomach begged to differ.

Over the growls coming from his midsection, Jude asked a farmer getting on in years, "Might this be for a grandchild?"

The man gave a sheepish smile and patted the copy of *Under the Window: Pictures and Rhymes for Children.* "For myself. Never got round to learning to read, so my wife means to teach me. I thought the pictures would help."

"What a clever idea, sir," Jude said and scissored a length of brown paper. He tied the twine into a double loop so that the spotted hands could carry it easily.

A short time later, Jude was assisting a boy of about twelve seeking Robert Ballantyne's latest adventure when Aurora Hooper entered, accompanied by a wispy girl with flaming cheeks. "Yoo-hoo, Mr. Pearce!"

No . . . no . . . not today.

Jinny, loyal as ever, rose from her nap behind the counter and trotted over for head scratches. Jude pretended not to hear as he took a novel bound in green cloth from a shelf.

"*Six Months at the Cape,*" he said, handing it over to the boy.

"Thank—" the boy got out before being nudged aside by Mrs. Hooper.

"There's a good lad. I mustn't leave my shop for long."

"Mrs. Hooper, I would appreciate your not manhandling my customers," Jude said quietly but tersely.

"Nonsense. I barely touched the lad." She chortled and turned to the staring patrons. "Pray tell, how can a woman *manhandle* anyone? Do pay a visit to Hooper's Fine Fabrics, by the by. Ten percent discount, today only, in honor of Saint George."

"Mrs. Hooper . . ."

She wheeled back to Jude. "Allow me to introduce my niece, Miss Caswell!"

With eyes averted, the girl dropped a lethargic curtsey.

"This is not a good time," Jude said to Mrs. Hooper.

"Ah, but my sister's family comes to town so infrequently." She prodded the girl's arm with a finger. "Bernadette! You have a voice! Don't stand there like a stump!"

Jude actually pitied her. "I really must insist you leave. I'm quite busy. I've not even had time for lunch."

Mrs. Hooper gave a pained sigh. "Very well, Mr. Pearce."

That was easy, Jude thought when the two were gone.

Which should have made him suspicious, for but half an hour later, Miss Caswell entered again with a small covered platter and wrapped parcel. There were then but two women in the shop, farmers' wives too absorbed in conversation to notice.

Miss Caswell murmured, eyes downcast, "From my aunt's restaurant. And a chop for your dog."

He did not ask what was beneath the pewter cover, but the aroma hinted at roast beef, Hooper's specialty.

"Here, allow me," he said gently, stepping over to take her elbow. He escorted her back through the doorway, for the women's conversation could not continue forever and he did not wish to humiliate her.

"It's very kind of you. But I cannot accept this. Do you understand?"

"It's roast beef and gravy and potatoes. With a fork, so you don't have to leave."

"You must take it back."

Finally, she met his eyes. "I didn't want to bring it, sir. My mother hates my beau because his father drinks and raises pigs. We've been in love since we were thirteen, but my aunt is trying . . ."

Her voice trailed and cracked.

"I'm sorry." Jude fished a handkerchief from his pocket, handed it to her, and took the platter. *Grandmother, perhaps you should have sewn more hankies after all.*

She wiped her eyes, blew her nose. "George is not like his father! He's apprenticed to a dentist in Birmingham and intends to make something of himself."

Casting about mentally for some encouragement beyond another *I'm sorry,* he looked past her shoulder and spotted Mrs. Kent moving up the pavement.

Mrs. Kent!

"Will you speak with someone much wiser than I am?" he asked Miss Caswell. "An older woman?"

She shook her head fearfully. He understood. It was *older women* who were making her life miserable.

"Please? You'll find her most sympathetic."

After a hesitation, she nodded.

When Mrs. Kent drew close, he introduced her to his young visitor. "Can you spare a moment to give Miss Caswell some advice?"

"Me?" Mrs. Kent said with hand to bosom. She smiled at

the crimson-faced young woman. "I can try. Shall we take a little stroll, dear?"

Three customers entered the shop. They were content to browse, so Jude gave Jinny the chop and then took the platter behind the counter and tucked into roast beef and potatoes. No sense in wasting food now that a young girl's hopes were not pinned to it.

Of Mrs. Hooper's hopes, he cared not.

When Mrs. Kent and Miss Caswell returned, both were smiling in spite of the girl's blotchy complexion. They approached the counter, where Jude was wrapping a copy of *The Return of the Native* for a patron browsing the shelves.

"Mrs. Kent advised me to apply to a college for the upcoming term," said Miss Caswell, "as George has two and a half years more of apprenticeship."

"Surely her parents would seize this as a means to distance them from each other," Mrs. Kent said. "And cease pressuring her to marry someone else."

"I did so enjoy schoolwork," the girl said. "I rather miss it."

"Thank you for allowing me to put you on the spot," Jude said to Mrs. Kent after the girl left with fork and empty platter.

"It was my pleasure," she said. "I trust she'll find academics a more fitting pastime than writing *Mrs. George Grigg* over and over in her diary. If George is as fine a fellow as she says, he'll wait until she finishes and begin the marriage on a more mature footing. Or it could be they'll both move beyond their youthful pledges."

"I was right to tout your wisdom, Mrs. Kent."

She snorted. "Any wisdom I may possess was forged in the kiln of folly."

"I highly doubt that," he said with a chuckle. "Have you received word from Miss Kent?"

She shook her head. "Soon, perhaps. She's been away but eleven days."

It seems much longer, Jude thought, walking her to the door. "You've been to the fair?"

"I took a turn around the green that proved most interesting. And now I shall go home and prop up my weary feet. Good day, Mr. Pearce."

"And to you," he said, finding himself adding, "I've decided to write to my father's parents."

She smiled. "Very good!"

That evening after a ham sandwich, he went to his desk and penned a simple page. He told of his parents' and siblings' deaths, adding that he earned a decent living in his own book-shop and wished nothing from them.

Yet, how to close?

Declare that he had forgiven them, when they had not asked for forgiveness? When it was his father, not he, they had injured?

He signed his name beneath *Regards.*

The letter which followed was easier. He smiled while penning her name.

22

"Pythagoras was a teacher and philosopher who lived on the island of Samos in the Aegean Sea, six centuries before Christ," Rosalind said to the thirteen girls in upper fourth-form geometry. "The Pythagorean Theorem is named for him; however, there is some evidence that the ancient Babylonians discovered it first."

Using a ruler, Rosalind drew a right triangle upon the chalkboard.

"The two sides connected by the right angle are referred to as the *legs*. This third side, opposite the angle, is the *hypotenuse*. If we assign a to the length of one leg, and b to the second, then we may determine the length of the hypotenuse with a simple formula: $A^2 + B^2 = C^2$"

Five hands rose. She called upon Margaret Whetstone, who wished to know if *discovered* was the correct term. "Should we rather say the theorem was *invented*?"

"A very good question, Miss Whetstone," Rosalind said as other heads nodded. "Let us consider a caveman with a family of six to feed. The hunting is sparse, but there are apples on the ground. Small apples, so each person would need two. Even if he has no words yet for numbers, he will discover that he needs twelve. He may invent a method for computing, such as having stones represent family members, but the sum was out there and does not change in any language or situation."

She smiled at her students. "But be it discovered or invented, it is time for us to put the theorem to use."

She solved the first example on the blackboard and drew more right triangles. The lesson moved along to a chorus of scratching pencils.

When the hour was finished, she dismissed the girls and crossed the courtyard to her tiny apartment in Fauconberg House. She had two hours before dinner and had just propped her feet upon an ottoman with a library copy of Mary Shelley's *The Last Man* when someone rapped at her door. She hopped up and opened it.

Lucinda Morris, instructor of botany and general science, stood in the corridor. Tall and athletic, she possessed a voice that made listeners take a backward step.

"Letters," she exclaimed, handing over envelopes. "Not one but two! Can the sky be falling?"

"I get letters," Rosalind said defensively. The rare ones from former students counted, although one satisfactory glance at the envelopes told her that these were not those. "Thank you for bringing them up."

"You're welcome. Tennis Saturday?"

"Very well." She was not good at the game, but anything to make Lucinda leave so that she could read her mail. Alone again, she sat and opened Mr. Pearce's envelope.

"Sorry, Mother!" she said.

Dear Miss Kent,

I pray this finds you in good health. How are your classes progressing? Do you still take morning strolls? Is there time, at the end of the day, for you to explore other worlds with our mutual friend Mr. Jules Verne?

The Saint George's Fair was a huge success, judging by the number of visitors in town. I closed shop only minutes ago, after a day of brisk sales. Your mother stopped by at the most opportune time, for a young woman was in dire need of some advice. Your mother is a kind soul, but then, you of all people know this.

I was pleased as punch to discover in my shipment on Monday past, a copy of Culinary Jottings: A Treatise in Thirty Chapters on Reformed Cookery for Anglo-Indian Rites. Yes, that is the title! I took it over to Mr. Galvez, and he graciously agreed to order the appropriate spices and prepare a special meal upon the date of my choosing. I would like to wait until your return, for it would be an honor to introduce you to the food I enjoyed as a boy. Will you think this over?

And now, Miss Kent, I have dominated your attention long enough. Odd, but it seems I just sat down to write. But if you will bear with me:

> *May your skies e'er be blue.*
> *One plus one equals two.*
> *May equilaterals dissect*
> *Whilst transversals connect.*

It is now well past midnight, for it took me two hours and a mathematics text to compose those last two lines. Robert Browning has no cause for worry.

> *Yours very truly,*
> *Jude Pearce*

Rosalind smiled. "You're an unusual man, Mr. Pearce."
Her mother's letter told of meeting Coral Shipsey's brother and sister-in-law from Buckfastleigh at the fair. Of convincing

Mrs. Deamer to gather seashells with her on Sunday afternoon past. Of purchasing an assortment of cold meats from
Grundke's and delivering them to Mr. Moore's. Of planting
petunias and convincing Mr. Hurst to turn a bit of ground for
a vegetable patch.

Absent was any mention of her helpfulness to the young girl
in Mr. Pearce's shop. Rosalind was beginning to recognize a
humility that was certainly at odds with a stage career.

*The apple trees are in full pink bloom, and Port Stilwell
is awash in scent. Though I miss you desperately, daughter,
I cannot recall ever being so happy. I feel there is some
deep purpose to my being here, apart from hiding from
reporters who have likely forgotten all about me.*

"Would that they could," Rosalind said to herself, recalling
three different articles Miss Beale had shown to her with the
same query: *Where is Charlotte Ward?* It seemed to have become
a game among theatre critics, a mocking and cruel one.

*May you never discover this, Mother . . . your happiness
never be tainted.*

23

"Coral is despondent over Mr. Clark again," Mrs. Deamer said while collecting Charlotte's dish and empty teacup in the dining room on the morning of the eleventh of May. "I fear I've made matters worse."

"What did you say?"

"That he's not worth all this angst. It upset her all the more." Mrs. Deamer sighed. "I would not be young again for all the fish in the bay. Wrinkles are fair trade for fragile hearts."

Charlotte clucked her tongue. "Indeed."

"I'll search for boots as soon as I've put these away," Mrs. Deamer went on.

"I may as well come with you and try them on."

Mr. Hurst would arrive any moment, and Charlotte did not intend he should do all the heavy work himself, not when the vegetable patch was her idea.

Mrs. Deamer carried a lantern to the door beneath the staircase, and Charlotte followed her down the steps into the dark, cool cellar. After a search that turned up chipped crockery, a coiled rope, a rounders bat and ball, and a basket of yellowed newspapers, they found four pairs of boots lined up against a wall.

168

Turning one of the most promising pair upside down, Mrs. Deamer shook it and then beat it against the wall for good measure. "You wouldn't want a spider."

"Nor a mouse." Charlotte eased off a slipper to try it on. She decided upon a pair and went through the kitchen, where Coral sat at the worktable with face bent over a bowl of potatoes.

"Why don't you sit at the terrace table?" Charlotte asked. "It's a fine day out."

"Thank you, Mrs. Kent," Coral murmured, not looking up from the potato she was paring. "Perhaps tomorrow."

With a longing glance toward the garden door, Charlotte went over to the table.

"Look at me, dear?"

Coral hesitated, then obeyed. Her cheeks were blotchy beneath reddened, swollen eyes.

Charlotte pulled out the adjacent chair. She prayed for the right words, however much she wished to echo Mrs. Deamer's.

"I shouldn't have snapped at Mrs. Deamer," Coral said.

"She took no offense. She cares for you, as do I."

"You tried to help me. And Amy. But now he ignores the both of us."

"You preferred fighting over him?"

"Well, at least I got his attention betimes."

Charlotte sighed.

"You don't know him," Coral said in a rush of words. "He can be kind and thoughtful."

"I've no doubt. When it suits him." Charlotte folded her arms upon the table. "What do you want from life, Coral?"

"Why, I want Noble."

"Is that the extent of your dreams?"

Coral opened her mouth, closed it.

"What is it?"

"I should like to own a bakery. I've been saving since I was fourteen, but it will take forever." She eyed Charlotte defensively. "I enjoy making cakes and tarts and such, and I'm good at it."

"I agree. And I do hope you realize that dream one day."

The girl's shoulders eased a bit. "Thank you, Mrs. Kent."

"What does Mr. Clark think of this?"

"Oh, he would approve."

"Wait . . . you've never told him?"

Coral blew out her cheeks. "I don't want to bore him. He has enough troubles."

"Troubles . . ."

"He so desperately wants a musical career. But if he quits teaching, his father will have him work in his mercantile, with no summer breaks to attend auditions."

"Ah." Charlotte nodded. "His dreams are more important than yours?"

She shrugged. "Aren't we supposed to put our loved ones' needs above our own?"

The question stung.

"We are," Charlotte said. "As much as humanly possible."

"The Bible says that love is not self-seeking," Coral went on a little righteously.

"Yes, it does. But there is a difference between needs and *wants*."

"Noble *needs* to perform, Mrs. Kent. As much as he needs water and air."

It took great self-control for Charlotte to resist rolling her eyes. "Those are Mr. Clark's words, aren't they?"

"Well, yes."

"I must ask why he should be eligible for the role of 'loved one,' when his affection is as fickle as April weather? When he has never bothered to ask about *your* dreams?"

"It'll be different once he gets a part." Coral swallowed. "If he'll only have me back . . ."

"Dear Coral," Charlotte cut in, "I can only hope that one day you'll understand your worth. You deserve better."

Fresh tears filled the girl's eyes. "Anyone in town will say I deserve nothing."

"The people living in this house would not say so. And, I suspect, many more."

Coral pressed her lips and shook her head.

"You are kind and intelligent," Charlotte added. "And deserving of good things. I shall pray every day that God allows you to see yourself through His eyes."

"Pride is sinful," Coral said in a small, dry voice.

"You are His beloved child. If you ever truly comprehend that, you'll be filled with awe. Not pride. Now, I must join Mr. Hurst. But please think on these things."

Rising, she patted Coral's shoulder and went out to a garden clothed in springtime glory. Drifts of lavender forget-me-nots and cornflowers were complemented by taller columbines. Tree peonies, poached-egg plants, and day lilies gilded the green throughout and picked up the gold edges of hosta leaves.

I could weave fancies around those colors, Charlotte thought.

She had decided upon a sunny patch for vegetables, ten feet before the clematis-covered stone wall that kept the woods at bay, and far to the left of the four slatted armchairs and two benches beneath the white-blossomed branches of the crabapple tree.

On the right side of the tree were a crumbling lavatory and gardening hut, where Mr. Alger Hurst was sorting tools. Short, thickset, and leathery, he possessed a limp he credited to a Cossack bullet in Kabul forty years ago, when he was an army corporal.

He was gardener and caretaker at Sea Gull Inn and had somehow allowed Mrs. Hooper to hire his free Tuesday afternoons. Either he had nothing better to do, Charlotte supposed, or he was paid far better than were the two women servants.

"Will you not wear gloves, Mrs. Kent?" he asked.

"Gloves are for milksops, Mr. Hurst," Charlotte said, kneeling to scoop out a pocket of dark earth. "I want to feel the soil."

"Aye, naught wrong with good honest soil," he said, grinning around his pipe stem before growing serious again. "Unless you're in a tent during monsoon, and the mud's so thick it sucks at your boots. Mark my words, Mrs. Kent. Our soldiers will still be in Afghanistan a century from now."

The only issue Charlotte had with Mr. Hurst was that any gardening lesson was sprinkled with diatribes against colonialism. She agreed with him on most points, but what could she do?

"I'm not even allowed to vote, Mr. Hurst. All I can do is try to grow some vegetables. Will you teach me to do that?"

With a grunt, he knocked out his pipe and put it into the pocket of his smock. He hefted a sack from the barrow and dropped it into the middle of the turned earth. "Too much acid. Fine for petunias but not for cabbages. I've got to spread this."

"And *that* would be?"

"Lime. But I'll do this myself."

"Nay, my good man! And allow you to take full credit?"

"You'll need the gloves, then. Soil is kinder than the hoe handle to the hands."

Less than half an hour later, Charlotte eased her hoe to the ground and attempted to straighten her aching back.

"You don't have to be a heroine, Mrs. Kent," the gardener said, hoeing in fluid motions as if he had just begun.

"Thank you, Mr. Hurst."

She sensed someone watching and looked to the right. The boy from Saint George's Fair stood across the side picket fence.

With forty feet between them, she could see fear in his eyes, as if he might bolt any second.

"Good morning, young man!" she called, hastening toward him.

"Er . . . good morning, Mrs. Kent!" Mr. Hurst called from behind.

24

Danny took a step back as Mrs. Kent drew closer.

"Danny . . . isn't it?" she said.

"Danny Fletcher, ma'am," he mumbled. "My brother fainted. Will you help him?"

He led her around the cottage to Albert, who was sitting on the middle of the three steps where he had left him, face resting against his propped knees, lunch buckets and Danny's arithmetic book scattered at his feet.

"Albert?"

His brother raised his face, blinked at him. Mrs. Kent took off her gloves and leaned to feel his face.

"Fever, I think." She straightened and turned to Danny. "Is your mother out?"

His plan on the way over was to say just that. But with Mrs. Kent studying his face as if she could spot a lie, he could not form the words.

"Stepmother," Albert mumbled.

"I see," she said.

Danny could tell that she did not see, not really. "She would make me go on to school, and I can't leave him with her."

Especially not today. She was so furious that she had rubbed Albert's face into the sheet, her own face as red as a radish.

"What of your father?"

"He's at the bank." Not that it would matter.

"I'll go for him."

"Please don't. He'll only bring Albert home." Danny's heart raced. This was a bad idea. The fear in his breast should have been sufficient warning. Better to tend to Albert in the Bickle ruins than to face Stepmother's wrath twice in one day.

He went over to take his brother's arm. "Never mind, missus. I'm sure he'll be better very soon."

"Wait." She glanced toward the lane as if she could see past the trees to their cottage, then came over to take his other arm. "Help me to bring him indoors."

"I can walk," Albert mumbled. Still, Danny kept hold of his arm, crossed the porch, and went through the door Mrs. Kent opened.

They walked through a small room with a staircase, into a parlor that looked like a place from a dream, colorful and restful. A woman with dark hair and an apron ceased dusting a lamp and hurried over.

"This is Albert, Mrs. Deamer," said Mrs. Kent. "He's taken ill."

Mrs. Deamer moved two embroidered pillows from a red sofa. They were not allowed to sit upon the parlor furniture at home, so Danny held Albert back when Mrs. Kent said for him to lie down.

"He smells bad," Danny explained as his brother leaned against him.

The women exchanged looks. Mrs. Deamer hurried across the room and through the door.

Mrs. Kent knelt before them. "Does your throat hurt, Albert?"

"Not hurt," his brother mumbled.

"Even when you swallow? When you had your breakfast?"

"Didn't."

"You had no breakfast?"

"We weren't hungry," Danny said quickly.

Mrs. Deamer returned with a bundle in her arms. She spread a sheet upon the sofa, put down a pillow. When Albert lay down, she removed his shoes and covered him with a second sheet.

"Shouldn't he have a blanket?" Mrs. Kent asked. "He's shivering."

Mrs. Deamer felt Albert's cheeks as Mrs. Kent had done. Remembering the feel of his mother's hands upon his own face, Danny envied his brother just a bit.

"A blanket would make his fever rise. A sheet will do."

"Danny here said that he fainted," Mrs. Kent said. "Should we send for the doctor?"

"No!"

Both women turned, and Danny felt heat in his own face. Mrs. Kent came closer and put a hand upon his shoulder. "I would pay, Danny."

He had but to picture their stepmother's face. "Please don't, missus."

His heart jumped when someone knocked at the door. Mrs. Deamer went to answer it and returned carrying book and buckets.

"That was Mr. Hurst." She handed Danny the book and one bucket but hefted the other by the handle, testing its weight.

"No wonder he's as thin as a rail." She raised the lid, peered inside, and looked at Danny. "Your lunch?"

What could he say? He burned with more shame and looked down at his feet.

"And no breakfast either? That's likely why he fainted."

"What if we sent for Mr. Moore?" said Mrs. Kent.

"Who?" Danny asked.

"The minister from Saint Paul's. Or would you rather send for the vicar? You attend Saint Michael's, perchance?"

"We did. But my stepmother hates the vicar. We don't want to see anyone . . . please. I'm going to have to take Albert away if you send for anyone."

The women looked at each other again.

"Coral's broth should be ready even if the vegetables aren't," Mrs. Deamer said.

"I'll see to that," Mrs. Kent said, smiling again at Danny. "Come, Danny."

"My brother . . ."

"He's in good hands."

He followed her across the hall into a warm kitchen that smelled savory and yeasty, and his stomach groaned. A fair-haired lady wearing an apron turned from stirring a kettle at the stove and gave him an odd look. He recognized her from about town. She was pretty but looked sad today.

"Miss Shipsey, this is Danny. I shall need a cup of broth for his brother."

"Only broth, Mrs. Kent?"

"He's ill. I may return for more. And will you give Danny something to eat?"

She smiled, and the sadness vanished. Danny wondered if kind ladies were aware of how magical their smiles were.

"Leave him to me, Mrs. Kent."

When they were alone, she said, "Do you like omelets?"

"Yes, miss."

She leaned her head, narrowed her eyes. "Do you know what they are?"

"Um . . . no, miss."

"Eggs." She took a butter crock from atop a cupboard. "Not Mrs. Beeton's way, God rest her soul, with the separating and beating. The French omelet is easier and better, in my opinion. I'll fry bacon, too. You've heard of that, haven't you?"

Her smile said she wasn't mocking his ignorance. She pointed a wooden spoon toward a door. "Now, if you're needing the water closet, it's through the pantry. Be sure and wash up. Towel's on the rack."

The water closet was tiny, with a toilet and basin. A cake of soap sat in a dish, and an embroidered towel hung from a hook. Danny washed his hands, trying to push dirt from beneath his fingernails as best as possible. The towel was too nice to use, so he dried his hands upon his shirt.

Seconds later, he sat at the table, tucking into more food than he had ever seen on one dish. Miss Shipsey had even brought over a beaker of milk and some toasted bread spread with marmalade. Wolfing food could get him a slap from his stepmother, but he knew instinctively that Miss Shipsey did not mind.

She pulled out the chair beside him. "I so enjoy seeing someone with a hearty appetite. How old are you?"

"I'm ten," he mumbled around a mouthful.

"You're in Mr. Clark's class?"

"Yes, miss."

Her smile faded into a wistful expression. "I'm told he's a wonderful schoolmaster."

"My brother's six," he said, hoping to steer the conversation in another direction. "He has Mrs. Fairburn."

"I had her too, when the infant school was in a wee building by the station. As poor as a beggar but sweet."

Mrs. Deamer brought the cup back into the kitchen. "More broth, Coral? And a tray and bowl and spoon this time. We've coaxed him to sit."

"May I see him?" Danny asked as Miss Shipsey pushed out her chair.

"But of course," Mrs. Deamer said. "After you finish your plate."

When he entered the parlor again, Albert was perched upon the sofa with the women on either side.

"Another bite?" said Mrs. Kent, hand upon his shoulder as Mrs. Deamer held bowl and spoon before him. His brother opened his mouth, obeyed. His face was flushed, but he seemed to have rallied a bit, for he gave Danny a weak smile.

"He could do with a lie-down whilst we're close by," Mrs. Deamer said.

Mrs. Kent eyed him. "Danny could do with one as well."

"Oh, I'm fine, thank you. I shouldn't leave my brother."

Truthfully, his eyes felt like chalk. The nightly ordeal of trying to keep Albert dry, the terror of being discovered whenever he failed, was draining. Still, he was relieved to know that they wouldn't be sent away just yet. Even though Albert seemed stronger, he would likely not fare well hiding in the Bickle ruins until school was dismissed.

The women exchanged glances above Albert's red curls, and Mrs. Deamer said, "Shall I . . . ?"

"Just continue spooning soup into him." Mrs. Kent smiled at Danny and left the room. She returned shortly with a pillow and folded sheet, which she spread upon the smaller sofa.

"I think you'll fit here."

He eyed the plump pillow. "What if I . . . what if I sleep too long?"

Thankfully, she understood. "School dismisses at five o'clock, yes?"

"Yes, ma'am."

"Rest, then. If you sleep though lunch, we'll feed you again when you rise."

Minutes later, his cheek was pressed into a pillow that smelled of the outdoors as the women's conversations melded into a pleasant hum. He drew in a sleepy, contented sigh. Kind people were taking up his burden of constant vigilance. For a little while, he could be just a boy.

25

When two hours had passed on Thursday morning with no literate foot over the threshold, Jude removed his coat, flipped the *Open* sign in the window to *Closed*, and took a rubber tennis ball from a counter drawer.

"I trust you won't carry this one off and chew it to pieces."

Jinny wagged her body and whimpered happily.

"Wait here," he said on the pavement. Pungent and sweet aromas wafted through the propped door to Pericles Blyth, Tobacconist. Mr. Blyth sat reading a newspaper with his boots upon a crate.

"You've got no customers either?" Jude said.

"Ah, there is a mild ague going about. Dr. Harris says naught to panic over."

"That explains it. Well, if anyone should ask, we'll be on the beach for a bit."

The water of the bay was dappled with shafts of light and color as it slapped and sighed among the shingles. With Jinny dancing about him, Jude rolled up his trousers, tucked stockings into shoes, and placed them upon an empty bench. Gingerly, he walked into the shallow surf, tossing the ball for Jinny to retrieve, over and over. Four women pulling kelp into buckets were their only witnesses, save the gulls screeching overhead.

"A little farther this time!" Jude said, drawing back his arm.

Jinny leapt to catch the ball. She brought it back, then shook her head and growled as Jude wrested it from her jaws. She was never so happy as when roughly mauled.

"Mister Pearce?"

Jude turned toward the sound. From Lach Lane, a well-dressed man in a gray suit and a low black topper hat waved.

"Give, Jinny." Jude took the ball from her jaws. She danced about, waiting, but when he shoved it into his pocket, she shook water from her fur and trotted ahead with tongue hanging. She reached the stranger first and licked the hand he held out to her.

"Good fellow," the man said. He seemed Jude's age, perhaps a bit older, with scant gray in his temples.

"She's actually female," Jude said as he closed the gap between them.

"Ah. My apologies."

Jude wiped his hand upon his shirt sleeves and extended it. "That's quite all right. Jinny doesn't take offense easily."

The man chuckled as they shook hands. "Well then, no wonder I mistook her for male."

Assuming this stranger had not sought him to discuss whatever misgivings he was having over the fairer sex, Jude waited.

"I intended to ask proof of your identity. But while you have your mother's coloring, there is no mistaking the Pearce cleft chin."

Time seemed frozen. Jude held his breath.

"I received your letter," the stranger went on. "Have you heard of me? Conrad?"

Letting out the breath, Jude said, "My uncle."

Now that he knew the man's identity, Jude recognized some of his father's pattern of speech. Tears stung his eyes as he turned to collect shoes and stockings. "Shall we go walk over to my shop?"

"Your shop is impressive from what I saw through the window. But may we sit here? I seldom have opportunity to be seaside."

They shared a bench. Jinny took that as permission to explore and loped off toward a clump of sea grass growing between stones.

"I'm overjoyed that you wrote," Conrad Pearce said. "Last summer, I went though every drawer of my father's desk, searching for any clue to your whereabouts. I even had my most trusted servants combing trunks in the attic."

That was gratifying to hear. "I knew my father had younger brothers, but you don't seem old enough to be my uncle."

"My parents would never have discussed something so intimate, but according to my old nursemaid, I was a surprise to them. Your father, David, was seventeen and at Cambridge when I was born. Our brother Emory was sixteen."

"Where is Emory now?"

"Deceased. Of a riding accident when he was but forty. He had daughters, thus the estate went to me."

"Father said the house was a palace."

"Our father had a shrewd head for business. Besides the land, he made fortunes investing in railways, coal, pig iron." Mr. Pearce gave him a sideways look. "Did it pain David to know the estate would never be his? Or yours?"

"I never sensed that he was bitter. Our home was a happy one."

"I'm glad to hear it."

"That being said," Jude went on, "the estrangement surely wounded him deeply."

"Surely." Mr. Pearce sighed. "My father was a difficult man."

"He's passed on, then."

"Last year."

Good! popped into Jude's mind in spite of himself. "I can't imagine disowning your own flesh and blood. My mother was an honorable woman."

"There was more to it than that. Emory confided to me when I was grown that David's leaving the Church of England infuriated our father. About the same time, he refused to court Pansy Truscott, whose father's estate joined ours, though she was besotted with him. Marrying an Indian woman was the proverbial straw that broke the camel's back."

Tact prevented Jude's thought from escaping his lips.

"Our mother passed on of a stomach abcess eight years ago," Mr. Pearce went on.

"Did she miss her firstborn?"

"I've no doubt she did. But she had not the fortitude to stand up to Father. She threw all her energies into me."

Grandmother Saroj came to Jude's mind. Soft-spoken though she was, she would have fought tigers to protect him. Tenderness and courage did not have to be mutually exclusive.

"She did ask for both of my brothers toward the . . ." Mr. Pearce's voice broke. "When she was delirious from pain. It's my hope that they're together now."

They shared a silence as Jinny chased waves in the distance, pity softening some of Jude's resentment. Grandmother Saroj was not married to a tyrant.

"I'm sorry," he said.

"Thank you." Mr. Pearce pulled a watch from his fob pocket and said, "My train arrives in an hour. Shall we proceed to the business at hand?"

"Business?"

"My memories of my eldest brother are hazy but endearing. I wish to do right by him . . ."

"I want nothing from you."

". . . as I do for Emory by providing for his wife and daughters."

Jude shook his head. "That wasn't my purpose in writing."

"I believe you. Please understand that I must do this for myself."

"Your coming here today is more than enough. I don't hold your father's actions against you."

"And yet I profit comfortably from those actions." Mr. Pearce took an envelope from his coat pocket and held it out to him. "This small token cannot repair the past but will allow me some peace of mind."

Jude shook his head. "No, thank you."

"Rest assured it's but a drop in the bucket. Will you grant me this?"

"I appreciate the offer. I do. But accepting money would make me feel beggarly."

"And yet I'm the one who is begging. This is family money, Jude. Please allow me to honor my eldest brother the only way I know how."

The envelope was being pushed into his chest. After a moment, Jude took it.

His uncle blew out his cheeks. "Promise you'll deposit and use it?"

"I promise," Jude said.

"Open it after I'm gone. You've made me a happy man."

Jude gave the man beside him a grudging smile. "I'm in a fair mood myself."

His uncle threw back his head and laughed. "I do like your sense of humor. Must have come from your mother. We Pearces are a stoic lot."

"Actually, I believe it did."

"Now, if you and Jinny would care to accompany me back to the station . . ."

Jude pulled on his stockings and shoes, then called to Jinny. As they walked up Fore Street, he prodded his uncle for recollections of his father. His mind pictured the Kent ladies. How happy they would be for him!

When they reached the station, he said, "I can't tell you how good it is to have family again."

His uncle gave him a sad smile and clamped his shoulder. "I like you, Jude. I almost wish that were not the case, for I shall likely never see you again."

Disappointment cut sharply. Jinny ceased her sniffing rounds to trot over to Jude's side and stare up with questioning eyes.

"My wife has not spoken to me for four days," his uncle continued, "ever since I declared my intentions. She would cut Emory's widow and daughters off in a trice if I allowed."

How did one respond to that? Jude took the envelope from his pocket and said, "If accepting this causes you family disharmony . . ."

"If not over this matter, it's another. I'm not the first man to be deceived by a comely set of eyes. But that's my burden to bear, not yours."

A whistle shrilled in the near distance.

"Still," his uncle said after some hesitation, "if you ever need me, do write."

"And the same to you."

A minute later, the Midland Railway locomotive pulled to a steamy stop to collect its lone passenger. The men embraced, and then his uncle boarded a first-class coach with a wave of his hand.

"Well, Jinny . . . this has been a most unusual day," Jude said when a cloud of smoke was all that was left of the train.

Jinny cocked her head.

"Shall we?"

He slipped a thumb beneath the seal, brought out the cheque, and stared.

One thousand pounds!

But no, his eyes had skimmed over another zero.

A ten-thousand-pound *"drop in the bucket."*

Jude's knees weakened, and he mumbled, "We must go to the bank."

Jinny wagged her tail.

But first, a letter to write before today's outgoing posts. And then, a visit to make.

26

The angst of the past two days knotted the muscles of Charlotte's shoulders and back. Seeking release, she sat at the pianoforte and ran her fingers over the keys. In time, she began playing the most depressing song that came to mind, "Little Barefoot." Softly, she sang.

> "Hundreds passing by unheeding,
> 'Cept to jostle her aside—
> There, with bare feet cold and bleeding,
> She in tones of anguish cried:
> 'Mister! Please give me a penny . . .
> I want to buy some bread for Ma!'"

She felt a presence, ceased playing, and swiveled on the bench.

"Pardon me, Mrs. Kent," Mrs. Deamer said, "but you barely touched your lunch. And now . . ."

"I can't stop thinking of those boys," Charlotte said. "Has little Albert recovered? What if he's much worse? There is nothing so maddening as not knowing."

"He was better when he left here, so he's likely recovered."

"Yes, that's true."

"But what if the stepmother discovered they were here and punished them?"

Charlotte frowned. "You're not helping my mood, Mrs. Deamer."

"I beg your pardon."

"No, no. It's something I've considered myself. In any case, their well-being is more important than my melancholy." A thought entered Charlotte's mind. She closed her eyes.

Are you offering me a means to atone for my failures with Rosalind? Is that why they're constantly in my thoughts?

When she opened them again, the housekeeper was turning.

"Wait, will you sit with me?"

"But of course."

"Has God ever spoken to you?" Charlotte asked as they settled into adjacent chairs.

"Not audibly, Mrs. Kent. No burning bush." Mrs. Deamer hesitated. "But I have felt . . . promptings at times during my life."

"Promptings. An appropriate description."

"Is God speaking to you?" Mrs. Deamer asked. "About the boys?"

"I believe He's urging me to help them. Not in a meat-pie-at-the-fair sort of way but dramatically. But what if it's my own empathy speaking?"

"Surely empathy is a gift from God."

"Surely," Charlotte said.

"And Scripture says whoever gives a cup of water to a child in His name . . ."

The uncertainty in Charlotte's mind faded. Why was it there, in any case? Age and experience had taught her caution, but when children were being mistreated, was not impulsive action appropriate?

"But what to do?" she asked.

"Visit their father? Appeal to his conscience?"

Charlotte thought for a second, shook her head. "Mr. Fletcher seems a decent man, but Danny may have good reason for not wishing him to be involved. At any length, I'm strongly inclined to believe the stepmother rules the roost."

"Appeal to *her* conscience?"

"Evidence suggests she has none."

"In which case, you would make matters worse." Mrs. Deamer shook her head. "I hope you don't assume all stepmothers are as Mrs. Fletcher. My husband's lavished him and his sister with affection. That Lowell took the wrong path was no discredit to her."

"I believe you," Charlotte said.

"Perhaps if you spoke with Mr. Moore for advice?"

"I hate to add another burden to his shoulders. Coral says that Mrs. Moore's family has been called."

"Oh dear," Mrs. Deamer said.

"But do you suppose it would do any good to speak with the constable?"

"Again, Mrs. Kent, you could make matters worse. There is no law against disciplining one's children."

"Discipline!" Charlotte snorted. "Is there a law against starving one's children?"

That sparked an idea.

"Regarding Mrs. Fletcher . . . what if I appealed to something else?"

"And that would be . . . ?"

"Greed. Nature abhors a vacuum, and I've noticed that people lacking in conscience possess an abundance of the stuff."

"Sadly true," Mrs. Deamer said. "Yet how would you appeal to her greed?"

"My allowance. My needs are small. What if I asked the boys to assist me in the garden on Saturdays? Just enough work to make my request honest. Mainly, they would be fed and safe. At least for a day each week."

Mrs. Deamer looked down at her hands. "I wish I had the means to contribute. But what I'm able to save . . . ."

"Goes to your visits to your husband and brother." Charlotte would never say so out of respect for the woman before her, but she suspected Mrs. Hooper was as stingy with her wages as she obviously was with Coral's. Another case of greed, this time feeding off desperation.

"Don't lose heart," Charlotte said to her. "I saw how you were with little Albert. The more maternal influences these lads have, the better."

"Thank you," Mrs. Deamer said quietly. "But I'm afraid there are two matters you should consider."

"Mrs. Hooper, yes?" Charlotte said. "Well, she made it clear that Mr. Hurst was retained for only the most rudimentary gardening and that I'm welcome to grow vegetables, but not to expect a reduction in rent. She wouldn't care a fig if I hired helpers."

"I suppose she would consider that she ultimately benefits."

"What is the second issue?"

"The cost of the extra food. The vegetables will take weeks, and you can't grow a ham out there."

"Oh dear, that's so." Charlotte mentally calculated her allowance. "I have enough to feed them, if Mrs. Fletcher doesn't demand too much money. She may appreciate having them out of her sight."

"Just mind that she doesn't think you disapprove of her. Don't give her reason to refuse from spite."

"That will be difficult. I *do* disapprove of her."

Mrs. Deamer gave her a little smile. "Not all stages are in London, Mrs. Kent."

Charlotte smiled back. "Thank you, Mrs. Deamer."

School was to dismiss in less than three hours. She would have to hurry, lest she place Danny and Albert in an awkward situation. But first, she stopped into the kitchen, where Coral was organizing spice containers.

"What a grand idea," Coral said after a quick explanation. "I don't mind cooking extra on Saturdays at all. Those boys need fattening up."

"You're a dear," Charlotte said before setting out on foot.

On Fore Street, she wasn't quite certain which of the white-washed cottages Rosalind had pointed out, nor could she recall the face of the woman leaving the bank that day. She went to the gate of the first cottage, where a young woman was sweeping the walk.

"Hallo there? I'm Mrs. Kent. Are you Mrs. Fletcher?"

The woman came to the gate with broom in hand. "I'm Mrs. Housely. The Fletchers is four down."

"Thank you. I'm sorry to have disturbed you."

"I never mind a break." She patted the broom handle. "Should you bring this to her? In case hers is broke?"

"I beg your pardon?"

The young woman tittered. "From riding."

"No, but thank you," Charlotte said, though she appreciated the humor and knew she would share the account later with Mrs. Deamer.

Four cottages down, she went through the gate, across the small porch, and knocked. Presently a woman of about thirty answered in a green print dress. She stared for a moment before saying, "Yes?"

"My name is Mrs. Kent. May I speak with Mrs. Fletcher?"

"I'm Mrs. Fletcher," she said warily. She was thin, with light-blond hair parted in the middle, plaited over the ears, and drawn back into a meager coil. Her cheeks were sallow, apart from two distinct spots.

Charlotte knew rouge when she saw it. *You vain thing.*

Large hands were clasped at her waist. Charlotte viewed them with disgust, imagining the inflictions they perpetrated upon Danny and Albert.

Still, she was onstage, so she smiled and warmed her voice.

191

"I'm delighted to make your acquaintance, Mrs. Fletcher. May I ask a minute of your time?"

Lids narrowed a bit over violet eyes that were Mrs. Fletcher's only redeeming feature. "Did the vicar send you?"

"Not at all." But it appeared their business would have to be conducted here on the porch. "I'm a widow, lodging in Mrs. Hooper's cottage on Orchard Lane. Do you know it?"

"I've seen it. It's yellow."

"It is indeed. And I believe you have sons of employable age?"

"Employable age?" she chortled. "They're but ten and six. And not very bright, truth be told."

"I'm speaking of light gardening on Saturdays. For wages, of course."

The violet eyes and door widened at the same time. "Won't you come in, Mrs. . . . ."

"Kent," Charlotte reminded her as she stepped into a tidy parlor.

"My baby is asleep upstairs, so . . ."

Relieved that Albert seemed to be at school, Charlotte put a finger to her lips and sat upon a plush yellow chair framed in mahogany. "How old is your little one?"

"Her name is Teresa," Mrs. Fletcher said proudly while settling into another chair. "She's twenty months."

"Lovely." Looking around, Charlotte said, "You have elegant taste. Most parlors are cluttered with bric-a-brac these days."

"I have only a day maid on Wednesdays and don't care to spend betweentimes dusting. Besides, Teresa would want to play with pretties, and it's not good for a tot to hear *no* all the time."

"What a thoughtful mother you are."

She beamed. "Now, how did you come to hear of Danny and Albert?"

"Actually, my daughter, Rosalind, took a stroll our first evening here, in March, and spotted them washing your fence. It was refreshing to know of children who aren't mollycoddled, so when I decided I needed help with my bit of gardening, they came to mind straightaway."

Mrs. Fletcher smiled and shifted forward. "Will you have tea, Mrs. Kent?"

"Ah, but no thank you. I must nip back soon." She searched her mind for an excuse.

Mrs. Fletcher had another subject on hers. "How much do you offer?"

"Sixpence per Saturday?"

"Each?"

"Well, for both." Charlotte rushed on. "Meals would be provided."

"Meals ain't such a bonus." She shrugged. "They have small appetites."

Charlotte had an unladylike and decidedly un-Christian urge to slap her.

What to do?

London isn't the only stage. She pushed to her feet.

Mrs. Fletcher stood as well, mouth agape.

"This has to do with your not wishing to be separated from them, good mother that you are," Charlotte said. "I admire you for that and will seek elsewhere. Perhaps you know if any of their playfellows—"

"Sixpence will do. Don't want it put about that I took advantage of a widow."

"How kind of you." Charlotte fished two shillings from her reticule. "Here are their first month's wages."

Mrs. Fletcher gave her a simpering smile. "You'll send the money to me directly every month, of course."

"But of course. Wouldn't want the sweet shop to tempt the little fellows." Charlotte paused at the door. "And don't worry. I'll not overwork them beyond their endurance."

"Thank you," Mrs. Fletcher said, not looking worried one whit.

Charlotte could have danced all the way home. The mental image of herself doing so made her smile. *A plump bird flapping its wings.*

Mrs. Deamer met her at the gate, wringing her hands. "Mr. Pearce is in the garden. He asked to wait. I'm afraid I was sorting the linen cupboard when Coral answered the door and told him your mission."

"Oh, I don't mind," Charlotte said, still floating upon a wave of euphoria. "I trust him to be discreet."

"Unlike a certain *cook*. I'll have a chat with her."

"Be gentle. I didn't swear her to secrecy. I could not keep a confidence myself when I was young."

Mr. Pearce rose from a bench near the crabapple tree, and Jinny trotted over.

"Hallo, dear Jinny," Charlotte said. Before she could offer the same hand to Mr. Pearce, her hand was scooped up and enveloped by both of his.

"Was your mission successful, Mrs. Kent?"

"Why yes, it was."

"I'm happy to hear it," he said. "You're not angry with Miss Shipsey, are you?"

"For sharing more than her shepherd's pie recipe? Not at all."

"I've come to thank you."

"You're quite welcome. However, that begs a question."

He grinned. "My uncle paid a call this morning."

"Oh my! You must tell me every detail!"

As they shared the bench, he related his morning adventure, adding, "I felt a connection to my father, just hearing his voice."

"To think you woke assuming this would be an ordinary day."

"Indeed." Mr. Pearce hesitated. "He insisted I take a substantial sum of money as my father's legacy."

"Why, this just gets better and better!"

"Do you think I was right to accept it?"

"Would your father have wanted you to?"

He nodded. "I believe so."

"Then there you have it," Charlotte said. "Whatever will you do with it?"

"I've been considering that while waiting for you. Firstly, I'd like to divide my tithe between Saint Paul's and the London Missionary Society, which sponsored my parents."

"How very admirable."

"And then I would buy my shop from Mrs. Hooper. No more renting."

"Won't that be liberating!"

"I should also go to London and meet with a couple of new book publishers. I haven't been in years."

"Now that you're a man of means, you must stay at The Langham, at least for one night. The hydraulic lifts are a marvel, and the food at the restaurant is superb."

"You've been to London often?"

"Now and again," she replied. "Will you also take a trip to India?"

"Perhaps." His face practically glowed. "When monsoon season is over."

"I'm so happy for you."

"Thank you. The bulk of it I'll save, of course. But it may be that I shall want to build a cottage one day. My loft is small."

The words came out a trifle too casually. He glanced away.

Charlotte smiled to herself. "You strike a nice balance of practicality and liberality."

He chuckled. "My grandmother's Indian frugality balanced my grandfather's Latin spontaneity. But there is one thing more I should like to do."

"And what is that, Mr. Pearce?"

"Now"—he held up a hand—"please hear me out. All the way over, I wondered how I could ever repay you."

She sat up straighter. "Surely you're not about to offer *me* money."

"I wouldn't insult you, Mrs. Kent. But after speaking with Miss Shipsey, the solution came: I would like to pay the boys' wages."

"No."

"If it weren't for you, this wouldn't have happened to me."

"You don't know such a thing. God could have made another way if He meant for you to have it." She shook her head. "You're very kind, Mr. Pearce. But I feel impressed to do this."

He sighed, stared at his crossed shoes, but then brightened. "Books!"

"Books?"

"Will you allow me to donate some books?"

"Well, there's a thought," she conceded. "Children should have stories."

"Stories opened up new worlds to me as a child."

"To me as well." Charlotte patted his shoulder. "That will be lovely, Mr. Pearce."

He hesitated. "May I include some for you?"

She opened her mouth to refuse, but then, how could she deny him the joy of giving, when she herself was spilling over with it?

And she did enjoy books!

"Very well, Mr. Pearce. If that is what you wish to do. And I thank you."

27

Danny could tell something was amiss the moment he and Albert stepped into the cottage. For one thing, they were met by a delicious aroma coming from the kitchen, accompanied by a song.

> "I wish he would make up his mind, Ma,
> For I don't care much longer to wait;
> I'm sure that I've hinted quite strongly
> that I thought about changing my state . . ."

His stepmother had a more pleasing voice than Mr. Clark, who began every morning belting out "God Save the Queen." Yet she rarely sang other than to put Teresa to sleep with a "Rock-a-bye Baby" so gentle and loving that Danny pressed his ears into his pillow when the notes drifted through their bedroom wall.

Albert inhaled as if about to plunge into the sea. "M-m-m, ginger biscuits?"

> "For a sweetheart, he's really so backward,
> I can't bring him out if I try;

I own that he's very good-tempered,
But then, he's so dreadfully shy!"

"Don't ask for nothing," Danny whispered.

His brother gave him a stricken look but accompanied him into the kitchen.

Teresa, playing with wooden spoons on a rug, pointed and chattered. Their stepmother looked up from sprinkling bits of rosemary onto a raw chicken in a pan.

"You're home. A Mrs. Kent asked to hire you to work Saturdays in her garden. She lives in the yellow cottage at the end of Orchard Lane."

Albert brightened. "We went—"

"We've picked brambleberries in the woods nearby," Danny cut in.

"Berries." She sighed. "My mum made the most marvelous tarts. She died when I was but ten, so I never learned her recipe."

"Yours are very good," Danny said carefully.

"Why, thank you."

It seemed a spell had been cast, warm and smelling of ginger. As if the woman who had boxed his ears this morning for leaving shoes upon the landing had taken a potion.

"I smell biscuits," Albert said, eyeing a tea cloth–draped plate on the table.

Teresa burst into tears while holding a spoon aloft. Mother hurried over to her, lifted her into her arms. "There, there. Did you hit yourself, mite?"

"Hold your tongue," Danny whispered to Albert.

She patted the child, rocking her back and forth until the tears abated. "Will a sweet make it better?"

Albert's eyes widened with longing, but Danny shook his head.

And then Stepmother lifted the tea cloth from the plate. She took a golden biscuit and gave it to Teresa, who pushed it into her mouth. She set Teresa to her feet and, incredibly, held the dish out to Danny.

"Have one. For him too."

No matter her mood, she still could not voice his brother's name.

Albert accepted his, grinning, and took an immediate bite.

"Now sit," she said with a nod to the chairs.

When they were seated, she put two more biscuits before each of them, then pulled out her own chair while hefting Teresa into her lap.

"If your father asks if you want to work for Mrs. Kent, what will you say?"

Danny could not dream of his father caring, but then, he had broken through his indifference for a little while on the day of the fair, hadn't he? Before Albert could swallow the mouthful of biscuit in his mouth and chirp out something incriminating, Danny said, "We'll say that we should like to work. It's good for us."

What a relief to speak the truth for a change. He did not need to ask how this came to be. Why Mrs. Kent took such pains for him and his brother, he could not fathom. But what a comfort to know she thought of them.

Stepmother looked at Albert. He nodded, wide-eyed.

"If you do as she says and she decides to keep you on, I'll give you each a penny every week."

A penny! Danny wondered if his joy could be contained. Not that the thought of spending time at Mrs. Kent's cottage every Saturday wasn't joy enough.

Later, Father sat at the table chewing listlessly, even though the roasted chicken and vegetables were the most marvelous meal they had had in months. Again, Danny wondered why bank clerking was so taxing.

"She can pay them only a tuppence," Mother was saying. "But it would be good for them to help a poor widow."

Father swallowed. "I don't know, Sabrina. We don't need the money."

The warning line appeared between her eyebrows. "Don't need the money, you say, when the town forces school fees upon us? It would be within our rights to send Danny out with the boats now that he's ten, but I'm not saying we should, am I?"

Danny shifted in his chair. Should he inject himself into the argument? Surely she would not make him pay for it later, especially for taking her side.

Before he could speak, she waved a hand toward him and his brother. "They wish to do it. Ask them!"

"We do, Father!" Albert piped. "She's nice!"

Danny felt the blood drain from his face.

Oddly, Stepmother was too pleased with the support to ask how he could possibly know this. Or perhaps she assumed Albert referred to her.

"You see?" she said.

Father gave Danny a questioning look.

"Yes, Father," Danny said, stretching his lips into a smile. "We wish to learn how to garden."

"Very well," he said wearily. "We shall see how it goes."

Stepmother's mood was so light that she allowed Danny and Albert each another biscuit for pudding, with well-sugared tea.

"Mother loves us now!" Albert said in bed.

"Sh-h-h." Danny glanced at the door and whispered, "She's not our mother. And she just wanted Father to agree. You still have to be careful."

"I'm tired of being careful!" Albert hissed.

He turned on his pillow and shoved a thumb into his mouth. The tea increased his chances of an accident, thus Danny slept fitfully when at all, rousing himself twice to have his brother use the chamber pot.

—◈◯◈—

By Saturday, Mother's mood had regressed.

"She said meals are included, so I'm thinking that means breakfast. You'll work hard so she'll keep you on. And no speaking of what goes on here. None of her affair."

"What will she make us do?" Albert asked Danny as they walked up Orchard Lane with empty stomachs. "Scrub the fireplace, like Cinderella? I would, for Mrs. Kent."

Danny snorted. "There aren't any fireplaces in gardens."

"Oh yes. We seen one behind a big house on fair day, remember?"

"That was the inn. Whatever it is, do your best, so we'll be allowed to stay."

On the porch of the yellow cottage, he spit into his hand and attempted to press down some of Albert's red curls. Mrs. Deamer answered his knock and smiled.

"Good morning, Danny, Albert. Come this way."

She led them into the kitchen. Danny was disappointed not to see Miss Shipsey, but a teakettle simmered upon the stove, so he reckoned she was not too far away. They continued on to the narrow white door leading to the water closet.

"You'll want to wash your hands."

"Why must we have clean hands to work in the garden?" Albert asked as Danny pushed back his sleeves at the sink.

"I don't know," Danny whispered. "But don't complain."

Again, the towel was too nice to use. He wiped hands upon his trousers and directed Albert to do the same. They followed Mrs. Deamer back through the kitchen and into a dining room, where Mrs. Shipsey was placing cutlery upon a white cloth, and Mrs. Kent was arranging flowers in a vase.

Danny did not know what to say. For once, he appreciated Albert's barging ahead.

"Hallo, Mrs. Kent! We're here!"

Mrs. Kent chuckled. "And so you are. We're celebrating your first morning of employment with a breakfast feast . . . a cold one, because I neglected to give you an arrival time. I do hope you're hungry."

Hungry? Danny approached the table, where a loaf of dark bread sat beside a crock of butter. Strawberries, as red as he had ever seen them. Cheese, pickled beef tongue, and scones. He could only stare. Even Albert appeared dumbstruck.

"Has the cat got your tongue?" Miss Shipsey said on her way to the door.

Albert laughed, and Danny eased into a smile.

Miss Shipsey returned with a silver teapot. They all took chairs, and Mrs. Kent said, "Shall we pray?"

A memory stirred of earlier prayers at table. Danny motioned for Albert to bow his head before bowing his own.

"Dearest Father, thank you for another day, and for allowing Danny and Albert to visit. Forgive us our failings, and give us the strength to honor you with our lives. In the name of your Son, Jesus Christ, amen."

While Mrs. Deamer poured two beakers of milk from a pitcher, Miss Shipsey put a bit of everything on their plates, including a piece of buttered bread as big as his fist. Danny tried to pace himself as his brother shoved food into his mouth.

The women did not seem to mind. They chatted. The greengrocer's wife, a Mrs. Stark, had been to Paignton to see a show called *The Pirates of Penzance*. Danny wondered if actual pirates were on stage, but children were not to speak at the table, and anyway, he was still too nervous to call attention to himself.

But minutes later, Mrs. Kent smiled at him and asked, "What did you learn at school yesterday?"

"Um . . . the solar system?"

"I could never remember their order," Miss Shipsey said. "Particularly Uranus and Neptune. Which comes first?"

"An acronym helps," Mrs. Deamer said.

Miss Shipsey blinked at her. "Acro—"

"Making a sentence from the first letters. I once had a schoolmistress who used them for everything. *My very elderly mother just sits up nights.* Mercury, Venus, Earth, Mars, Jupiter, Saturn, Uranus, Neptune."

"Well done, Mrs. Deamer," said Mrs. Kent. She turned to Albert. "And what did you learn, young Albert?"

He scrunched up his face. "A song about boats."

"Will you sing it for us?" Miss Shipsey asked.

With the women smiling and Danny holding his breath, Albert wiped his mouth on his sleeve and piped,

> "Sail-ing, sail-ing, over the bounding main.
> Where many a stormy wind shall blow,
> 'Ere Jack comes home again!"

The women laughed in a delighted, non-mocking sort of way. The knots in Danny's stomach eased. No angry outburst loomed on the horizon. Not all kind people in the world turned on you. What a marvelous thought!

Afterward, Mrs. Deamer and Miss Shipsey collected the dishes onto trays as Mrs. Kent led Danny and Albert into the parlor.

"We have a bit of weeding, but it's not good for digestion so soon after a meal. Let us rest a bit." She lifted a book from the sofa and then sat in the middle. Albert, hesitating, climbed up to sit upon her left. Danny took the other side.

She held up the book in her lap, *The Swiss Family Robinson*. "Mr. Pearce of the bookshop brought several over for you. I chose this one because I so much enjoyed the story when I was a child."

Danny knew of the shop, had seen the man with spectacles sweeping the pavement and sometimes walking a small dog.

"What's it about?" Albert asked.

"Why, a family who find themselves shipwrecked on an island."

"Why did he give us books?" Danny asked.

"Because he's a kind man who remembers how fond he was of stories when he was a boy. I'll show you the rest later."

She opened the book, but Albert said, "May we bring them home, Mrs. Kent?"

"No, Albert," Danny said.

Their stepmother would disapprove. He knew this instinctively, though he would be at a loss to explain.

"To keep them here is best," said Mrs. Kent, moving pages. "But they will always belong to you. Perhaps when you're grown men, you'll read them to your children."

The concept of being *grown* had never occurred to Danny. *Now* was all he had, save those trips to a happier past.

"The tempest had raged for six days, and on the seventh seemed to increase. The ship had been so far driven from its course, that no one on board knew where we were. Every one was exhausted with fatigue and watching. The shattered vessel began to leak in many places, the oaths of the sailors were changed to prayers, and each thought only how to save his own life."

Birdsong floated through the window, and in the distance, gulls squawked faintly. Danny closed his eyes, leaned back against the seat, drew in a deep breath of pine and salt and flower-scented air and imagined himself onboard the doomed ship, rocked too and fro by the sea.

⋙◈⋘

His shoulder was being given gentle shakes.

"Danny?"

He forced open his eyes. Mrs. Kent smiled down at him.

"You both dropped off like Rip Van Winkle. It's been two hours. I fear if you sleep longer, you'll toss and turn tonight."

He sat up, looked to the bare place to his left.

"Albert went to the water closet."

Danny did not smell anything, nor see any dark spot on the cloth. Still, he had to ask. "Did he . . . have an accident?"

"No." She sat beside him, her eyes studying his face. "Does he have them often?"

"Oh, not at all," he assured her. "But he's a heavy sleeper. So I wondered . . ."

Albert skipped through the doorway, licking his lips.

"Miss Shipsey gave me a chocolate! There's one for you in my pocket."

Mrs. Kent smiled and rose. "Shall we do some gardening?"

The vegetable patch was comprised of a half-dozen fresh-looking rows, about twice as long as Father was tall. Short sprouts of various kinds were spaced out across the tops of five, like soldiers on hillsides.

She bent with a soft grunt, pulled a small shoot of grass from the soil. "Some weeds and grasses are trying to elbow themselves in. Mind you pull from the base, to get the roots. I shall be thinning tomato seedlings at the table on the terrace."

It took Danny what seemed half an hour to finish three rows. He stepped over to Albert's second and soon met him in the middle.

Brushing his hands, Albert gave the patch a worried look and whispered, "We should have worked slower."

"That would be dishonest," Danny whispered back, though he had thought the same.

"Will she send us home?"

"Perhaps she has something else for us to do."

Mrs. Kent walked over. "Finished, are you?"

Danny's heart sank. "I'm sorry . . . there weren't many weeds."

"Ah, but a stitch in time saves nine."

"What does that mean, ma'am?" Albert asked.

Brushing her hands against her apron, she gave him a

thoughtful look. "That it is best to attend to small things right away whilst they're more easily mended."

"But we've no more work to do."

"I didn't hire you just for the work. I hired you to keep me company as well. My daughter, Miss Kent, has returned to school, you see."

"So that you won't miss her too much?" Albert asked.

"Yes," she said.

"What should we do now?" Danny asked.

"Well, I wouldn't mind reading some more. What about you?"

28

"Remember your vocabulary test," Rosalind said to her algebra students at the end of the hour on the twenty-fourth of May. "If you'll memorize three terms every day, you'll fare better than waiting until Thursday evening to cram it all in."

Choruses of "Yes, Miss Kent" accompanied the shuffling of fifteen pairs of feet as they gathered books and pencils. When the last student had left, Miss Beale came through the door as if she had been waiting.

"There is a solicitor here asking for you. A Mr. Pankhurst."

"A solicitor? But why?"

"He said this regards your mother."

Divorce, Rosalind thought with quickening heartbeat as she started for the door.

Miss Beal caught her arm. "There is no hurry. Take some breaths."

Rosalind breathed in deeply, and it occurred to her to wonder aloud, "How did he know where to find me? Mother never publicized my whereabouts."

"Lord Fosberry, very likely. They were married, after all. Would you like me to stay with you?"

"Yes. Please."

In the principal's open office, an older gentleman looked up and stood. He had a kindly face, like someone's benevolent uncle. Shadows from dimpling showed through a graying beard. Eyes the color of stone were softened by laugh lines. And so with some reservation, Rosalind gave him her hand and the benefit of the doubt.

"I'm delighted to meet you," Mr. Pankhurst said, clasping her hand as Miss Beale closed the door.

"Thank you, Mr. Pankhurst. You wish to speak with me about my mother?"

"Shall we sit?" Miss Beale said, scooping Hetty from her chair.

Rosalind took the corner chair.

Mr. Pankhurst remained standing. "I do beg your pardon, Miss Beale. But this is a private matter."

"I asked her to stay," Rosalind said.

"Again, my apologies," he said gently, "but I'm afraid I must insist."

Never having had a father or any other dominant male figure in her life, Rosalind wavered. What if he took offense and left without revealing his mission?

She turned to Miss Beale. Her expression said, *"Whatever you decide."*

Rosalind decided she needed moral support more than she needed to appease someone she had not even invited into her day. She gathered courage and said, "I'm afraid *I* must insist, Mr. Pankhurst."

"Yes, of course. First, allow me to say that I was a great admirer of Lady Fosberry's work. As a Londoner, I had the pleasure of seeing her in many productions."

"Lord Fosberry wishes to divorce her," Rosalind said with a little chill. As much as she wished her mother to be shed of him, divorce was a harsh reality, the very word whispered as if it were something tainted. A second divorce was akin to a scarlet letter.

"My dear Miss Kent," he said in gentle voice, "I have distressed you. Whilst I cannot predict the future, that is not the reason for my visit."

He withdrew an envelope from his breast pocket and handed it over. It was sealed and blank but for a three-shilling stamp and the return address of the firm of Pankhurst and Snelling. "I have here an apology from Lord Fosberry."

Rosalind snorted. Unladylike, but then, the provocation was great.

"I understand why you should have misgivings," he said.

"Misgivings indeed! It was a letter from him which caused her breakdown."

He gave her a pained look. "We men often act rashly when our pride is wounded. But after counseling with his vicar, he fervently desires to clear his conscience."

"She's never going back to him," Rosalind said.

"He does not ask her to do so."

"Why do you assume Miss Kent has knowledge of her mother's whereabouts?" Miss Beale asked, making Rosalind glad again of her presence.

"Surely Lord Fosberry informed you we're estranged," Rosalind added.

"Because I myself have grown daughters." He gave Rosalind a tender smile. "Daughters tend to feel a keen responsibility for their parents."

Miss Beale cleared her throat. "Mr. Pankhurst, that generality is pleasant but lacking."

He smiled at her. "I can appreciate why Miss Kent asked you to stay."

To Rosalind, he said, "I desired not to imply some great intrigue. But yes, I happened to make some discreet inquiries, and a nurse described a young woman of your appearance removing Lady Fosberry from the Royal Free Hospital."

"All this effort for an apology?" Rosalind said. "He accused her publicly. He should be making retractions in newspapers, not disturbing the only serenity she's had in years."

The solicitor sighed. "In due time, Miss Kent. This is but a first step. And there is no guarantee that Lady Fosberry would *see* the retraction . . . wherever she may be."

"I'll not give you her address."

"Yes, I imagine not." The stone eyes glinted above the kindly uncle smile. "Your feelings do you credit. I would not think of asking. Simply that you post it."

"Does this contain a cheque for the money he took from her?" Rosalind could not refrain from asking.

"In a sense it does, yet another reason to keep this between the two of them. He proposes the terms of repayment."

"He intends to repay her," Rosalind said flatly.

"With interest. It's only fair."

She looked at Miss Beale.

The headmistress gave her an uncertain look, straightened in her chair, and said, "Do you give her your word as a gentleman that the envelope has what you claim?"

"You have my word," he said with fervent earnestness.

Where was the harm, then?

"I'll send it to her," Rosalind said.

The kindly uncle smile resumed in force. "I'm in your debt, Miss Kent."

He rose with a little bow, wished them good-day, and escorted himself from the office.

"Will wonders never cease?" Rosalind said.

"My very thoughts," Miss Beale replied. "Will you post it in the morning?"

"I'm not sure. Half-term break is but a week away, so I may just bring it to her myself. It would take almost as long to get there in any event."

She thanked Miss Beale for her support and crossed over to Fauconberg House to freshen up for dinner. A letter from Mr.

Pearce waited in the basket upon the foyer table. She carried it upstairs to her parlor and opened it. He asked how her classes were progressing. There was no poem, but he did relate a joke from *Punch*.

> *Why do chickens dislike Shakespeare?*
> *Because Macbeth did murder most foul.*

She smiled. Two paragraphs later, the page trembled in her hand.

"His uncle visited?" she said to the fireplace.

He wrote of his disappointment that there could be no relationship with his father's family, now that he wished to have one. But at least he had answers to some questions and part of what would have been his father's inheritance.

He closed with, *After I post this, I will share my news with Mrs. Kent. I thank God for leading you both to Port Stilwell. And not only because your mother's counsel led to my sudden monetary gain, although, quite frankly, it does not hurt. I plan to order a diamond-studded toothbrush for myself and a crystal water bowl for Jinny.*

Smiling again, she put his letter aside to read again before bedtime. A glance at the clock spurred her into action. She refastened her comb, smoothed wrinkles from her gown, and crossed the courtyard. In the dining hall, one hundred and seventy girls stood at their places. She was the last to the faculty table.

"I beg your pardon," she said to Miss Beale and the other teachers.

Miss Beale sent her a stern look before leading in prayer, which rattled Rosalind. The principal was a stickler for promptness. She did not dwell on this, nor join the others in conversation, instead thinking of Mr. Pearce's good news.

"I thought you didn't care for veal," said Janet Shergold, who taught history.

Rosalind looked down at the half-eaten stew upon her plate. "I didn't notice."

Janet glanced at Miss Beale and lowered her voice. "I was late twice last term and received the same sour look. Nothing came of it."

But then, after the last crumbs of almond cake were eaten and everyone dismissed, Miss Beale approached with a somber expression.

"I'm sorry I was late," Rosalind said.

Miss Beale waved a hand. "Do you have the letter with you?"

"Why, no. Shall I fetch it?"

"Bring it to my apartment."

⌦◇⌫

Miss Beale's parlor was crammed with a settee and an overstuffed chair, a lamp table and writing desk, and shelves of books. A basket filled with newspapers and periodicals rested beside her chair, with Hetty curled at the apex.

"I'm having second thoughts over Mr. Pankhurst," Miss Beale said. "Why did he ask you to post the letter?"

"Because I refused to give the address," Rosalind replied. Wasn't she there?

"But why did he say *post*? Not *deliver*? How does he know that your mother isn't here in Cheltenham?"

"Do you think I'm being watched?"

"There seems more to this than he's letting on. And why would he ask you to post the letter with half term so near?"

"Perhaps he isn't aware that it's near."

Miss Beale's brows lifted. "I can't imagine anything catching Mr. Pankhurst unawares. What if he wants to *ensure* that you go to your mother? One way would be to give you a letter of supreme importance . . . within days of a school break."

"So that I could be followed."

"It's possible." Miss Beale pursed her lips. "And then again, this could be an old woman's delusions. I may be looking for monsters that aren't there."

Disappointment tightened Rosalind's chest. "I won't chance that there aren't monsters. I shall have to stay here."

"That might be best, dear."

"I'll post the letter, then. I can't keep it until July. But I so wish I could be there when she opens it. What if it's not what Mr. Pankhurst claims?"

"Would she mind if you read it yourself?"

Rosalind grimaced. "I shouldn't want anyone reading my mail."

"But of course."

"Still, she would understand my motive."

Especially when reminded of the inquiries she had made into Mr. Pearce's character. A daughter had a duty to protect her mother too.

"You don't have to do that here, if you'd rather . . ." Miss Beale began.

"No, I trust you. And I may need your counsel."

Rosalind broke the seal and took out two pages. The script was precise, with little flourishes, as if the writer had labored for artistic perfection. For some reason, this annoyed her. She read aloud.

"My dear Charlotte,
  How can I begin to say how wretched I am? My sleep is haunted by memories of my actions. I beg forgiveness for every grief I have heaped upon you."

She let out a breath and exchanged smiles with Miss Beale. "A promising start."

"I intend to repay the seven hundred pounds you so generously lent to me. To double it! Fourteen hundred pounds would ensure a comfortable future, thus relieving your daughter of the burden of providing for you."

Kind words, but Rosalind was beginning to feel uneasy.

"Being that there is no hope for our marriage, I believe it is in both our best interests to end it on amicable terms. You have obviously settled somewhere peaceful. For my part, I wish to marry again. Lady Blake is of kind and generous character, and most eager to join her life with mine."

"He doesn't allow grass to grow beneath his feet," said Miss Beale.

"But alas, there is only one legal ground for divorce. I cannot force my pen to write the word! Granted, there would be publicity, but far more if there were a lengthy trial, where Jack Boswell would have no choice but to testify under oath to your secret meetings."

"Who is *he*?" Rosalind muttered. "Lord Fosberry accuses my mother of adultery yet again?"

"I do not cast stones, dearest Charlotte. Had I been more attentive, you would not have sought solace in the arms of a stableboy and footman. A brief appearance before the High Court of Justice in Westminster, before reporters get wind of it, and you will become the independent woman you once were."

Pulse pounded in Rosalind's temple. "You serpent!"

In haste to digest the rest, no matter how repulsive, she read silently, then said to Miss Beale, "If mother does not go to London and admit to . . . secret liaisons with the footman, Lord

Fosberry will be forced to keep the money for the hiring of a skilled detective to find her and serve a claim form, and then there would be expenses for staying in a hotel during a lengthy trial."

"That's extortion, plain and simple," Miss Beale said.

"How does he think he can succeed? Did he not read the stableboy's denial of his charges?"

"Where there is smoke, there's fire, in many people's minds. Perhaps he counts on your mother considering that some already assume she's guilty, simply because it was in print. And that she needs money desperately."

"Well, she doesn't, thanks to Aunt Vesta. Why would this . . ." Rosalind shook the accursed letter. ". . . this Jack Boswell . . . why would he testify against her?"

"For payment? Lord Fosberry seems to have a lot of it to throw around now." Miss Beale angled her head. "I wonder . . ."

"What is it?"

"I find it odd that your mother had but seven hundred pounds to give him. It would be a fortune to me, but given her long career . . ."

"She had me to support for most of my life, long distance though it was. Still, you would think she would have had more."

"Your aunt Vesta. Was she wealthy?"

"Comfortable," Rosalind replied. "She had two servants."

"Yet she left you a sizeable legacy."

Rosalind pondered this. "When I arrived here, I ceased contact with my mother. Do you think the legacy actually came from her? Is it possible to do that?"

"I shouldn't think it would break any laws."

"It would be just like her. Imagine! For years, I thought she was the most selfish woman alive."

"You were a child. And taught to think that way."

"Still, it hurts. I intend to ask her."

"Should you? If she wanted you to think it was from your aunt . . ."

"She feels as if she's taking charity from me. It would relieve her of that."

Miss Beale nodded at the letter in Rosalind's hand. "You should show that to her straightaway."

"Straightaway." Rosalind nodded. "I'll post it in the morning."

"In person. They'll expect you to go home for half-term break. You'll leave on Wednesday instead. Catch them off guard."

"Two days? But I can't just up and leave again."

"I'll take care of your classes until I find a replacement. We have applicants to spare." Miss Beale folded her arms. "It pains me to lose you, Rosalind. You will always have a place here, when this issue is settled. But for now, your staying is no good. You've received letters from Port Stilwell, yes?"

"I have."

"It's but a matter of time before the wrong person intercepts one, or strikes up conversation with a Fauconberg House resident who may have seen your mail."

"But how am I to get away undetected?"

"Hmm. We'll find a way."

"What will you say to the staff?"

"That you've eloped with Mr. Slater, of course."

Rosalind had to smile. Mr. Slater was a philanthropist whose donations earned him the right to a rambling and disjointed speech of at least an hour every Founders Day.

Miss Beale became serious again. "You should encourage your mother to speak with a local solicitor. They're not all bad apples."

"I'm sorry to have involved you in this melodrama," Rosalind said.

"Nonsense. I pressured you into this 'melodrama,' as you say. May as well see it through. For now, get some sleep."

29

Conversing with Mrs. Deamer after five years in Lincolnshire was feast after famine. Charlotte was mindful that she must not interfere with her duties. Yet where was it written that she could not lend a hand? The chats were well worth the effort.

"Now, we make a pleat here, before you tuck in the corner," Mrs. Deamer said at the foot of Charlotte's mattress.

Twenty years ago, she would have felt domestic work beneath her. Not in an arrogant sort of way, but simply because that was the mindset of most British.

"I believe this is the first time I've ever changed bedding," Charlotte confessed. "Or rather, *helped* change bedding."

"I had to ask my former housekeeper to teach me before I arrived here."

"We're quite the pair," Charlotte said. "Women of reduced circumstances."

"Port Stilwell is a far cry from the Strand," Mrs. Deamer said, tucking in the other corner.

"As it's a far cry from Egypt. Where was your favorite place to travel?"

"Oh, that would be Tuscany. The food . . . nothing in England compares."

"Don't say that too loudly," Charlotte said, pointing to the floor.

"Ah, you're right." Mrs. Deamer brought the folded counterpane from the chair. "What was your favorite play?"

"Most likely *Lady Audley's Secret*. Have you ever seen it?"

She shook her head. "I'm surprised, though. Not Shakespeare?"

"Brilliant though he was, his were never my favorites to perform."

Mrs. Deamer started spreading the counterpane with Charlotte's help. "My ears reel from disbelief."

"Well, most of the audience will have read the play, and thus are predisposed to appreciate it. All that is required is to act your part with passion, or at least competence. They know that Ophelia will be tragic, Lady Macbeth treacherous, and so forth. But with a clever contemporary work, they hang on to every word, looking for clues in your character, wondering how it will all tie together in the final act. The tension is delicious."

"What did you like about *Lady Audley's Secret?*"

"Playing the villainess. I actually had them hissing. Once, someone threw a shoe at me! The Adelphi had to post a guard at the stage door every night."

"And that's good?"

Charlotte sighed at the memory. "It was grand!"

"Do you miss it?"

"At times." Charlotte picked up a pillowcase. "But that part of my life is over. And this part, well, it's very good."

"I'm happy for you," Mrs. Deamer said and turned to collect the pillows.

Not before Charlotte caught the pain in her face. She went over to her, rested a hand upon her shoulder. "You'll have a better life one day, Mrs. Deamer. I pray that every night. Please don't give up hope."

Mrs. Deamer, face turned away, nonetheless nodded. "Thank you, Mrs. Kent. It has already gotten better. I had friends once. If you'll forgive my presumptuousness, you've filled that void."

"And you for me," Charlotte said, gently jostling her shoulder. "We're two characters in a play. Come, time for the big musical scene. What shall we sing?"

"Sing!" Mrs. Deamer laughed.

"What's so amusing?"

Both heads turned. Rosalind stood in the doorway smiling, but with dark circles beneath her eyes.

"Have you taken ill?" Charlotte asked, hurrying to embrace her.

"Oh, not at all." Her daughter set down a Gladstone bag and gave her a squeeze. "I haven't slept the past two nights. And I reek."

Charlotte took a sniff. "Tobacco?"

"The school doctor, Mr. Arnall, smuggled me out. He asked if I minded his pipe, and what could I say?" Rosalind yawned. "It was his coach. Only, we were forced to creep nine miles in a torrent so that I could leave from Gloucester Station, and I could not open a window because of the rain."

"Shall I draw a bath, Miss Kent?" Mrs. Deamer asked.

"If you please."

When she was gone, Rosalind leaned to fish around in her open bag. "I brought just a nightgown and some linens. Miss Beale is sending my trunk to Exeter on Saturday, under the name Hetty Whitecrest. That's her cat."

"But why did you leave early?" Charlotte asked.

Straightening, Rosalind handed her an envelope. "This will explain. Lord Fosberry's solicitor brought this to me. I felt compelled to read it. I hope you don't mind."

"Of course not."

"You'll want to sit."

"I'll be fine. You sit."

Neither sat. Charlotte unfolded the two pages. Her pulse jumped at the sight of Roger's pretentious script. Her stomach knotted when she read the accusation.

"How dare he!"

"Is Boswell the footman he mentions, Mother?"

"Yes. And just the sort of weak man Roger can easily dominate." She looked up at her daughter. "I never . . ."

"But of course you didn't."

Tears stung Charlotte's eyes. "If you have doubts . . ."

"None at all." Her daughter shook her head.

"Thank you, Rosalind." She swiped her eyes with her fingertips and shook the accursed pages. "He's right. Others will believe it."

"Perhaps if you went to the newspapers? Gave your side? We could leave for London in the morning."

"I won't drag my life out into the court of public opinion, Rosalind. In any case, it would be like throwing paraffin into a fire. Scandal is so much more fun than the benefit of the doubt."

"Very well," Rosalind said. "We should at least leave Port Stilwell."

"Leave?"

"And soon. People have seen my letters."

"Wherever would we go?"

"We found this place. We can find another."

Charlotte put a hand to her racing heart. "I need some time. Go and have your bath."

Alone, Charlotte went to her window. Saturday would be Danny and Albert's third visit. Last week after a hearty breakfast, they planted tomato seedlings, and then she read them to sleep again. After lunch, she taught them to play dominos, which led Albert to exclaim that this was the best day of his life.

She could not seesaw from believing that God was directing

her to help them, to abandoning them. There was no middle ground.

And what of Mrs. Deamer? Would the next tenants seek her friendship, or play Lord of the Manor?

Yet a third reason came to mind. There was mutual admiration going on between Rosalind and Mr. Pearce. How could Charlotte pluck that seedling from the ground before it had a chance to grow?

She waited until Rosalind had finished her bath before knocking upon her door. Her daughter sat at her table, clad in a dressing gown with a towel turbaned about her head.

"We're staying," Charlotte said.

"But if they find you—"

"I shall go to court and fight. I'll not allow Roger to make a fugitive of me."

"Are you certain?" Rosalind asked, a hint of relief in her eyes.

"Quite so."

"Miss Beale says you should see a solicitor."

"I'll call upon Mr. Lockhart tomorrow."

"How do we know that he's honest?"

"Well, Mrs. Hooper had him draw up our lease, yes? She knows Port Stilwell's people better than anyone, I expect."

Rosalind hesitated, nodded. "I shouldn't judge everyone by Mr. Pankhurst."

Charlotte smiled. "Caution is only natural. Once bitten, twice shy."

"May I come with you?"

"Of course."

After supper, Rosalind went to bed. Charlotte tucked covers about her shoulders and said, "At least there is some good news."

"Does it concern Mr. Pearce's uncle?" Rosalind said while covering another yawn, so that Charlotte had to lean close.

"It does."

"He wrote to me. Mr. Pearce, that is. Not the uncle."

"That's very nice, dear," Charlotte said, turning off the lamp. "Sleep well. Don't trouble yourself tonight."

She need not have added the latter, for the sound of soft snores accompanied her across the room.

30

Mr. Lockhart's office was tidier than Rosalind expected, given the cracked windowpane and peeling signboard. The carved oak claw-foot desk and Persian carpet were awe-inspiring. An immense colored print of the Bay of Naples almost covered one wall, and on another were six framed paintings of Mount Vesuvius in all stages of eruption.

Mr. Lockhart inspired less awe, with wild muttonchops sprouting from cheeks, crumbs in his moustache, and vocal cords of gravel.

"I had neither the time nor the inclination for theatre while at University College, Mrs. Ward," he said. "Which was fortunate, for I had not the funds either."

"Mrs. *Kent* for the time being," Rosalind reminded him.

"Yes, of course."

Her mother smiled, though her eyes were shadowed. "It is not a crime not to go to theatre, Mr. Lockhart."

"Thank you for saying that . . . Mrs. Kent. And I strongly advise you to stay close to home."

"She hardly goes anywhere as it is," Rosalind said.

"Mostly to church," Mother said. "But no one will bother me there."

Mr. Lockhart sighed and folded his hands upon the desk "If I were searching for someone in an unfamiliar town, I would make it a point to watch church doors."

"If I wore my veil?"

"Have you been wearing it?"

"Not since I arrived."

"Then you may as well perch a stuffed peacock upon your bonnet. You'll draw the same attention."

Moved by her mother's pained expression, Rosalind said, "I'll stay home with you."

"No. You've given up—"

Mr. Lockhart cleared his throat. They turned to him again.

"Don't accept anything offered you, unless you trust the giver. You cannot be summoned unless the claim form is delivered to your hand. Never open the door yourself. These people are clever. I have heard of a claim form presented as a wrapped gift."

"Should I share my identity with our cook?"

"She needs to know nothing but that it's a divorce." His eyes studied her beneath bushy brows. "Have you shared your identity with anyone in Port Stilwell?"

"Our housekeeper, Mrs. Deamer."

"Mother . . ." Rosalind groaned.

Her mother met her eyes. "I would trust her with my life."

"I would not have a profession if most people were so trustworthy," Mr. Lockhart said. "But absolutely no one else. An ounce of prevention, and so forth."

He turned to Rosalind. "How many from Cheltenham know that you're here?"

"Just Miss Beale. She was to have the postman deliver my mail to her and warn the staff to alert her if anyone approaches with questions over my sudden absence."

"That's quite a weak link," Mr. Lockhart said to Mother. "I cannot advise strongly enough that you should leave Port Stilwell."

Mother shook her head. "I cannot do that."

He sighed. "Very well. But again, discretion is of the utmost importance."

"Please take no offense, Mr. Lockhart," Rosalind said. "But can we trust *your* discretion?"

He gave her an understanding smile and touched Roger's letter upon his desk. "I am embarrassed whenever one of my profession compromises his integrity. Anything Mrs. Kent says to me regarding this situation I must keep to myself."

"I'm grateful," said her mother. "But if he finds me and this goes to trial?"

"As you may be aware, solicitors are not qualified to argue in court. But I maintain contact with some of my fellow alumni in London."

"Barristers," she said in a flat voice.

"Hopefully, it will never come to that."

He placed fountain pen into its holder, signaling the meeting was over.

Charlotte's mother began opening the drawstring to her reticule. "Your fee, Mr. Lockhart?"

"I send out invoices at the beginning of the month." He winked at her, adding, "Depending upon my inclinations to chuck it all and go fishing. In any case, you'll find me reasonable."

The tension in Rosalind's shoulders eased a bit. For his folksy ways, the solicitor inspired trust and competence.

"What is wrong with hiring a barrister?" she asked her mother as they walked back up Fore Street under steel gray clouds.

"They're expensive. I was forced to retain one for my . . . divorce from Mr. Gilroy. Before your father."

"Whatever happened to Mr. Gilroy?"

"Bad habits dug his grave years ago."

"Well, we have the money."

"You've spent enough on me."

Rosalind linked arms with her. "I know all about Aunt Vesta's supposed legacy."

Her mother stopped walking. "Who told you?"

"You just did," Rosalind said, smiling.

"I didn't mean to imply . . ."

"Mother, it's too late to deny it. I've figured it out, with Miss Beale's help."

Appearing on the verge of tears, Mother said, "I wanted your future to be secure. You've had to leave Cheltenham because of me. And now . . ."

"And now, I'm happy to be back."

"Do you mean that?"

"Yes." She drew in a breath of salt air. "I was too busy to realize how much I missed being here."

Mother patted her hand. "What a treasure you are."

They continued on in companionable silence, turning up Orchard Lane and passing trees in young leaf. At length, Mother said, "It was so very kind of Mr. Pearce to send those books. The boys were delighted."

"I beg your pardon?" Rosalind said. "What books? What boys? The fence boys?"

Her mother related her visit to the stepmother and the events which followed.

"Marvelous!" Rosalind said. "But she charges you a hefty fee, I imagine?"

"She tried. I'm sure she meant it for their university fund."

Rosalind smirked at her. "How did Mr. Pearce come to be involved?"

As she explained, Rosalind found herself wishing they had stopped by the bookshop. But then, Mother needed to stay close to home. Perhaps the timing of the Fletcher boys' needing her was fortuitous.

"I should visit the shop after lunch so that he doesn't continue to write," Rosalind said. "I'm sorry you'll not be able to come along."

"I wouldn't even if I could. I plan to have a good, long lie-in."

At the cottage, Mother showed her the books Mr. Pearce had brought over. They were beautiful copies, most bound in leather.

"What a timely gift," Rosalind said, pressing her fingers over the embossed cover of *The Coming Race* by Edward Bulwer-Lytton.

Mother picked up a copy of Percy Greg's *Across the Zodiac*. "Why do you suppose he sent that one? And this one? They're too advanced for the boys, and I've never expressed interest in science fiction."

The gleam in her tired eyes spoiled her attempt at an innocent expression.

⟡

Voices came from inside the bookshop. Perhaps Mr. Pearce had forgotten to turn the *Closed* sign after his lunch? She stepped closer and pressed her cheek against the glass. Mr. Pearce was leaning against the counter with arms folded, conversing with Mrs. Hooper.

"Oh, crabshells!" Rosalind muttered, jumping back as Jinny's paws hit the glass. She was four steps away when the door opened behind her.

"Miss Kent!"

Rosalind turned. Mr. Pearce grinned from his doorway while Jinny bounded over with welcoming barks.

"I can hardly believe my eyes!"

She leaned to pat Jinny's head. "I see that you're occupied."

"Not at all," he replied, but then Mrs. Hooper loomed at his side.

"Good morning, Mrs. Hooper," Rosalind said, straightening again. "I'll just . . ."

"But the term isn't over," Mr. Pearce said. "Is it?"

"Perhaps she heard of your mysterious financial windfall?" Mrs. Hooper said with a chuckle.

Rosalind stared at her. "I do beg your pardon!"

"Mrs. Hooper, that was uncalled for," Mr. Pearce said.

"Oh, you young people!" She rolled her eyes. "Surely you recognize jest? No doubt Miss Kent has some compelling reason to share. Do come in, Miss Kent. Mr. Pearce, nip upstairs and make some tea, will you?"

"Another time, Mrs. Hooper." He took her elbow. "We're to meet at Mr. Lockhart's at four o'clock tomorrow?"

"Yes, four," she huffed and pushed past him. "Good day."

Rosalind stepped aside lest she be trampled.

"Come in, please," Mr. Pearce said.

She did. It was improper that they be alone, now that unspoken feelings lay between them. But propriety could surely be pragmatic. This was a public place, and they stood just inside the door. She could very well be shopping for a book.

And there was the dog.

"What happened?" He closed the door. "Are you unwell? Your mother?"

"No, we're fine. My mother needs me."

"How can I help?"

"You helped by giving books to her. But I'm afraid that's all I'm able to say."

"Very well," he said after a moment. "I apologize for Mrs. Hooper. She brought over some documents regarding my purchasing the shop."

"Congratulations on your good fortune," Rosalind said.

"It still seems a dream."

"But how sad that your uncle desires no future contact."

"I can only hope he'll change his mind one day."

"Well, don't give up hope. People do change. And thank you for the books."

He smiled. "Did you notice the two science fiction novels?"

"Yes, so thoughtful. I look forward to reading them."

Silence followed. He glanced down at his feet and said, "I've thought of you every day."

The abrupt change from books to feelings caught her off guard.

"We've spoken so few times," he went on, "yet . . ."

She found her voice. "It seems we've known each other for ages."

"Truly, Miss Kent?" He grinned, patted his chest. "My heart races."

She smiled. *And mine.*

"Your eyes make little half-moons when you smile," he said. "It's endearing."

"Thank you."

"Would you take offense if . . . I asked you to move away from the window?"

"You must find out for yourself," she replied, surprised at her own boldness.

He took her elbow and led her over to the corner, beside the rack of stationery goods, then turned and faced her. As he removed his eyeglasses, his green eyes were warm upon her.

She lifted her chin. Should she close her eyes? She had so little experience, having been kissed by but one man, and so long ago.

Don't think of Reginald.

Mr. Pearce's expression sobered. He stepped back and cleared his throat.

"Forgive me, Miss Kent."

"What is wrong?" she asked.

"I quite forgot myself. Do forgive me."

"Will you stop saying that?"

"Yes, of course." He gave her a sad look and moved over to open the door. "I don't wish to be rude, but will you please go now?"

Three steps away from his shop, she realized his misgivings.

Humiliation spun her around. He was standing in the same spot, watching her through the window, and moved aside when she pushed open the door.

"I'm happy for you, but I don't care a fig about your money."

"Not for one moment did I assume so," he said. "Mrs. Hooper has no barrier between brain and vocal cords."

"Oh."

He shifted his feet. "Why didn't I . . . carry through?"

Staring at his shifting feet, she replied, "Yes."

"Well, you seemed repulsed."

"I did?"

"Your frown said as much."

She looked up again.

He shrugged. "It is one thing to befriend someone who is basically a mongrel."

"Mongrel!"

"Quite another to—"

"You think I care about your lineage?" she asked with heat in her face. "Actually, I do. I think it's lovely how your grandparents found each other and meshed their cultures so well."

He looked relieved. "Thank you for that. Then why the expression?"

"I was thinking . . . of my former beau."

For a moment, he stared. Then a slow smile. Folding his arms, he said, "I see. Still feel something for him, do you?"

"That's not amusing, Mr. Pearce."

He sobered. "Pardon."

"I couldn't help . . . well . . ." She shuddered at the memory of Reginald's viselike embraces, the feel of a wet sponge across her lips.

"You're making that face again, so I have my answer. I quite traumatized you, didn't I?"

"No trauma," she assured him. "Just an unpleasant memory."

"I'm sorry. But does that mean I can only go uphill from there?"

She smiled, removed her hat again.

He stepped forward and took her into his arms. She closed her eyes, tilted her chin. The kiss was sweet. Dry. And made her light-headed.

"This is the best day of my life," he murmured into her hair while her head rested upon his shoulder.

"Mine too," she murmured back.

"Perhaps that's why my grandmother sewed all those hand-kerchiefs. She had an inkling you'd come along."

She smiled to herself, glanced at the door, and stepped back from his arms. "We quite forgot the window."

"I didn't forget. But I didn't want to chance your changing your mind again. By the by, perhaps you wouldn't mind addressing me as Jude?"

"Only if you don't mind my being Rosalind."

His eyes glinted again. "I would never mind your being Rosalind."

31

Infinitely soothing, Charlotte thought at the garden table while pulling seedlings from cucumber sprouts in trays. Clearly God had planned it so, so that His creation would not starve.

She heard hinges creak and looked over at Rosalind, coming through the gate. "Hello, Mother. Did you rest?"

"My limbs, yes. My head, no."

Rosalind slipped into the seat facing her. Her face fairly glowed in spite of her hat; Charlotte suspected it was only partly because of her walk.

"I'm sorry," Rosalind said.

"Please, don't be. I feel much better now with my hands in soil." She smiled at her daughter. "May I assume your meeting with Mr. Pearce went well?"

Rosalind smiled. "You may assume my meeting with *Jude* went well."

Charlotte raised her brows.

"He's invited me to lunch on Tuesday. Mr. Galvez will prepare an Indian dish. Do you mind?"

"Of course not. I'm delighted for you."

"And I'm delighted that my trunk arrives tomorrow. I'll have something to wear."

Charlotte studied her gown. Brown, trimmed in blue, and rigidly tailored. "As you'll be in Exeter anyway, why not buy a ready-made gown? I'm sure Mrs. Deamer would be quite happy to accompany and advise you."

"I have gowns."

"Yes, well . . ."

"You take issue with the way I dress?"

"To be frank, your clothes are like uniforms." Charlotte cast for the right words. "I just wonder if your generation . . . you women who are educated . . . fear that accenting your femininity would be at odds with your newly won rights."

Rosalind smiled. "Miss Beale does say 'frilly is silly.'"

"Well, it can be, taken to extremes. Imagine a woman of my age and size in laces and flounces. I would resemble a Christmas tree."

"Now you exaggerate, Mother," Rosalind said, but smiling as if picturing the thought.

⚬◇⚬

Saturday morning, Danny sat almost mute, avoiding looking at Rosalind though she sat directly across from him.

"Miss Kent is my daughter, remember?" Charlotte said from the head of the table, wondering if he had forgotten. "She's home for good now, or at least for a very long time."

"You're the lady who got lost," Albert said. He was perched on the very edge of his chair, more standing than sitting, apparently so as to reach his food better.

"Indeed, I am," Rosalind replied. "I would be wandering still had you boys not set me in the right direction."

Albert smiled. "Perhaps you would have gone into the woods."

"Oh my!" She feigned a shudder, which made him chortle.

Charlotte smiled and looked at Danny. "Miss Kent and Mrs. Deamer are to take the train to Exeter after breakfast."

"Exeter has the big church," Danny murmured, pushing eggs

around his plate with his fork. "I went there with Mother and Father. Before Albert came."

Danny had never spoken of his mother. Charlotte's heart ached at his blank expression, as if his grief had turned into dull acceptance over the years.

"What a sweet memory you must have of that day," Rosalind said.

"I can't remember all of it," he said, adding to Charlotte, "Father bought fish and chips. Not at the cathedral but a café. And chocolate cake."

"Chocolate cake," Albert said wistfully. "I saw one in the kitchen."

"It's not polite to hint, Albert," Danny whispered.

Charlotte raised brows at Coral, bringing in some tea. She nodded and smiled back.

Silence passed other than the clicks of cutlery against china.

"Boys, can you guess this riddle?" Rosalind asked. "What has a face and hands . . . but no body?"

After a moment, both heads shook as if they had a string attached.

"A clock!"

Albert laughed, and Danny pushed his lips into a strained smile.

"Could it be that they were punished for speaking to me the evening they were washing the fence?" Rosalind asked Charlotte while the boys helped Coral take dishes into the kitchen. "Does Danny resent me for that?"

"I shall certainly ask."

After seeing Rosalind and Mrs. Deamer off from the porch, Charlotte turned to the boys. "Albert, please ask Coral if you might assist her in the kitchen."

He scampered away without asking why his brother wasn't included.

"Danny, what is wrong?" she asked.

"Nothing is wrong, Mrs. Kent," he replied.

"You couldn't even look at Miss Kent. Why?"

He crossed his arms, holding himself, and began to sniffle. She took the handkerchief from her sleeve and handed it to him.

"Will you stop having us here?" he asked after blowing his nose.

"Whyever would you think that?"

"You hired us because you miss her terribly."

Charlotte leaned to draw him into her arms. "Nothing will change. Why, I should miss *you* terribly if you weren't here."

She felt his small body relax, heard his yawn.

"You're sleepy."

He tensed again. "No, missus."

"Danny, I'm not angry," she said, straightening to stare into his eyes. "You've done nothing wrong. But it's unnatural for children to be so tired."

She waited.

A goldfinch twittered.

"Albert wets the bed if I don't put him to the pot," Danny blurted.

"During the night? Does he not go before turning in?"

"He does."

"And so you must stay awake to do this?"

"He sleeps so hard."

"Is he punished if he has an accident?"

Danny was trembling. "Yes."

"By your father and stepmother." She said it this way so he would not have to name names, merely eliminate one. *Please let there be only one.*

"Not Father."

"What does your stepmother do?"

"Um . . ."

"Does she strike him?"

The trembling increased. "Please don't speak to her."

235

"I won't." Not that she did not wish to march over there this minute and give her a piece of her mind, but the boys would suffer reprisals. A benefit from having lived with Roger was the awareness of how brutes conducted themselves. In their pettiness, they consistently had to have the upper hand.

"Are there marks on Albert?" she asked. "Is that why he wouldn't sit?"

He turned his face to her. "Please, please don't look at them. *Please*, Mrs. Kent! Albert speaks without thinking and would mention it. We're not even to tell Father."

"What would happen if you did?"

He shook his head. "We can't."

"Surely there is a way I can help you."

"You do! That's why I was afraid you would stop."

Charlotte sighed and wished Rosalind and Mrs. Deamer had not left. Holding this in without exploding was going to be difficult.

She brushed back his hair. "Very well, Danny."

For now.

32

"We should see the cathedral before burdening ourselves with packages," Mrs. Deamer said to Rosalind.

"Have you been many times?" Rosalind asked.

"Many. We attended services when my husband was on official business."

This she said with voice lowered, though the man, woman, and four children several feet away from the railway bench were caught up in conversation.

"May we get ice creams too?" carried over in a young voice, causing Rosalind and Mrs. Deamer to trade smiles.

They got to their feet as the South Devon line locomotive sounded from the west, prompting the family and a half-dozen other passengers to crane their necks and gather bags.

"Why, Miss Kent!"

Noble Clark approached, bedecked in a well-fitting black suit and eye-catching red-striped cravat. He switched his satchel to his left hand and then grasped hers.

"You're home! But when?"

"Since Wednesday."

"Well, such an extraordinary coincidence! You're off to Exeter, then?"

No, we thought to dress up and watch trains, Rosalind thought but was then ashamed. She despised sarcasm.

"We plan to visit some shops and collect my trunk. You've met Mrs. Deamer."

"I have had that pleasure." Beaming, Mr. Clark said, "You cannot imagine how good it'll be to have friendly faces along on the journey, for I'm on pins and needles!"

"Whatever do you mean, Mr. Clark?" Rosalind asked, but his attention was diverted by the locomotive squealing to stop. A guard ran down the line, opening doors.

Mr. Clark bounded past other passengers to an open carriage, turned, and waved.

"We've no choice, have we?" Rosalind muttered.

"You need your trunk," the housekeeper reminded her.

He offered his hand, assisting them into the carriage. Rosalind nudged Mrs. Deamer to the forward-facing seat and settled beside her.

He owes us, she thought.

Mr. Clark seemed content as he boarded, but then having an audience was likely worth riding backward. Perching hat upon shelf and satchel upon the seat, he said, "No doubt you're wondering why I'm bound for Exeter. Auditions are to be held today for the chancel choir."

"In the cathedral?" Rosalind asked.

He nodded. "One of the tenors suffered a heart attack in the midst of the 'Tyrolese Evening Hymn' a fortnight ago, poor chap."

"I read of his death in the *Gazette*," Mrs. Deamer said.

"He was fifty-seven and had a good run, don't you agree? If I'm performing at that age, I'll consider myself to have led a full life."

I wonder if the tenor felt the same. Rosalind turned to Mrs. Deamer. "We shall have to see the cathedral last, then. Will the shops hold our parcels?"

"But wait!" Mr. Clark said. "You mean to go to the cathedral? Excellent!"

"After the auditions, of course," Rosalind said.

"You could accompany me. Two birds with one stone. Please?"

Rosalind could only stare at him.

"It's that I'm most anxious. The auditions are *a capella*, naturally more difficult. And there will be tenors from all about Devonshire."

"We can't spare that much time, I'm afraid," she said. "My mother's expecting us to take the three o'clock return train."

"But you planned the cathedral tour, in any case. You'll have a good view of Lady Chapel whilst auditions take place. You could take in the rest beforehand."

His voice broke. "My mother and father refused, saying it's a wild goose chase. How do you think that affects my courage? This means more to me than anything."

Stifling a sigh, Rosalind looked at Mrs. Deamer, who smiled back.

"Very well."

"Oh, thank you!" He clasped his hands against his chest. "Can you imagine what I chose as my audition piece?"

"Mozart's *Requiem*?" Mrs. Deamer asked.

He eyed her with obvious fresh respect. "I'm quite sure you'll hear that today, but not from me. You see, most singers will choose somber pieces. Joyful would seem flippant in light of the recent tragedy."

"That seems reasonable," Rosalind said with grudging interest.

He tapped his temple. "I've given this much thought. But the choral director, being only human, will grow fatigued with a parade of melancholy."

"What is there besides joyful or melancholy?"

"There is *sweet*. Hence, I decided upon Brahms's 'Cradle

Song.'" If the director has children, this will surely bring on fond memories. He may even recall his own mother singing it. And, as sleep is likened to death, any thoughts the song prompts toward the unfortunate tenor will be comforting, not morbid."

"I think you've made a wise choice, Mr. Clark," Mrs. Deamer said.

He beamed at her. "And here is the genius part! I shall sign up as 'Noble Young,' almost ensuring that I am last."

"But if you're chosen, will not the director take issue when you confess your actual name?" Even knowing the point was moot, Rosalind had to ask.

"I'm not the first performer to adopt a stage name, Miss Kent. Why not now, as this will surely lead to greater things? And *Noble Young* has a great, positive quality to it. You would be predisposed to favor a man with such a name."

Oh my. Rosalind realized her mouth was open and closed it.

Mr. Clark gave her an appreciative smile. "I was also struck mute when the idea first came to me."

Closing his eyes, he sang softly,

> "Lullaby and good night,
> With roses bedight . . ."

Rosalind winced when he hit the first off note.

> "With lilies o'er spread
> Is baby's wee bed."

He continued on, and when finished, opened his eyes. Rosalind let out the breath she had been holding.

"Brahms was indeed the perfect choice," Mrs. Deamer said.

"There you are! And now, the *coup de gras*! The original Prussian. It's a mite tricky, for I learned it but two days ago."

"Guten Abend, gute Nacht,
Mit Rosen bedacht,
Ich werde toten
Meine Katze—"

"Mr. Clark?" Mrs. Deamer said.

"I beg your pardon; I wasn't finished."

"You just sang that you wish to kill your cat."

"I'm quite sure you're mistaken. I don't own a cat." But he looked a bit concerned as he sang on.

"Da das Weinen
Halt mich wach . . ."

"Because its mewling disturbs your sleep." Mrs. Deamer shrugged under Rosalind's stare. "Our housekeeper of twenty years was from Frankfurt."

Mr. Clark blinked. "Why would Mrs. Grundke sabotage me? She's quite fond of me! When I was seeing Gisela, she would serve me sausages and potatoes."

"Ah," Rosalind said, "and you broke off with her daughter."

"No, I simply stopped coming by. In any event, that was two years past, and Gisela is happily married to Mr. Healy, who owns four fishing boats."

"Still, you owed her an explanation."

"Well now, you see, *that* would have been unkind." He rolled his eyes. "What was I to have said, that her accent was beginning to grate upon my nerves?"

"Whatever the reason, it isn't decent to drop people like a child weary of a toy."

Mr. Clark's face reddened. "Miss Kent, I thought better of you. I can scarcely believe I considered courting you."

"Please clear your mind of that notion straightaway." Rosalind was about to mention Coral Shipsey when she felt a touch upon her sleeve.

"Simply leave it off and repeat the first stanza," Mrs. Deamer said.

He gave her a grateful look. "Or perhaps you could teach me the correct words?"

"In your anxious state, your mind would not retain them."

Sighing, he sank against his seat. "A minor setback. Still, the perfect song."

He gave Rosalind a wounded stare, and she averted her gaze to the window. She didn't even *like* him, yet she felt ashamed for inserting discord into his fantasy. No matter that this day would not end well for him, unless no one else auditioned.

At least there was a silver lining. He would not want them to accompany him.

"You'll still accompany me?" he beseeched.

Rosalind dug her fingernails into her palm. "Very well."

"I'm ever so grateful. Matter of fact, I'll hire a cab!" He gave them a hopeful look. "Though High Street is actually a pleasant stroll."

"A cab would be lovely," Rosalind said.

The train halted at St. David's Station on the River Exe. Mr. Clark exited first and scurried off to lay on a cab.

"I'm in a nightmare and cannot wake," Rosalind muttered against the babble of voices in the flow of departing passengers.

"But we'll be treated to a free concert," Mrs. Deamer said. "Surely most who audition can sing. And I do so enjoy a tenor voice."

"For how long? Mr. Clark is to be among the *last*, remember? And they're coming from all over Devon."

"How many can relocate on a fortnight's notice? In any event, there is another train at five. We'll have ample time to shop."

Impulsively, Rosalind linked arms with her. "You're so kind."

"Well, we're both heading in the same direction."

"That is so. But I'm certain I would not have warned him

of the faulty lyrics. It would have been a fine story for Mother and Coral."

"There is still enough of it to make a fine story," Mrs. Deamer said.

From the carriage, Rosalind admired the city's old Roman town, its castle ruins, Elizabethan houses with projecting storeys, gardens, quaint shops, and spires.

The long gray line of the cathedral, with its two Norman towers, stood serene above the lime trees. The driver brought them to the west front, and Mr. Clark paid the shilling fare without grumbling. They took some time to admire the choir screen displaying effigies of prophets and saints, martyrs and kings, until Mr. Clark grew noticeably agitated. As they entered through the propped center door, three heads turned upward as one to look at the vast ribbed and vaulted roof.

"The longest unsupported roof in England, over three hundred feet," Mrs. Deamer murmured in the reverential quietness. A sign upon a post directed them to the Lady Chapel's carved pews in the very back, where at least twenty people were gathered. There seemed to be no one in charge as of yet.

"What time will they begin?" Rosalind whispered.

"At ten," Mr. Clark replied.

She pushed back her sleeve, looked at her watch. Quarter past nine. "We have time to look about."

"You'll join me before?" he pleaded. "You won't leave?"

"But of course."

Mrs. Deamer leaned close to say, "As you wait, take deep breaths."

"Will that help him?" Rosalind asked on their way to inspect the stained-glass windows of the south side.

"His nerves, yes." Mrs. Deamer gave her a sad smile. "His voice? Now, *that* would be a miracle."

33

Rosalind and Mrs. Deamer moved from windows to chapels to tombs, a speck of what there was to see. But unease over abandoning even Mr. Clark was heavy to bear, and Mrs. Deamer reminded her that they could return one day.

About forty were seated in the Lady Chapel, some women, clearly there to give the same moral support Mr. Clark had asked of them. He grinned and jumped up to offer entrance to his pew. Rosalind stepped first so that Mrs. Deamer would be the one to sit beside him. After all, she felt the most sympathy.

Only, Mr. Clark moved into the pew after her so that he would be in the middle.

"Do you mind?" Rosalind heard him murmur.

"Not at all," Mrs. Deamer murmured back.

A gentleman wearing thick eyeglasses and a black suit approached the pulpit.

"Good morning and welcome. I'm Mr. Thurman, choir director. When your name is called, come to the podium and announce what you will sing. If you have not given your name to Mrs. Hall in the pew to my right, please do so at once."

With a shuffling of feet, three sheepish-looking men hurried over.

"Amateurs," Mr. Clark snorted below his breath, and Rosalind elbowed his side.

When the men were back in their seats, a Mr. Adams was called up to the podium. He fixed his eyes unwaveringly upon a woman in the pew he had left, and cleared his throat.

"*Requiem aeternam dona eis . . .*" came out thinly, but his voice grew stronger, clearer. And on key.

"No stage presence," Mr. Clark whispered as the man left the podium.

Rosalind frowned, whispered back, "Stop, or I will leave!"

Mr. Aunger, next, beautifully sang from Beethoven's *Missa Solemnis*, and with eyes taking in everyone in the pews. Mr. Clark shifted in his seat.

Mr. Candler was either nervous or as delusional as Mr. Clark, for his voice was so painful to hear that Rosalind was embarrassed for him. She tensed, waiting for comment from beside her, but Mr. Clark had apparently taken her command to heart.

Messieurs Hinshaw and Julian sang equally well. Rosalind did not envy the choir director for having to choose. Mr. Clark fidgeted more and more.

When Mr. Libby was called, he strode easily up to the podium and smiled.

> "Awake my soul, stretch every nerve,
> And press with vigor on;
> A heavenly race demands thy zeal,
> And an immortal crown . . ."

His voice was as clear as a bell and met high notes effortlessly. As he returned to his seat, the stillness was as thick as held breath. Even the director waited.

"Mr. Lloyd," he called at length.

Mr. Clark coughed as Mr. Lloyd was leaving his seat, and then again.

Faces turned in their direction. Rosalind whispered, "Mr. Clark?"

He gave her a pained look, coughed again, and started getting to his feet.

"I beg your pardon," he said to the director. He coughed while moving the length of choir and nave, so swiftly that Rosalind and Mrs. Deamer lagged behind.

"Well, that was delightful," Rosalind muttered as they spotted him outside, bent over and panting into a handkerchief.

She felt some guilt when Mrs. Deamer went over to rest a hand upon his back. "Are you going to be ill, Mr. Clark?"

"No!" he sobbed.

Heads turned from passersby on the walk, and from people studying the choir screen.

"Come," Mrs. Deamer said, leading them to a park on the north side. Under stately elms, she and Mr. Clark shared a bench. Rosalind settled upon one nearby.

"Mrs. Grundke's fault," Mr. Clark murmured into the handkerchief. "She destroyed my confidence!"

Rosalind sighed but gentled her voice. "You won't be the only one not chosen."

He looked over at her with teary red eyes. "But I need it most!"

"You have Saint Paul's," she reminded him.

"Saint Paul's!"

"Why was this so important to you?" Mrs. Deamer asked.

His shoulders rose with his sigh. "It would have been a stepping-stone. I've not had the training for the likes of London or even the Bristol stages. This would have sharpened my talent."

He's crushed, Rosalind reminded herself. Besides this not being the proper time, nor her place, to insert some reality, he was unlikely to listen.

"I'll be teaching school when I'm an old man," he said flatly.

"Well, surely there are rewards to it," Mrs. Deamer said.

"Rewards! It's so tedious that I want to scream!" He panted a minute, blew his nose, rasped, "I want to perform somewhere where audiences don't smell of fish!"

And I want to be Princess Beatrice, Rosalind thought.

Even Mrs. Deamer seemed at the end of her patience. But at a gentle end, for her tone was still laden with compassion. "Mr. Clark, sometimes our grand plans simply do not happen. But we must move on, make the best of it. Now, shall we accompany you to the station? Miss Kent and I really must do some shopping."

He blew his nose again. "I can't go back alone."

Both faces turned to Rosalind, Mrs. Deamer's weary and Mr. Clark's pleading.

"I could carry parcels," he said.

She shrugged. Why should he stop at ruining the morning, when the whole day lay ahead as a plum to be picked?

"Thank you!" he cried. "May we have lunch first? I'm quite famished."

Mrs. Deamer suggested the tea shop connected to Bournemouth's, their first shopping stop. They ordered sandwiches and cucumber salads and some strong Earl Grey tea, as well as iced lemonade for a morose Mr. Clark. His gratitude did not extend to offering to pay, but then, his schoolmaster wages may not have allowed. In spite of herself, Rosalind regretted the hired carriage.

"Lunch is my treat," she insisted. When Mrs. Deamer protested, Rosalind reminded her of the purpose of this mission.

Bournemouth's should have been named Behemoth's for its size, Rosalind thought. Two shop assistants in identical white blouses and navy serge skirts assisted her in the fitting room. When she could not decide between a handkerchief dress of moss green batiste with a red-and-pink border, and a second of yellow print with a side flounce, Mrs. Deamer suggested she get both.

Rosalind took her advice. It felt very good to feel feminine.

"Now, I should like to buy one for you," she said to Mrs. Deamer.

"No, thank you," Mrs. Deamer said firmly. "I have several gowns."

Mr. Clark said, "I could do with another hat."

When she did not yield to his hint, he shrugged and took the parcels. He waited on a bench outside Mrs. Sutten's Ladies' Shop, where she purchased underclothing and stockings, and Gladdishe's Fine Shoes, where she bought a pair of low boots with a modest heel.

On St. David's platform, Mr. Clark and Mrs. Deamer settled upon a bench with parcels piled between them while Rosalind went inside the station house.

"Are you holding a trunk for Hetty Whitecrest?" she asked at the clerk's desk.

The clerk opened a narrow box. Fingers spidered through some cards. He took one out, handed it to her with a pencil. "Here we are, Miss Whitecrest."

"Will you have it loaded on the South Devon to Port Stilwell?"

"But of course."

On the platform, Mr. Clark jumped up to give her his place on the bench.

"Thank you, Mr. Clark," she said, "and for carrying my parcels."

"You're welcome." Nearby benches were occupied, so he leaned his back against a post with arms folded.

"MISS WHITECREST?" a voice boomed.

Faces turned toward the porter near the station doorway.

"MISS HETTY WHITECREST?"

What was there to do? Rosalind bounced to her feet and hurried over.

The porter took off his cap. "I regret to say this, Miss Whitecrest, but your trunk fell when they was puttin' it into storage.

The corner got crushed, but we wrapped string around it so naught would fall out. Would you care to see before we load it?"

"No, thank you. I'm sure it's fine."

"Who is Hetty Whitecrest?" Mr. Clark said at her elbow.

Rosalind turned. Mrs. Deamer, standing at the bench, sent her a worried look.

"None of your affair," Rosalind said.

But he brought it up again from his backward-facing seat in the railway carriage.

"You're a dark horse, Miss Kent. First, your mother claims you're too busy to receive letters. Then you're home before end of term. Are you a schoolmistress at all?"

"Of course I am. Would you like to hear the Base Angle Theorem?"

"The what?"

"Mr. Clark, that will be quite enough," Mrs. Deamer said softly but authoritatively. "Has no one ever given you a nickname?"

He looked wounded. Staring at his knees, he muttered, "Clara."

"Clara?" Rosalind said.

"Because of my love for music, I was a target for every schoolyard bully. That's why I don't wish to work with my father in the mercantile and be forced to wait upon those same brutes."

What was there to say?

Mrs. Deamer said it. "I'm sorry, Mr. Clark. No child deserves that."

"Nor any man," he said. "Everyone in town will gloat over my failure today."

"What failure?" Rosalind said. "You didn't audition."

"You simply changed your mind," said Mrs. Deamer

After a moment, his face brightened. "Why, that is so. Thank you, Miss Kent, Mrs. Deamer."

He winked at Rosalind. "Or should I say, Miss Whitecrest?"

"It's your choice," Rosalind said. "But if you address me as

Miss Whitecrest, I shall never speak to you again, so choose wisely."

"Kent, it is," he said with a little chuckle that made her smile in spite of herself. Still, she was happy to be shed of him at Port Stilwell Station.

34

Coral stood at the stove, muttering. "Light, you old dinosaur!"

"Coral?"

She spun around, a flaming match in hand. "You gave me a start, Mrs. Kent!"

"Forgive me." Charlotte stepped closer. "Don't burn yourself."

Coral shook out the match, lit another. She put the iron kettle on the burner flame. "Just a bit and I'll have you a cuppa. You've risen early, Mrs. Kent."

"I thought to have a chat with you. Shall we sit?"

With a worried expression, Coral followed her to the worktable.

"I have retained Mr. Lockhart," Charlotte said. "Do you know of him?"

"The solicitor. He owns the orchards. But why?"

"My husband, Lord Fosberry, wishes to divorce me."

Coral blinked at her. "But you're widowed."

"I was, yes. Before Lord Fosberry."

"You're married to a *lord*? But why would he divorce you, such a lovely person?"

"As are you, dear. But to sum up a dreary tale, he desires another woman, one of considerable wealth. Which is what he assumed of me before we married."

"Men!" Coral frowned. "Are there no good ones?"

"There are. But Lord Fosberry is not, as he threatens to accuse me of adultery. And people will believe it."

"*I* don't believe it!"

"Thank you, Coral. Most will not be so charitable."

However trustworthy she believed Coral to be, Charlotte thought again of her wee-hours decision to be transparent. On the one hand, it would save her, Rosalind, and Mrs. Deamer of having to guard their speech. But on the other, nothing delighted youth and impulsivity more than a good secret.

Coral touched Charlotte's sleeve. "Mrs. Kent? I know how it is to have your goings-on traded from cottage to cottage like a cup of sugar. I'll cut off my tongue before causing you harm."

Charlotte's eyes filled even as she smiled at the severity of that grim pledge. She filled in the details of her life for Coral.

"Oh my!" Coral said. "It's like something from a novel!"

"I confess I fear the ending."

"Well, you're not to worry. If any stranger comes asking for you, he'll feel the underside of my skillet!"

"I would appreciate your not going that far," Charlotte said with a little chuckle. "But thank you. By the by, until I'm able to venture out again, Miss Kent and Mrs. Deamer and I will have our worship here."

Coral looked uneasy. "I have choir, or I would . . ."

"Of course. And you must go."

She left the kitchen with a lighter burden.

Rosalind attempted to heap bricks upon it over breakfast.

"But why, Mother?"

"I have to trust her," Charlotte replied. "Let us say no more of it today, please."

After breakfast, Charlotte, Rosalind, and Mrs. Deamer gathered in the parlor. It seemed more in the spirit of corporate worship to sit together upon the sofa, rather than in separate chairs.

"I'm not certain how to go about this," Charlotte confessed.

"I have had students who were of the Society of Friends," Rosalind said. "As one explained it, every member is a minister but speaks only when led to do so. They call it *waiting* worship."

"Waiting for someone to speak?" Charlotte asked.

"Most definitely. For God. When you think of it, prayer is conversing with Him. But too often it's one-sided, at least on my part."

Charlotte nodded. "Mine as well."

"'Be still, and know that I am God,'" Mrs. Deamer said. "Should we close our eyes?"

Silently, Charlotte made her usual requests for the health and safety of everyone in her life. She asked forgiveness for failings and gave thanks for blessings.

And then she waited. After a while, listening to her own breathing, she had the irreverent thought, *How long should this take? Forgive me, Father. Please speak to me.*

Waiting. God was not to be summoned with the snap of a finger like some cosmic errand boy.

The clock ticked on. The silence thickened, swelled.

Rosalind's hand slipped into hers, squeezed, and Charlotte's eyes teared.

No audible voice. Something so much better. She felt enveloped by love, compassion, strength.

On her other side, Mrs. Deamer sniffed.

Albert and Danny entered Charlotte's mind. As much as she cared for them, this was not the time, she said to herself, and she focused upon the powerful silence.

Another picture came to her mind. A bank teller with a bulbous nose.

This time, she smiled.

◆━━◇◇◇━━◆

At ten o'clock on Tuesday morning, knocks came at the door. Charlotte lowered her copy of *The Hand of Ethelberta* and traded glances with Rosalind, sharing the sofa.

Mrs. Deamer led Mr. Fletcher into the parlor. He was dressed in a black suit with a starched collar and conservative yellow cravat.

"Good morning, Mr. Fletcher," Charlotte said. The wait had been difficult, but yesterday had held the risk of Amy Hugo coming for the laundry at the wrong time.

"Good morning, Mrs. Kent . . . Miss Kent," he replied, hands twitching at his sides.

"Please, do have a chair."

He sat in the paisley chair, and Mrs. Deamer took the other armchair. Coral brought in a tray and set it upon the round table.

"Will you have tea, Mr. Fletcher?" Mrs. Deamer asked.

"Yes, if you please. Two sugars."

Silver clicked against china. Coral brought him a cup and saucer and then, as prearranged, took a place upon the settee.

"And how is the weather?" Charlotte asked.

"I believe it means to rain, though not for hours yet."

"What a relief. We shouldn't wish you to get soaked upon your return."

After a polite sip from his cup, he looked at Rosalind and cleared his throat. "Miss Kent, when Mr. Trussell discovered your note beneath the door yesterday, he wondered why you didn't ask for him."

She gave him a wide-eyed smile. "Well, since I opened my account, I've conducted my business exclusively with you, Mr. Fletcher."

"Um, quite right . . ."

"But it is my understanding that there is a bank in Seaton as well."

"Seaton?"

"It's but one railway station away."

"I know where . . ." He drew a breath. "Begging your pardon, Miss Kent. Are you displeased with our service?"

"Quite the opposite, Mr. Fletcher."

"Then may I ask, whyever would you change banks?"

"You suggest I do not?"

"Most emphatically."

Charlotte cleared her throat, caught his eye. "Mr. Fletcher, my daughter has not threatened to change banks. She merely asked your opinion."

His expression revealed the thought he was constrained from voicing. *You asked me out here for this?*

She gave him an understanding smile. "And so now you may relay to Mr. Trussell a truthful account of your call. Or at least the first part."

"The first part?"

Taking a deep breath, Charlotte said, "We wish to assure you that you have friends. Every one of us supports you. Picture us as holding up your arms, as Aaron and Hur did for Moses during the great battle."

"Battle?"

"You must fight for your sons."

She took advantage of his stunned immobilization to press on. "They're being starved . . . or have you not noticed? Their clothes are filthy. Albert is beaten severely for wetting his bed."

"He's but six, Mr. Fletcher," Rosalind said.

He got to his feet. Setting cup and saucer onto the table, he said, "I must return."

Mrs. Deamer rose as well, went over to the door, and stood with her back to it.

"No, Mr. Fletcher. You will hear us out."

He stared at her, his lips moving as if to call forth words.

"Please," Rosalind said.

He sat once more, this time perched upon the edge of the chair, seemingly ready to take flight at any minute.

Charlotte began again. "There is a secret, Mr. Fletcher, that is hidden from parents of young children. Time is deceptive. It seems to crawl. You will look back one day and wonder how you did not notice its wings. Once they are adults, they have a choice whether or not to have anything to do with us. They have leave to spit in our faces if they so desire."

"M-Mrs. Kent," Mr. Fletcher stammered. "I love my sons."

"But Mrs. Fletcher does not."

He gave a weak shrug. "She's mother to my daughter. I cannot leave her."

Charlotte swallowed her disgust. Who was she to judge? With gentled voice, she asked, "Why do you fear her so?"

"I don't fear—" He lowered his head. "She was so kind before we married. Now she has such fits of temper! I cannot bear to be in the same room with her."

"Does she beat you, Mr. Fletcher?" Rosalind said with a chill voice.

His face jerked toward her. "Of course not."

"You fear her raised voice. Your small boys fear her fists. Does this seem fair to you? Would you hide behind them if a wolf attacked?"

"Rosalind . . ." Charlotte cautioned.

Mr. Fletcher closed his eyes.

Coral moved to the edge of the settee, expression urgent. Charlotte nodded.

"I've heard that your late wife was a gentle soul, Mr. Fletcher," Coral said. "What would she wish of you?"

He buried his face in his hands, shoulders shaking with quiet sobs.

Very good, Coral, Charlotte thought. On the faces of the others she saw reflected her own thought, that tears were a hopeful sign.

At length, he pulled a handkerchief from his coat pocket and mopped his reddened eyes.

"How can I stop her? I cannot stay at home all day."

"You must find a way, Mr. Fletcher," Mrs. Deamer said.

"And bear in mind that you're not alone," Charlotte said.

"We are committed to praying that God gives you strength. Any time you need encouragement, we're here."

He nodded, blew his nose, and pushed to his feet.

Mrs. Deamer stood aside.

Charlotte watched him leave, heard the front door close.

Coral, gathering his cup and saucer, murmured, "I cannot abide cowardice in a man."

"Because he didn't take up arms at once?" Charlotte said. "That is not how men think on matters fraught with emotion. He'll need some time to digest all of this. Would you agree, Mrs. Deamer?"

"Most definitely," she replied.

"What if you're wrong?" Rosalind asked. "What if you were mistaken about God wishing us to do this?"

Coral sniffed. "And the boys pay for it with their flesh?"

Charlotte shook her head. "That would be most horrible. We would be forced to seek more drastic measures. But let's not fall before we're pushed."

35

The fourth time Jude stepped out and looked northward, he was rewarded with the sight of Rosalind advancing down Kleef Lane. In a green dress and straw bonnet, she looked stunning.

"You see?" he said to Jinny. "I didn't frighten her away. You worried for nothing."

He lifted a hand, and she returned his wave.

Jinny was on alert, wagging her tail.

"Off with you, then!"

The dog bounded away to catch up with Rosalind.

A throat cleared. Jude turned, met Dr. Harris's bearded grin.

"So, the talk is true, then. And she's a comely lass indeed."

Jude grinned back. "Indeed, she is, sir. And I'm afraid I'm closing for lunch."

Hand to heart, the doctor said, "You would choose your sweetheart over your best patron?"

He had not yet dared think of her as *sweetheart*. The thought gave him enormous pleasure. "You're not offended, are you?"

"Now, I would not be much of a man if I were not." He held up a parcel. "But the fact of the matter is I've just been to Grundke's for wurst and sauerkraut. And I'm still wading through the last stack of books you pushed upon me."

Before Jude could protest the friendly barb, Dr. Harris wished him good-day. He doffed his hat to Rosalind as they passed.

Jude went back into the shop to grab his hat and turn the sign, catching up with her outside Flores.

"I'm so terribly late," she said.

"Not at all. I'm happy you're here. When I didn't see you at church, I worried that you were unwell. Is Mrs. Kent all right?"

"Yes, quite, thank you." The smile she turned to him did not mesh with the dent between her brows.

He wanted to ask if something were troubling her, but others were passing, shop patrons and employees returning to the fishery after their lunches.

Most of Flores's round tables were filled. He escorted her over to one near the window. Mrs. Galvez came over, patted his cheek, and said to Rosalind and everyone in the dining room, "Ah, what a good boy you are, Jude, and with the pretty Miss Kent again! And my Paul is preparing for you chicken *makhani* and asparagus with ginger."

Jude made a great show of thanking her. "We can hardly wait."

"I have never had Indian food," Rosalind said, smiling, but the dent remained.

When they were alone again, or as alone as a couple could be in a restaurant, Jude said below the chatter going on about them, "I sense something the matter."

She stared across at him for a moment, then let out a low breath. "I'm sorry."

"No, please don't be. But I would like to help you if I can."

After a moment's hesitation, she said, "I trust your discretion, Jude. But I must ask you to keep this to yourself."

"Of course."

He listened to her account of the morning and shook his head. "I'm sorry to hear it. I assumed your mother hired the boys because their family was poor."

She hesitated again. "Not poor. Their father is a teller at the bank: Mr. Fletcher."

The news did not surprise him. He had conducted business with Mr. Fletcher for years, and he could easily imagine the man's being cowed by someone with overbearing ways.

"You fear he'll do nothing?" he asked.

"I do. But Mother says we should pray God gives him courage and wait."

"Well . . ."

She gave him a dry smile. "You agree, of course."

He smiled back. "No doubt there are subjects in which Mrs. Kent and I would be at odds. But being that her counsel dramatically affected my life, I tend to agree."

"For how long? Bearing in mind how much is at stake."

"I understand that. But just a few days longer may make the difference between the solution you desire and some action that could make matters worse."

"Umm. I see."

"If you're going to pray, then don't try to force God's hand. I'll pray as well."

"Thank you, Jude. How very kind."

His cheeks warmed. One compliment from her, and he felt as if he could fly!

"You should meet them," she said. "Can you get away for Saturday lunch?"

"I should be delighted."

"That is, if Mr. Fletcher allows." She pulled a frown. "Forgive me, raising doubts again. It's just that I've always held this image of fathers as lions, ever ready to pounce if their cubs are threatened. But I never knew mine, so perhaps I live in a fantasy."

Jude put down the fork halfway to his mouth. He had assumed Mrs. Kent was recently widowed. "What happened to your father, Rosalind?"

"He drowned the day before I was born."

"How tragic!"

"To compound tragedy, he was celebrating my imminent birth."

"Have you any mementos? Photographs?"

"Yes, photographs. And Mother saved some playbills."

"He was an actor?"

The dent reappeared. "Um . . . I don't believe he was well-known."

"But that's fascinating. Was your mother an actress? Is that why she's so well versed in Shakespeare?"

She gave him a pained look.

"What is it, Rosalind? I know so little about you. Why such mystery? You said you trust my discretion."

"I do."

"Well then . . ."

"I would explain anything you ask," she said. "But it's not my secret to share."

"Meaning, it's your mother's."

"Yes. Trust me, she's done nothing wrong."

"That thought never entered my mind."

They fell silent, Rosalind staring at her fingers folded upon the cloth.

None of your affair, he reminded himself.

But that Rosalind and her mother had shown up in Port Stilwell for seemingly no reason, that she left her classes so abruptly and now was not at liberty to discuss her basic family background, was troublesome.

An old, familiar aroma hit his nostrils. Spices unlike any he had ever tasted in England. Mrs. Galvez, beaming again, set two plates before them. "I hope you enjoy!"

Jude and Rosalind picked up their forks. A bite of chicken and Jude's eyes watered at the overabundance of seasoning.

Fortunately, three managers from the quarry chose that time

261

to enter. With obvious reluctance, Mrs. Galvez moved over to greet them.

He gulped water from his beaker. Rosalind did the same from hers.

"This is awful," he leaned to whisper.

"Yes!" she whispered back. "But they took such pains. We must eat it."

"Is everything all right?" Mrs. Galvez said from his right with worried expression.

He hefted a forkful, smiled. "It's lovely."

"Lovely," Rosalind said. "Thank you so much."

Her smile returned, and she left them again.

"Are you terribly disappointed?" Rosalind whispered.

"Not with you here, sharing the adventure."

She gave him a droll smile. They ate doggedly, swiping eyes with their handkerchiefs when Mrs. Galvez's back was turned.

I love her, he thought, watching her struggle to swallow.

He dared to suppose she might feel the same for him in time. But Phoebe had taught him that secrets were an unstable foundation for a courtship. A man could step from happiness one day, to devastation the next.

Rosalind sniffed, and he looked up. She was staring at him, eyes shining.

"Forgive me," she murmured.

"Forgive *me*," he said, "for pressuring you."

"One day I'll be able to tell you everything."

"I look forward to that. But for now, will you make one promise to me?"

She was watching his face, and it seemed, holding her breath.

"That if you ever find yourself . . . not desiring my company . . . you'll give me fair warning? Not discard me out of the blue?"

"I promise, Jude."

That made him feel better. If he was not yet secure in the longevity of her feelings, he was in her integrity.

He watched her fork a mouthful of asparagus, wince, and swallow.

And in her kindness.

36

Danny and Albert tarried at the schoolyard as long as they dared, taking turns pushing each other upon the wooden swing that hung from a stout oak.

They took slow steps walking home. This could work out for or against them. One day their stepmother would growl that they were always underfoot, another, rage because they weren't there for chores.

"Mrs. Fairburn showed us a picture of a camel," Albert said, giving a swift kick to a knot of wood that clattered down the paving stones. "They carry water in their backs."

"Their humps," Danny corrected. "How many humps did he have?"

"Two." Albert kicked the wood again. "They all have two."

"Some have only one big hump. I've seen pictures too."

Albert pursed his lips. "It would be easier to ride one with two humps. You sit in the middle."

"People don't ride camels."

"They do ride them. Mrs. Fairburn said."

"I'll wager Mrs. Kent has seen a camel," Albert said. "She's been to lots of places."

Mrs. Kent. Thinking of her, of all the ladies on Orchard Lane, made Danny smile and long for the week to move faster.

As usual, Albert allowed him to enter the cottage first. The kitchen smelled of cabbage and boiled ham, making Danny's mouth water. Their stepmother was rolling out pastry dough and handing little bits to Teresa, who babbled something through floury lips. "We're home, Mother."

"I have eyes." She glanced at him, then back to her rolling pin. "You took long enough."

"Mrs. Fairburn had us clean the blackboard." He hoped Mrs. Kent would never know what a liar he was.

"Well, go and sweep the back walk."

Danny went out to the garden with a sense of relief. He took the yard broom from the potting shed and began sweeping the path from back door to privy while Albert placed hands on the ground beneath the elm and crept his bare feet backward up the trunk.

"Look, Danny!" he called, propped upon his head.

"Um-hm." When Danny finished sweeping, he went indoors to report to their stepmother. She was carrying dishes to the table, with Teresa pulling on her skirt and whining.

"Finish this so I can change her nappy." She put the stack on the cloth and narrowed her eyes. "And leave the pot alone, mind you."

She scooped up Teresa and left. Danny went to the sink.

"Can I come in?" Albert asked from the garden door.

Danny shook his wet hands. "I think so."

His brother came close, whispered, "Give me a taste?"

"Watch the door." Danny went to the stove, raised the lid, lifted a bit of ham on the tip of the stirring spoon, and blew on it. Albert came over and gulped it like a baby bird.

"Mmm."

"Wipe your mouth."

Albert's tongue darted out and around, collecting the bit on his lip.

Danny was taking out a bit for himself but put it back at the click of the parlor door opening and closing. Father's muffled steps did not stop at the chair where he usually sat until supper. Footfalls carried on until he appeared in the doorway.

"Hallo, sons."

His sagging face was grimmer than usual, which filled Danny with a fear he could not identify.

"Hallo, Father!" Albert said.

Danny said the same while gathering dishes to set the table.

"Where is your stepmother?"

Stepmother? Father always referred to her as their mother, as if by saying it enough, he could make it so.

"She's upstairs with Teresa," Danny replied.

Father left the doorway. The raps of shoes upon staircase were sharp and quick.

"Something's happened," Danny said.

Albert caught his fear. "He won't leave us, will he?"

"No," Danny said, though his stomach was tight. Voices drifted from upstairs. "Will you put the forks around?"

"But where are you . . ."

He shook his head, went to the doorway, and took two quiet steps into the parlor. His heart jumped when Father appeared at the head of the stairs.

"Danny! Come and mind Teresa!"

He was halfway up the staircase when he heard Albert behind him.

"Me too, Father?"

"Very well," Father said, face crimson.

When Danny reached the landing, Father nodded toward the nursery.

"We're not allowed," Danny said, holding back.

"Come!" Father said.

Danny followed him into the nursery, Albert on his heels. Their stepmother stood by Teresa's crib, clutching her as if she had just pulled her from a river.

"You'll not take her from me!"

"No, no, no!" Teresa cried, clinging to her neck.

"Put her down, Sabrina." Father's voice was as low as their stepmother's was loud.

Her eyes were slits through which her rage seemed to intensify. To Danny and Albert, she screamed, "Get out!"

Teresa shrieked. Danny wanted to close his ears, his eyes, and curl up in a corner. Albert's thumb went into his mouth.

Father went over and pulled Teresa from her mother's arms. Above her wails, he said, "You've gone and frightened her. They're her brothers!"

Their stepmother burst into tears, sobbing into her hands. Father held the girl on his shoulder and patted her heaving back. "There, there now. There, there."

"She wants me!" Stepmother sobbed when Teresa strained to reach for her.

Danny's heart thumped in his throat.

Albert took thumb from mouth, went to the window seat, and picked up Teresa's doll. As he brought it over and held it up, his sister's wails grew less intense.

"Want to play with her?" Albert cooed.

"There you are," Father said, patting her back.

She quieted, seemed to think over the situation, held out her hand. "Mine!"

Albert handed her the doll, and she wrapped an arm around its neck.

"You see?" Father kissed the top of her head and set her down.

She grinned at Danny and Albert. "Baby. Mine."

"Keep her from the window," Father said. "Come, Sabrina. We must talk."

Their stepmother looked at Teresa, lip trembling. "Leave the door open."

"Very well."

267

On his way out, Father put a hand upon Danny's shoulder. The light pressure made him want to weep with happiness even as he feared what was to come.

Their stepmother followed Father through the doorway, turning midway to mouth *Door open!* Danny flinched at the look she shot him. He assumed they would go into their bedroom. But from the sound, he could tell it was his and Albert's.

"Why are we . . ." his stepmother began, but the door closed. And then came murmurings, too low to discern, especially over Albert and Teresa.

"Nose!" Teresa said, pressing a finger to the tip of Albert's, then her own.

Albert touched his ear. "Ear?"

"Keep her here," Danny said to his brother.

He feared going to the door of his and Albert's room but realized the voices had escalated. He could make out words simply by moving into the hall.

". . . not fit for animals, Sabrina. How could you allow them to live in such filth!"

"You live here too!"

"Aye, and twice the shame on me."

"Animal is what he is! Lies there and wets himself!"

"He's but a boy! Would to God I never brought you here!"

"That wasn't your tune when your precious Marjorie lay dying!"

"Don't you dare say her name! You took advantage of us in our grief, pretending to have a decent heart!"

She said something through sobs, something Danny could not understand.

Father's voice again. "I shall buy a new mattress. We will clean this room."

"He'll only stink it—"

"I'll get a sheepskin mat . . . something! I will take them

to Exeter on Saturday and buy new clothes, and you will see they're kept clean!"

Saturday? But what of Mrs. Kent?

Still, the thought of returning to Exeter, of spending time with Father! Even if they didn't get chocolate cake, what a wonder that would be!

". . . will treat Danny and Albert decently. They'll serve their own plates, however much they want, and you'll not say a word, whether I'm here or away. If it's not in you to be kind, then you're to stop being hateful!"

"You care only about those boys. Teresa's yours too!"

The familiar weariness crept into his father's voice. "I confess I've not had the strength to be a proper father. Especially to Albert."

"See? You cannot even speak of Teresa without turning it about to your boys!"

"She's not suffering from your hand as they are. But yes, I will do right by her."

"Well, very good for you. And I need to see to her!"

"Not until we're finished here!"

"What more is there to say?"

"There is *this* to say! That I would *hope* you haven't gone low enough to beat any of the children. If you ever do, I shall pack you up and deliver you back to Branscombe."

"You'll do no such thing! Teresa will go there over my dead body!"

Her sobs came again, loud now. Danny stepped back into Teresa's room. Albert and Teresa were taking turns running into the wall, crashing to the carpet and laughing.

He smiled at his brother's endless capacity for fun in the bleakest of situations. And this one was bleak, for Father would return to work tomorrow, and Stepmother would take out her anger on them.

The sobs abated. He moved back into the hall.

"Whatever your father did to twist you so, Sabrina, is a pity. And no, that rakeshame will never see our daughter. But I mean every word about taking you there. I can hire someone to keep house and mind the children, just as I hired you."

"Will you hire someone to share your bed?"

His father snorted. "You jest? That part of our lives died long ago. I mean to live for my children. And trust me, I shall ask them every day how they're being treated!"

He returned to the nursery. Albert lay upon the rug, pretending to sleep, while Teresa tugged at his shirt and laughed between hiccups.

A glimmer of hope came to Danny. Mother had surely asked God to put Mrs. Kent into their lives. Now she had asked Him to make home a better place. A safer place.

Tears stung his eyes. He did not deserve all this.

But Albert did.

"I will be a good brother," he said to Mother under his breath. "I'll stop stealing and lying. Please tell God."

37

The highlight of Charlotte's afternoons were when Rosalind returned from the pillar-box with the *Exeter and Plymouth Gazette.*

"Here is also a letter from Mr. Fletcher," Rosalind said, entering the parlor on Thursday.

"What does it say?" Charlotte asked as the envelope was placed in her hand.

"It's addressed to you." Her daughter frowned. "I shouldn't have insulted him. I'm quite sure I made matters worse."

"Well, let us see." With Rosalind and Mrs. Deamer looking on, Charlotte removed the seal and drew out the page.

"Dear Mrs. Kent,

Albert and Danny will not be there on Saturday, as we intend to visit Exeter for sightseeing and the purchase of new clothing."

"Oh my!" Charlotte said, then continued to read aloud.

"They do, however, wish to remain in your employ and will return the following week. I am grateful beyond words for your kind attention to them, and wish you all the best. The same to Miss Kent, Mrs. Deamer, and Miss Shipsey.

> Very truly yours,
> Irving Fletcher"

"Marvelous!" said Mrs. Deamer.

"Indeed!" Rosalind said. "But Jude was to meet them over lunch. I hope he won't be disappointed."

"I doubt so." Charlotte smiled at her. "And it gives us reason to invite him the following Saturday."

"May I read the letter to Coral?" Mrs. Deamer asked.

"But of course," Charlotte replied and handed it over.

Later, with mutual rustlings, she and Rosalind shared newspaper pages.

"Here it says that the Foundling Hospital in Exeter needs blankets," Charlotte said. "Will you buy some yarn and needles on your return walk tomorrow?"

Rosalind lowered the front page. "You can knit?"

"My grandmother . . . your great-grandmother Davis taught me. It helped pass the time in greenrooms whilst awaiting my scenes. It was that or gossip. Some actresses managed both, but I've always had to keep count of my stitches."

"Will you teach me? I should like to help the babies too."

Charlotte set the newspaper into her lap. "One hermit is enough."

"I go places."

"A morning walk and an occasional lunch with Mr. Pearce hardly fill your days. Why don't you apply to the school board? Perhaps there will be a position in the fall."

"Only if Mr. Clark's voice improves," Rosalind snickered.

"The infant school . . . Albert says his schoolmistress is very old. Perhaps she intends this to be her final year teaching."

"In Albert's eyes, *I'm* very old."

Charlotte frowned. "Will you be serious? I'm attempting to discuss your well-being. I don't see the humor in it."

"Forgive me," Rosalind said. "It's just that I love being mothered by you."

"Thank you for saying that. I love mothering you." She wagged a finger. "But don't distract me."

They traded smiles, and Rosalind said, "Two reasons I would rather not apply . . . at least not now. Firstly, our situation here is too tenuous. We could be forced to leave at any time. It would be unfair to the students, having to adjust to a new teacher."

"We're not leaving. If he finds me, he finds me."

"But have you thought of what a trial would do for your privacy? Would you want reporters lurking about here?"

"I can't bear to think of it," Charlotte admitted. "Still, we wouldn't leave."

"Not even if the boys no longer needed you?"

Charlotte shook her head. "You and Mr. Pearce . . . I see a bright future in it."

"We shall see," Rosalind said with a little smile. "But all that aside, I'm not ready to apply to the school board. There is that second reason."

"And it is . . ."

"If a vacancy lies ahead, the logical one would indeed be at Albert's school. And as fond as I am of him, I have neither the patience nor the experience for children so young. I need for them to be old enough so that we can converse like adults."

"What will you do with your time, then?"

"Well, take walks. Read. Knit, once you've consented to teach me. I'm not suffering, Mother. It's good to have a little time to contemplate life."

━━◇◯◇━━

"Miss Kent is a truthful young woman," Mrs. Deamer said while polishing silver at the dining room table the following morning.

Charlotte, darning a stocking, nodded. "But also a kind one. She loved teaching at Cheltenham. Can I believe her when she says she's content?"

Mrs. Deamer held up a spoon to the sunlight slanting through the curtains. "Would it please her for you to believe her?"

"Yes, of course."

"Then there is your answer."

Charlotte studied her. "As simple as that."

Mrs. Deamer smiled. "*Simple* is an undervalued concept, I believe."

"You're right, you know."

"Who is right?" Rosalind asked, entering with a large paper parcel.

"Mrs. Deamer," Charlotte replied. "My! Did you get enough yarn?"

"Three dozen." Rosalind set the parcel on the table and took out a skein of pale blue. "Mrs. Hooper said the dye lots never quite match, so it's best to buy it all at once."

"I'm sure the babies will appreciate the consistency. The needles?"

Rosalind pulled out a chair and sat. "She must unpack them from a shipment and will deliver them herself after lunch. I said that wasn't necessary, that I could get them tomorrow, but she insisted."

Coral entered carrying a tarnished fork and handed it to Mrs. Deamer. "Look what was hiding under the cupboard."

"Thank you," Mrs. Deamer said. "By the by, Mrs. Hooper is coming over."

"Oh dear!" Coral said. "I should mop."

"You mopped last night."

"She's only coming to deliver knitting needles," Rosalind said.

Coral twisted the hem of her apron. "She found out about the margarine."

"The margarine?" Charlotte asked.

Her face reddened. "It's not fit for animals. May as well spread paraffin on our toast. She orders it and says to use it. But I buy the butter from my own pocket, so it's not as if I'm stealing."

"What do you do with the margarine?" Mrs. Deamer asked.

She stared down at her apron. "Pitch it over the wall into the trees."

Rosalind laughed, rose, and embraced her from the side, pinning her arms. "I, for one, thank you! And I shall buy the butter henceforth."

Charlotte raised her water beaker. "Hear, hear!"

Coral gave them a worried smile.

"I wish you would have come to me with this," Mrs. Deamer said.

"I didn't want to put you in the midst."

"Well, you don't *know* that's the purpose of this visit. Go back into the kitchen and compose yourself. And stay there when she arrives, unless I come for you. You look as guilty as a cat in the larder."

◆❖◆

As it so happened, Mrs. Hooper's visit had nothing to do with margarine, had little to do with the knitting needles she delivered, and had mostly to do with the tall young gentleman accompanying her.

His face was clean-shaven, with thick lashes fringing brown eyes, full lips, and an aristocratic nose. The brown suit coat did not disguise a muscular frame, therefore Charlotte reckoned him to be some sort of laborer, carrying tools in the satchel at his side. If so, she should mention the squeak on the fourth stair.

"Mrs. Kent, Miss Kent. It is my privilege to introduce Mr.

Tobias Smith," Mrs. Hooper said in the parlor, beaming as if presenting the crown prince. "He's an artist."

"I'm very pleased to meet you," he said with an anxious little bow.

Trading glances with her daughter, Charlotte thought, *Artist?* Perhaps Mrs. Hooper intended a fresco on a wall? "Would you care to sit?"

As Mrs. Hooper and Mr. Smith took chairs, Mrs. Deamer said, "I'll get tea."

"We have just had some," Mrs. Hooper said. "And you should hear this too. Mr. Smith will be moving here tomorrow."

"Here?" Charlotte said. "To Port Stilwell, you mean."

"Yes, to Port Stilwell." Mrs. Hooper waved a hand. "And into the room upstairs."

Silence fell. Rosalind's expression mirrored Charlotte's gnawing sense of dread.

"This wasn't a good idea," Mr. Smith said to Mrs. Hooper. "I should return to—"

"They're merely surprised, Mr. Smith," she cut in.

"This does come from out of the blue," Rosalind said.

"You yourselves came 'from out of the blue,' if you will recollect," Mrs. Hooper said. "The room sits empty. There was always the probability of its being let."

Charlotte studied his face. He seemed decent enough. But if she had learned but one lesson in life, it was that appearances could be deceiving. An argument entered her mind. A valid one. She had lived in close quarters with men for most of her life, but Rosalind was the product of all girls' schooling.

"I mean no offense to Mr. Smith," she said to Mrs. Hooper, "but we assumed that if you ever let the room, it would be to another woman."

Mr. Smith gave her an understanding nod. "I didn't give the inn enough time."

Raising a silencing hand, Mrs. Hooper said, "We've never

discussed this subject, Mrs. Kent. Thus I never led you to believe so. Mr. Knight was here nine months."

"With his *wife*." Charlotte lowered her voice, though Mr. Smith could hardly escape hearing. "And there is the matter of the bathroom."

"Stuff and nonsense! You share them in most railway stations and hotels. There is a clever invention called a *door* you may have heard of. And you can bear this for a month."

"One month?" Rosalind said.

Mr. Smith cleared his throat. "Six weeks at the very most. I'm commissioned by Macmillan Publishers for a series of sketches of the area for a collection. I had hoped the inn would suit me, but after three nights, I realized the noise is not conducive to work."

Charlotte recognized the self-satisfaction in Mrs. Hooper's eyes. *This is about my advising your niece that day. About Rosalind and Mr. Pearce. You're certain enough that we won't move to risk digging back at us.*

"Mrs. Hooper?" said Coral Shipsey from the dining room doorway.

This is not the time to confess to the margarine, Charlotte willed with her eyes.

"If Mr. Smith stays in my room, he may have the bath off the pantry to himself."

Mrs. Hooper glared across at her as if she might explode any second.

Coral spoke faster. "It's tidy, with a good mattress, and the cross breeze through the windows smells of the garden."

"That will be quite enough." To Mr. Smith, Mrs. Hooper said, "Coral Shipsey is my cook. I apologize for—"

"How very kind of you, Miss Shipsey," he said with a smile.

Mrs. Hooper gave a nervous chuckle and said, "Servants quarters, Mr. Smith? Simply out of the question."

"My mother cooks for the Marquess of Bath. Father is head

gardener. I spent my childhood in servants quarters, and happily so."

Charlotte smiled to herself at Mrs. Hooper's discomfort.

"But then, where would *you* stay, Miss Shipsey?" Mr. Smith asked.

"There's a second maid's room in the attic."

All eyes went to Mrs. Hooper. She dragged out a pained sigh. "Very well."

That settled, Charlotte asked to speak with her privately. Mrs. Hooper pushed to her feet and followed her into the kitchen, where Charlotte closed the door and said, "May I ask how you happened to make Mr. Smith's acquaintance?"

"Why, when the inn didn't suit him, he inquired at the desk for other options. Mrs. Fallon gave him my name."

"You know nothing more about him?"

"I know more than I knew about you, Mrs. Kent. But one can see that he's a gentleman." She chuckled. "You won't have to lock your bedroom doors."

How I love your sense of humor, Charlotte thought.

They returned to the parlor. The three women were gathered around Mr. Smith as he held up a page in his sketchbook of seaside Port Stilwell.

"You can see the whitecaps on the water in this one," Mrs. Deamer was saying.

"I drew it just this morning," he said. "But it isn't finished. I add the fine details at night, or during inclement weather. Gulls' nests, leaves, shingles, and so forth. That way, no time is wasted. I expect I'll be far more productive in this tranquil setting."

"But how do you remember how those looked?" Coral asked.

He tapped his temple. "I am blessed with a keen memory. And details do not have to be one hundred percent accurate. I allow myself some artistic license, if you will."

If he were working for Roger, Charlotte thought, he would have served his claim form upon introductions. Why tarry? If he were a reporter, would he have invented an occupation that kept him away most days?

In any case, London has forgotten you, she said to herself. But to ease nagging doubts, she asked, "Do you ever use a camera, Mr. Smith?"

He shook his head. "I don't think I ever would care to, Mrs. Kent. There is much more challenge and fulfillment in creating a scene with pencil."

Coral and Amy will be at fisticuffs over this one, Charlotte thought.

"Pencil . . . and talent," Rosalind said.

"Thank you, Miss Kent," he said, smiling at her.

Charlotte watched her daughter return his smile. *Oh dear.*

38

"Please stop fretting," Rosalind said to Coral Shipsey as they carried the mop bucket up the stairs, one hand each clasping its wire handle. "This is the least I can do after you solved the bathroom problem."

It was not that she was a prude. Though her aunt had striven to hide it from her, she had learned boys were different the first time she witnessed a nanny changing her little charge in a park. Years later, she had seen canvas and marble nudes in museums.

But a bath was the most intimate room in a house. Sharing with strangers at hotels was different than with a member of the household, whose bedroom would be just across the landing. No doubt Mr. Smith was just as relieved at this new arrangement.

She had never ventured up to the attic. How nice to have an excuse.

On the landing, they eased the pail to the floor. Rosalind stepped back and allowed herself a peek through Mrs. Deamer's doorway, taking in the dormer windows, colorful blanket, and row of books upon the chest of drawers. She did not fear being caught. Mrs. Deamer was obviously put out with Coral for asserting herself without her input and was allowing her to handle the consequences. This pettiness was unlike her, but then, with everything else taken away, her job was all that she had.

Coral's new room across the landing mirrored the layout of Mrs. Deamer's. Together, they cleaned and opened the two bay windows, removed and folded dust sheets. Rosalind stood, then, in the doorway while Coral mopped.

"What do you think of Mr. Smith?" Coral asked.

"He seems quite pleasant," Rosalind replied, wondering if Mr. Clark was being nudged aside in Coral's affections.

"He didn't have to let on that his mum and dad were in service. I like that he doesn't put on airs."

Rosalind had to say it. "Quite different from someone else, don't you think?"

"Ah . . . Noble." Coral swished the mop, shook her head. "He's seeing Amy."

"Oh dear. I spoke out of turn. I'm so sorry."

"You've no cause to be. Mrs. Kent made me see that I've wasted enough time waiting. It doesn't hurt so much anymore. And now that I've stopped paying him any mind, he tries to chat me up. Poor Amy!"

"Poor Amy," Rosalind echoed.

"But I'm not pinning my hopes on Mr. Smith."

"Well, no. You've only just met him."

Coral laughed. "Wouldn't have mattered, weeks ago. I'd be dreaming up my wedding gown, thinking with my heart instead of my brain."

"And what is your brain saying to you?"

"That he'll be gone soon enough. If I allow myself to get all fluttery, I'll only be hurt again. That I should keep my eyes on my goal of having a bakery."

"I'm impressed, Coral," Rosalind said. "That's very wise thinking."

Footsteps sounded. Coral ceased mopping.

"Miss Kent? Coral?"

"Yes, Mrs. Deamer?" Rosalind asked, stepping out onto the landing.

The housekeeper reached the top step. "Mr. Smith is here."

"But he doesn't move in until tomorrow. We aren't prepared."

"He offers to assist in moving Coral's belongings."

Coral said from her doorway, "Oh, we can't allow that. He's a guest."

"As is Miss Kent," said Mrs. Deamer but with more warmth than censure.

"I say we accept his offer," Rosalind said. "He certainly looked strong enough. I'll ask him to wait for the floor to dry. Is Mother with him?"

"He asked to see her garden."

"How quickly did she spring from the sofa?"

"Miss Kent . . ." Mrs. Deamer said with a look of mild reproof.

"I shouldn't have said that."

The housekeeper's eyes shone a bit. "She was in a chair."

Rosalind laughed, relieved that the tension was gone. She accompanied Mrs. Deamer down the staircase. "I'll bring tea out there. What do you think of him?"

Mrs. Deamer was silent for a moment. "The timing causes me some suspicion."

"For Mother and me as well."

"Perhaps you should inform Mr. Lockhart?"

"I shall. But Mr. Smith seems to have no motive other than to sketch."

In the kitchen, Mrs. Deamer brewed some tea and said, "It may be good for Mrs. Kent to have someone new with whom to chat."

Rosalind looked up from arranging macaroons in a dish. "I only hope Mrs. Hooper doesn't try to fill the unused bedroom any time soon. One new face is enough for the time being."

"Indeed." Mrs. Deamer placed three cups with saucers beside the pot.

"Will you join us?"

"I must change the bedding for Mr. Smith and get out some fresh for Coral."

"You're no longer angry with her?"

Mrs. Deamer gave her a little smile. "I had to remind myself that being young and impulsive is not a crime."

On the terrace, Rosalind set the tray on the table and watched Mother give Mr. Smith the grand tour of the garden. Mrs. Deamer was right, she thought. It would be refreshing for Mother to have someone new about.

However did she keep her sanity on Lord Despicable's estate?

Mr. Smith looked over Mother's shoulder and lifted a hand. He had a handsome smile, she thought. It softened the Spartan-warrior features of his face. It would be interesting to see if Coral could keep her resolve not to have romantic notions about him.

Mother beckoned, and when Rosalind neared, leaned down to push aside a cluster of velvety leaves to reveal a green ball the size of an acorn. "Our first tomato!"

"It's adorable," Rosalind said. "Let's celebrate with tea."

"Thank you," Mr. Smith said. "But I'm here to help."

"We must wait for the floor to dry upstairs."

They sat in the wicker chairs about the table. As Rosalind poured, she asked, "Tell us more about your book, Mr. Smith."

"I'm very excited over it," he said. "I made the rounds of publishers with some sketches from a visit to Cornwall, and Macmillan commissioned me to sketch towns in the shires which border water. Those off the tourist paths."

"When will you be finished with the whole project?" Mother asked.

"Eighteen months, perhaps. And what of the two of you? I don't detect the Devonshire accent."

"Oh, from all over," Rosalind replied. "Will you have milk or lemon?"

"Milk, please, with four sugars." His large hand dwarfed

the Spode cabbage rose teacup as he took a sip. "Earl Grey. My favorite, and my mother's."

"Please, have some macaroons," Mother said. "Miss Shipsey's a gifted baker. She hopes to open her own shop one day."

He took a bite, chewed, swallowed. "Quite delicious. I enjoy hearing of people who reach for the stars."

"Is your book of sketches your star, Mr. Smith?" Mother asked.

"It is indeed, Mrs. Kent." He smiled at her. "If it's a success, I shall be able to buy my parents a little farm where they'll be accountable to themselves alone."

"How lovely. Have you siblings to help you?"

"Three sisters. All married, so naturally unable to set aside as much as I can."

"Your parents are fortunate to have you," Mother said.

"Thank you, Mrs. Kent. I'm fortunate to have them."

"And Coral and I are fortunate to be spared lugging her belongings upstairs," Rosalind said.

Mr. Smith chuckled, raised his cup. "To everyone's good fortune, then."

❖◇❖

Rosalind returned from her walk the following morning to find Mr. Smith carrying a writing table down the staircase, with Mother and Mrs. Deamer watching.

"Mr. Smith is here," Mother said, as if Rosalind could not figure out whose face was hidden by rosewood.

"Careful, Mr. Smith," Mrs. Deamer said.

When he reached the ground floor, he set it down, blew out a breath, and grinned at Rosalind. "Good morning, Miss Kent. I asked to borrow this from the spare bedroom, and Mrs. Deamer kindly obliged."

"You've moved in, then?" Rosalind asked.

His eyes searched her face. "I assure you I shall be as quiet as a mouse."

"Well, not *too* quiet, we hope, Mr. Smith," Mother said. "You'll be expected to hold up your end of conversation during meals. There is nothing so tedious as a dining room with only the sounds of slurping soup."

His laugh came deep from his chest. "You and I shall get on just fine, Mrs. Kent."

During a lunch of cold boiled beef, young carrots and new potatoes, and salad, he followed Rosalind's directive by telling of the farmhouse where he had lodged in Bigbury-on-Sea and how the wife had made pets of a half-dozen silkies.

"They had names and would sit in her lap in the garden. Ofttimes, one would roost in her hair."

Rosalind was first to ask. "Silkies, Mr. Smith?"

"Beg your pardon . . . a breed of chicken. They're small and colorful and docile, with lustrous, silklike plumage. And they have five toes instead of four."

"Chickens have toes?" Mother asked.

He gave her an indulgent smile. "I came here just in time. You have much to learn about poultry."

Mother smiled back, and Rosalind asked, "Did the family ever . . . cook them?"

"Alas, that fate befell the ordinary chickens without names."

"And with but four toes, I presume," Mother said. "Tell me, Mr. Smith, did you sketch the woman and her pets? It would make an interesting addition to your book."

"She declined my request to do so, and that was that." He eyed the slice of beef upon the serving dish. "May I pass this to either of you?"

This, after having had three servings to their one each.

"Please, go ahead," Rosalind said. As he forked it onto his plate, she said to herself that it wouldn't be so bad, having a man living under the same roof. Already his presence brought an air of energy to the place.

Hours later, when he was out with his sketching pad, she

found herself stepping onto the porch to look down the lane more than once. *You have a beau,* she reminded herself on her fourth and final look. And she was eager to see him tomorrow.

❧⟨⟩❧

She decided to wait at the pillar-box the following morning, but then entertained second thoughts. Would Jude think her overeager?

You've kissed, she reminded herself. Meeting at the corner was far more benign on the list of courtship rituals. In any event, he was approaching from the distance. She returned his wave.

Jinny reached her first, as usual. Rosalind knelt to allow her chin to be licked while averting her mouth. When Jude was close enough for her ears and not the whole countryside's, he said, "I couldn't wait to see you again!"

She smiled, lowered Jinny's paws, and stood, for it was obvious from his face that he intended another kiss. She did not run to meet him, proving she was not an overeager woman, though she did take two steps.

The kiss was warm and sweet. Even better than the one in the shop, for no misunderstanding had preceded it. But on a Saturday morning, one was enough for a man to whom she was not betrothed.

Jinny's *arf!* implied the same.

On their way up Orchard Lane, Rosalind said, "Danny and Albert aren't coming."

"Oh no."

"But that's good news. Mr. Fletcher is taking them to Exeter for school clothing."

"Why, that's splendid, Rosalind."

"Apart from my wanting you to meet them. Can you come again next week?"

He gave her a look of mock worry. "Should I go home now?"

286

She laughed. "I think we can feed you two Saturdays in a row. Oh, and I have more news. We have a new lodger."

"A friend of your mother's?"

"Would that it were so. But actually, he's an artist."

"He?"

"Mr. Tobias Smith. Mrs. Hooper bullied us into this. But it won't be for long, and he's taken the apartment behind the kitchen so we have a degree of privacy. You may meet him. He went sketching this morning, but I think he intends to return for lunch."

She did not add that happenstance found the two of them leaving the cottage at the same time this morning and walking a good way down Fore Street together before parting ways at the beach. There was nothing to it, but she did not want Jude to think she was the sort of silly girl who would attempt to make her beau jealous.

"Hallo!"

They turned. Mr. Smith hastened toward them. Returning his wave, Rosalind whispered, "There he is."

"I thought to stay nearby to be in time for lunch," Mr. Smith said when close enough for conversation. "I found a nice copse of apple trees to sketch. May I walk with you?"

"Of course," Rosalind said, "May I introduce—"

"Mr. Pearce, of the bookshop?"

"How do you do?" Jude said, proffering a hand.

"Very well, thank you." Mr. Smith switched his satchel strap to his left arm and shook his hand.

Jinny took this as a reason to jump up and rest her forepaws on his thigh.

"Down, Jinny," Jude said. "I beg your pardon, Mr. Smith."

"Not at all." Mr. Smith set the bag upon the ground and knelt to rub her shoulders while his face was tongue bathed. "Aren't you a sweet pup? I wish I had a treat for you."

Rosalind traded smiles with Jude and said, "Miss Shipsey

287

will see that she has plenty. Speaking of . . . we should go so she doesn't have to hold lunch."

"Oh, of course." Mr. Smith took up his satchel, brushed his knees, and got to his feet.

"How did you know this was Mr. Pearce?" Rosalind asked as they walked.

"I spent a fair amount of time with Mrs. Hooper on Thursday. She mentioned several names, but I remembered Mr. Pearce's especially, for mercenary reasons." He leaned his head forward to grin at Jude. "I hope you'll carry my book of sketches one day."

"I'm sure that would be my pleasure," Jude said. "I'd like to see some, if I may."

"It would be *my* pleasure."

"But still, how did you know he was *the* Mr. Pearce?" Rosalind pressed.

"Umm, she said also that you were . . . seeing each other. When I noticed . . ."

His voice trailed.

Rosalind's face heated, and she exchanged looks with Jude.

"Forgive me," Mr. Smith said. "I spend so much time alone that I forget one shouldn't blurt out one's every thought."

"It's a common affliction about here," Jude said.

"She said you had a rough beginning. Sorry about what happened to your family. I can't imagine getting over something such as that."

"Thank you. It was a long time ago."

"Mrs. Hooper is the one who blurts every thought," Rosalind muttered.

Mr. Smith grimaced. "I resolve here and now to mind my words more carefully so that I don't become as Mrs. Hooper."

"I'm fairly certain there is no danger in that," Jude said with a forgiving smile.

"Oh, but she said some good things as well," Mr. Smith went

on. "That you've apparently come into sudden wealth. That cannot change the past, of course, but that's not a bad thing to happen, is it?"

"It's better than a sharp stick in the eye."

Mr. Smith laughed and touched the tip of a finger, as if to count. "But there is bad again. You were left standing at the altar."

"I was hardly standing at the—"

"You're doing it again, Mr. Smith," Rosalind warned.

"No, that's quite all right," Jude said. "I'm curious. Continue, please."

He touched a second fingertip. "Well, she seems to take issue with you for refusing to court her niece, a brilliant lass who would make an excellent wife."

"A child. Did she happen to mention that she was a child?"

"Not to my memory. But she did express regret that I move about so much, otherwise she would arrange an introduction."

"That poor girl," Rosalind said.

"And . . ."

"There is more?" Jude said.

"Only that her son defended you in grammar school when you were mocked for having Indian blood."

"Defended me? Bartholomew Hooper was the worst of the lot."

Why did you ask, Jude? Rosalind thought. The crunches of soles upon the roadway were the only sounds.

Mr. Smith kicked a stone. "There is no shame for having been bullied, Mr. Pearce. I was for having parents in service. Until I outgrew my tormentors."

"Lucky you," Jude said. "I used to daydream of that very thing . . . discovering some magic potion that would turn me into Hercules."

"But you became wealthy instead. What did George Herbert say? 'Living well is the best revenge'?"

"I don't seek revenge. Bartholomew has apologized. Some of my old schoolmates are my best patrons now."

"So . . . you're not the least bit happy that they may be a little envious?"

"Not at all." Jude smiled over at him. "But that's a good saying."

Rosalind marveled at how men could be so brutally frank with each other without taking offense. Still, she was relieved at the sight of Mother at the cottage gate.

"It is always a pleasure to see you, Mr. Pearce!" she said.

He took her hand. "A pleasure to see you as well, Mrs. Kent."

"I realize you can't leave the shop for very long. Coral has lunch ready. Shall we?"

In the dining room, Mr. Smith put fork and knife to work with his usual enthusiasm, but he did pause to say, "You have a fine dog, Mr. Pearce. From where did you get the name? Surely there is an interesting story."

Jude shook his head. "Sorry to disappoint, but it was the name of a neighbor's especially good-tempered beagle when I was a boy. I suppose I thought the name would ensure like behavior."

"And obviously did."

"She's yet to bite anyone."

"I was bitten on the hand by a dog when I was a girl," Mother said. She held up her left hand. "You can barely see the scar."

"I'm sorry to hear it, Mother," Rosalind said, then realized that was something she should have known. Even Aunt Vesta had been fond of relating events from her own childhood. But Rosalind was weary of the deception, and in any case, the men had not seemed to notice.

"Oh, it frightened me more than hurt," Mother said.

"I can relate to that," Mr. Smith said, and soon they were laughing at his account of a snake dropping down his collar in

Hyde Park as he listened to an orchestra performing the works of Rossini.

"I sat propped against a trunk, my collar loosened, as it was an especially hot August day. At the first bite, I jumped up dancing like a lunatic, which caused the snake to do the same! Nannies covered the eyes of their wee charges! People pointed! I tore buttons and a sleeve in my haste to shed the shirt . . . and it was a new one!"

"How many times did it bite you, Mr. Smith?" Mother asked.

"Five, Mrs. Kent. Ten punctures! Fortunately, it wasn't an asp, just a grass snake. But to this day, I avoid low-hanging branches like the plague."

"And what of Rossini?" Jude asked.

Mr. Smith grimaced at him. "Not quite so fond of him anymore, truth be told."

On the porch a while later, Rosalind thanked Jude for being so kind to Mr. Smith. "I gather he is lonesome for male company during his travels. You men seem to have a language all your own."

Jude smiled and squeezed her hand. "It was no burden. I like him."

"So, you're not jealous?" she teased.

"Should I be?" he asked, his eyes playfully narrowing.

She pecked his forehead. "No. Now go and open your shop."

On her way to the parlor, she thought of how Reginald would have sulked. Not that she had ever had a male friend when they were courting, but he was jealous even of her school acquaintances.

Fear of spinsterhood had almost led her into a grave mistake. Rosalind could picture herself now, bound into marriage, perhaps with a child or two, while dying inside. How grateful she was to God for giving her the wisdom to veer from the path she was on when she had no way of knowing if others lay in the shrouded future.

Jude turned to send her a wave from the end of the fence. She smiled and waved back. Was Jude the right path? She hoped, for she was certain that she loved him. *"Too soon,"* her mother would say. And too soon to admit as much to him. The man was supposed to say it first. That was a law set into stone.

39

Danny and his family had a railway carriage to themselves on the way home. Father and Stepmother, cradling a sleeping Teresa, shared the forward-facing seat. Danny and Albert knelt upon the opposite seat at opposite windows, the parcels and folded sheepskin between them.

All this time, Danny had thought they were poor, but in the shops, Father had purchased two sets of clothes and a pair of shoes for each. Even after their stepmother reminded him that summer break was near! As hills and trees, cattle and pastures, moved by, Danny stretched out his arm and relished the breeze against his skin.

A westbound train whooshed by with a gust of hot air. He jerked back his arm.

Father chuckled.

"May I see?" Albert hopped down as the train clicked by.

"Mind you keep your arm inside," their stepmother warned.

It was not like her to concern herself with their safety, particularly Albert's. As his brother squeezed to share the window, Danny turned to say, "I'll watch him."

She smiled, closed her eyes, and nuzzled her nose into Teresa's silky curls.

A rush of happiness came over him. This was the most perfect day in his life. The cathedral was bigger than he had remembered, the fish and chips the best meal he had ever had, though he would never say that to Miss Shipsey. Afterward, chocolate ice cream!

And in the luggage carriage was a new mattress!

"How will we get the mattress home?" he asked after the other train had passed.

"Mr. Ford will have someone on hand," Father said. "Most likely Mr. Plummer."

"Who is Mr. Ford, Father?" Albert asked, moving over to his knees.

"The stationmaster, Albert."

"And who is Mr. Plummer?"

"The Methodist minister. He lives near the station and drives people when they need him."

"He didn't drive us there."

Father tousled his flaming hair. "Why, we had no parcels then, did we?"

"Do you know everyone?" Danny asked.

"Everyone with two shillings to rub together."

"Mrs. Kent?" Albert asked.

Breath held, Danny glanced at his stepmother. Her eyes were still closed.

"But of course," Father said. "You're her gardeners, yes?"

Danny eased out the breath. But of course Father knew her. Hadn't he sent a letter that they would not be there today? He hoped Mrs. Kent was not too disappointed. They would work twice as hard next Saturday to make up for it.

Too soon, the train hissed to a stop at Port Stilwell Station. Teresa whimpered and raised her head, blinking. She pointed to Albert, whose hair was wild from the wind and father's tousling, and laughed. "Look!"

That made Father laugh, and Albert. And miracle of miracles, so did their stepmother. Happiness so overwhelmed Danny that his eyes teared.

Mr. Plummer seemed as wide as he was tall, and sometimes jabbed Danny with his elbow, but Danny relished sitting high in the wagon seat behind the team of horses. Father, his stepmother, and Teresa sat just behind them, on a wide bench fastened into the bed. There was no doubt as to Albert's enjoyment, for from Mr. Plummer's other side, he called to every person they passed.

"Hallo! Hallo!"

At the cottage, Danny and Albert followed as Mr. Plummer and Father lugged the mattress indoors and up the stairs.

"What will you do with this one?" Mr. Plummer said of the old mattress.

"I haven't thought," Father said.

"My wife and the ladies at the church . . . they take apart, patch, and clean them, then give them to pensioners and poor families."

"Very good."

"He shouldn't have charged you," Stepmother muttered when Father returned from helping Mr. Plummer load it into his wagon.

Danny's stomach felt the familiar knot.

"Sabrina, we don't need the money."

When she did not argue, Danny relaxed a bit and went back upstairs. Albert lay curled upon the foot of the bare mattress. But for the slight indentation made by his brother's body, it was the same height all around. And the blue-and-white ticking was not stained! Which brought on the old panic. He shook his brother's shoulder. "Albert!"

Father came into the room. "Tired him out, did we?"

Not yet used to his being interested in their lives, Danny said, "He's not been to the bathroom since Exeter."

"Wake up, son," Father said, scooping him into his arms.

Albert stirred enough to use the chamber pot, but with eyes

closed and mouth agape. Father hefted him onto his shoulder and turned to Danny, studying him as if for the first time. "How long have you been waking him to go?"

"Just before you came in."

"No. Before that."

Danny tried to think, shook his head. "I don't know. But sometimes I can't wake myself."

"But of course. You're a boy yourself." Father's eyes were fixed upon him as if he were some new discovery, some wonder.

Please, Mother, ask God to have him stay this way. For Albert.

Danny's conscience felt a pang. He wanted it as much for himself as for his brother. Albert had never known Father any other way, so he could not have the same yearning.

God knew Danny's thoughts. Would He make his father the way he was before, to punish him?

That was a lie, Mother. Please tell God that I want it for me too. Please tell Him that I'll never be dishonest again.

His throat swelled. In a tinny voice, he said, "I stole a sheet."

"You what?"

Danny hung his head. "Took a sheet from Mrs. Winter's wash line. Before Christmas. It's in the attic."

"But why?"

"So we would have a dry one whenever Albert had accidents."

The old weariness settled into Father's face. Danny had apologized to God too late. But then, Father reached his free hand between Danny's shoulders and pressed him into his side. The strength of the hand upon his back, the cloth against his cheek, brought fresh but good tears.

"I expect we'll need to buy Mrs. Winter a new one."

"I'm sorry," Danny said into his side.

Father released him, stepped back. "It's a sin to steal, Danny. But the greater sin would have been to watch your brother be punished without trying to put a stop to it. I'm sorry you couldn't come to me. I've failed you both."

Lips pressed tight to keep tears in check, Danny shook his head.

"But I have. Never again!"

"Teresa has ice cream on her nose," Albert murmured upon his shoulder.

Father laughed.

Danny laughed as well. He reckoned he had laughed more today than any day in his life.

His stepmother served coddled eggs and toast for supper, because, as she said, she had had no time to prepare anything else.

"I like coddled eggs," Danny assured her. Not from affection, for the beatings were still sharp in his memory. Even though life was so much better now, he still feared her power to change Father. He resolved to say nice things to her, to help more and keep her happy.

He had not realized how bad the room had smelled until Father tucked them in that night. The breeze from the windows felt as crisp as their new sheets. Albert lay upon the sheepskin, which Father said would dry quickly and could even be washed.

"So sleep, Danny." Father said with a kiss upon his forehead.

He did, face pressed into pillow, and woke Sunday morning to the familiar smell. But this time, Father came in and bathed Albert's naked body at the washstand with a flannel.

"I tried not to muss it up, Father," Albert said.

"That's why it's there, Albert. No matter. Let us dress for church."

"But Mother hates the vicar," Danny blurted before thinking.

It had to do with his calling upon Father and Stepmother some months ago because someone had spoken to him about a bruise covering Albert's cheek.

Danny reckoned that person to be Mrs. Fairburn, and the odd thing was that a fall from the elm in the garden had caused the injury. With Albert and Danny to confirm her innocence in this case, their stepmother had ranted and raved, thus ending their church-going days at Saint Michael's.

His father gave him a sad look. "Mr. Plummer has always been a decent fellow. I thought we should give the Methodists a try."

◆─◇◇◇─◆

Danny and Albert set out on Monday morning with full stomachs and clean shirts and trousers. At the schoolhouse, Danny handed his brother his lunch pail, heavier than it had ever been, and said, "Mind you don't go mucking about in the dirt at recess."

"But I have more clothes now," his brother said.

"We don't want Stepmother to have to wash too often."

Albert's forehead furrowed. "She wouldn't be angry. Would she?"

Torn between admitting the worry in the back of his mind, and not spoiling his brother's newfound happiness, Danny chose the latter and patted his shoulder. "We want to be nice boys for her, don't we? And nice boys stay away from dirt."

On the grammar school side of the building, some children gave him bemused looks, but most treated him with the same disdain.

"Stinky has new clothes! Did your father rob the bank?"

Mr. Clark came out to the steps and rang the bell. Danny filed past with the others, head tucked as far into his new shirt as possible, expecting more abuse.

"Will you read the morning prayer, Danny?"

Danny jerked his head up as his cheeks burned. "Um . . ."

"Very good," Mr. Clark said. And smiled!

At the end of the day, Danny sprinted to the other side of the building to find Albert, two other boys, and a girl playing tag. He sighed at the dirt upon his brother's shoes and trousers. Perhaps he could brush it off with his hands.

But even that could not dampen his spirits! While his school-mates still shunned him at recess, they had spared him the usual taunts. And Adelle Whitaker had thanked him for picking up her pencil from the floor! Adelle, who looked down her nose at everyone because her father was postmaster!

"Emery says his uncle walks with a wooden leg," Albert said during their walk home. "He straps it on under his trousers."

"What happened to his real leg?"

"I don't know."

"Are you sure he said it at all?"

"He did!"

"Well, ask." Danny opened the front gate. "And listen."

Teresa's shrieks met their ears before they stepped onto the porch. Danny ran inside and tossed their lunch pails onto a parlor chair.

"Mother?"

"Mo-ther!" Albert called.

Danny hustled up the steps into the nursery. Teresa sat at an angle in her crib, with one chubby leg stuck out between the iron bars to just above the knee. Her face was wet, and she sobbed more loudly when he approached.

"Go and find Stepmother!" Danny shouted as Albert came huffing through the doorway.

To Teresa, he soothed, "Don't cry . . . Mother's coming."

He was too short to reach over the railing and lift her. Pushing on her leg did not work. Her howls made him want to cry himself. But then, the leg seemed to loosen a bit when he raised it. Gently, he wiggled and raised some more.

It worked! She drew in her leg and pulled herself to a wobbly stand.

"Da-ey!" she sobbed, straining arms to reach him.

He took her under the arms and pulled. Her belly, then legs, slid over the railing, so heavy against him that he stumbled backward a step.

"There, there now," he said, rocking her from side to side as his stepmother did.

She wept against his shoulder. He took a couple more backward steps, patting her back. Seconds later, she raised her sodden face and twisted to point to her doll in the crib. "Baby!"

"I'll get it." Before he could put her down, rapid footfalls sounded upon the landing. His stepmother rushed in and pulled her, arms flailing, from him. The suddenness caused her to shriek again.

"There, there now," his stepmother said, rocking her as he had just done.

"She wants her doll." Danny went over to reach through the bars. He handed it to Teresa, which calmed her at once.

Albert entered. "The kitchen smells good, Mother. What are you cooking?"

She glanced at him, not smiling but neither was she frowning. "Come with me."

A treat? For saving Teresa? Danny and Albert traded cautious smiles as they followed her down the staircase. In the kitchen, their stepmother set Teresa in the corner with her doll and blocks. She went over to the stove to lift the lid from a kettle and stir with a wooden spoon.

"What are you cooking?" Albert asked again.

She replaced the lid, set the spoon upon the stove, and moved over to face them.

"Sit."

They climbed into chairs. She took Father's, at the head of the table.

"I wasn't to be away long. Can't have her wander about when I'm in the privy."

"Her leg was stuck," Danny said, just in case Albert had not explained. His stomach was beginning to feel queasy. But why?

"I know," she said, eyes narrowing. "But next time, wait. I was on the way."

"Aren't we to have a treat?" Albert said.

She pressed her lips for a moment. "I wish to say something to the two of you. How old do you think your father is?"

Danny could only stare at her while Albert shifted in his chair.

"Well?"

"F-forty?" Danny stammered.

"Forty-six. And I'm twenty-nine. Do you know what that means? It means he'll die before I do. Maybe not this year, maybe not the next, but before you're grown. People die, as you well know. And I'll be in charge of you. No one else. Not even your Mrs. Kent, who'll be dead before even your father goes."

Danny sat frozen to the chair, his nose as wet as his eyes.

"Even if you go running to your father again, and he sends me away, when he dies you'll be handed over to me."

"Father said you won't hit us again," Albert squeaked.

"I won't hit you. I'll clean your sheets and your clothes and feed your bellies. We'll get on just fine. But you are never to hold my daughter again, or I'll make you pay when your father dies. Do you hear me?"

If only Father would come home early! Danny found his voice. "Her leg—"

"I know what goes through your minds!" She was fairly hissing. "That she's only your half sister. Well, I'll smother you in your beds before I allow you to do things to her. Now . . . out of my sight!"

Teresa burst into fresh tears in the corner. Danny jumped down from the chair, took a crimson-faced Albert by the hand, and led him through the door to the garden. They sat upon the bench and wept in each other's arms.

"I thought she loved us." Albert sniffed.

"She loves only Teresa." He had figured out long ago that his stepmother did not love Father, could not possibly. "But it's not Teresa's fault."

"Will we tell Father?"

"No!" She was right; people did die. Mother. Grandmother and Grandfather Fletcher. "She said she won't hit us. We mustn't touch Teresa, ever."

He flinched at the squeak of the door. Their stepmother advanced with Teresa on her hip and a dish in her hands.

"Bis-cuits!" she sang. She slid Teresa to her feet, motioned for Danny and Albert to sit apart, and placed the dish between them.

Danny could only stare at Stepmother.

Albert hesitated, then reached for one. "Chocolate!"

"Mine!" Teresa said, lunging for the dish.

His stepmother held her back and scooped up two biscuits. "Two, darling. One for each hand."

As Teresa shoved both into her mouth, their stepmother pulled a handkerchief from her apron and leaned to wipe Danny's face. "Now, now. Dry those eyes. We understand each other. Everything will be fine. Have a biscuit."

The biscuit was dry in his mouth. Any tenderness she had shown them over recent days was not real. Everything was not fine.

"Thank you," he mumbled.

But the past few days had been far better than when they were hungry, beaten, and neglected, he reminded himself. Every night henceforth, he would ask Mother to ask God to allow Father to live for a long time.

Chewing, drooling chocolate, Teresa reached for the dish.

"No more, darling," Stepmother said. "You'll spoil your supper."

Her quick little hands snatched two more biscuits.

"No, Teresa!" While Stepmother struggled to open her fist, Teresa pushed the other biscuit into her full mouth.

Albert laughed.

"Shut up!" Stepmother hissed, and he fell sober. Her voice softened for Teresa, though it shook. "Give . . . give to Mother, darling."

"No, no, no!" Teresa cried and slapped her.

"Stop that!" Stepmother held her out to avoid flailing arms and legs. When Teresa could not reach her mother's reddened cheeks, she sank her teeth into her wrist.

"Ouch! Stop!"

Stepmother was able to wrestle her arm away and set the girl down. Rubbing her wrists, she said through tears, "Why did you bite?"

But Teresa turned and made for the dish. Stepmother scooped her up again, this time from behind, where hands and feet and teeth had no place to strike.

"Door!" Stepmother shrieked.

Danny jumped up, ran around her, and opened the door for her to carry the screaming girl through. He stuck his head around and waited for any more commands. But she continued through the kitchen.

One biscuit remained upon the dish when he returned to the bench.

"I'm sorry," Albert mumbled, cheeks full.

"It's all right. You may have it."

He listened to his brother's crunching and thought of the stricken look upon his stepmother's face. The only person she loved in the world had turned against her, at least for a while. When you loved but one person, he thought, your happiness rose and fell, depending upon that person's treatment of you.

Not that he felt any pity. Teresa would calm herself. His stepmother would cuddle her, kissing the top of her head.

If she could have but *attempted to* love him and Albert, and Father, perhaps she would not allow a baby's fit of anger to make her so sad. Perhaps, even, she would be three times as happy!

Albert paused from slurping his fingers. "Why are you looking at me?"

"I love you."

His brother's grin exposed brown teeth. "I love *you*."

303

Danny decided he would try to love as many people as he could. Already, besides Father and Albert and Teresa, he loved Mrs. Kent, Miss Kent, Mrs. Deamer, and Miss Shipsey. So why not ask Mother to ask God to give them *all* long lives?

Or perhaps he would try asking God himself. After all, he was ten years old.

40

Charlotte padded into the kitchen in slippers and a wrapper on Tuesday morning. Between last night's window-rattling thunder and her own episodes of intense body heat, she had hardly slept.

"Ah . . ." She sighed at the sight of steam rising from the kettle.

Coral, slicing bacon, said, "You're awake early, Mrs. Kent."

"I've been awake for hours. But you know, inertia is the strongest chain."

They spoke in low tones, though larder, pantry, and bathroom buffered Mr. Smith's bedchamber.

"Inertia?" Coral asked.

"The force which keeps you in bed or chair when there is something you need to do."

"Ah. Please take no offense, Mrs. Kent. This doesn't apply to you. But inertia sounds a lot like laziness."

"Well, it's not." Charlotte thought for a second. "Though they may be cousins."

Coral laughed, set down the knife, and went over to the sink to wash her hands. "I'll have you some tea in a tick."

"Thank you. I hope you'll have some too." Pulling out a chair at the table, she eyed the stack of bacon slices. Mr. Smith's appetite was a wonder to behold. "Your toast and marmalade mornings are over."

"But only for a little while." Coral poured hot water into the teapot and added a pinch of leaves. She brought the pot to the table, then collected cups and spoons, milk and sugar.

"Let's allow it to steep a bit longer." Coral leaned closer and lowered her voice even more so. "This is probably nothing. But Mr. Smith asked Sunday why you and Miss Kent and Mrs. Deamer don't attend church."

A warning bell rang in Charlotte's mind. But then, was that not a perfectly natural question? "What did you say?"

"That I *couldn't* say."

"Did he persist?"

"Not at all."

"Well, then." She smiled. "I'm sure he was good company for you."

Coral nodded. "Reminds me of my oldest brother, Jack. Big lumbering giants, they are. It was nice of him to walk with me and not mind going early. I thought Noble's eyes would pop out."

"No . . ." Charlotte groaned.

"I'm over him, Mrs. Kent. But I have to admit I enjoyed seeing him stare at us. Poor Amy was practically dancing to keep his attention."

"Oh my. Poor Amy, indeed."

"Saving for my bakery is the most important thing now," Coral said, pouring tea into cups. "Though I would have to leave here, as Owen's is so popular."

"I would hate to have you leave, but I do understand. Where would you go?"

"Anywhere. As long as there's a train station, so I can visit my family."

"Exeter?"

"That would be ideal. But I look over the notices in the *Gazette* when you've finished, and rents are higher than here."

After a sip of tea, Charlotte said, "But so would be the wages, wouldn't they? What if you applied for a position in an established bakery or restaurant?"

Coral tapped her chin thoughtfully. "Where I could *bake*, instead of having to concentrate on meals."

"You would gain more practical experience whilst saving and waiting for the right opportunity."

"But where would I live, then? If I must pay for a room . . ."

Charlotte sighed. "Coral, do you really want this bakery?"

"More than anything."

"You don't have to say you do to please me. Truly."

Eyes watering, Coral said, "Anything, Mrs. Kent."

"Then you must ask more questions. You cannot assume that all hotels and bakeries don't provide rooms for staff. Or pay enough to live on and continue saving."

"You're right." Coral added a fourth spoonful of sugar to her tea. "I've been waylaid by, what did you say? Inertia!"

"And not laziness. Will you ever drink that?" Charlotte pointed to her tea.

"Oh. Yes." Coral took a sip from her cup and drew up her lips. "Too sweet."

"Imagine that."

From the pantry corridor came the squeak of door hinges. Mr. Smith entered in pajamas and wrapper, his black hair sticking up on one side. He yawned, scratched his face, and looked about, eyes finally stopping on Charlotte and Coral.

"Oh . . . I beg your pardon." He started to turn.

"You don't have to leave," Charlotte said. "I'm in a dressing gown as well."

He gave them a sheepish smile. "Good morning. I was hoping to make some tea."

Coral rose. "I'll freshen the pot, Mr. Smith. Please, have a seat."

"Thank you." He pulled out a chair. "The thunder woke you too?"

"It never allowed me to sleep." Charlotte glanced at the window. "We may be in for more. It's a pity for your work."

"Such is the life of a traveling artist. I have some detailing to do. And perhaps I could sketch the cottage between showers. It's quite unique."

Casually, Charlotte said, "You'll not ask us to pose on the porch, will you?"

"Would you care to?"

"I'm shy. *And* fat."

He winked at her. "You're not exactly Humpty Dumpty, Mrs. Kent. But no, the cottage alone will suffice."

Coral brought over the teapot. "We've some bread pudding left over from last night, if you can manage sweets this early."

"None for me, thank you," Charlotte said.

"I would enjoy some," Mr. Smith said. "It's a wonder you had any left. I daresay I had three dishes last night."

Four, Charlotte thought, smiling to herself. "Miss Shipsey plans to have her own bakery one day."

"I endorse that plan heartily. You're an artist with flour and sugar."

"Oh now, you flatter me," Coral said, setting a dish of bread pudding before him. "Mrs. Kent advises me to apply somewhere in Exeter where I can gain more experience."

He set his teacup into the saucer. "Don't just apply. Promote!" Forefingers drawing a square in the air, he unfolded his plan. "Fill a half-dozen flat boxes with samples, and carry them to the best hotels and restaurants there."

"Why, that's an excellent idea, Mr. Smith," Charlotte said.

They both looked at Coral. All animation had left her face.

"Miss Shipsey?" Mr. Smith said, fork raised to his mouth.

"Mrs. Hooper," she said. "She does some business in Exeter

and knows everyone from miles about. If she learned I was applying elsewhere, she would give me the sack."

This was no surprise to Charlotte.

Mr. Smith chewed, swallowed. "You need a promoter. Allow me that honor. I would reveal your identity only to those who are interested in hiring you."

"You would do that for me? But I can't allow you to take time from your work."

"I wouldn't be. I'm to meet my editor, Mr. Kaye, in Exeter on the twenty-eighth of June, returning the day after. I could catch the early train and deliver your boxes. That would give you nearly three weeks to plan."

"That's very kind of you," Charlotte said.

He ducked his head modestly but then said, "I gained my book contract with tenacity. Muscling my way in to see the right people . . . with utmost courtesy, mind you. I would be representing the head baker at an esteemed lodging house in Port Stilwell."

Coral laughed. "Mr. Smith! I'm not—"

"Is there any untruth to that?" he asked, holding up the dish of half-eaten pudding.

"Well . . ."

Charlotte had to smile and wondered that he had not found his way into the theatre business.

"I would ask for appointments. That way, when you go up there on your own, you won't be facing some great unknown. We could rehearse your interviews so that you'll have the confidence you need. Just as if you were to be in a play."

"Rehearsing would be good," Charlotte said. Her confidence in Mr. Smith's genuineness became more solid. If he knew who she was, he would never have made the theatre reference.

He pushed out his chair. "I've enjoyed our visit. But I must dress and finish some detailing before breakfast."

Breakfast? Charlotte thought.

Coral smiled at her as if to say that it didn't matter. And why should it, when he was so willing to help her?

That gave Charlotte pause.

She asked to speak with him on the porch after lunch, while Rosalind was reading in the parlor, Mrs. Deamer upstairs, and Coral in the kitchen. The rain had lightened into a mist that blurred the trees on either side of the lane like an impressionist painting.

"Is something wrong?" he asked with a worried expression.

He was young enough to be her son, so she gave him what she hoped to be a look of motherly concern.

"You must get quite lonely in your travels."

"My work dominates so much of my energy that I don't notice," he replied, but the sadness in his dark eyes said she was not far off the mark.

"Coral . . . Miss Shipsey . . . she's a wonderful girl."

He nodded. "You're concerned that I'll hurt her?"

"She's been hurt before."

"I'm not interested in having a girl in every port, Mrs. Kent. I feel a bond with people from humble beginnings. I would have done the same had she been a man."

Charlotte let out a breath. "I'm so happy to hear it. I hope I've not offended you."

He shook his head. "It's good that you look out for her."

"I feel that bond with her too, Mr. Smith. I'll leave you to return to your work."

"Allow me." He stepped over to take the door handle, pausing to give her the tenderest of smiles. "If I were to have romantic notions, Mrs. Kent . . . they would be for someone else."

You can't possibly be saying . . .

She had known of young swains who pursued much older women, but always wealthy ones. Silly, wealthy women. The theatre world was full of such cases.

"But she has a beau," he went on. "I hope he knows how fortunate he is."

She felt fortunate herself, for the years of training that had kept her from revealing her ridiculous thoughts. "I believe he does, Mr. Smith."

41

Fog swirled about Jude's feet. Shouts came from the bay, and the sound of the steam engine winching fishing boats ashore. Mrs. Galvez answered his knock, holding a scrap of red meat.

"Mr. Pearce! You're just in time."

He grimaced. "When you said breakfast . . ."

"For Jinny, as if you did not know!" She laughed and tossed it to the pup.

Jinny carried the offering in her teeth to her usual spot beside the door. No animals were welcome in Flores. Mr. Galvez had such fear of hair, animal or human, finding its way into food, that he kept his own as short as a Caesar's.

"I appreciate the invitation," Jude said as he followed Mrs. Galvez through the empty dining room. "My usual is boiled egg and toast."

"It will not be breakfast fare. We decided it is high time to have a Spanish dish on the menu."

The kitchen was well lit, with whitewashed cob walls, windows on either side of a long worktable, and another to the right of the stove, where Mr. Galvez was dishing something into a bowl. He was a thick man, with full lips and a jutting brow.

"Ah, good morning, Mr. Pearce!"

"Whatever you're cooking smells good."

"It's *paella*! Sit, sit!"

Mrs. Galvez slid into the chair Jude held out for her and began pouring tea into cups. "Thank you for agreeing to be our little pig."

"Your what?" Jude said, chuckling as he took his own chair.

"*Guinea* pig," Mr. Galvez corrected on his way to the table.

"Ah yes." She laughed at herself and handed Jude his cup.

"Now, be honest. Brutal, if you must," Mr. Galvez said, passing around steaming servings.

The three picked up forks and blew in unison. Jude tasted, chewed, and swallowed the mixture of rice and vegetables, prawns and sausage. Tears burned his eyes.

Mr. Galvez spit his out into his dish. His wife swallowed and drew up her lips.

"As I feared . . . too much salt," Mr. Galvez said.

"Too much everything," said Mrs. Galvez. "But it's the most popular dish in Spain. That's what *Woman's Gazette* said."

"Is that where you found the recipe?" Jude asked. "May I see it?"

Mr. Galvez rose and fetched an open magazine from the counter near the stove. With Mrs. Galvez leaning close to look, Jude scanned the ingredients. There seemed nothing harmful.

Tomatoes, green beans, chicken stock, saffron . . .

He looked at the measurements. "You realize these are metric, don't you?"

"They are?" said Mr. Galvez.

"Spain uses the metric system. Whoever translated this did not convert the measurements." Jude pushed the magazine across the table. Mr. Galvez held it about seven inches from his nose and squinted.

That explains the Indian meal, Jude thought.

"Mr. Galvez, you need spectacles."

He set the magazine back onto the table. "No."

"I never realized," said his wife. "He's cooked the same dishes for years, never needed recipes."

"Don't want spectacles hanging on my face, steaming up in the kitchen," Mr. Galvez said. "I can see fine except to read. Which I almost never do."

He pushed the magazine back to Jude. "Can you convert those numbers?"

Jude nodded. "I'll copy the whole recipe in large letters."

"The problem is solved, then."

"I'll fetch some paper," Mrs. Galvez said, pushing out her chair. "But it is time to prepare for lunch."

Mr. Galvez got to his feet as well. "It hasn't been on the menu for twenty years. A day or two more will not matter."

He went into the larder while Mrs. Galvez went to the tiny office. Both returned at the same time; he with a joint of beef, and she with a writing tablet, blotter, and fountain pen.

Jude set to writing, and Mrs. Galvez returned to the table shortly with a large pan of red potatoes. She sat and began peeling, her knife leaving long strips.

"Are you still seeing Miss Kent?" she asked.

"Thirty grams equal two tablespoons," Jude said under his breath. "I'm having lunch with her today."

"Why did you not say?"

He shook his head. "Not here. At the yellow cottage."

"Do you love her?"

While this woman's abrupt frankness could make him squirm, he appreciated her concern for his welfare. "I can't wait to see her."

"Does that mean yes?"

He gave her a long-suffering smile.

"Why is that difficult to say?" she asked.

"Um . . . because I'm an Englishman?"

She sighed. "I shall never understand why Englishmen are so cold."

"Cold?" Jude said. "I beg to differ. Our hearts are big and near our skins, so we feel the need to armor them."

"Isn't it time you put away the armor and say it to her?"

"We've been acquainted but three months. I don't want to frighten her away."

"Ah." She nodded. "Yes, once you've said the words, the thought of marriage will always be there. You'll seem a cad if you don't propose in due time, but you cannot possibly know a person well enough in three months."

She was echoing his own attempts to temper his impulsive heart.

"Same as kissing," she said. "Too soon."

"Um-hm." *One cup chopped onions,* he wrote, staring down at the page. She was probably right. Kissing Rosalind was tantamount to a declaration of love. But that ship had sailed, and he was loath to call it back to shore.

Such a lovely ship.

"Why do you smile?" Mrs. Galvez asked.

"Didn't realize I was," he said, sobering his expression.

"Um-hm," she said with a droll smile of her own.

He blotted the pen and sat it in its holder. "Well, here you are. I must open shop."

"You'll return when we have another go at it?" Mr. Galvez asked from the stove.

"Yes, of course."

He almost ran into Mrs. Hooper outside, crouched and kneading Jinny's shoulders.

"Yes, yes, we love Aunt Aurora, do we not?"

Aunt Aurora?

She smiled up at Jude. "Dogs love this. Their muscles grow stiff, just like ours. I massaged Cedric every day, and he lived fifteen years."

"Why don't you get another, Mrs. Hooper? Perhaps another schnauzer?"

Straightening, she shook her head. "I wept for months after he passed. I cannot go through that again. I'll content myself with chats with my wee friend here."

Jinny thumped her tail, asking for more, but Jude said, "I'm afraid your wee friend and I must open shop."

"And I wish to discuss an important matter." She fell into step with him. "The school board is talking of founding another grammar school, on the east side of town."

"Indeed?" Perhaps Rosalind would be interested, he thought. "When?"

"Not for another two or three years. Such things take time. But it goes to show you that Port Stilwell is growing. You should expand, prepare for more patrons."

Their steps halted at the shop door. As he took his key from his pocket, he took perverse pleasure in saying, "Thank you for your advice, Mrs. Hooper. Good day to you."

But she followed him indoors with Jinny close behind. "Please close the door. This is a private matter."

He frowned but obliged.

She walked about the shop, marble-like eyes scanning about. They stopped at the counter, where sat the travel brochures he had received in the post yesterday.

"India, Mr. Pearce?"

He chided himself for not taking them upstairs last night. The less she knew of his affairs, the better. "Mrs. Hooper, if a patron appears I must open the door."

She motioned toward the south wall. "You could break down that wall."

He raised his brows. "I'm afraid Mr. Blyth might object."

"Not if you owned the space. I'm his landlady, remember."

"He's been there since I was a boy. Why would you kick him out?"

"Don't look at me that way, Mr. Pearce," she said, wagging a finger. "It was Vincent's idea to buy up half the properties in town. I'm seventy years old. Better to have money in the bank than have to collect rents. Not everyone pays promptly, as you did."

"Hire Mr. Lockhart to do it for you."

"And give up a percentage to that pettifogger? I think not."

"Bartholomew . . ."

"The restaurant is more than enough for him to maintain."

Why are you even trying? he asked himself. "I do hope you'll not take away Mr. Blyth's livelihood, Mrs. Hooper. In any case, I wouldn't be interested in buying."

She opened her mouth as if to argue.

He shook his head.

With a sigh, she stepped toward the door. "By the by, have you met Mr. Smith?"

"I have."

"Charming fellow, isn't he?"

"Charming." He opened the door and stood aside.

"His height doesn't hurt, mind you. Women are naturally drawn to the tall ones."

"I have books to shelve."

"And a delightful sense of fun! It's not all work, work, work for Mr. Smith. Small wonder that Miss Kent seemed quite keen on him."

"Um-hm."

"Have I mentioned that Bernadette is making excellent marks at Girton College? There's a girl who appreciates a diligent worker. She would not find you dull at all."

"Good day, Mrs. Hooper."

She gave him a sage grin. "And to you, Mr. Pearce. We'll speak again."

I can scarcely wait.

Customers began drifting in. Jude sold mostly copies of the *Gazette*, a few magazines, a dozen envelopes, and one copy of *The Duke's Children*. He had opportunity to think over what Mrs. Hooper had said to him later, on his way up Orchard Lane.

"Do you think I'm dull?" he asked Jinny, trotting a couple feet before him.

Jinny paused to give him a worried look and then went over to the side of the lane to sniff a clump of grass.

Rosalind doesn't think so, he assured himself. Hadn't he made her laugh on their first meeting, when she entered the shop needing a handkerchief?

That was before Mr. Smith.

Tall, affable, witty Mr. Smith. *Fun* Mr. Smith. Under the same roof.

Doesn't matter. Jealousy is childish. He's a gentleman.

And Rosalind had promised to inform him if she no longer wished to keep company. He trusted her integrity.

"Do come in," said Mrs. Deamer at the cottage door, seeming a bit ill at ease. "Miss Kent should be here very shortly."

"Did I misunderstand the invitation?"

"Not at all, Mr. Pearce. We're expecting you. She's on the green. Mr. Smith offered to teach the Fletcher boys to play rounders after breakfast." She looked past him. "And I hear voices . . ."

Jude turned. From down the lane, two boys advanced, chattering like magpies, with Rosalind and Mr. Smith following.

Rosalind and Mr. Smith lifted hands. He waved back. Jinny took that as an invitation to dash through the garden and whine at the gate.

"We'll go and meet them," Jude said to Mrs. Deamer.

Jinny bounded ahead and went to Rosalind, but then diverted her attention to the boys and their enthusiastic pats of her head and back.

"I'm sorry you had to wait," Rosalind said when they caught up to each other. She looked as fresh as sea air in a simple blue frock and a straw bonnet that did not conceal her flushed cheeks. "The boys begged for more innings."

"We had only just arrived," he assured her.

She nodded toward Albert and Danny, their faces being bathed by Jinny, and lowered her voice. "Mr. Smith drew other boys to the game like a magnet, and they were part of a group for possibly the first time in their lives."

Jude looked over at the two. If sheer joy could be personified, it would be their faces. He smiled. "I'm happy for them."

Mr. Smith came forward carrying ball and glove, a wooden bat tucked under one elbow. His face was sun reddened under dark hair standing in sweaty peaks. "Hallo, old chap. Wish you could have been there! Do say you'll join us next week."

"Thank you, but I would have to close shop for too long."

"Can you not wait and open after lunch on Saturdays?"

"It's my biggest day. Some of my patrons are from outlying farms and come to town only then."

He waited for Mr. Smith to echo Mrs. Hooper's sentiments regarding work and dullness. Instead, the man clapped him upon the arm and said, "Well then, it's no wonder your shop is successful. People appreciate a merchant who appreciates them."

"It's kind of you to say," Jude said, warming to the man. "By the by, I have my catching glove put away somewhere. It's quite worn, but if you can use it . . ."

"We can!" Mr. Smith said, proffering the one tucked into his elbow. "I daresay it's not as worn as this one."

Jude took the glove. The leather was indeed stiff and creased and mottled.

"It's suffered some abuse, all right. I carry it with me wherever I travel."

"It was a gift from his parents when he was fifteen," Rosalind said.

"At no small financial sacrifice to them. When Mrs. Kent mentioned the bat and ball in the cellar, it seemed meant to be." Mr. Smith shook his head and smiled sheepishly. "Enough sentiment for one day. Miss Shipsey is holding lunch."

"But first . . ." Rosalind turned to the boys, "Danny? Albert? Come and meet Mr. Pearce."

They got to their feet and closed the gap between them, Jinny trotting between.

"You must be Danny," Jude said to the older.

The boy gave him a shy nod but took the hand he extended. "And this is Albert. My brother."

"We like your dog," Albert said as they shook hands.

"Why, thank you. You must come to the shop and play with her."

"The shop?"

"His bookshop," his brother said. "Mr. Pearce sent those books to us, remember?"

"Will you send more?" Albert asked. "I don't much like the *Wonderland* book."

"Albert!" Danny and Rosalind said in unison.

Jude laughed. "Stop by, and we'll choose a better one together."

Miss Shipsey and Mrs. Deamer served roast leg of mutton at the dining table, where Albert and Danny took turns giving accounts of the game.

"I hitted the ball my first time!" Albert said.

"Because Mr. Smith pitched from up close," Danny said, though seemingly without malice. Indeed, the boy seemed protective of his younger brother, pulling out his chair and tucking a serviette under his chin. He validated Jude's observation by adding, "He stepped close for me too."

"You'll grow better with practice, lads," Mr. Smith said. "Just remember the first rule of rounders . . ."

"Is to have a jolly good time!" Albert said.

"That's the stuff!" Mr. Smith exclaimed.

"And did you do that?" Mrs. Kent asked. "Have a good time?"

Danny nodded. "I never wanted to stop."

Rosalind and Mrs. Kent listened to their accounts like doting mothers, and Jude was filled with boundless admiration. What could be more fulfilling than to change the course of a child's life?

"And we're to play again Saturday next!" Albert went on.

"Can you take time away from your work again, Mr. Smith?" Mrs. Kent asked.

Mr. Smith waved a hand. "I can make up for it weekdays. Besides, having taken time for play will enhance my work, so there is some selfishness here."

"Selfishness?" Rosalind said with a little smile.

The boys shook their heads, and Rosalind and Mr. Smith exchanged glances of such camaraderie that Jude felt a little pang.

You trust her integrity, he reminded himself.

Integrity was one thing, though.

Feelings were another.

He could not control hers. Nor would he wish to do so. He could only hope that his heart would not be broken yet again. He would be forced to leave Port Stilwell. *A man can endure only so much.*

42

First day of summer break! Noble thought, setting out on foot early Monday, the twenty-eighth of June. He minded not one whit, having his father wake him before sunrise. Better than having to help at the mercantile!

Thankfully, Father had jumped at his suggestion of a music box for Mother's almost-forgotten birthday. Where else but in Exeter? Why, he might just take his time. A good steward compared prices and quality, after all.

He was delighted to find only two other passengers at the railway station. Mr. and Mrs. George, farmers with some grown children in Ottery St. Mary. Perhaps he would have a carriage to himself.

They seemed equally delighted to see him, for Mrs. George waved him over to say, "Another grandson, Mr. Clark!"

"Outstanding! May he bring you much joy." Noble was happy to brighten their morning, for Mr. George was thoughtful enough to compliment his singing every time they crossed paths.

"Why, thank you, Mr. Clark," Mrs. George said, and to her husband, "Did you hear that, Alpheus?"

"DID WE BRING A TOY?" Mr. George shouted.

Mrs. George leaned closer to him. "HE HOPES HE BRINGS US MUCH JOY!"

"AH!" The man beamed, nodded. "THANK YOU, MR. CLARK. FINE SINGING, SUNDAY PAST!"

Noble thanked him, and when the locomotive steamed to a stop, escorted them to a carriage.

"Will you join us, Mr. Clark?" asked Mrs. George.

"I'm afraid I would be bad company." He touched his forehead. "Headache."

She clucked sympathy. Her husband gave him a blank smile. Noble bade them farewell, then passed three carriages before netting an unoccupied one.

As the final boarding whistle shrilled, he spotted a tall man dashing across the platform with a satchel and stack of small boxes tied together with ribbon. The fellow who had been escorting Coral to church, Noble realized. Mrs. Hooper's new lodger, Mr. Smith!

Coral . . .

Her sweet face came to his mind often of late. What a fool he was, courting Amy and attempting to court Miss Kent, when all along Coral was meant to be his true love!

He sighed, folded his arms, and propped his feet upon the facing seat. Would she forgive him? She had so many times, but that was before this giant lumbered into the picture. Noble burned with dislike. What was his business in Exeter? To buy a gift for Coral? Why had he himself never thought of doing so?

He spent the rest of the journey in a dark cloud. Insult to injury was when a man entered his carriage at Feniton and attempted to chat him up about the inquiry into the Tay Bridge tragedy of December past. What did Noble know of collapsed bridges? Pity that people lost their lives, but he could do nothing for them, and he was dying inside!

When they pulled into St. David's Station, he watched Mr. Smith cross the platform. Only then did Noble exit his carriage.

He threaded his way around departing and waiting passengers before drawing to a halt.

Some eight feet away, Mr. Smith stood with a lone box in his hands, his satchel resting beside a wastebin.

Noble sidestepped to behind a wide post and angled his head to watch.

Mr. Smith sent a glance to the right and left, then dropped the lid of the box into the bin. He scooped something bread-like with his fingers and shoved it into his mouth. Chewing, he tossed the box, wiped his hands with a handkerchief, and took up his satchel.

Noble watched him enter the station house before moving to the wastebin. The boxes were easy to spot on top of the other contents. Most of the lids were dislodged, revealing crumbs and bits of custard in some, full pastries in others.

He's insane! What other reason was there for such bizarre behavior? He would have to warn Coral. He imagined her smiling, beaming with gratitude while wiping a tear.

"You've saved me from a horrible mistake!"

As he entered the station house, Noble made a plan. He would begin his foray at Brown's Haberdashery. They did not carry music boxes, but he needed a new silk cravat for when he spoke to Coral.

Fleur-de-lis, he thought. Claret red and gray, perhaps?

The combination of her gratitude and his being dressed to the nines, and she would be his again! Amy would be heartbroken, of course, but such was life. He was beginning to tire of Amy, as it were, with her hints about marriage.

The boarding whistle shrieked behind him. Just before the arched doors leading to the city, a laughing small girl was lifted into the air by a pair of hands. A smartly dressed woman beamed at the scene and held a familiar-looking satchel. A porter pushed past with a trunk, and Noble could see the back of the man.

Mr. Smith.

He set down the girl and gave the woman a quick embrace. She stepped back with eyes shining while he took the little girl's hand.

Married!

The woman met Noble's eyes, gave him an odd look. Spinning around, Noble hurried to another exit, then out onto Station Road. A hand upon his shoulder jerked him backward. He found himself staring up at Mr. Smith.

"Why, hallo! You're the singer, aren't you? Why are you here?"

The giant hand still clamped his shoulder. Noble swallowed. "To purchase a music box for my mother."

Mr. Smith smiled. "Small world, isn't it? I'm here to meet with my editor for lunch, and my sister and niece insisted upon meeting my train."

"Lovely." Noble stretched his lips to show his sincerity.

He gasped as fingers dug into his shoulder bone.

"But I don't wish to have my personal business bandied about Port Stilwell. I shall have to insist that you forget that you saw me."

"Y-yes."

Mr. Smith studied him for a moment and moved his hand to clap his back. The motion propelled Noble a step forward.

"Good man! I look forward to hearing you sing on Sunday. A gift from God, your voice. Now, go and buy your music box. If I hear gossip, I will know its source."

Noble watched him walk back toward the woman and child just outside the station house. He realized that his hands were shaking.

Any joy from the prospect of browsing shops was gone. Noble entered a clock shop on Howell Road and purchased the first music box the assistant showed to him, a handsome wooden case with eight bells which played six tunes. Carrying the parcel to the station, he found an empty bench. Never had he felt so alone.

When the ten o'clock train pulled in, he did not look for an empty carriage but took one occupied by a pair of older women in animated conversation. They gave him terse nods and lowered their voices.

"I said to her that Milton is a hardworking man and deserving of shirts that are ironed."

"You did? And what did she say?"

"She said, 'What does it matter, when it's only the fish that sees him?'"

"Oh my!"

"Who sees our sheets? We iron them, don't we?"

The train started moving. Noble sighed, set his hat beside him, and rested the back of his head against his seat. If only Mr. Smith had not seen him. If only he had gone about his business instead of standing there and staring!

He sighed again. The women silenced and turned faces toward him. He did not recognize them from Port Stilwell.

"Forgive me," he said. "It's just that I've witnessed a tragedy."

Both sat straighter. One, with silk flowers upon her hat, said, "What happened?"

"Um . . . from where do you hail?"

"Feniton," both replied.

"Ah."

They were waiting, but Noble's hands began trembling again.

"Did someone die?" said the second woman. No hat covered her gray topknot.

He glanced at the windows and lowered his voice, as if Mr. Smith were sprinting alongside. "It concerns a young woman's beau."

"He's unfaithful!" the hatless woman hissed.

"I saw the evidence."

"Just like my sister's husband!" the hatted one said.

"But my life is in peril if I warn the young woman."

"Your life? He threatened you?"

A chill ran through him. He rubbed his shoulder. "Most emphatically."

They exchanged looks and stared. The sympathy upon their lined faces made him feel a bit better, not so alone in the world.

"Do you love her?" asked the hatless woman.

"But of course he does!" her companion said.

To Noble, she said, "What will you do?"

"Nothing," Noble said with a shudder. "I dare not."

The hatted woman stretched forward to pat his hand. "We can't fault you for being afraid. But how many chances does a young man have to be a hero?"

Noble's eyes watered. "None."

43

Early Tuesday morning at the front gate, Charlotte asked Mrs. Deamer, "Did you pack a wrap?"

"Yes." Mrs. Deamer lifted her portmanteau. It was especially fine, of burnished leather, and spoke of a more genteel life.

Charlotte was certain that her friend would rather possess a carpetbag and an unruffled past. Were Roger in prison, could she be as decent? She found herself rather enjoying that mental picture, so she pushed it from her mind.

"I changed the bathroom linens," Mrs. Deamer was saying as Rosalind joined them. "There are more in the cupboard if you need some before Friday."

"Don't worry," Charlotte said, and then looked out into the lane, toward the rattle of hooves and wagon springs. "Do I hear a carriage?"

Her daughter winked at her. A pair of horses came into view, followed by Mr. Plummer's wagon. Rosalind clapped her hands. "Very good!"

The plan was for Rosalind to accompany Mrs. Deamer to the station as part of her morning walk. Charlotte asked, "How did you arrange this?"

"I didn't. Jude insisted."

"I'm overwhelmed," Mrs. Deamer said. "Please thank Mr. Pearce."

Mr. Plummer led the horses to turn the wagon around and helped her into the seat beside him. From the gate, Charlotte and Rosalind wished her a safe journey.

"This cottage is too quiet," Rosalind said as they entered the hall.

"That will change when Mr. Smith returns." Charlotte turned to her. "What would you think of having the boys here every day for the summer? Except Sundays, of course."

"Have you the energy?" Rosalind asked.

"Oh yes. You?"

Rosalind nodded. "I could tutor them. I miss teaching."

"They're bright enough to become heads of class. Why don't you stop at the bank during your walk? Ask their father?"

Though Danny had assured them, perhaps too fervently, that their stepmother no longer mistreated them, Charlotte preferred to have all future dealings with Mr. Fletcher.

"Should we ask the boys first?" Rosalind suggested.

"They'll love the idea."

Her daughter frowned.

"What is it?"

"Please don't think I mean this to hurt you, but Aunt Vesta made every little decision for me, even chose my friends. I had no confidence in my own judgment. I didn't particularly care for Reginald upon first meeting, but when people said how perfect we were together, I assumed they knew more than I did."

Eyes clouding, Charlotte said, "I'm so sorry."

Her daughter put a hand upon her shoulder. "I would not appreciate these days so much had my past been perfect."

"Thank you, daughter." Charlotte patted her hand. "We'll speak with the boys, then."

Rosalind set out upon her walk, and Charlotte went inside,

into the kitchen. Coral stood polishing a copper pot, three more on the table before her.

"Can you do that sitting?" Charlotte asked.

Coral gave her a weary smile. "Not as vigorously."

"The cabbages are ready. Shall I pick one for supper?"

"You have a green thumb, Mrs. Kent. I'll cook it with some salt beef." She covered a yawn and glanced at the clock. "Ten of nine. The morning is crawling."

"He'll be here. Perhaps we shall need two cabbages."

The quip did not lighten Coral's expression. "What if Mrs. Hooper finds out?"

Charlotte sat at the table. "You used your own funds for ingredients, and baked during the time you would still have been abed."

"Even so, she could sack me for disloyalty."

"That's a huge *could*. Rosalind and I would stoutly protest."

Voices came from the hall, and Coral's face blanched.

"That's not her," Charlotte said, though in truth she wondered.

Rosalind entered, frowning. "I came upon Mr. Clark halfway down the lane. He says he has an urgent private message for Coral."

"Noble?" Coral blew out her cheeks. "Amy must have come to her senses. Would you please say to him that I want nothing to do with him?"

Quick footfalls sounded, and Mr. Clark sprinted into the room with blond hair wild about his head.

"I *must* speak with you, Coral!"

She shrugged. "Speak, then."

He swiveled glances at Charlotte and Rosalind. "Privately?"

"No," Coral said, setting the pot onto the table with a sharp rap.

He sighed and looked about. "When is Mr. Smith due back?"

"The eleven o'clock train," Charlotte replied.

He closed his eyes and groaned. "That's when I'm to leave. My bags are at the station. I shall have to get there early enough to hide."

"And why would you do that?" Rosalind asked.

"Because he threatened to harm me if I inform anyone that he's married! I saw him yesterday, with wife and child in Exeter Station!"

"I believe you're mistaken, Mr. Clark," Charlotte said after exchanging looks with Rosalind. "Perhaps his editor is a woman, who brought along her child? A sister?"

"This was his *wife*," Mr. Clark said. "A man can tell."

Coral pursed her lips. "He said his editor was a mister-something. Don't you remember, Mrs. Kent?"

"Why yes." Charlotte felt a bit queasy. Not only had he never mentioned a wife, but he'd given them to understand that he was a bachelor. Why, then, the deception?

"And he threw away some boxes," Mr. Clark went on.

"What did you say?" Coral asked.

"Pastries. They were yours, weren't they?"

"Mr. Clark, please have a seat," Charlotte said. "Let us all sit."

They gathered at the table, and Mr. Clark began. "I spied upon him from behind a post. He gobbled down two or three pastries and dropped the rest into a rubbish bin."

Covering her face with her hands, Coral cried, "Why did he offer? I never asked him to!"

"I would have thought better of him," Rosalind said. Her eyes met Charlotte's again. "Mother, are you all right?"

Charlotte nodded back, insides knotted. One did not have to be in theatre to be an actor. Were this an ordinary household, she would simply have been mystified, but she was certain now that Mr. Smith was either a reporter or connected to Roger.

With a strained voice, she said, "We are grateful to you for bringing this to our attention, Mr. Clark."

"I didn't intend to. I tossed and turned all last night, from fear of his finding out."

"Mr. Smith threatened you?" Rosalind said.

He rubbed his shoulder. "I have the bruises to prove it."

"Oh dear!" Charlotte exclaimed.

"That part, at least, was a blessing in disguise." Mr. Clark pulled in a breath. "I needed the push to get out of Port Stilwell."

Coral uncovered her tear-stained face "That's quite drastic, don't you think?"

Rosalind nodded. "What if you spoke with the constable?"

"You don't understand. I've no desire to be teaching when I'm forty, or working in the shop." He took his watch from his pocket, glanced at it. "I must leave soon."

"Where will you go?" Rosalind asked.

"London. It's been my dream since childhood. With so many performing venues, surely I'll find a place. I've got a bit of money saved."

He's going to starve, Charlotte thought. This was not the time to inform Noble that he greatly overestimated his gifts.

"Perhaps if you gave yourself a trial period," Rosalind was saying. "A fortnight?"

Tears sprang to his eyes. "I'll sweep streets if I must, until opportunity comes my way. If I don't do this now, I never will. Can you not understand?"

"I can," Charlotte said. "Wait here." Ignoring her daughter's odd look, she went upstairs to her writing table.

Dear Mr. Irving

I trust this finds you well. Can you possibly find some position for the bearer of this letter, Mr. Noble Clark? As a stagehand? A cleaner? He is desperate to perform, but I believe you will find his hands more practical than his voice.

Back in the kitchen again, she handed the envelope to him and said, "I cannot promise anything. If there is a position, it will be labor. But you would have access to trade newspapers and learn of auditions."

He stared at the envelope. "Mr. Henry Irving? But how do you . . ."

"It's a long story. Farewell, Mr. Clark."

"Thank you." He got to his feet and gave Coral an earnest look. "I'll come for you when I've made my mark. You'll forget all about Mr. Smith by then."

She frowned at him. "He *wasn't* my beau, Noble."

"He wasn't?"

"Never."

"Oh. I thought . . ." He cleared his throat. "I'll see myself out."

Safe journey, Charlotte thought as they listened to his footfalls.

Rosalind turned to her. "Could Lord Fosberry have sent Mr. Smith?"

"Why would he stay so long, then?" Charlotte replied. "He's surely a reporter."

"We should search his room."

"We can't intrude upon his privacy."

"We have due cause, Mother," Rosalind said.

Coral pushed her chair away from the table. "And, begging your pardon, but it's *my* room."

They entered and set to work. At the writing desk, Charlotte thumbed through blank sketching pages and *Johnson's Dictionary*. Rosalind and Coral unmade the bed and raised the mattress.

Nothing.

Charlotte moved on to rifle through the few clothes hanging in the wardrobe, Rosalind to the chest of drawers. Coral grimaced and felt inside a boot, then its mate.

"Would he have hidden anything in another part of the house?" Charlotte asked.

"He would want to keep it close," Coral said. She looked about the room, eyed the top of the wardrobe. "I wonder . . ."

She pulled the chair from the desk, dragging it across the carpet.

"Wait, Coral," Rosalind said. "I'm taller."

With Charlotte and Coral at either side of the chair, Rosalind lifted her skirts, climbed upon the seat, and looked over the top of the wardrobe.

"Eureka."

She brought down a handful of papers to spread upon the writing table.

An unsealed envelope bore the name *Thomas Smithson.*

"Could this be his actual name?" Charlotte said.

"If so, he's clever to use one similar to his own," Rosalind replied.

Also there were a railway timetable from Paddington Station and a torn sketch that had been wadded and then smoothed.

"Why, that's me," Charlotte said.

Her image sat upon a garden bench, reading a book. A long eraser tear scarred the paper. She assumed he had decided against tossing it into the stove, with the intent to copy it over.

"So it is you, Mrs. Kent," Coral said.

"He made me slim, at least. A camera would have alarmed me, so he was forced to improvise."

Rosalind opened the envelope. Inside were a half-dozen pound sterling banknotes. She tucked the flap again.

"One would expect him to hide his money," Charlotte said.

The banknotes and timetable could have been related to the assignment he claimed to have. But the sketch, combined with Mr. Smith's deception, was enough evidence against him.

"We should leave these where they are," Rosalind said.

"But what if he comes into here first?" Charlotte said. "I

would like the advantage of surprise, not give him time to make excuses."

"Very well." Her daughter scooped them up and stepped onto the bench again.

They straightened the room and returned to the kitchen, where the drama had begun. Coral filled the teakettle at the sink.

The safety she had felt but an hour ago was an illusion, Charlotte thought.

"Lavishing attention upon the boys," Rosalind said with tight expression. "Offering to help Coral. It was all calculated to win our trust. And our affection."

"Could it be that he was truthful in his reason for being here?" Charlotte ventured. "But then he recognized me and realized there was money to be had on the side?"

"I doubt that," Rosalind said. "There is likely no contract for a book. He's with a magazine or newspaper."

"I should have known," Charlotte said.

"How could you have?"

"He never questioned me about my life, my background. I'm certain it was so as not to arouse my suspicions, but it's unnatural for people who spend time together."

"How do you suppose he found you?" Rosalind asked.

Coral moved from the stove. "I've spoken to no one of you, Mrs. Kent. Not even to my family. I've learned to be discreet, as Mrs. Deamer put it."

"Thank you, Coral," Charlotte said, both relieved and guilty, for the thought had entered her mind.

"But . . ." Coral went on. "Mr. Smith did ask certain questions. Sometimes. In the course of conversation."

"Besides the church question you mentioned?"

"Yes."

"Such as?"

"Why do you never go anywhere . . . why is it that you and Miss Kent seem never to discuss any past happenings . . ."

Charlotte's pulse quickened. "And how have you answered?"

"Always the same. That I'm not at liberty to discuss."

"Why didn't you speak with us?" Rosalind said.

"Well, they seemed natural questions from someone under the same roof. And he would say he understood and change the subject, but it was harder and harder to keep things from him." Her lips tightened. "Especially after he offered to help me."

"I'm grateful to you, Coral," Charlotte said. And she felt the overwhelming urge to be alone. Mr. Hurst would not arrive to tend the garden until well after lunch. "I need to be out of doors for a while."

She went through the kitchen to a bench near the crabapple tree. Garden warblers sang a throaty contralto from the nearby wood, where salt breezes rattled the leaves. Gulls called to one another over the bay. The sounds of home.

Father, have I trusted the wrong man yet again? What should we do now? Your Word promises wisdom to those who ask for it. Please, please grant me that wisdom now.

44

"I won't allow this to involve you," Charlotte said when Rosalind joined her on the bench half an hour later.

"Don't say that, Mother." Her daughter took her hand. "We're a team."

Charlotte had to look away as she squeezed her hand.

"I wonder if our trust in Mr. Lockhart was misplaced," Rosalind said.

"Surely you don't suspect him."

"Who else can it be? Coral seems truthful. Mrs. Deamer's above reproach."

Coral brought out tea. Rosalind moved to the side so that she could put the tray between them. As she poured, Coral said, "Would you mind if I went up to the attic before Mr. Smith arrives? I can't bear the thought of facing him."

"Of course not," Charlotte replied.

"I'll leave sandwiches out for him."

"Why would you?" Rosalind asked.

"Because it's what Mrs. Hooper pays me to do," she said flatly.

"Oh dear. Well, don't poison him."

"I shan't, Miss Kent." She turned to leave, saying over her

shoulder, "Though I can't promise not to overcrank the pepper mill."

That made Charlotte chuckle.

Stirring sugar into her tea, Rosalind said, "It's good to hear you laugh."

"Churchyard humor."

"We should rethink moving. If he's a reporter, then it's but a matter of time before Lord Fosberry finds you."

"It'll be a matter of time for the remainder of my years," Charlotte said with a sigh. "People depend upon us. People whom God put into our lives. I don't believe He means for us to abandon them. We've put down roots that I'm not prepared to rip from the ground."

Rosalind's eyes narrowed. "You aren't referring to cabbages, are you?"

Charlotte laughed again and took a sip from her cup.

Mr. Smith came through the kitchen door, scanned the garden, and brightened. "Ah, my favorite ladies!"

"And so it begins," Charlotte murmured.

"For shame, Mr. Smith!" Rosalind said when he was but eight feet away.

He stopped short, smiling still, though cautiously. "I beg your pardon?"

"Or shall I say, Mr. Smithson?"

His brow furrowed. "You . . . went through my belongings?"

"You have *no* right to be outraged!"

Charlotte's racing heart made her lightheaded. She was glad for Rosalind's control of the situation.

He took a step closer, palms outstretched. "I can explain. I adopted a pen name. It's not so uncommon . . . George Eliot, Mark Twain."

"And the woman and child you were seen with in Exeter?"

He blew out a sigh, dropped his arms. "They're my sister

and her daughter, from Lynton. I breakfasted with them before meeting my editor."

"You never mentioned that they would be there," Rosalind said.

His expression tightened. "Miss Kent, do you suggest I'm obligated to give you every detail of my life?"

"Why did you discard Miss Shipsey's pastries?"

Cheeks flushed, he replied, "I meant to protect her. The creams had soured. She wouldn't have wanted me to give them out. I could have discarded them at Port Stilwell Station, could I have not?"

"Someone may have seen you here," Rosalind said. "And if they were spoiled, why did you eat some?"

"How else would I have known they were spoiled? She gave me one for the journey. Ask her."

The umbrage in his face weakened Charlotte's certainty of his guilt. But the fear in Mr. Clark's had seemed equally genuine. She said, "The person who saw you said he was threatened."

"The singer!" He folded his arms. "Odd fellow. He frightened my little niece, Betsy, with his standing there and staring. He wouldn't leave when I asked politely; thus, I helped him to see the wisdom in it. I'm not sorry to say I would do it again."

"Um . . ." Rosalind said while Charlotte also floundered for words.

"Miss Kent . . . Mrs. Kent." He took a step forward, his expression earnest. "It's me. Tobias. I like to think that we're friends."

There was still something troubling to sort out, Charlotte reminded herself. "Why did you sketch a picture of me when I asked you not to do so?"

He halted. "Actually, you said you would rather not pose for one. I sketch all the important people in my life, to have something to give to them when I leave."

"Whom else have you sketched?"

"Why, Miss Kent. Danny and Albert. Mrs. Deamer and Miss Shipsey." He gave a dry chuckle. "Mrs. Hooper . . . naturally."

"Are there any more of me?"

"None, Mrs. Kent." His expression seemed without guile. He was either innocent or a very good liar. "Why should there be?"

Danny and Albert were fond of him, Charlotte thought. As was Jinny. Weren't children and dogs supposed to be keen judges of character?

"May we *see* the contents of your satchel?" Rosalind asked. "Now?"

"If you please. If we're wrong, you'll have our deepest apologies."

Charlotte waited. What a relief it would be, and not only for the peace of mind she could enjoy for a while longer. Mr. Smith had brought lightheartedness and energy into the cottage. Even laughter. She did not want that to end.

His shoulders sagged, and he covered a yawn. "Very well. But I've had just three hours' sleep. May this wait until after I've rested?"

It was tempting to agree. Yet if he had extra sketches of her or a story, or both, where would he hide them this time?

"What do you think, Mother?" Rosalind whispered.

If he's indeed devious, he'll find a way, Charlotte thought. *And wouldn't an innocent person insist upon showing the evidence at once?*

She got to her feet. "This will take but a moment, Mr. Smith."

Rosalind stood as well.

Mr. Smith stared at them, seeming to cast about for words. At length, he walked to the second bench, lifted it, and placed it three feet away, facing them.

"A gentleman doesn't sit when ladies are standing," he said with a dry smile.

Charlotte and Rosalind sat.

Folding himself into the bench, he clasped hands upon a crossed knee. "Thomas Smithson is my name. I'm a reporter for *The Cornhill Magazine.*"

Charlotte closed her eyes and groaned.

"Why?" Rosalind asked.

"My family's livelihood," he replied. "To make a name. Why does one do anything of worth?"

"You count invading my privacy as a thing of worth?" Charlotte asked.

"I beg your pardon, Mrs. Kent, but when one decides upon a stage career, is it not disingenuous to speak of privacy?"

"*One* should have a choice as to how much *one* wishes to expose. Do you not have curtains in your windows?"

He shrugged.

Glaring, Rosalind said, "You fooled us completely, didn't you?"

"A tool of the trade, Miss Kent. I took no pleasure in it."

He turned to Charlotte, softening his voice. "It may be that this could benefit both of us. Of late, actual photographs are beginning to crop up in magazines and newspapers. If you would but allow me to hire a photographer—"

"No."

"Please bear with me," he rushed on. "The magazine would pay twice as much. I would gladly share that with you."

"Absolutely not."

He gave her a sly look, alarming in what she had once considered a pleasant face.

"As the story will come out in any event, would you not rather have some control over it?"

His message was clear: He could write anything he wished. Her life here was too mundane for an interesting story. Make her a drunkard, give her a lover. Or three. Not only would Roger find her, but with more ammunition for the divorce.

"And you offer this because . . ." Charlotte said.

"I truly admire you. My parents saw you in several productions in your day."

"Your *servant* parents?" Rosalind said.

"Please forgive me that bit of fiction," he said sheepishly. "They're far from peerage, in any event. My father owns a tailor shop and is solidly middle-class."

"You played upon our sympathies to earn our trust," Charlotte said. "The same reason you befriended Danny and Albert and pretended to help Coral."

He actually looked embarrassed.

"Please . . . Mr. Smith . . . Smithson," Rosalind said, as if encouraged by this small evidence of humanity. "You have no idea of the harm you'll cause my mother."

"Harm? Having a reporter knock now and again? You're not obligated to invite us indoors, you know."

"There is more to it than that."

"Is there?"

The corners of his mouth twitched and then froze, as though he was working hard to restrain them. Meeting Charlotte's eyes again, he said, "I'm ambitious, Mrs. Kent, but not without heart. You have been kind to me. I would cut off an arm before doing you actual harm. What is it that you fear?"

She had a ready answer. "I fear men such as you, Mr. Smith. You offer me money, not from any kindness but because it would advance your reputation. You offer sympathy to prod for more information to print."

Frowning, he got to his feet. "Very well, ladies. It appears I have a train to catch."

Rosalind rose as well. "Wait, Mr. Smith."

He continued across the garden.

"Who informed you that Mother was here? You owe us that much!"

But he left without turning.

Charlotte sent up a prayer. *Thank you for prompting me to ask about the etchings.*

"So, we're back to where we began," Rosalind said, sinking back onto the bench.

"I'm afraid so." Charlotte was still in a prayerful mode, and the thought that followed was, *Is there any way to stop this from happening, Father? I'm not after vengeance, and I understand that we're to turn the other cheek. But if I can prevent or even lessen the blow beforehand, will you show me how?*

"Mother?"

Charlotte blinked at Rosalind. "I was praying for direction."

"And did you get an answer?"

"Not as yet."

"Well, I shall set out in the *direction* of Mr. Lockhart's office and demand explanation."

"We're not certain it was him," Charlotte said.

Coral hurried from the cottage. "Mr. Smith just left!"

"He confessed," Charlotte said. "He's a reporter."

Closing her eyes, Coral groaned. "I'm so sorry . . ."

"What is it?" Charlotte rose and went over to her with Rosalind following.

Coral wiped her eyes upon the end of her apron and said with a thick voice, "I may have said too much. A fortnight after he arrived, he asked how Danny and Albert came to be here. He promised not to say anything."

"You mentioned the stepmother?" Charlotte asked.

"I was so proud of what we . . . what you've done for them." With a pitiably hopeful expression, she said, "But he won't write anything about them, will he? They're not even famous."

"They're a major part of Mother's life," Rosalind said. "There isn't much else taking place here."

"I'm so sorry!" Coral cried again. "What have I done?"

What have you done? Charlotte asked herself even as she patted Coral's back.

45

Rosalind waited until Mr. Smith was a speck in the distance. Never did she want to see his face again. Years of daily walks had made her fast on her feet. Within twenty minutes, she was peering through Mr. Lockhart's dusty window.

He sat at his desk, writing on a tablet. She had to rap upon the door twice before he raised his head and squinted in her direction.

"Miss Kent?" he said, holding open the door. "Is something the matter?"

"There is something very much the matter, Mr. Lockhart."

"Please." He took her elbow and led her to a chair, then sat in the one beside her. "How may I assist you? Is your mother all right?"

The concern in his expression almost disarmed her of the righteous anger that had fueled her walk. Almost.

"Did you betray us?"

His brows lifted. "Someone found her. It was only a matter of time. She was served a claim form?"

That his initial concern was for her mother and not to defend himself tempered Rosalind's hostility a bit. In any event, she had no choice but to relate today's events.

"Will she consider moving?" he asked.

"She's set firmly against it."

"Pity. Why did you not inform me that another lodger had arrived?"

Why, indeed? she asked herself.

"We meant to. But then he seemed so benign and pleasant, and we assumed if we were careful about what we said . . ."

He gave an aggrieved sigh.

"Mrs. Hooper pushed him onto us," Rosalind said by way of defense. A thought struck her. "Do you think she's behind this?"

"Who can say? Probably not. But it wasn't I. At this point, whether you believe that is not important. Just that you trust me enough to take action."

She pulled in a breath. "What sort of action?"

"Immediate action. You must go to London."

"Mr. Smith's train has not left. Can you not go to the station and confront him?"

"To what avail, Miss Kent? He knows that my effectiveness is limited."

You could punch him, Rosalind thought.

"Now, it would be best if your mother accompanied you. But would she be able to bear London again?"

"You're serious."

"Indeed."

"I shall have to ask. It'll be a shock."

"Remind her that no one expects her, thus I do not think she would be harassed."

"She has a half veil," Rosalind said.

"Perfect!"

He went around to his desk and took a sheet of paper from a drawer.

"The last train leaves at half past four, which would have you arrive at nine."

"Leave today?"

"Yes. Visit Mr. Benjamin Miller at this address before eight o'clock in the morning. He's a highly respected solicitor, the top of our class at University College. Bright enough to be a barrister, would that his nerves allowed him to argue in court."

"But he doesn't know us."

"He knows me." He scribbled onto the paper, folded it, and brought it to her. "Have you currency enough for the journey?"

"I have." Rosalind had stormed off without reticule, so she slipped the paper into her sleeve.

"Good. Your withdrawing money could arouse suspicion. We cannot risk someone telegraphing to warn him. The fewer people aware that you're leaving, the better."

This could be an act, she thought. *He could be the one to telegraph Mr. Smithson.* But she so wanted to trust.

"Miss Kent?" His voice broke into her thoughts.

"It wasn't you?" she asked.

He chuckled. "You would be dense not to suspect me. But we haven't time to gather character references. Now, go straight home. I'll come for you in an hour and a half to drive you to the station. Pack light. I expect you'll be there but a day or two."

"Thank you, Mr. Lockhart."

"My pleasure."

She set out up Fore Street with thoughts occupied over how Mother would react to her news. At the first corner, she automatically looked to the left.

Few people were out and about. Where was the harm in veering over to the bookshop? It did not seem right to up and leave town without informing Jude.

Just a day or two, she reminded herself and continued on. They had seen each other just yesterday. She would be back before he realized she was away.

In the parlor, Mother sat with eyes closed and head against the back of the sofa.

"Mother? Are you asleep?"

She raised her head, looking very weary. "Just resting my eyes."

"Can you bear to go to London with me? You could wear your veil."

"But why?"

"To see a solicitor whom Mr. Lockhart highly recommends. We would need to leave in an hour."

"Today?"

"I'm afraid so. I'll do this alone if you—"

"No. We'll both go." She rose to her feet.

Rosalind packed her bag and went into the kitchen. Coral stood at the table, chopping a cabbage.

"Mother and I need to go to London."

Coral's knife went still. "Now?"

"When Mr. Lockhart comes for us. We should return in a day or two. Will you pack some sandwiches?"

"Of course. This has been a day for trains. Will Mr. Lockhart go as well?"

"No, but he directed us to another solicitor."

"You trust him, then."

"I do." Rosalind shrugged. "I think."

She thought of asking her to speak to Jude. But he would want to know the reason, and she wanted it to come from her. He had surely had enough of *"Trust me, I'll explain later."*

Little over an hour later, Mr. Lockhart was stashing their bags and Coral's basket beneath a train carriage seat.

"Go with God, ladies," he said.

46

Jude stepped outside his shop. His last patron had departed with a copy of *Fry's Almanac* an hour ago. In either direction, a half-dozen townspeople went about their affairs. None were headed in his direction, so he went back inside to lock the moneybox.

"Stay," he said when Jinny had taken a couple of hopeful paces toward the door. "I'll be but a moment."

Jinny gave him a wounded look but went back to flop against the counter. Just in case a customer did enter while he was away, her presence would signal that he would return shortly. His regulars would feel free to browse the shelves.

He passed Mr. Blyth's tobacco shop and walked into Clark Mercantile.

"Have you any rounders catching gloves?" he asked. "Small, that is. I should like to buy two."

Mr. Clark scratched his blond beard, turned to the shelves behind and took down a box sandwiched between badminton birdies and shoelaces. "There has been a sudden interest in the game."

"Yes, I offered my old one to a friend a fortnight ago but can't locate it. I may have donated it to the church jumble sale."

Mr. Clark moved aside the lid and handed over two gloves.

Jude held the supple leather of one and imagined the dull smart of ball against padded palm. *I should hire an assistant. Make time for such—*

"More padding there," said Mr. Clark. "It's a new company. Even sent a left-hander, which I sold to Mr. Travers for his son. The boy was so grateful, I thought he would weep."

"How nice that they make a left-handed glove."

"It actually goes on the right hand, as you can imagine." A frown tugged the corners of Mr. Clark's mouth. "Yes, the Travers boy knew how to express gratitude. Unlike *some* sons."

"I'm sorry," Jude said, hoping not to be pressured to listen to a tale of family dispute while needing to return to his shop. The brand name embroidered near the hem of the glove caught his eye.

Urry.

Identical to that on Mr. Smith's glove. Which was, as Jude recalled, well padded.

"This isn't a new company."

"Aye, but it is. Relatively speaking." Mr. Clark lifted the box, showed him the smaller script beneath the brand name. *Established 1877.*

"Perhaps they went out of business for a span of time? I saw an old glove recently bearing the same name."

"That's highly unlikely, Mr. Pearce. I had never heard of them before and have been doing this for nigh forty years. Besides, you can believe they would use the earliest date they have. We Brits appreciate dinosaurs."

Jude fished three shillings from his pocket. *Don't ask. None of your affair.*

"Is anything the matter, Mr. Pearce?" Mr. Clark asked.

"Have you sold these to only boys?" Jude found himself asking.

"Yes, apart from a tall fellow who required one for a nephew."

Carefully, Jude asked, "What if I wished to age this glove?"

"Age?"

"Make it appear well used. Older."

Mr. Clark pursed his lips. "Wouldn't be difficult. Soak it in seawater, dry it in the sun. Pound it with stones. But why, in heaven's name, would you do such a thing?"

"I wouldn't. Just one of those things to wonder. Such as . . . where do odd stockings go?"

"Ah. Curiosity killed the cat, Mr. Pearce."

Jude smiled. "Good that I have a dog."

On his return walk, he thought that it was obvious why Mr. Smith would do such a thing. Men, himself included, would do almost anything for a woman's praise. It began with their mothers, he suspected, for one of his earliest memories was of perching upon the side of a pool, calling for his own to watch him jump into the water.

His eyes smarted, and he reined his thoughts back to the situation at hand.

Women were blessed with deeper sentiment than men. He envied them that. A glove with a poignant family history would be more appreciated than one purchased after Mrs. Kent mentioned the ball and bat in the cellar.

But to invest such effort for fleeting praise meant, surely, that Mr. Smith was keen on Rosalind. How could Jude fault any man for recognizing what a gem she was?

Did he wish Mr. Smith would leave Port Stilwell?

Yes! Tomorrow!

But could he fault him? No, of course not.

Something troubled him about the man, though.

It's your own jealousy, he said to himself.

47

Darkness made strings of jewels of the lamplit windows of the tenements branching out from Waterloo Bridge Station.

A different story behind every one.

One part of a transient childhood was curiosity over the lives of stationary people. Did any look from their windows and wonder at the people in moving trains?

"Mother?"

Charlotte turned. Rosalind's face was somber with concern.

"I'm fine," she murmured over the rustle of belongings being gathered by Mr. and Mrs. Vacher.

They had not had the liberty to speak of their situation since the young couple boarded at Bridgwater, but then, what more was there to say? Her fear that London would chew her up and spit her out yet again? As comforting as it would be to lean on her daughter, Charlotte had been a burden long enough.

And there was an advantage to knowing the city like the back of her hand.

"We shall need to stay on Waterloo Road for the night," she said as they disembarked onto platform 7. Beneath the four-faced clock reading twenty past nine, some four-dozen passengers moved toward exit doors, their voices echoing through the almost-empty station.

"Perhaps tomorrow we'll have opportunity to look for something clean but reasonable in Kensington," she went on.

Rosalind smiled, some of the worry leaving her face.

A man upward of forty advanced, with trim beard, fine clothes, and an intent expression. Charlotte tightened her grip upon her bag and nudged Rosalind's arm. The best thieves did not look the part.

He glanced over his shoulder and said softly, "I beg your pardon, ladies, but would you happen to be acquainted with a Mr. John Lockhart from Port Stilwell?"

Charlotte stared at him, needing a moment to absorb his unexpected appearance.

Rosalind was quicker. "Mr. Miller?"

"I am," he replied.

"We were to look you up tomorrow," Charlotte said with recovered composure.

"Mr. Lockhart telegraphed, asking if I would meet two women, one wearing a veil and a younger with brown hair. I was intrigued. May I ask your names?"

"He didn't say?"

"He wanted as few people as possible to know we were leaving," Rosalind said, "and he wouldn't have been able to include your name on a telegram in any case."

Rosalind offered her hand to Mr. Miller. "I'm Rosalind Kent, and this is my mother, Charlotte Ward."

"Indeed?" He smiled at Charlotte. "What an honor! Mrs. Miller and I were among the audience hissing you in *Lady Audley's Secret.*"

Charlotte offered her hand. "Thank you, Mr. Miller."

"My pleasure. May I carry your bags? My coach is outside."

He was inviting them to stay in his home, Charlotte realized. "You're very kind, but we wouldn't think of imposing."

"I beg you to reconsider," he said. "When my wife learns whom I was to meet, she'll be gravely disappointed at the missed opportunity to have you stay under our roof."

And thus it was that, minutes later, they were crossing Waterloo Bridge in a plush coach behind a team of four horses. The relief over having been met so warmly and not having to find a hotel room so late made Charlotte almost giddy.

"How did you come to be acquainted with Mr. Lockhart?" she asked with hat and veil in her lap.

"We shared a staircase at University College London and became fast friends. I've tried to persuade him to join my practice here, but to no avail."

His tone became serious. "We have a half-hour ride. Given your identity and that this is the first favor Mr. Lockhart has asked of me, I assume your situation is urgent?"

Charlotte explained from the beginning, then gave over to Rosalind to recount her meeting with Roger's solicitor, Mr. Pankhurst.

Mr. Miller listened with head tilted, the light from gas lamps moving across his face at intervals. "It's good that you did not delay. I shall visit the office of *The Cornhill Magazine* in the morning."

"Can you stop the story?" Rosalind asked.

He shook his head. "I'm afraid not. But we'll threaten a lawsuit for libel if a grain of it is untrue."

"A lawsuit." Charlotte sighed.

"I realize that theatre people have learned that fighting scandal fans the flames," he said, "hence, even the most outrageous claims see print. But you already have one falsehood to disprove in a divorce court. You simply cannot afford more."

And Danny and Albert cannot afford to go back to where they were, Charlotte thought. There was no guarantee that Mr. Fletcher would stay strong in his family were his reputation ruined.

"Will they take your threat to heart?" Rosalind asked.

He fell silent for one, two, three, four shifts of light across his face. The fifth reflected a smile. "I believe they will."

The coach turned northward and slowed. Through the left window, Charlotte thought she recognized the dark forms of the trees of Hyde Park, which would mean they were on Park Lane. They rocked to a gentle stop outside a three-storey mansion of ghostly white stone. Seconds later, the coach door was opened by the driver, a young man in livery dress.

"Mr. Miller, I am certain we cannot afford you," Charlotte said.

"Ah, but you can, Mrs. Ward. As I made mention, this is the first favor Mr. Lockhart has ever asked. My assisting you would go toward the great debt I owe to him."

"And what debt is that, may I ask?"

"Few students at university desired to room with the Hebrew fellow."

"You're Jewish?" Rosalind asked.

"Miller is a common name among us. John Lockhart thought nothing of it and became a fast friend."

He motioned toward the open coach door. "Shall we?"

A housemaid in black and white opened the door. They went from a marble-floored hall with a massive staircase, into a parlor with warm paneled walls. A woman with startlingly short auburn curls put aside her needlepoint canvas and rose from a sofa.

"And so these are our mystery guests, Mr. Miller? Welcome to our home."

Charlotte warmed to her at once. She crossed the carpet and took the proffered hand.

"Mrs. Miller . . . your husband is a true Galahad."

Mrs. Miller nodded. "Always."

"I'm pleased to introduce . . ." her husband began.

His wife touched a finger to her lips and studied Charlotte. "Theatre?"

"In another life," Charlotte replied.

"Are you Charlotte Ward?"

"I am. I was. And this is my daughter, Rosalind Kent."

"Oh my!" Mrs. Miller squeezed her hand, then went over to offer hers to Rosalind. "We must have a long talk about your experiences. There is so much I am keen to know."

"Ruth . . ." said her husband. "They've traveled a long way."

They had indeed, and both were on the waning side of an emotionally draining day. But like her host, Charlotte believed one good turn deserved another.

"If I may freshen up and see my daughter off to bed, we'll have our long chat."

Mrs. Miller endeared herself even more by shaking her head. "Over breakfast."

She rang for a housemaid, who led them upstairs to elegantly appointed bedchambers and offered to run baths. For all her exhaustion, and in spite of a bath and clean sheets, Charlotte tossed and turned, her mind dragging her again and again through the day's events.

⊷⟨⟩⊶

Too early, someone rubbed her shoulder.

"Mother? It's ten o'clock."

Charlotte opened her eyes, roused herself from her pillow, and took note of her daughter's dress and straw hat. "Why didn't you wake me earlier?"

"Mrs. Miller forbade it."

"What a dear woman. Have you breakfasted?"

Rosalind smiled. "I have and took a turn through the park. I've been invited to look over their library but thought to look after you."

Charlotte hurried through her toilette, downstairs, and into the parlor.

Mrs. Miller brushed aside her apologies and rang for a tray. "I've had more time to think of questions to ask."

Between bites of the toast and jam and tea, Charlotte answered those questions. Her hostess, as she suspected, had had aspirations toward theatre in younger years.

"Is Edward Sothern as amusing in person as onstage?" Mrs. Miller asked.

"Even more so. He has almost a mania for practical jest."

The conversation distracted Charlotte from thinking of the trouble at hand. Still, the day crawled. Mr. Miller returned after lunch, when Charlotte, Rosalind, and Mrs. Miller were ensconced in wicker chairs in the luscious garden.

"They have lost readership to more recent magazines and cannot afford to lose a libel suit," he informed them. "I gave them to understand that I work closely with Barrister Emil Helsby. He's well-known for having won the verdict for the defendants in the Peerless Case."

All Charlotte recalled of newspaper accounts of that case was that it had to do with shipping.

"They have agreed to allow you to read Mr. Smith's story before it is published and will remove anything you perceive as injurious to your reputation."

That was good, or at least the best she could hope for.

"Can we afford Mr. Helsby?"

Mr. Miller smiled. "He'll be most reasonable. It is good to have friends. And should there be a divorce trial, he would consider it a privilege to represent you in court."

Charlotte breathed a sigh. "I'm so grateful, Mr. Miller."

"But there is more," he went on. "The Fletcher boys are to remain."

Voice flat, she said, "Their story isn't 'injurious to my reputation.'"

"Exactly so."

"Why is including them so important?" Rosalind asked.

"Because this is the age of Dickens, may he rest in peace. It tugs upon the heartstrings, the failed actress putting aside her misery to lift them up from abuse. Pardon me for putting it that way, but that's how the magazine plans to tell it."

He leaned forward. "As your attorney, I must advise you that such a story would help your case in a divorce court."

"No. They can accuse me of failure and misery if it so pleases, but I'll not have the boys suffer. Is there anything you can do?"

"I assumed you would reply so. They've offered a compromise. If you'll pose for a photograph and allow them to publish it, they will omit all reference to the boys' troubled home life. Only that you struck up a touching friendship with them."

This was greatly disappointing but better than the worst she had feared.

"Will they hold to that?" Charlotte asked.

"I have it in writing. A lawsuit for breach of contract is more easily won . . . and less sensational . . . than one for libel."

"Mother?" Rosalind asked.

Charlotte's eyes stung. "I have no choice. But I ask one thing."

"And that is?"

"That we do not see Mr. Smithson throughout this entire process."

48

The tree behind the Bickle cottage sagged with plums. Now that they had regular meals, Danny and Albert did not have to set upon them like locusts. Sweetness was their goal more than sustenance. The lowest limb, which Danny jumped to bring lower, provided enough fruits to satisfy.

"Let's bring some to Miss Shipsey," he said to Albert while wiping juice from his chin with his sleeve.

"We haven't a basket," Albert said.

"We can carry them in our arms."

"I want to climb."

"Very well. I'll help you up, and you can toss them to me."

He gave Albert a boost and was soon catching plums and picking missed ones from the grass. When they had a good number, he helped his brother from the tree. They sat upon the grass and sorted out those with visible wormholes, leaving fourteen with unblemished satiny red skin.

Albert took a bite of the biggest.

"Why did you do that?" Danny asked.

His brother looked apologetic but continued chewing.

Rather than trust him to carry, Danny took off his shirt and bundled the plums into the cloth.

"Perhaps she'll make a pudding and invite us to stay," Albert said between chews as they set out for Orchard Lane.

"It's not Christmas."

"But if we ask?"

"You don't give a gift and then ask for it to be returned, which would be the same."

When their knocks were not answered at the yellow cottage, they went around to the garden. No one. Danny decided they should leave the plums upon the porch.

"Let's look for a basket in the hut."

The kitchen door opened, and Miss Shipsey exclaimed, "I *thought* I heard voices! I was upstairs, packing my room."

She exclaimed over the fruit and invited them into the kitchen. Everyone was away, she said, but the dairyman had delivered, thus she needed them to help drink the milk before it soured.

"Where are they?" Danny asked as they stepped inside.

"Away. As I said."

"In the shops?" Albert asked.

"No," she replied.

"Mr. Smith too?"

"Yes."

"When did they leave?"

"Yesterday. Will you have almond biscuits with your milk?"

"Yes, please," Danny said.

She handed him his shirt. "Then go and wash your hands."

When they returned with decidedly cleaner hands, two beakers of milk and a plate of biscuits waited upon the table.

Danny sat, took a biscuit, and thanked her before taking a nibble.

Albert shoved two in a row into his mouth and gulped from his beaker. Turning to Miss Shipsey, he said, milk drooling down his chin, "Are they in Exeter?"

"No. Wait and swallow before you speak, Albert. And do try and keep crumbs from the floor."

Miss Shipsey's pinched expression worried Danny. Had something happened to Mrs. Kent and the others?

Still, he nudged his brother. "Stop asking questions."

"But will Mr. Smith return by Saturday to play rounders?"

"Mercy!" Miss Shipsey exclaimed. "You do go on and on!"

Albert ceased chewing. His milky bottom lip began to tremble.

She stepped closer and put a hand upon his shoulder. "I'm sorry, Albert. I'm just out of sorts. None of your doing."

He swiped a hand under his nose and blinked up at her. "You're not out of sorts. You're nice."

That made her laugh. She patted his shoulder, went around the table, and pulled out a chair. Resting elbows upon the table and leaning forward, she said, "You're dear boys. I can't bear the thought of your hopes being crushed. Mr. Smith's job finished early so he returned home."

"He's gone?" Danny said.

She mumbled something he did not understand and nodded. "He wasn't meant to be here forever, remember?"

"Where does he live?" Albert said.

"He lives in London."

Danny watched his brother wipe his eyes. He did not wish to think ill of Mr. Smith, but it was unkind to up and leave without a good-bye. It left a person empty. Mother had done so, only she had had no choice.

"Is that where Mrs. Kent and Miss Kent and Mrs. Deamer are?" he asked.

Miss Shipsey locked eyes with him. "The *three of them* are not in London. And that's enough of that."

Danny nodded.

Knocks sounded.

"Mrs. Kent!" Albert exclaimed.

"She wouldn't have to knock," Danny reminded him.

Miss Shipsey wore the pinched expression again as she got to her feet. "Finish your milk and biscuits."

At the doorway leading to the hall, she looked back at them before closing the door with a decisive click.

"Something's wrong," Danny whispered to Albert.

Albert stopped chewing again, eyes wide. "Did they die?"

"No!" Of that, he was certain. Or almost certain. Danny slipped from the chair.

"Where are you going?"

"Sh-h-h! Stay put!"

It was wrong to spy upon Miss Shipsey. But Danny had to have relief from the dread growing inside. He crept across the kitchen to the door and angled his head down so that his ear met the keyhole.

"—the loveliest pup in the world? I wish I had a treat for you!"

A man's voice came next. Mr. Pearce's, he realized. "I assumed she would have long since returned from her walk. Perhaps I'll happen upon her on my way back."

"Um . . . she's not in town. She and Mrs. Kent are away."

"I see. Are they in Exeter?"

"No, sir."

"Is everything all right, Miss Shipsey? I don't mean to pry, but I was told it's important that Mrs. Kent stay close to home."

Another silence, then, "They're in London, Mr. Pearce."

Danny thought, *London?* But Miss Shipsey had said otherwise at the table. He pressed his ear harder.

"I don't think she will mind my saying as much," Miss Shipsey went on, "but only to you. Please keep that to yourself."

"Are they in some sort of trouble?"

"I'm sorry, Mr. Pearce, but it would be best to come from them."

"Have you any idea when they'll return?"

"Soon, I should expect. You'll understand when Miss Kent explains."

Another silence fell, and then Mr. Pearce said, "Will you

give these rounders gloves to Mr. Smith, then? I've misplaced the one I promised, but the Fletcher boys should each have one in any case."

Danny's pulse leapt.

"How very kind of you," Miss Shipsey said.

Wait! Danny thought. Why did Miss Shipsey not say that Mr. Smith was in London as well?

"And when you see the boys," Mr. Pearce went on, "do invite them to come round and choose more books."

"I shall."

Mr. Pearce said then that he must return to his shop. Even from his listening point, Danny recognized disappointment in his voice.

He crept back to his chair.

"Who is it?" Albert said.

"Later. Don't ask *any* questions."

The door swung open, and Miss Shipsey breezed into the kitchen. "That was Mr. Pearce. He brought these gloves. Wasn't that lovely?"

"For us?" Albert said and winced at Danny.

"But of course!" She laughed and held one up in each hand. Placing the smaller before Albert, she said, "They're certainly not for me. Will you have more milk?"

"If you please?" Albert replied.

"No, thank you," Danny said, trying on his glove. The leather smelled sharp yet sweet, and it was soft against his skin. He stretched out his fingers and thought he had never owned anything so fine.

Later, they walked down the lane with full bellies and gloves upon left hands. Danny felt uneasy, relating everything he had heard at the door, but there was no one else in whom he could confide with Mrs. Kent away. Father spoke more nowadays, but he still looked tired around the eyes, and so Danny did not wish to trouble him.

"Why did she not say to him that we were there?" Albert asked.

"I don't know why."

"Will they come back? Miss Kent and Mrs. Kent and Mrs. Deamer?"

"She said that they would."

"They must!"

"Yes."

Three or four steps later, Albert turned to him. "We should thank Mr. Pearce. You're supposed to show gratitude."

"I don't think now is a good time."

"But he has more books for us."

"That's why you want to go. Not to thank him."

"I want to do both," Albert said.

As did Danny. More books *would* be nice. What else had they to do?

"As long as you don't mention what I heard at the door."

Mr. Pearce's dog, Jinny, rose from beneath the bookshop window as they drew close. They crouched beside her on either side and laughed when she licked crumbs from their faces. Mr. Pearce came out.

"Good afternoon, boys."

Danny got to his feet. "Good afternoon, sir. Thank you for the gloves."

Mr. Pearce's brows lifted over a smile. "You're welcome. But how did you get them so quickly?"

Danny had not considered that the man would wonder. Stretching his lips, he said, "We're very quick."

"Indeed. Well, come inside, then."

Jinny led the way and flopped down before the counter. Mr. Pearce helped them decide upon books: *A Great Emergency* and *From Nowhere to the North Pole* for Danny, and *Jan of the Windmill* and *Carrots: Just a Little Boy* for Albert.

"May we bring one to our sister?" Albert asked.

"You mustn't ask that," Danny said.

"No, I wish I'd thought of it myself." Mr. Pearce took a wide and thin book from a bottom shelf, *Mother Goose Rhymes*.

He was as kind as Mr. Smith. Perhaps kinder. After all, Miss Kent seemed to spend a lot of time with him.

The knot inside Danny's chest softened a little.

"I like the pictures," Albert said, leafing through the book of rhymes.

Mr. Pearce nodded. "As do I."

The door opened a couple of inches but clicked shut again. Jinny rose and trotted over to wait. A woman was visible from the back as she waved to another woman in the near distance.

"We must go," Danny said. He thanked Mr. Pearce and was pleased when his brother did as well.

Mr. Pearce folded his arms.

"Say . . . if you play on the green Saturday, ask Mr. Smith to send one of you by. Perhaps I can close shop for an hour or so."

"Mr. Smith's returned to London," Danny heard himself blurt.

Mr. Pearce cocked his head. "He has?"

"You weren't supposed to say that!" Albert said but added to Mr. Pearce with a catch in his voice, "He's not coming back!"

The door opened, and the woman entered. Danny recognized her vaguely; she bought fish at the beach at times. Her brown hair was caught up into a straw hat.

She smiled at the three of them, stooped to pet Jinny.

Mr. Pearce said, "Good morning, Mrs. Fallon."

"We have to go," Danny repeated to Albert.

On the walk home, his brother said, "Why did you say that to him, if Miss Shipsey didn't want him to know?"

"I don't know," Danny said. "You spoke too."

"Only after you did."

Albert was right, and there were too many unanswered questions. He had hoped Mr. Pearce, being an adult and friend to Miss Kent, could have sorted them out. But a backward glance on their way through the bookshop had told him that Mr. Pearce was just as baffled.

49

A Mr. Crocker arrived just after Thursday breakfast with camera and stand. He was polite and soft-spoken, not attempting to coax a smile from Rosalind's mother, who sat in a parlor chair with hands clasped, her faraway look unruffled by the powder flash.

"May I take two more, Mrs. Ward?" the photographer asked, pushing aside his cloth.

"She agreed to *one*," Rosalind said sharply.

He nodded understanding, and she felt guilty for directing her anger at him.

"The others are in the event of a developing error," he explained. "Only one will be used."

"As long as it's the same pose," Mr. Miller said to Mother, "I can't see the harm. You wouldn't wish to sit through this again."

"Very well," Mother said.

The draft of Mr. Smith's story was not due to arrive until sometime tomorrow. Over breakfast, Mr. Miller had advised Mother that they should prepare for the eventual claim form. Thus, when Mr. Crocker left, Mr. Miller had notebook and pencil ready.

"I'll need a list of your friends in Lincolnshire to start," he said from the chair adjacent to Mother's.

"I had none."

"Servants," Mr. Miller went on. "Tenants. Merchants."

"A housemaid, Alma Willis, risked her position to help me."

"What of the stableboy?" Rosalind said from the sofa.

"Yes, I meant to mention him next," Mother said. "Oswald Green."

Mr. Miller penciled into the notebook balanced upon a crossed knee. "Did you have much association with Oswald?"

"He helped me to escape."

The pencil froze.

"He also contacted *The Daily Telegraph* to refute the charges Lord Fosberry made in that same newspaper," Rosalind added.

"How may we contact him?" Mr. Miller asked.

"Why, through his employer," Mother replied. "Mr. Perry, who owns a courier service. He came to my aid as well."

"In Spilsby?"

"No, here in London."

Mr. Miller got to his feet. "Excuse me. I must send for my secretary."

As he left the parlor, Rosalind's mother turned to her. "You don't have to sit through this."

"I should be here for you."

Mother smiled, shook her head. "I'm fine. It's a relief, actually, not waiting for another shoe to drop."

"I wouldn't mind a stroll," Rosalind admitted.

"Well, then. Off you go."

A housemaid directed her to the morning room, where Mrs. Miller sat in an overstuffed chair reading a newspaper. After reporting how the photography session went, Rosalind asked, "Is there a post office nearby?"

"Oh dear. The nearest is Charing Cross Road, almost a mile and a half. Mr. Miller sent our driver on an errand. Feel free to use carriage and driver when he returns."

"Thank you, but I enjoy rambling about. And Mr. Miller may need the carriage again."

"Well, you'll be close to Trafalgar Square. Have you ever been to the National Gallery?"

"I haven't."

"Oh my. You simply must. Shall I come with you?"

"You're very kind, but I shall be fine on my own. Will you explain to Mother if I'm not back for lunch?"

"But of course. I'll give you directions. By the by, if you go to the gallery, you'll want to purchase a keepsake guide. Follow it backward, and you'll avoid most of the crowd. And there is a tea room around the corner on Orange Street."

Rosalind set out southward, passing charming limestone houses in the villa style, with irregular balconies, rotundas, and verandahs for viewing the breadth of Hyde Park, to her right. It was a perfect distance, not only for the exercise. The thought of telegraphing Jude had occurred to her during the photographer's visit, and thus she needed time to consider whether or not she should.

They were not engaged. Would accounting for her absence be presumptuous?

But what if he discovered she and Mr. Smith were away at the same time? That had not occurred to her during the rush to leave Port Stilwell. What if he assumed the worst? After all, his former fiancée's change of heart had come out of the blue.

You can explain when you return, she said to herself. Jude was reasonable. He would understand. It would be a relief to have nothing more to conceal from the man she loved.

She sighed happily. She had assumed love was breathless, the overwhelming stuff of novels. Instead, she simply wished he were walking here beside her.

By the time she reached the stone cross on Charing Cross Road, Rosalind had her answer. They were not schoolchildren. If Jude should think her presumptuous for not wishing to cause him worry, she had his character all wrong, and it would be good to find that out.

She entered the post office. Could she say what she must in one line? One line, which would be read by at least one other on the receiving end?

The solution came to her.

"I would like to send a telegram to Mr. Lockhart in Port Stilwell," she said to a young male clerk.

Please explain all to Mr. Pearce.

Rosalind paid the sixpence admittance in the entrance hall of the Grecian-style building on the north end of Trafalgar Square, and paid another sixpence for *The Pall Mall Gazette Guide to the National Gallery*. She started in the glass-domed vestibule of the main staircase, with its large paintings of the British school, but then moved on as advised to room 22 and its collection by J. M. W. Turner. In general, there were more and more visitors in each room as she went down the numbers, but she was able to see every painting with little hindrance.

Her stomach sent up growls at half past three as she left the Florentine School in room 1. She easily found Mrs. Northey's Tea Room and smiled at the waitress's raised brows when she ordered two watercress sandwiches, two honey cakes, and tea.

This is London. She'll forget me before the top of the hour.

Another thought occurred, albeit one most reluctant. Had Noble Clark procured employment?

None of my concern.

But it was. Mother would ask when this business with the magazine was over. And they were rather in his debt.

Her meal finished, she returned to the square, to a hansom cab stand she had passed, and asked the driver, "How far away is the Lyceum?"

He doffed his cap. "But a half mile, miss."

Half a mile was an easy stroll, even a London half mile. But that would put her two miles from the Millers', and she had been away far too long as it was. She asked the driver to take her there.

As the horse *clip-clopp*ed up Wellington Street, she spotted a familiar head of flaxen hair sweeping beneath the Lyceum's six-columned portico. She had her answer and was tempted to call to the driver to carry on. But what if Mr. Clark were to hear as well, look up, and see her? She sighed, waited for the hansom to stop, and stepped down onto the pavement.

"Please wait," she said to the driver. "Mr. Clark?"

The broom went still, and he turned his face toward her. His amber eyes widened. "Miss Kent?"

"I see you were hired."

His face was flushed, whether from the work or embarrassment or both. "It's my first day, actually. Why are you here?"

"Mother has some business with a solicitor."

He nodded at the broom in his hands. "Until I can find a part onstage. I was anxious in Exeter but am much better now. I've been practicing my vocals."

"Very good."

"Please say to Mrs. Kent that they've offered me a room above stage. It's got but a cot and pegs on the wall, but I don't have to pay rent."

"She'll be happy for you." Rosalind smiled and offered her hand. "And I'll leave you to your work. Wouldn't want to cause you to get sacked on your first day."

He said thickly, "It's good to see a familiar face, Miss Kent."

She was glad then that she had stopped. She turned again for the cab.

"Oh, Miss Kent?"

She turned again.

"Mr. Irving asked your mother's address yesterday. I didn't see the harm in giving it. He said someone had sent a letter days ago, but he didn't know where to forward it."

Rosalind groaned inwardly. More Lord Fosberry threats? "Did he mention the return address?"

"He didn't. But you could ask. He's in the office."

She followed him through an arched doorway, a poster to the right announcing the latest production, *The Bells: A Drama in Three Acts*.

In the office, Mr. Irving rose from his desk chair to clasp her hands.

"Why, Miss Kent. How good to see you again. Is your mother here as well?"

"She is not. But she will be as grateful as I am that you hired Mr. Clark."

"Mr. Clark arrived at a good time," Mr. Irving said, "as Mr. Rook decided to retire."

"Mr. Clark said that a letter arrived for Mother? Do you remember from where it came?"

He went over to another desk, fished into a basket, and drew out an envelope. "It's not yet been posted."

Her stomach churned at the sight of the Lincolnshire return address. Still, she thanked him.

"Please give your mother my regards," he said.

On the steps again, she bade another farewell to Noble Clark.

"I hope your dreams come true."

He smiled. "There is nowhere to go but upward, yes?"

The maid who answered the Millers' door directed Rosalind to the garden, where Mother and the Millers sat at a table set for high tea.

"Why, you're just in time," Mrs. Miller said as her husband got to his feet. "We have your place here."

Rosalind thanked both and explained that she was not hungry, though she did accept tea from Mrs. Miller and a sponge cake Mr. Miller proffered.

"Did you enjoy the gallery?" her mother asked.

"Very much so. Apart from Da Vinci, I had no idea how

many artists were also mathematicians." She stirred sugar into her tea. "Did you locate Oswald Green?"

"He left two hours ago," Mother said. "It was good to see him."

"His testimony will be invaluable," Mr. Miller said. "If we should have to call upon him."

"I hope so." Rosalind pulled the envelope from her pocket. "Because I fear that we may."

50

The return address gave Charlotte a start, but the handwriting was not Roger's pretentious script. She took a steadying breath and opened the envelope.

Dear Lady Fosberry,
Do you remember me? I am Alma, upstairs maid.

Alma. Had Roger found out that she had helped her? Charlotte read on.

We miss you. Even Mrs. Trinder speaks well of you now, with Lord Fosberry gone nigh three weeks. It was wrong of me, but I listened to him and Lady Blake easy through the grate from the parlor. She could no longer live with her conscience, said she, and would not marry him. He begged her to change her mind. I heard weeping. In the end, she said the only way would be for him to live six months in Sweden, after which he may divorce you without a trial.

The page trembled in Charlotte's hands.

"Can you keep it still, Mother?" Rosalind said, leaning against her shoulder.

"Does this relate to your case?" Mr. Miller said.

Charlotte took a breath. "It does."

> *I hope you will not mind Lady Blake marrying Lord Fosberry afterward. She is most kind. She pays our wages to keep up the house and grounds. Even Jack Boswell seems content these days. I hear him whistling in the hall. It was him who urged me to write to you. He said, only to me, that when Lord Fosberry was in his cups, he declared he would not honor his word to relay to you that there would be no trial.*

How typical of Roger to want to keep her in torment! How did a person go through life with such a streak of petty spite?

> *There is more, Lady Fosberry. Jack said that his lordship refers to you as a word I must not write. I only inform you of this now if ever you suffer any regret over leaving.*

Charlotte thought, *Only that I waited so long.*

"Mrs. Blake has to be insane," Rosalind muttered.

"There were some obvious eccentricities," Charlotte said. "But I'm grateful to her."

"To whom?" Mr. Miller said.

Charlotte nodded and hurried through the final paragraph, which expressed Alma's best wishes.

"May God bless you too, Alma," Charlotte murmured, passing the letter across the table to Mr. Miller.

After reading, he lowered the page and smiled. "This is quite extraordinary."

His wife stared down at her teacup with an expression of curiosity and acceptance.

"Please, you may see it as well, Mrs. Miller," Charlotte said. "You've been most gracious. And there is too much good news here for three people to contain."

"I quite pity this Mrs. Blake," Mrs. Miller said when finished. "Should you not write to her and warn her?"

"She should not," Mr. Miller said before Charlotte could even consider this. "That she was aware of his original plan shows a willingness to overlook his character failings. A letter from you will not change her mind."

Charlotte felt selfish relief. She could not imagine the revenge Roger could concoct were she to break up his engagement. And perhaps he would treat Mrs. Blake well, given her vast wealth.

Mr. Miller clapped his hands. "We must celebrate! Dinner at Verrey's!"

The wave of euphoria gave way to heaviness of heart, and Charlotte found herself asking, "May we not? Or rather, will you go without me?"

"But of course," Mr. Miller said.

"We'll stay in," said his wife, who turned to Charlotte. "Are you unwell, Mrs. Ward?"

"I'm afraid I'm not ready for London." But there was more to it.

Rosalind studied her. "You should turn in early tonight, Mother. You've had an exhausting two days."

Charlotte did not argue.

Cocooned in bedclothes that evening, she thought of her two failed marriages.

Would have been three, perhaps, had Patrick lived.

She had read Scripture enough to know that God did not desire broken marriages. Her failure, she realized, was in not taking the vows seriously. For allowing infatuation, loneliness, ego, and the desire to be as her peers to propel her into hasty unions. Did not the gospel of Luke admonish those who chose to build a wall to count the cost beforehand? Could marriage be likened to a wall?

She shifted from the sodden part of her pillow and wiped her eyes with her fingers.

And yet, in spite of my failures, Father, she prayed, swallowing past the lump in her throat, *you've killed the fatted calf for me.*

—×<>×—

The following morning, Mr. Miller returned to work in his office. Mrs. Miller went the second mile by insisting upon showing Rosalind some of the London sights. Assuring both that she did not mind the solitude, Charlotte spent most of the day in the garden, reading the three newspapers the Millers took, and simply meditating. As painful as her latest London memories were, she did enjoy the sounds of the park and the aroma of plane trees in summer leaf.

Rosalind and Mrs. Miller returned just before six. Charlotte joined them in the parlor, where they described tours of the South Kensington Museum, including its new India Museum. Mr. Miller arrived soon afterward.

"You will be pleased," he said, handing her four typed pages.

Mr. Smithson's article was surprisingly fair. Almost to the point of boredom. He wrote of her day-to-day goings-on in the house, from gardening to reading to playing piano to chess to conversing over dinner.

The boys were portrayed as overactive lads who appeared on her doorstep when the youngest suffered an injury on his way to school. Three sentences were devoted to her reading to them, teaching them gardening.

"Surely Mrs. Fletcher will not take issue," she said.

Mrs. Hooper would, however, for he labeled her the town gossip, with ears raised to hear any scrap of scandal she could pass on.

"That was unkind."

"Balaam's ass spoke the truth too," Rosalind muttered.

"Rosalind!" Charlotte said, stifling a laugh.

She continued reading aloud. Three entire paragraphs described how Mr. Smithson taught Danny and Albert to play rounders, along with every other town boy.

"What an egotist," Rosalind said.

"He kept his word, though," Charlotte said. "Perhaps there is some decency in him after all."

"He was constrained to keep his publisher's word, rather," Mr. Miller reminded her.

"Still, if not for him, we would not have the letter from Alma. Like Joseph's brothers' ill deed, good came from it."

"You are far too charitable, Mother," Rosalind said, though with an affectionate smile.

"Perhaps. Perhaps not." Charlotte read aloud the article's final paragraph.

"We parted ways most amicably, with my stating my wish to see her on the London stage again one day. 'I am too happy here in Port Stilwell' was Mrs. Ward's quick reply. And why should she not be? She has her garden, her lovely daughter, the affection of two boys, and the culinary delights of Coral Shipsey, the most skilled pastry cook in Devonshire."

51

Mr. Lockhart met Charlotte and Rosalind at Port Stilwell Station the following afternoon.

"Mr. Miller telegraphed," he explained. "*Arrive 2:30, all well.* I cannot wait to hear the rest."

He was forced to wait because of five others upon the platform, but only until they were settled into his carriage.

"Splendid!" he said, after handing Alma's letter back to Charlotte. "But do save this. If he were to change his mind, you have some proof there of his intent."

That put a small damper on Charlotte's mood. "I shall."

Rosalind frowned. "If he changes his mind, Lady Blake will break their engagement, and he won't have the funds to bring her to court."

"Yes, of course, Miss Kent," he said. "But save the letter."

He either resented Rosalind's intrusion upon his instructions, or was simply weary, for he drove in near silence, shoulders hunched, not bothering to ask of their trip, nor of the health of his dear friend.

At the cottage, he helped them down from the carriage, removed his bowler hat to mop his brow with his handkerchief, and turned to Rosalind.

"There is other news."

"Yes?"

"When I received your telegram, I went straightaway to Mr. Pearce's shop, only to find a note in the door that it would be closed for an indeterminate amount of time. I saw Mrs. Hooper walking with his dog some time later and asked his whereabouts. She replied that he had left for India on the previous afternoon."

Rosalind blinked at him. "India?"

"By way of Bristol, I would suppose."

"Oh dear," Charlotte said.

The door opened, and Mrs. Deamer stepped onto the porch, as grim faced as Mr. Lockhart. Charlotte shook her head, and Mrs. Deamer stepped back into the house.

"Are you quite certain, Mr. Lockhart?" Charlotte asked.

"Quite certain. Mrs. Hooper said . . ."

He mopped his brow again.

"What did she say, Mr. Lockhart?" Rosalind pressed.

"That his heart was broken from Miss Kent chasing after Mr. Smith."

"That woman!" Charlotte hissed.

Rosalind's face went pasty white. "I should have asked you to speak with him before we left."

"I'm very sorry, Miss Kent. Perhaps he'll regret his hastiness and return before the ship sails."

"He may indeed, Rosalind," Charlotte said, one hand upon her shoulder.

"No. Thanks to Phoebe Drummer, he won't."

⊰⊱⊰⊱⊰⊱

"Coral blames herself," Mrs. Deamer said in the kitchen. "She informed Mr. Pearce that you were in London."

"Without saying why?" Rosalind asked Coral, seated at the worktable, her face buried in her arms.

She raised her pink and damp-eyed face. "I said that you would return soon and explain. But I didn't let on that Mr. Smith was there. I allowed him to believe he was still here."

"Mrs. Hooper must have informed him," Mrs. Deamer said. "According to her, Mr. Smith sent word through the stationmaster that he would post the remainder of his rent from London. She's been here twice, demanding to know what we did to drive away such a wonderful man."

"She'll not think so kindly of him when his story is printed," Charlotte said as she wrapped an arm around her quietly weeping daughter.

"Mrs. Deamer, will you draw a bath? And, Coral, please bring some warm milk upstairs."

Later, when Rosalind lay upon her pillow, Charlotte brushed her damp hair from her forehead with her fingers.

"My fault," Rosalind rasped. "I praised Mr. Smithson in his hearing."

"Not your fault," Charlotte soothed. "Are we to point out the good deeds of women only?"

"But I can't recall praising Jude for *his*."

"I'm sure you did."

Her daughter blew her nose. "I ache all over."

"Yes, there is no feeling like it." Charlotte sniffed, tears fresh in her own eyes. "You poor darling."

"He has to come back *sometime*. His shop . . . Jinny."

"I expect he'll return."

"He *must* allow me to explain."

"Yes." Charlotte rubbed her shoulder.

An hour later, when she was certain Rosalind was asleep, Charlotte slipped from the bedroom and went downstairs. She eased into a parlor chair, hip aching from lying so long propped upon an elbow.

Mrs. Deamer entered. "How is she?"

Charlotte shook her head. "Will you sit for a while?"

"Of course." Mrs. Deamer took the paisley chair.

"Did Albert and Danny come today?"

"They did. We read together, they weeded the garden, and Coral fed them. But we were worried for you, and our hearts were heavy over what we learned of Mr. Pearce. We sent them home soon after lunch. I hope you don't mind."

"No, of course not."

"I feel so sorry for her."

With a sigh, Charlotte said, "I should have urged her to tell Mr. Pearce my background as soon as I realized they were serious."

"I don't know. I was stunned that he would react in such haste. He seemed to be of such steady temperament."

"I thought so as well." Charlotte shook her head. "Reasonable people *speak* to each other. Is a man who would stalk away under a presumption one she would wish to have in her life? What of later misunderstandings?"

"I hate to say it . . . but perhaps Mr. Smithson brought on a blessing in disguise?"

Charlotte had to smile. "More than one, actually."

Upstairs, she told her of the letter.

"Incredible!" Mrs. Deamer said. "You'll not have to hide anymore."

"I shall become a fixture in town."

"But what of future reporters?"

"Mr. Smith's article proved that I'm dull as dishwater."

Mrs. Deamer clucked her tongue. "Not so!"

"Well, they're not likely to come just to report that I still play piano in the parlor. And he praised Coral's baking skills in his article to be published. I should expect she'll not be working for Mrs. Hooper for much longer."

"Sadly for us; happily for her."

"Is she all right?" Charlotte asked.

She tilted her head. "Time will heal."

"I hope." Charlotte paused, said carefully, "And how were your visits to your husband and brother?"

"The same. One belligerent; one contrite."

"Ah. I'm sorry. We have all had an emotional week."

"Indeed," Mrs. Deamer said. "We should stay indoors tomorrow, lest a meteor drop upon us."

"I would chance that to go to church," Charlotte said. "It's been a long time. But I shan't leave Rosalind alone. She may seek out that meteor."

52

"Please go," Rosalind said from her bed as her mother propped the breakfast tray upon its legs on either side of her. "All of you."

"I'll not leave you."

Fresh tears stung her eyes. She fished a wadded handkerchief from beneath her pillow and blew her nose. "I need to be alone, Mother."

Answering questions, even hearing voices through the walls, agitated her senses. She wished simply for quiet, to curl up under the bedclothes and sleep.

Mother went over to the chest of drawers, brought back a fresh handkerchief from the top drawer, and handed it to her.

"Only if you'll eat, then."

The smell of the bacon made her queasy, but Rosalind forced down half the coddled eggs, a bite of toast, and the cup of tea while her mother watched.

She set the cup back upon its saucer. "No more."

"Very well." Mother moved the tray and set it upon the foot of the bed. "Now to dress."

"I'm not going to church," Rosalind reminded her.

"But you must wash your face. Brush your teeth and hair.

And go downstairs. Staying in bed in your nightclothes will only feed the despondency. I know this."

Rosalind had not the strength to dress, but she had less to argue. The sooner she complied, the sooner her mother would leave her to her own misery.

Swollen eyes stared back at her in the bathroom mirror and stung when she pressed the wet cloth to them. When she returned to her room, her mother was taking from the wardrobe the yellow calico Rosalind had purchased in Exeter.

"That's not a housedress," Rosalind said.

"Today it is," her mother said. "Yellow is the most cheerful color."

She sighed and allowed herself to be bullied still more.

From the parlor sofa, she responded with a nod to the subdued farewells of Mother, Mrs. Deamer, and Coral.

Coral hesitated at the door, dark circles under her eyes. "You won't know I'm here unless you need me . . ."

Rosalind shook her head and watched her turn with defeated posture.

"Coral?"

She turned.

"But thank you for offering."

Coral gave her a grateful little smile.

The sounds of footfalls against the porch and the steps drifted through the open windows, along with murmurings at the gate. Then silence, but for the clock's ticking and birdsong.

Where is your ship now, Jude? Will you look up at the stars at night and think of me at all?

Five weeks to reach India, and the same to return. He would spend at least that much time there, would he not? Perhaps he would meet an Indian woman.

Tears burned her eyes again. She blew her nose.

Rosalind heard the squeak of the gate. Footfalls again. Knocking.

Mother and the others had left but twenty minutes ago. Had someone forgotten something? But none would knock.

More knocks sounded, followed by three distinctive barks.

Her heartbeat quickened. She started to rise but sank back into her chair.

Mrs. Hooper!

The desire to feel a connection to Jude by seeing Jinny was strong, but not as strong as the desire *not* to see Mrs. Hooper. *Go away, go away, go away!* she thought to the clock's rhythm.

"Rosalind?"

She cocked her head at the muffled but familiar voice.

What did Coral put into my tea?

"Please, Rosalind?"

She crossed the room into the hall and opened the front door.

To the sight of Jude! Grinning at her!

She fell into his arms. Or did he fall into hers? It mattered little. All her worries fled in the face of his embrace while Jinny yipped happily.

"I thought you were on your way to India," she said against his shoulder.

"Mrs. Hooper's doing," he said. "When I asked her to keep Jinny, I did not wish her to know my affairs, so I said I had a personal matter to attend. But she had seen travel literature on my counter some days ago and assumed so."

"Where did you go, then?"

"To London . . . to look for you."

She stepped back from him. "You were in London?"

"May I explain in the garden?" he said. "I left Jinny so abruptly that she needs to stay close."

Rosalind knelt down to stroke her furry back. "I understand, Jinny."

They shared a bench, holding hands, Jinny resting her snout upon Jude's boot.

"When I learned you were in London . . ."

385

"From Coral."

He winced. "I was most persistent."

"I'm not angry with her," Rosalind assured him, then confessed, "I *was*."

"When I learned that Mr. Smith was also there, I feared you realized some attachment to him."

"That's why you went? To try and persuade me to change my mind?"

He shook his head. "I was devastated but would not dare to presume to ask you to change your mind. Your mind is your own."

Hearing this made her appreciate him all the more. "How did you learn he was there?"

"I'm not at liberty to share that. Do you mind? It was not from Miss Shipsey."

"Very well."

He squeezed her hand and said that, shortly after hearing Mr. Smith's whereabouts, he assisted Mrs. Fallon from the Sea Gull Inn.

"Mr. Smith was constantly in my thoughts. I asked if she recalled his staying. She recalled very well, but for one night and with no complaint over the noise."

"That's not what he said to us. How naïve of him not to realize that word would have gotten out eventually."

"Perhaps this was his first experience with small-town life," Jude said, then went on. "I had learned of another misrepresentation from him and was concerned that he might be connected with your mother's need for seclusion, if you were in some danger."

After a sleepless night, he said, he went to London the very next morning. He stayed at the Langham and haunted the entrance and restaurant for three days.

"And then I gave up and came home last night," he said, "only to happen upon your mother outside Saint Paul's this morning, with Mrs. Deamer and Miss Shipsey. She explained what led you both to go to London. She was an actress? Somehow, I am not surprised."

"She has that way about her," Rosalind said.

"She urged me to come here straightaway, that she believed God would understand."

"I believe so too. By the by, her name is actually Mrs. *Ward*."

"Mrs. Ward. I shall try to remember."

"And Mr. Smith's is actually *Smithson*."

"I may forget that one," he said and leaned in for a kiss.

53

Rosalind and Mr. Pearce and Jinny came around from the garden when Charlotte, Mrs. Deamer, and Coral returned from St. Paul's.

Jinny, being no one's fool, trotted directly to Coral.

Charlotte laughed with the others. How happy her daughter looked! Such a far cry from this morning!

"Will you stay for lunch?" she asked Mr. Pearce, who looked every bit as happy.

Over a plate of fried sole, peas, and potatoes, he described his stay in London. "I never ventured from the Langham, truth be told. The lift was an adventure. I could have ridden up and down all day were it not for my quest to keep a lookout in the lobby."

"That was terribly kind of you," Charlotte said. "I'm amazed at how everything sorted out so."

"But I'm not sure how to address you now," Mr. Pearce said. "Rosalind said your name is 'Ward.' Will you return to that?"

"I have already in London. It's my family name, so I'm happy to have it again. And Rosalind doesn't mind."

Her daughter smiled and shook her head.

Charlotte smiled back. *She's not likely to keep* Kent *for very long either.*

"But you didn't learn who put Mr. Smith on to you?" Mr. Pearce asked.

"I don't suppose it matters now."

"Wouldn't you like to know, Mother?" Rosalind asked. "For curiosity's sake, if nothing more?"

Charlotte thought this over. "Yes. For curiosity's sake."

◆◇◆

The Congregationalist minister from Seaton, a Mr. Povey, concluded Paulina Moore's funeral a fortnight later with a Scripture from the Psalmist. "'Weeping may endure for a night, but joy cometh in the morning.'"

It seemed most of Port Stilwell was at Saint Paul's. Several men, including Jude, stood in the back to allow pews to women and the elderly.

After the burial and closing prayer in the churchyard, Charlotte and Mrs. Deamer, Rosalind and Jude, and Coral stood in a queue to pay their respects to Mr. Moore.

"I wish I could have known her," Charlotte said to him when her turn came.

"Thank you for saying that," he said with a sad smile.

◆◇◆

Mrs. Fletcher answered Charlotte's knock the following morning, carrying a blond-haired tot.

"This is Teresa?" Charlotte said. "What an adorable little girl."

"Thank you," Mrs. Fletcher said with a begrudging smile.

"May I speak with you and Mr. Fletcher?"

Her smile tightened into wariness. "Why?"

"May I explain just the once?"

She was led into the kitchen, where Mr. Fletcher looked up from coffee and newspaper with a concerned expression. Danny and Albert gave her cautious looks.

389

Charlotte understood. As a rule, those who mistreated others were insanely jealous of their victims' affections.

"Do you think the boys could go outside?"

Relief flooded their young faces, and at the nod from their father, they sprinted through the kitchen door.

"But why are my sons news?" Mr. Fletcher asked when Charlotte informed them of the upcoming story.

"Because I was once an actress, Mr. Smithson chose to write of my life here. The boys are mentioned but briefly, as visitors to the cottage."

Mr. Fletcher shook his head, as if to help his mind absorb it all. "It does not mention me, nor Mrs. Fletcher?"

"Not at all," Charlotte said.

"Still, I would rather it were not in print."

Charlotte nodded. "As would I. My solicitor fought to suppress this."

Mrs. Fletcher hefted the child higher up on her hip. "We could reconsider if the reporter agrees to add something of Teresa."

Her husband gave her a pained look.

"It's only fair," she whined.

Can you be any more ignorant? Charlotte thought. "I am truly sorry. It's quite set in stone. And I hope it doesn't predispose you against the request I'm about to make."

She asked if the boys could come over six days weekly until the start of school. "The garden demands lots of attention during the summer."

"And how much more are you willing to pay?" Mrs. Fletcher said.

"Not a penny more, Sabrina," said her husband, adding to Charlotte, "We'll call them in and ask. But I should think they would be delighted."

On Wednesday, the twenty-seventh of July, Rosalind brought *The Cornhill Magazine* from pillar-box to parlor and looked on as Charlotte read to Danny and Albert the portion having to do with them.

"Are we famous?" Albert asked.

"A wee bit," Charlotte replied. "But you must not let it go to your head."

He looked askew at her.

"Become a snob," Rosalind explained. "Think yourself better than others."

Danny looked at the article again. "But Mr. Smith didn't play rounders with us *every* day."

Rosalind coughed.

"I suppose he remembers differently," Charlotte said, giving her daughter a warning look.

⊷⟨⟩⊶

Port Stilwell residents went about their business after the article, save Mrs. Hooper, who called at the cottage on Friday afternoon after the boys had left for home.

"You were an actress!" she gushed in the hall. "You know, I had an inkling."

"Did you?" Charlotte said.

"I'm extremely disappointed in Mr. Smith . . . son," she said with a frown. "To libel me so, when I provided respite from his desperate situation!"

"You can't always know what goes on in someone's mind."

"Indeed!" Mrs. Hooper excused herself and went then into the kitchen and, according to Coral later, raised her wages thirteen shillings per month.

"And she insisted upon my having tomorrow off," Coral said while bringing a dish of crimped salmon and caper sauce into the dining room for supper. "She'll send over restaurant meals."

"How will you spend the day?" Mrs. Deamer asked. "Visit your family?"

Coral shook her head. "Show Mr. Smith's article to restaurants and bakeries in Exeter."

"Clever girl, you!" Rosalind said.

"Why, thank you, Miss Kent. But is that wrong? To take advantage of her giving me the day?"

"Did she ask you not to seek employment in Exeter?" Rosalind asked.

"She did not."

"Then the day is yours to do as you please." Charlotte took a sip of tea. "It is truly an ill wind which blows no good."

⋯⟨◇◇⟩⋯

Charlotte answered the door on Saturday morning, expecting Danny and Albert, but finding instead Mr. Moore clutching his hat, mourning band around his coat sleeve.

"Mr. Moore?" she said. "Do come in."

"May we speak out here?" he said. "It's rather private."

"But of course." She stepped onto the porch. "How are you?"

His face clouded. "I thought I was prepared, but it's more difficult than I imagined."

"I'm so sorry. How may we help you?"

His shoulders rose, then fell. "You can forgive me . . . if you've a mind to. I have wronged you greatly, Mrs. Ward."

"Why do you say that?"

He glanced away. "I recognized you at first sight. I was assigned to Marylebone for six years, and Mrs. Moore and I went often to the theatre. But when you introduced yourself as Mrs. *Kent*, I assumed you desired privacy after . . ."

"You read of my breakdown," Charlotte said to make it easier for him.

"Paulina so enjoyed news of the theatre. I knew she would be delighted to learn you had chosen Port Stilwell as your haven."

"I had not asked you to keep confidence," Charlotte reminded him.

"That is so, but it was implied when you introduced yourself."

"If it gave her some joy, I'm glad you shared that with her."

"There is more," he said. "By the time her brother and his wife visited, she was delirious from laudanum and imparted that information. I asked both to keep this in strictest confidence. But when I saw the article in *The Cornhill Magazine,* I noticed that the author's name, Smithson, is the maiden name of Paulina's sister-in-law. I feel this was no coincidence. *And* I fear this has caused you undue harm."

Charlotte needed a moment to absorb this information, and then said, "Far from it, Mr. Moore. You will be comforted to learn what a marvelous gift your wife gave to me."

54

"Multiplying by two-digit numbers is not as difficult as it appears," Rosalind said on Friday, the fifteenth of October, while chalking *23 x 871* upon the blackboard.

She turned and faced thirty dubious looks from nine- and ten-year-old faces.

"How many of you know how to add?"

All hands rose.

"And how to carry?"

Hands went up again.

"But of course you do!" She smiled. "We shall simply combine adding with multiplying, one step at a time. Why, you'll soon be able to do this in your sleep."

Her students laughed.

Rosalind taught mathematics first subject of the day, when the children's minds were fresh, then went on to grammar, her least favorite, while hers was somewhat fresh. But she worked just as hard to make it interesting.

At lunch recess, she held the door and watched her students carry their pails down the steps. By calling back offenders to spend recess at their desks, it had taken her but a fortnight to train them not to bolt like cattle.

Teaching younger boys and girls of fishermen and shop-keepers and quarry workers was vastly different from teaching older girls from the upper class. But Rosalind had learned from Miss Beale the keys to discipline: preparedness and consistency. The rewards were great. She was learning family connections and finding her own place in Port Stilwell's community.

Danny Fletcher sent her a wave from a group of school-mates. She returned his wave, happy to see how sociable he was becoming. She gave Jude much credit for that, with his Saturday afternoon rounders games on the green. The solution he found for keeping his shop open was simple. Young Amos White was quite competent and delighted to earn extra wages. It mattered little to Jude that the occasional fish scale turned up upon a shelf or in the money box. This was a fishing village, after all.

On the seventeenth of October, Jude came to lunch after church. Mrs. Meeks, the new cook, served a decent grouse pie with turnips and mushrooms. Forty-three years old and widowed, with children and grandchildren in town, she was unlikely to leave for some hoity-toity restaurant in Exeter, as Mrs. Hooper had stated so eloquently of Coral Shipsey.

"Anyone care for a game of Twenty Questions after dessert?" Mother asked as Mrs. Deamer brought a compote of apples into the dining room.

"I was hoping Rosalind would go for a walk," Jude said.

"You were?" Rosalind teased. "Have I offended you?"

He mugged a face at her. "A walk *with me*."

"You know that's not possible." The six members of the school board had made it clear when they hired her that unmarried women teachers were to be chaperoned when appearing in public in the company of any non-family male. Not fair, considering how Noble Clark had courted with impunity, but her only choices were to teach, or to sit home and complain over the rules.

She had had a third choice, actually: Miss Beale had asked her to return to Cheltenham. Her mother was becoming involved in the community, was even on the committee to plan the Christmas pantomime. But Rosalind no longer wished to live with one foot in one life and another here.

Jude, with whom she would love to be sitting in the garden, unchaperoned, had much to do with that decision.

"Shall I come with you?" Mrs. Deamer asked.

Jude thanked her, and they set out later, Jinny exploring ahead, Mrs. Deamer in the middle so there would be not even a hint of impropriety. They made small talk until Jude came to a halt at the Bickle cottage.

"Mrs. Bickle's son desires to sell. But I'd like your opinion."

Rosalind eyed the crumbling stones, rotting wood, and weed-choked garden. "Whatever would you do with it?"

"Have it torn down and build another using the same stones, plus more from the quarry to make it larger. It's in a good spot, close to the shop and school. The garden is well shaded and could be lovely."

Close to the school . . .

"You should show her the garden," Mrs. Deamer said. "I'll wait."

Rosalind gave her a suspicious look. What whispered conversation had occurred when she answered Jude's knock? But Mrs. Deamer gave her a benign smile.

She glanced about. Cottagers were at Sunday dinner or resting. Apart from Mrs. Deamer, there were no witnesses to their picking their way through calf-high weeds with Jinny in the lead.

The garden was bigger than Rosalind would have supposed, surrounded by a lichen-covered wall crumbling in spots. The earth was packed and scattered with yellow leaves from a decent-sized plum tree. Beneath it, Jude smiled, took her hand, and got upon one knee.

"Jude?" She had known this moment was inevitable, but still, her heart raced.

Jinny trotted over with leaves clinging to her coat and nudged his free hand.

He laughed and rested that hand upon his dog's head. "Will you marry *us*, Rosalind?"

She smiled, took a breath. "I will, Jude."

"Thank you, my darling. You've made me a happy man."

Getting to his feet, he removed his eyeglasses and kissed her, Jinny barking her approval.

Rosalind closed her eyes and relished being in his arms.

Thank you, Father. Thank you for nosebleeds and good men . . . and second opportunities.

At length, Jude stepped back and reached into his waistcoat pocket. The ring he brought out was gold, with an oval amethyst stone surrounded by seed pearls.

"I've wanted to show this to you since you first smiled at me with those half-moon eyes. My grandfather bought it in Bombay for my grandmother. She would have loved you. But if you would prefer a new one . . ."

"No. It's beautiful." She allowed him to slip it onto her third finger, at least to the second knuckle. "Oh dear. She had small hands."

"We'll take it to a jeweler in Exeter. But what of this place? Can you imagine living here when it's rebuilt?"

"I can imagine that easily."

They kissed again. "July? The cottage should be finished, and you would have the summer break for our honeymoon. I assume you'll want to resume teaching?"

"Yes," Rosalind answered. "But there won't be enough time to journey to India unless I resign."

His green eyes met hers. "India? If you're unable to sit backward on a train, I fear such a journey would make you miserable."

"But it's been your dream."

"A person should have more than one dream. I would love to explore the Continent with you. Wouldn't you like to see Paris? Rome?"

"Very much," she replied. "But are you certain you'll not have regrets later?"

"I've come to realize I've romanticized India because of my family. But I carry them in my heart. Geography has nothing to do with that."

She touched his clean-shaven face. "You're a good man, Jude."

"I hope so," he said, smiling back at her. "But what do you say? If we packed lots of ginger biscuits, could you bear two to three hours on a Channel steamer?"

"Two to three hours? I can bear that."

In front of the cottage again, Mrs. Deamer kissed Rosalind's cheek. "Your mother will be delighted."

"She wasn't in on this?"

"I want to ask her formally," Jude said. "After. It would have put her in an awkward position had you turned me down."

You knew that wasn't going to happen, Rosalind said to him with her eyes. She fingered the ring in her pocket on the return walk, too caught up in a wave of euphoria to add to the discussion of a European honeymoon.

"Thomas Cook tours are the best," Mrs. Deamer was saying. "Tickets, currency exchanges, meals—they handle it all for you, yet allow some time for exploring on your own."

When they reached the porch of the yellow cottage, Mrs. Deamer turned to say, "I'm flattered to be included in this happy occasion. But I'm going upstairs. It should be family now."

Her mother sat upon the parlor sofa, knitting her fourth, perhaps fifth, blue blanket. "How was your walk?"

"Quite eventful," Rosalind said.

Jude walked over to the side of the sofa and knelt.

Her mother set her knitting into her lap and smiled at each of them. "I expect you have something to say to me?"

"Rosalind has consented to be my wife, Mrs. Ward. May we have your blessing?"

With eyes shining, Mother replied, "You shall always have my blessing."

Epilogue

The birthday cake rose three layers, a mountain of flour and butter, currants and sugar, nutmegs and cloves, eggs and almonds,
candied citron and lemon peel, beneath peaks of white icing.

"That's the most marvelous cake," Charlotte said to Coral
in the kitchen.

"Marvelous," Mrs. Deamer echoed.

"Now you see why I wanted to bake it here?" Coral said. "It
would have fallen apart on the train."

"She helped me put together the sandwiches as well," said
Mrs. Meeks.

"We cooks must stick together," Coral said to her.

She was more than a cook, however, as the proprietor of
Shipsey's Fine Confections and Pastries on Exeter's Queen
Street, and the wife of one Patrick Teague, who kept books
for her and three other establishments. They lived above the
bakery with their fourteen-year old son, James, who was accompanying his Teague grandparents on a visit to Wales.

"Your wife is an artist," Charlotte said to Mr. Teague in the garden, where Rosalind directed men arranging chairs.

Mr. Teague placed a chair at the end of a semicircle and smiled. He was as tall as Coral was short but with the same strawberry-blond hair.

"She has a shrewd head for business as well. Did she say to you that her own brand of tinned biscuits are to debut by Christmas?"

"Wonderful! And no, she did not."

"I knew I should have married her when she asked me," Noble Clark said, hoisting another chair from the stack.

Coral's husband straightened. Charlotte exchanged worried looks with Jude.

And then Mr. Teague laughed. "Sorry, mate, but you're not her type."

Mr. Clark winked at Charlotte.

She wagged a finger at him, relieved that the former Amy Hugo had not yet returned from visiting her family in town. But then, after sixteen years, Amy surely knew her husband's quirks.

Mr. Clark had found his own unlikely success, sour notes and all. In fact, those were his claim to fame at the Vaudeville Theatre in London's West End. Charlotte and Mrs. Deamer had caught his act in a musical comedy two years ago. He would appear onstage with a cello, played with startling competence, and belt out modern tunes.

Years ago, the management had figured out to have him serenade a comely actress, thereby stopping the patrons from pelting the stage with fruit. Even those in the cheap seats respected women. This was no longer necessary, and audiences cheered at his appearances, even sang along.

The memory of his butchering "Lead, Kindly Light" during Charlotte's first visit to Saint Paul's made her smile. Had it really been nineteen years ago?

I'm actually seventy! Charlotte said to herself. Apart from swollen knuckles and a lower back which had to be coddled, she did not feel old.

You've been most kind to me, Father. Most kind. Every year, bad memories faded while new ones were created. She could hardly wait to see what surprises the next century held.

"Mother?"

Rosalind stepped to her side. Her daughter seemed not to have aged at all but for faint lines at the corners of her eyes. A checked teal-and-white serge summer gown with a wide tan belt complemented her slim figure. Upon her mahogany pompadour perched a wide-brimmed straw hat with ostrich plumes.

"We have forty chairs from the guildhall," Rosalind said. "Should we bring some from the kitchen and dining room?"

"Forty should be more than enough."

Her daughter looked doubtful. "When is the train to arrive?"

"In an hour."

"Does *she* know?"

"I doubt it. I suppose I should stop by and ask."

"When has that ever been of any use? She made her own bed, Mother."

"Still, may I steal Jude away early?"

Her daughter sighed but then wrapped an arm around her for a sideways embrace. "But of course, Mother. You can't stop trying to bring out the best in people, can you?"

Charlotte patted her cheek and walked over to the cake table. Alice and Beth, ages seventeen and fourteen, were pinning purple and green crepe paper streamers in loops around the edges of the cloth while Jinny's grand-pup Lottie watched from a patch of sunlight.

They were lovely girls, Alice with her father's wheat-colored hair and her mother's half-moon eyes, Beth with Rosalind's brown hair and the Pearce cleft chin. And both with a faint olive patina to their complexions.

Charlotte had had to learn, years ago, that every grandmother considered her grandchildren the brightest ever born, and that boastings to fellow members of Saint Paul's auxiliary were not welcome.

"Your decorations are very nice," she said.

"Is it time to bring out the cake, Grandmother?" Beth asked.

"Not until after lunch, I'm afraid."

"I don't mind," Alice said. "I want everything to stretch out as long as possible, because it's your special day."

Beth nodded, and Charlotte thought, *Not only are they bright but kind.*

Ten minutes later, she sat beside Jude in his two-seat phaeton behind a pair of red Cleveland bays, Pete and Peggy.

"I'm quite happy to be pulled out of chair duty," he said, taking up the reins. "I suppose it's the mathematician in Rosalind that makes her want them arranged so precisely." He looked at Charlotte sideways. "In strictest confidence, mind you."

"'Seal up your lips, and give no words but mum,'" Charlotte said. "From *Henry VI*."

He chuckled. Her son-in-law had gained a little weight since marrying Rosalind and shed some hair. More important, though, his laugh lines were deeper.

When Mr. Blyth, the tobacconist, passed on eight years ago, Jude bought the shop and expanded Pearce's Books. Amos White became his assistant full-time, and fish scales stopped showing up in odd places.

Jude flicked the reins, and the horses *clip-clopp*ed past trees loaded with waxen green apples. Snowy cumulous clouds with ragged edges floated overhead.

"The sky is beautiful today," Charlotte said.

"I forget to look up," Jude said. "A hazard of working indoors. But just think: If clouds formed only on one small spot on earth, multitudes would pay to visit there."

Charlotte looked at her son-in-law. "I have thought that myself."

He tapped his temple. "Great minds, eh?"

She laughed and patted his sleeve. The party would be grand, but better yet, in the scheme of things, were the heart connections with family and friends.

While helping her from the carriage in front of the Fletcher cottage, he asked in a tone that begged refusal, "Shall I come with you?"

"Only if you wish," she replied with a droll smile.

"Um . . . I should keep the horses company."

Sabrina Fletcher answered the door with a hopeful expression that faded straightaway.

You get the face you deserve, Charlotte thought. Bitterness had a way of seeping through the pores, tightening the eyes, pulling the mouth downward.

Dashed hope had ravaged the woman's looks even more so. It was not for Danny and Albert she pined, but Teresa, who, at fifteen, escaped her suffocating affection by marrying a young farmer she had met on May Day. They raised sheep and two small children fourteen miles away in Musbury, visiting but rarely.

"Good morning, Mrs. Fletcher," Charlotte said, moving forward so that the woman had no choice but to stand aside. This was not for the neighbors' amusement.

In the parlor, she turned and said, "Mr. Pearce and I are on our way to meet Danny and Albert's train. Will you come with us?"

Her frown deepened. "Why should I?"

"They send funds to keep you from the widows' home. Does that mean nothing?"

"Only for their father's sake. I could move in with Teresa's family any day I choose."

When pigs fly, Charlotte thought. "Life is short, Mrs. Fletcher. You'll want to have people to love in your old age."

Mrs. Fletcher's eyes clouded, but from her mouth came, "Whatever would we have to say to each other?"

"You could say how proud you are of them, to begin with."

She rolled her eyes.

That raised Charlotte's ire. "Better still, you could beg forgiveness."

"They should beg *my* forgiveness! I hear things! Once, twice a year, they visit you, their sister, their parents' graves, but never once do they stop by to ask how I'm faring!"

Enough, Charlotte thought. "They're not likely to do that until you apologize for the cruelties you inflicted upon them."

"How Christian of them! Supposing I was stricter than I ought to have been at times. It's hard work, tending family! What happened to turning the other cheek?"

"Turning the other cheek is what has kept you in this house," Charlotte said with great restraint. "I'm sorry to have wasted your time."

"Perhaps she'll change her mind one day," Jude said as they set out again.

"That's been my prayer," Charlotte glanced back at the cottage. Mrs. Fletcher skirted away from the window.

What a sad little life.

And mine could have been likewise.

How utterly foolish, to be unable to ask forgiveness. To allow pride so much importance when it was the sorriest of companions in old age.

Danny and Albert disembarked from the train, Danny, age twenty-nine, clad in conservative summer tweeds and a felt homburg hat, and Albert in tan linen with a straw boater atop his copper hair. They set their satchels on the platform to embrace Charlotte and even Jude, trading greetings until Jude said, "Let's catch up on the way, shall we?"

They were great successes. Jude and Rosalind had played no small part in that, having funded their fees at University College after Mr. Fletcher passed from an aneurysm. Danny, a solicitor, was attached to Mr. Miller's practice, and Albert was an insurance underwriter for Lloyd's of London.

"I'm to be on my own soon," Albert twisted around to say from beside Jude in the front seat. "Danny's found a more appealing flatmate-to-be in Mr. Miller's niece."

Charlotte turned to Danny next to her. "Julie Miller? I met her last visit. She's a lovely girl."

"The wedding is to be at Christmas. Please say you'll come." Danny cuffed his brother's shoulder. "And *I* wanted to be the one to give her the news."

"Um . . . sorry. Forgot," Albert said.

"A Christmas wedding will be great fun," Charlotte said.

Four carriages with horses lined the lane, and two wagons. Mrs. Deamer waved from the porch and walked out to meet them.

"What a sight for sore eyes you are!" she said to the boys as they traded embraces.

While she retained the title of housekeeper, she was more of a companion, the housework taken care of by Lynette, the day maid Charlotte had hired in 1882, shortly after purchasing the cottage from Mrs. Hooper, now deceased.

This was made possible when the newlywed Roger returned the money she had lent him, in return for her signing a letter drafted by Mr. Lockhart, agreeing never to mention him in any future interview. That was the last thing she would wish to do, but the money was welcome in any case.

Charlotte's three favorite men and Mrs. Deamer accompanied her around the cottage. She heard the strains of "Hearts and Flowers" as they turned the last corner and discovered that the house chairs had been moved into the garden for the members of the Port Stilwell Orchestra.

"Rosalind's idea?" Charlotte asked Jude.

"The girls', actually," he replied.

"I love this."

Guests milled about chairs and refreshment tables, setting down dishes to applaud her. Rosalind and the girls advanced.

Because the party was planned, Charlotte did not expect to be as struck with emotion. Tears blurred her eyes, and she was glad for Jude's supporting arm.

You are the most blessed woman on earth, she said to herself.

"Come, Mrs. Ward, let's join the celebration," Albert said.

"He can't wait to get to the food," Danny said to her, and his brother mugged a face at him.

Charlotte laughed. *Some things never change.* "Yes, let's."

Lawana Blackwell has thirteen published novels to her credit, including the bestselling GRESHAM CHRONICLES series, set in the countryside of late nineteenth-century England. She and her husband live in Texas.

You May Also Enjoy . . .

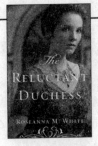

After a shocking attack, Rowena Kinnaird is desperate to escape her family and her ex-fiancé. She finds an unexpected protector in the Duke of Nottingham, but will she ever be able to trust him— let alone fall in love—when his custody of the Fire Eyes jewels endangers her once more?

The Reluctant Duchess by Roseanna M. White
LADIES OF THE MANOR
roseannamwhite.com

Lady Miranda Hawthorne secretly longs to be bold. But she is mortified when her brother's new valet mistakenly mails her private thoughts to a duke she's never met—until he responds. As she sorts out her feelings for two men, she uncovers secrets that will put more than her heart at risk.

A Noble Masquerade by Kristi Ann Hunter
HAWTHORNE HOUSE
kristiannhunter.com

After the man she loves abruptly sails for Italy, Sophie Dupont's future is in jeopardy. Wesley left her in dire straits, and she has nowhere to turn—until Captain Stephen Overtree comes looking for his wayward brother. He offers her a solution, but can it truly be that simple?

The Painter's Daughter by Julie Klassen
julieklassen.com

◊ BETHANYHOUSE

Stay up-to-date on your favorite books and authors with our free e-newsletters. Sign up today at bethanyhouse.com.

Find us on Facebook. facebook.com/bethanyhousepublishers

Free exclusive resources for your book group! bethanyhouse.com/anopenbook

More Fiction From Bethany House

In Scotland's Shetland Islands, a clan patriarch has died, and a dispute over the inheritance has frozen an entire community's assets. When a letter from the estate's solicitor finds American Loni Ford, she is stunned. Orphaned as a child, Loni has always wanted a link to her roots. She sets out on a journey of discovery, but is this dream too good to be true?

The Inheritance by Michael Phillips
Secrets of the Shetlands #1

At Irish Meadows horse farm, two sisters struggle to reconcile their dreams with their father's demanding marriage expectations. Brianna longs to attend college, while Colleen is happy to marry, as long as the man meets *her* standards. Will they find the courage to follow their hearts?

Irish Meadows by Susan Anne Mason
Courage to Dream #1
susanannemason.com

Stella West has quit the art world and moved to Boston to solve the mysterious death of her sister, but she is in need of a well-connected ally. Fortunately, magazine owner Romulus White has been trying to hire her for years. Sparks fly when Stella and Romulus join forces, but will their investigation cost them everything?

From This Moment by Elizabeth Camden
elizabethcamden.com

◈ BETHANYHOUSE